WHO IS LEE?

BY ZAINAB F. RAZA

John Perkins – *Author of Confessions of an Economic Hitman**

"The world is ruled by institutions that refuse to be held accountable to the people they were created to serve."

TABLE OF CONTENTS

"If there is a reason I believe in my ability to achieve a life in accordance with my heart, it is because of my parents."

ACKNOWLEDGMENTS

I believe writing is a personified form of company, yet the art I carry conceptually could not have been tangible without the people I've bonded with along the way. I needed to know that the stories I interpret from inspiration can be real and brought to life on pages. Because of the relentless confirmation of this possibility, I finished *Who Is Lee?* Thank you to Zehra and Raza Hassan, Kisa Zaidi, Suekayna Asgari, Dominick Pilli, Austin Kolodney, and Kevin Avery. While I may continue to believe that writing consoles the common isolation writers often feel, each of you made me feel seen.

Without this incredible constituent, everything I am would remain only conceptual.

INTRODUCTION

It was long believed that life on Earth evolved in isolation. However, new evidence suggests that opt inhabitants may have been present for millions of years. First introduced to Earth during the Eocene era, approximately 55 million years ago, opt inhabitants in mammal-like forms coexisted and competed with proto-primates. These early opt inhabitants were largely indistinguishable from Earth's native fauna.

Charles Darwin's groundbreaking theory of evolution, presented in 1859, would eventually lead to deeper questions about the origins of Earth's species. By the early 1900s, it became clear that some of the primates inhabiting our planet were more socially complex than apes and had off-world origins. In a revelation that shook the scientific community, it was discovered that these primates were not Earth natives.

By the late 20th century, governments around the world publicly acknowledged what had long been speculated: extraterrestrials had been living among us. Surprisingly, despite their advanced technology, these opt inhabitants were less intelligent than humans. UFO sightings over the centuries, previously dismissed as hoaxes or hallucinations, now took on new significance.

In the present day, researchers have identified that the opt inhabitants we've coexisted with throughout the animal kingdom occupy a space between apes and humans, playing critical roles in our ecosystems. Many theorists suggest that these creatures were sent to Earth millions of years ago and that the more recent arrivals may need human assistance. The general consensus is that there is no hostile intent. Some researchers even posit that the beings responsible for sending these primates may be hyper-intelligent extraterrestrials monitoring our planet.

The United Nations has confirmed that Earth has been receiving harmless extraterrestrials for the past 200 years. The U.S. government sought to expedite opt inhabitant evolution in order to establish contact with the original hyper-intelligent genus, as it was confirmed that we are not alone and, therefore, are in preemptive need of galactic allies.

Public opinion, however, remains staunchly against establishing contact with potentially hyper-intelligent extraterrestrials. In response, the government falsely shifted its narrative, claiming that the ongoing research on these familiar opt inhabitants serves different purposes. "Officially," the aim is to either militarize the opt inhabitants or use them in pharmaceutical testing.

The aim is to bring these beings to human-level sentience through intravenous experimentation and then submerge them into complex human societies. But is this fair?

As humanity navigates its complex relationship with these sentient beings, ethical questions continue to arise about the future of this research.

PREFACE

The decision to become a writer was made at a young age, and though my reasons for continuing this pursuit evolve with time, the fundamentals remain the same. I want my work to mean something for the better. Beyond the primary morals and constructs we generally abide by, I've come to understand that only you can establish secondary beliefs that align with your personal experience. No one else has lived your life. I cannot promulgate beliefs, as they are endemic to my condition, experience, and resolution. However, if there is anything I can offer, it is the suggestion to reflect on an individualistic scale. I believe that is respectfully unassuming enough.

I cannot fully endorse any of the characters, nor does the unfolding of the plot mirror my own experiences. *Who Is Lee?* wrote itself, and I didn't attempt to force meaning into it. Yet, the story is deeply about relevance. I think that's what's most valuable: to be misunderstood, to mask, to project, to accept that we are novices at being human—since it's our first and only time living—and to bear the pressure of making something of ourselves. It's all too familiar.

PROLOGUE

Dr. Masklig stood at the edge of the hangar, staring at the mangled remains of the alien craft under the harsh, fluorescent lights. The Air Force facility was buzzing with activity. He pressed the phone tighter to his ear, listening as Richard's cool, detached voice echoed from the other end of the line.

"We've recovered another one," Masklig began. "The hovercraft is damaged beyond repair, but what's left… it's remarkable. No combustion, no fuel—just a silent propulsion system, unlike anything we've ever seen. And the occupant didn't survive the crash."

Richard's tone remained flat. "Unfortunate. But that's not our concern. We'll await government approval to move forward with Project O.H.I. This information stays between us until the green light is given. Clear?"

Masklig glanced over at the containment unit where the deceased extraterrestrial was being examined. The creature looked disturbingly familiar—primate-like, almost human in some ways. He felt a pang of guilt. "Another O.I. died during your last experiment,"

Masklig said, unable to keep the edge from his voice. "How many more of them need to die before we treat this as something other than an asset grab?"

Richard scoffed. "They're not *animals*, Doctor. Don't confuse them for something they're not. These are biological entities with extraterrestrial relationships far beyond our reach. Our job is to understand—and use—these beings, not waste time on sentimental nonsense."

Masklig's grip tightened. "I'm not sure this is the right thing to do anymore. This isn't good for my career."

The silence from Richard was chilling before he spoke again, his voice low and measured. "If this job is such a moral burden, why are you even calling me then?"

Masklig hesitated, feeling the weight of Richard's words. He had called, after all. "Because I'm torn," Masklig admitted, his frustration boiling over. "These experiments— they're crossing a line."

Richard's response was swift and cutting. "We have a world to defend, and Project O.H.I. is key to that. What's more important to you? Your reputation, or securing the future?"

The question hung in the air, unanswered. Masklig glanced back at the ruined hovercraft, at the lifeless form of the extraterrestrial inside. The future Richard spoke of seemed as dark and uncertain as the one staring back at him from the other side of the containment field. "I'll think about it," Masklig finally said, though the truth was, he wasn't sure how much longer he could pretend that the line between right and wrong hadn't already blurred beyond recognition.

"If that doesn't move you," Richard replied, his voice as steady as ever, "keep in mind we have one O.I. left at our agency. Who knows? It might die like the other two in your absence."

The call ended before Masklig could retort; surely the death of the other experiments at Richard's agency wasn't *his* fault.

CHAPTER 1

BAIT OVERTURE

It's not the same anymore. I'm not a public atrocity nor an attraction. Anymore, at least. And I prefer it this way. I mean, there's not much to elaborate on, and I don't think I really could if I tried. The simple reason is people treat you the same as the next. The next being, the next scientific discovery or innovation, and I am an innovation. I'm not proud of it, but that's because the concept of pride is not equivalent to a neurotypical experience of such a feeling. I also can't elaborate.

Maybe I should journal this, but I can't focus because I haven't said what I want to say, and what I want to say isn't necessarily an elaboration, but it counts for something. I don't know who's counting, though. I just hope that one day, the rustling of my windbreaker will be the most apparent distraction on this train.

The train's fluorescent lights remind me of everything familiar: the lab, the call center pushing weight-loss pills without FDA approval, and the bathroom where I masturbate daily. I really like the idea of masturbation. I've learned that people do it to diffuse their constant melancholy. I should say incessant since people masturbate a lot. I think the fact that I do it and the fact that I know why most people do it counts for something, too.

If I had it all, I'd say there's something safe about the train—the steady chug, the tunnel's void without a hint of light, monotonous expressions huddled together, calm yet impatient, waiting. Sometimes, being in transit distracts me in a good way because it's immersive. This energy is in unison, and if my regulations would supply me with the freedom or auxiliary, I suppose I'd be less concerned about my vulnerability. But I am a product of IRAAB, which is better than being a space alien, but it makes you wish that you didn't exist in the first place. It's also kind of like waking up and wishing your family isn't yours. You want to *continue* being alive or never have been born in the first place.

International Research and Administration of Animalia Biotechnology (IRAAB). That's home. They made me. I should say they made me conscious; on another note, it's up to me to prove that. The best thing to do is to act like one of them. Those passengers who work nine-to-five and prefer Whole Foods but succumb to anything cheaper. Those who entertain sociability and participate socially just to assert themselves. I suppose it's a means to implement an inherent hierarchy, and I could continue on that frequency… for about two more months. And then I'll have to prove myself again with another intelligent breakthrough generated through my own consciousness. Otherwise, I'll be put down like a stray. So, I guess someone's counting.

IRAAB is counting, and Dr. Alec Masklig is counting on me, and I don't think he'll let me die. I don't want to, and that doesn't really qualify me, give me points, or display much progress because it's an instinct. My actions, efforts—they all appear transparent lately. If I don't provide any breakthrough that proves my existence is the equivalent of a human being, the subject, being me, is terminated. But I mean, neurotypical people aren't the only ones to consider, right? That's a bad joke. Sorry, I can't tell.

I'm not the first to be introduced. There are superior aliens who don't need to jerk off to understand what it's like being human, but IRAAB is striving for a comeback. It's like they're saying, "Hey, look! We *also* made a talking alien, and we did it with minimal effort!" I am the world's cheapest model. So yeah, I don't have pride. And if I were the best alien everrr, shit, maybe I would have *some,* given the biotechnological advancements. Actually, the longer I think about it, the more I believe I probably still wouldn't. It's hard to explain, and it's always so hard to explain, and that's obviously a problem right now.

My fame peaked when an indie-rock band asked me to be their album cover. I did it because Dr. Alec always urges me to obtain new and unique experiences. I just went along with it. And honestly, while I was shooting for the cover, all I felt was fear…

And that's not my fault. It's IRAAB's fault. As I said, I'm not well equipped, and even if I were in a situation where I'd have to return the violence for defense purposes, I couldn't. I'm not allowed to. All I'm told is that I'm in the real world, and there's shit I have to deal with inevitably. If those greasy fuckin' kids wanted to do something, I can't do anything back. Sometimes, I feel robbed of the autonomy of self-preservation, like I'm not actually living *my* life.

Sure, the law protects me as I am a citizen, but I mean, come on. IRAAB'S lawyers would file a case against the perpetrator, but would they fight to win? Besides, that's a right most have. Sometimes, I wonder what will happen if a passenger rises to tower above me, forcing me to meet his sight. What if the passenger's hand is in one pocket and the other doesn't know what it's doing, and his chest expands, and his breath reaches me before the exhale is even complete? And I can then tell his breathing is hitched or something. Locking eyes, he draws a shitty fuckin' jackknife that you can buy from a vape shop. I'll know at that moment that if I am to stand, my defensive instinct will kick in, and before I can even make a gesture, my consequences will consume me… I'll seize until I am powerless. Because that's what the consequence is. So I'll just sit here, engaged, afraid. I'll just have to let it happen.

By the time my droning thoughts of rebellion—and the reasons for that lack—conclude, the train screeches to a halt, the brisk air punctuating our temporary traveling purgatory. I pull the sleeves of my trench coat down to cover my wrists. Fuck off. Despite the arboreal microhair, I do get cold. As the doors slide open, the world shifts into the following mode, and people become less of a passenger and more of a cog in the "American Dream." Their steps become strides, and their cortisol increases. It's pretty interesting to witness, but if I catch a glimpse of my reflection somewhere—either in the puddle of homeless piss by the stairs or the metal sheets drilled into the walls, I'll find that I'm one of them. *Almost.*

I work at a call center that sells diet pills without FDA approval. That's where I'm headed right now. One foot after the other, I know the dance of dodging men in suits and the occasional jaywalking. But I rarely need to jaywalk. I have nothing to make me late unless it's a progress report or a technical emergency. My job is a place where recovered addicts go because it's a one-two-step career. *Career*, Jesus. I mean, it's a white-collar job, but I like to wear blue. It's like a fun little statement… because I'm a fuckin opt. Opt inhabitant is the scientifically correct term, and 'alien' is just a colloquial way of naming my genus. The term no longer correlates with a recognized scientific taxon, but I feel calling me an opt is the same as calling someone a slur. Dr. Alec called me that once for fun, and honestly, I laughed. A fat while ago, laughter gave me a renewal on my life's lease. Every sixty days, I have to exhibit neurological biomarkers during my electroencephalography and MRI scans measured by specific gradients to earn another sixty days until I've reached my potential. Then I'm a free man.

I get to work. My designated seat, headset, and desktop are at the end of the row, and these rows are lined with burn-outs, drop-outs, every-out. All of them and their eyes are hollow, and their only burden is in the past, which is why they work—to compensate. No one gives a shit that I work here. Sometimes, I wonder if they are just deliberately negligent or simply accustomed to an alien in a suit because if it's the former, then my intuition is correct. The atmosphere is careless on purpose, and I get the sense that these low-lives don't really like me. I'd still call them low-lives even if they were welcoming. I've had four conversations here in the past year, half of which have been with the manager, Mel, who either conducts an employee evaluation or asks how I'm doing in front of HR. I think that department is vacant because, last I heard via eavesdropping, our HR rep was doing lines of amphetamine in the back. I don't think he was fired the first time around. It was when he punched Mel. I don't particularly dislike Melman, but punching him for absolutely no fucking reason sounds pretty alright, considering his tone is more or less a flat line on a bedside monitor. And his voice is nasal. And he's so white; he looks like his ancestors raised pigs or were pigs. It's just sad. I think if I were Melman, I'd be sad. Bald and sad.

I smirk at my internal monologue as the belt of my briefcase slides off my shoulder. I sit down, turn on my desktop, and stare at a screen that's as blank as the bubble above me. Being thoughtless invokes a steady rhythm of anxiety because I feel myself at my roots. An observing creature of survival and nothing more, having the inability to generate epiphanies or anything short of epiphanies is rather terrifying, given that the nothingness festering in my mind leads to my individualistic extinction. So, I process occurrences in my peripherals and find my neighboring colleague doing the same. I want to assume he has kyphosis from the way he's sitting and wonder which will kill him first: the excessive amount of cheap European drugs or his own body. But I also sit like that. I shit like that, stand like that, walk like that. Fuck him anyway.

"Hey." I don't know his name. I stretch my lips to form a non-threatening smile. But I don't like to show teeth.

He looks me up and down. I don't know if I'm plagued with impatience. Seconds have passed. He shoves his hair to the side to meet my eyes. Oh God, is he going to get up and pull out a shitty jackknife that he most likely bought at the local vape shop? No. He just utilizes his chair to swivel back to staring thoughtlessly at the screen. Yeah, fuck him. Neither of us has a genuine reason for why we don't like each other.

On some level, I envy the kid. But that same energy is applied to everyone; it doesn't even matter if I know them. I'd kill for their freedom, and I suppose no one is free, so maybe I should just chill the fuck out. But also, the kid's been recently promoted. Hence the swivel chair. I could really use a swivel chair.

I don't let the awkwardness of our lame exchange sink. I nod my head while looking down at the floor. My eyes find the next task. As people do, I open my briefcase and use my index and thumb to pull a lead file. I hear the crackle of unfamiliar, soft plastic. I know I didn't pack anything for myself, so I inspect the noise. It's a bag of extruded biscuits. So, food you'd buy for a quarter at a petting zoo. They make a great energy booster since they're full of protein. It's basically dehydrated alpaca meal. I know it's from Dr. Alec, that son of a bitch. I smile to myself, knowing he is determined to tell me that he gives a shit about me. I reach in and grab a bite, only to pause. *Something feels wrong about this.* Why is it animal meal? As much as I want to give credence to Dr. Alec's sincerity, I can't help but think this is a test.

"What is that?" I look over to find the kid interested in not me but my food. Ha!

"It's a snack, my… I packed it for myself and didn't really want it." I laugh.

"Can I try?"

I want to tell him that I don't know if he can. "Yeah."

It won't kill the guy. It might make his stomach upset at most. *But.* What if this is also a test? What if causing harm might reflect poorly on me? It would. But if I'm the only one who knows that, I don't care. I don't have a thought about my identity. I am; that's all there is to it. People seriously give a shit about who they are to themselves, and I care to know what the opposing theory might do to them. It would kind of be hard to digest.

Because it's the truth.

Like that snack, the meaning of existence has a lot to do with being perceived. Therefore, this widely marketed concept of self-reflection is nothing but a sham, designed solely to sell products and services that ultimately contribute to the same illusion. The "inner peace" market pushes essential oils, Pilates classes, and imported coffee to make you feel good about yourself. However, I believe how you present yourself to the world directly influences how people recognize and remember you. This presentation is a crucial part of how you immortalize your existence—through the documentation of your actions and the perceptions others have of you. If you manage to do something truly memorable, people will carry that memory of you for a lifetime.

"Sorry." I jerk my hand back.

"Uh." The guy looks at me in slight disbelief. He smirks.

"You can't have this."

"Why?"

Fuck. I stammer. "Be—because it's inedible. Because it's old!" I find my excuse halfway through. Then we both just sit there twiddling our thumbs. I have little interest in the life taking place next to me, but I need more content to discuss with the scientists at the facility.

I lean towards him to an unnoticeable degree. "What's your name?"

"Caleb."

"Why are you here?" I already know the sob story. It's shared among most employees who barely co-exist here. Caleb squirms. It's a hard memory for him. I study his expression as it transfers from indifference toward me to grave bitterness toward his reason for applying for this job. Caleb tries to hide it, but his naivety gives it away. He looks down, letting the bangs of his fine hair hide his darkened eyes. It's starting to feel uncomfortable. I can't put my finger on it. Before I open my mouth to stop him or even save him from what seems to be humiliation, he tells me.

"I just need to pay rent."

Does he just need to pay *rent*? I try to swivel back but I obviously can't. Caleb can. The ring of my desk phone interrupts my premature thoughts about Caleb.

I answer. "Cut Theory. We *cut* your weight. How may I assist you?" What a shitty slogan.

I think I'm zoning out as I recall the newfound curiosity about Caleb's expression. I can only imagine what I witnessed: exploited youth, severity, and the wrinkle formed between his brows. I believe he felt interrogated for a second. I wish he could think otherwise, but it's not like I wanted to get to know him out of genuine concern.

"I'm sorry. Could you repeat that? You cut off, unfortunately." I'm pretty good at lying.

The customer groans and then reiterates faster than a boat propeller. Jesus, the high- pitched tone, the urgency to drop forty pounds in a month, the disgusting desperation. The worst part is that this woman's tone is accusatory. "I've been taking Cut Theory for about a month and haven't seen a difference. I know there's a thirty-day trial, and I'd like a refund. I did not see much of a difference, unfortunately, and I have this wedding to get to—"

"Ma'am," I cut her off *right* there. I don't care about weddings, and I don't care to hear her say that it's our fault. "We understand that Cut Theory was not a successful experience and are happy to help you. Can you please provide me with your order number?"

She quits her bullshitting and gives me the number. I click and click and type until I locate her order, only to find that she ordered and received Cut Theory like two months ago. Ah, fuck. I break the news to her. "So, unfortunately, we cannot refund you because you received your order two months ago, which is above our thirty-day refund policy."

"Yeah, but I started it a month ago!" She groans again. It's so annoying.

"I understand." I don't understand. "But since the order was shipped two months ago, we cannot offer a refund. We have a new Cut Theory line that might better suit you. We can offer you a thirty-day free trial—"

She hangs up. IRAAB said customer service is a big positive in my life since I'll frequently engage with people, but I think it's to avoid paying for school. Other aliens of other agencies get to go to school.

But work is just that. One situation after another—mitigating, communicating, and sticking to the god-awful script Mel copied from one of those free template websites. I wish IRAAB were like other facilities that paid for college. I'd probably want to study anthropology to figure out people more as a whole. I'd probably be able to make friends by the time I graduate.

The employees here don't give a shit about anything other than things they can benefit from. So they care about making money, they care about their two cents, their two-cent promotions, and they care about the people they'll deal with after their shift ends. I guess I kind of fit in here, but even that's a paradox in itself.

I sneak a glimpse of Caleb. It seems his tension has subsided. That's… Good?

"Hey," I whisper to him. "Are you okay?"

"I'm okay, Prometheus." Good one.

"You just didn't look right for a second."

"…How do I know you're worth talking to?"

For a moment, I'm taken aback by his philosophical utterance. Speechless, I scoff. I mean, I get it. I'm a science project, not a therapist. "I get it," I say softly to him.

I remember when I first started this job. Melman was excited to be affiliated with IRAAB. The employees were sort of wide-eyed. They were still the same unhealthy people, but they appreciated the newness of it all, unaware of what the general public had to say. They just asked questions that matched the capacity of their intellect.

That's the best way I can put it. They also asked which meds scientists would use to sedate me if I ever became hostile. I'm not sure if they were interested in the sedatives— or if I've ever been hostile. I told them that they didn't administer drugs and that I had microchips implanted to shock me.

The attention was fun because it was an opportunity to build something worthy of presenting to my creators. But it never led to any real connection because this sort of thing happens all the time. Even Wall Street has an alien now. Humanity has evolved—our boundaries, perspectives, and tolerance have all expanded. We're all just used to this.

I really do appreciate the type that gives a shit about me, though, not on a personal level. It reflects well on them. And it appears that the subset of people who take a genuine interest in me are healthy or just super kind. It's strange but true. You can't get any change out of me, though. That said, it's only been two months since I started at Cut Theory.

Individuality deserves a more in-depth study because it lies beneath the thick layer of one's archetype. People aren't exploited; it's their archetypes that are. We're... *we're*. Ha. People are constantly categorized into types—Type A and Type B. What's your Zodiac sign? Your Enneagram number? How about your Myers-Briggs type? Are you a middle child or an only child? What about those with divorced parents? And this one is my favorite: people often judge you based on your economic class.

I think I should observe people in that light to get perspective and then later claim it as intuition when I enforce that "astute" judgment. I judge people by the way they talk to me. Do they blink or stare? How do they phrase their questions? Are they two feet away from me? These are fundamental factors to consider, given that I'm not a person. No matter how hard IRAAB tries.

My name is Lee. I am an Enneagram type five. I'm an ISTJ. Dr. Alec is an ISFJ—so close, but not quite. My birthday is December second, so I'm a Sagittarius. I've heard that those born in the winter months are often Vitamin D deficient, which increases the likelihood of depression. I don't know much about my past or my biological parents, and I doubt IRAAB would disclose that information. They're afraid I might want to seek them out and eventually desire to become one of them. Sometimes, I wonder if I'd want that, too, envisioning an easier life surrounded by foliage and forage. Leaves of green and rich agricultural soil seem appealing, but even with all of that, my life wouldn't truly come to fruition.

I simply wouldn't grow, right? I'd just stare at my pack and parents and make noises. I'm not even sure if I'd learn their tongue! Regardless, I am more advanced and would simply get bored. I'd want to maintain my sociability even as a possible introvert. I think I'd miss Dr. Alec a little bit, too, for reasons that aren't considered progressive.

The phone rings. I read my script. "Cut Theory. We *cut* your weight. How may I assist you?"

"Yeah, hi," a shy man with a thin voice responds. "I tried your product and received excellent results." Great.

"We are so glad that Cut Theory benefitted your weight loss journey. How may I assist you?"

"Oh! No need for assistance. Just wanted to let you guys know. Have a great day now."

"Thank you. We will go ahead and renew your subscription." I hang up. He sounded sweet. I don't care for his triumph, you know? But good for him. Behaviors classified as instinct are a subject of debate. I'm unsure why I'd want to speak to Dr. Alec again if I were living in the jungle, but I can anticipate the feeling. Perhaps it's because he is the head of Project Opt Homo-Inhabitant (*Homo*) and ultimately decides whether I live or die unless a substantial unanimous vote goes against his decision. The only authority above him is the CEO. Essentially, I need Dr. Alec to survive. That said, he's generally a nice guy. He's an alcoholic, but I suspect that many scientists are discreetly in the same boat. And he's funny.

One of my biggest achievements at IRAAB was my ability to process humor. While aliens can recognize humor, understanding complex humor is noteworthy. Dr. Alec would play George Carlin specials, and I grasped most of it. So, I don't get my kicks from simple things like peek-a-boo.

By five, I grab my coat and briefcase. I take one last look at Caleb, who's barely getting his shit together metaphorically and currently.

I adjust to the city's bustle with rigidness as the fall air antagonizes my paper skin. There's something about the end of the day. It's more vibrant. I feel like a child again because these natural pinks, blues, greens, and random neons on liquor store windows stimulate my eye. However, it's hard to focus when you have to meet deadlines.

I'm meeting mine pretty fucking soon, and I don't have anything tangible to report.

I can lie. I can lie very well, but it doesn't get past many. There's a whole procedure for determining whether I've made progress. One of the more significant steps is an MRI scan to check if there's any development in my cerebral cortex. First, I submit my claims of emotional discovery recorded in my journal for scientists to identify development by matching information from page to screen. MRI and EEGs can't identify specific emotions, so my entries help define progress in certain regions of the brain. As I'm undergoing scans, I have to think of the claims in my entries to have synapses fire. They particularly search for proliferation among implemented organoids formerly created in Petri dishes from reprogrammed progenitor human cells. Our species comes physiologically and neurologically equipped to reach human-level evolution, but humans decided to expedite this process. An act of probing, if you will.

I can lie about an experience, and they'll pencil it down, monitor my journaling, and schedule sessions to study my emotional process. *Then,* they do a brain scan. If my reports don't match the scan, I'm in trouble. It's happened only once, and scientists of Project Opt Homo-Inhabitant justified it by classifying it as critical thinking… which is technically considered progress. *Progress.* I hate that word like most people hate the word *practical.*

As mentioned, processing complex humor is just one of my many advancements. I have interests, too, and have determined which political party I represent. I'm a Democrat, and I prefer capitalism as opposed to socialism. I also accept that every economic function has its faults, and I also say, 'fuck the one percent.' So, I also understand injustice. I like bars even though I can't drink, and it is against my instinct to guard my vulnerability against drunks. I like the beach and whale watching. I like *some* music, and if I could drive, I'd probably play jazz in the morning—the kind of jazz that has life—and I'd play folk in the evening.

I spot my diner, past the crowds of miraculous colors, the barred pawn shops, and liquor stores hanging on their last thread. It's a Thai place with just four walls and a kitchen so small you can hear every exchange. The manager spots me from the window before I even pull instead of pushing the wooden door. The lady rushes with steps as little as her height. Her eyebrows lift the soft, warm skin pressed to her cheekbones. She opens the door for me.

"Lee," Miss Tangerine exclaims. I'm not all too sure if that's her name. That's just what I heard the first time around. She looks so happy to see me, and I know why. I'm sure her devout urgency to greet me is sincere on some level, but the primary motive is to vlog me placing my order, which is a dinner combo.

We don't have to do this dance every time.

Why Thai food? Why this diner? It took me years to adjust to a meal outside of alpaca meal, and some of the fucking scientists suggested I try flavors beyond my palate as if it would spark any development. It surprises me that the assholes at IRAAB have doctorates. I'm too afraid to try any other diner, as the amount of MSG here perfectly accommodates my digestive limitations. Technically, I can eat nearly anything; I'm simply not adventurous.

"Lee!" She repeats my name. "It's so good to see you!" I bet her nerves are shot every weekend. She never actually knows if I'll return on a Monday or not. The first few times Miss Tangerine posted me, many people came around to witness me eat with chopsticks. Then, like my life's notoriety, the public's attention at this Thai "restaurant" gradually subsided.

I put my hands in my pockets casually. Miss Tangerine glances down watchfully. I warm my voice up to interrupt her suspicions of me potentially going homicidal because that's what everyone thinks. "Hi! Good to see you again, Miss Tangerine." I have to say I kind of like returning here because this lady doesn't give a fuck about what I call her.

She pulls out her phone for the sake of viral cinematography and closes in on my uncomfortable expression. I purse my lips and look down because what the fuck else am I supposed to do every time?

"Say 'hi'!"

I look back into the camera and wave. "Hey, folks."

"So… Uh… What are you having today, Lee?"

I awkwardly make a beeline to the register, where a stack of dusty menus sits, waiting to be reviewed by people who indulge in cultural appropriation. I act as if I'm reading through even though I'd like to cut the bullshit and just pass on my order like any other white man who knows how to say papaya salad in Thai. "I will have… A dinner combo. Fried rice and egg. Beef."

She turns the camera to herself. "Excellent choice! Join Lee every Monday evening. Bye-bye."

Oh my God. The woman's smile stretches like a rubber band. She returns to me with relief. "I'm so glad you came, Lee." She's motherly. I need to jerk off and study Freud later.

After a soft pause, I ask for the bathroom. I rush down the hall, abandoning my briefcase and coat. One hand pressing my dick, the other reaching for the door to quickly secure much-needed privacy. I make sure no one else is shitting in the stalls and promptly burst into one of them, twist the lock, and unzip my pants.

On the way to the bathroom, I saw the lazy chef in the back and endorsed his face, too. I think about him. Obviously, I don't think about fucking inhabitants.

One big fucking orgy. I'd fuck Miss Tangerine if I could, I'd fuck the lard-chef in the back. I wouldn't fuck an animal, but I wouldn't care *who* I'd fuck otherwise. I rush through my climax and make sure my dick is under the belt that is meant to secure khakis. I wash my hands afterward… I'm not an animal.

Miss Tangerine waits for me with a bag tied and ready. "Thank you, Miss Tangerine." I pay with the company card. *Daddy's* money. She pats my back, unafraid of me.

"Take care, Lee."

Oh, Jesus. She says that as if I'm about to be placed in hospice. I smile one last time before looking away. I need to breathe. My heart rate increases, and I hope the scientists who are facilitating surveillance know I'm safe and mindful and that this surge isn't a defensive rush of adrenaline. I have to speak to myself and tell myself I'm okay. I think I feel bad for myself, and it's ironic because everyone at home is going to celebrate it. Pity isn't necessarily a new discovery, and even I know that. I also know that if the board witnesses falsification, our lawyer will step in to deliberate through fine print about the qualification of pity and if there has been a previous synonymous experience.

Take care, Lee. I feel chills down my spine as my body generates homeostasis. I keep my sight below eye level because I suddenly feel endangered. In fact, I feel more susceptible to harm as if the law of attraction had been reinforced during that exchange.

I reach the train station's platform and wait for my ride home. A tedious journey, honestly, and what's worse is that I have to return to a bullshit facility only to sleep for eight hours in a pod that hums like an oven fan. I can handle it, but it's not conducive to IRAAB's goals, you know? It's like I'm being ripped out of a simulation. It makes me *feel* like I'm in a simulation.

This janky locomotive can only take me so far. Sometimes, Dr. Alec is there to pick me up at an intersection reminiscent of *North by Northwest.* He's mentioned a shortcut before, but I'm not a man of risk. Most of the time, I walk on the rural path of gravel and dried, yellow grass. This short journey feels less real than my existence. And it's funny because I've spent most of my life here. This is my hometown, and I was raised here. I look up at the sky, settling into the evening routine. If I try hard, I can remember my childhood. I remember playing outside in the grass when the grass was lush. I remember myself tumbling and what the world looked like upside down. I can't tell you if my development was from child to adult. I was just 'programmed,' and adjusting to the implemented maturity took time. Until then, all I did was play.

I remember what it was like behaving as a kid, but even more so, I remember the reactions and the energy radiating through my perceivers, observers. They didn't like that I played and roamed in a diaper. It was ostensibly deemed unfit for this project, but that memory stings. The ability to be aware of motives and potential ulterior motives makes a motherfucker feel lonely, I suppose. No one is sincerely asking how I'm doing; they just need some rendition of an answer to transliterate into a report. It's Monday, which means weekly evaluations and blood tests are to be conducted. After all, I am prone to diseases.

Recalling the dreaded day of the week encourages me to drag my feet. I feel this dangerous urge to walk barefoot, to test the gravel's strength against thick skin. If I let these mere desires trespass, then what's next? Commuting through branches? I hear my species do that and roll through the foliage to avoid predators. That probably looks dumb as shit.

I want to try that. Fuck it.

Thick rows of evergreen border the vast acres in which IRAAB resides. I use my right shoe to push the heel of my left shoe off and repeat the process. I tie the laces of my loafers to the briefcase's handle and make for the woods. The coarse but cold grass delights my senses. I accelerate my pace until I'm running homeward bound. I may be tired, but I refuse to overlook this freedom to compensate for the remainder of my energy that will be drained when I return to the facility.

I stumble and roll into the tall strands of yellowish green. The brisk wind softens itself to brush through my hair. I don't have much time to lie there, yet I allow myself to soak up the image of the sun setting as I try so hard to keep the facility out of my peripherals. And then I close my eyes for a gentle moment. I wish I could hold this feeling forever, and I wish I could unearth it to my defense when angst riddles my streams. I pick myself up and run to the pines of daunting heights and lunge onto the bark. Blood swells where splinters push. What a beautiful thing to feel pain on behalf of your intention. I extend my right to grip the branch and let myself depend on it. Hanging there, I feel great, but I don't feel like myself. This is what I think depression is. When nothing makes you feel okay about yourself.

So, this experience is irrevocably disappointing, but I suppose I can enjoy the short-lived liberty of knowing I am solely to blame for my recently acquired wounds. I swing in the direction of the winding gravel roads as they lead to the gated entrance of the facility. A block of concrete attached to other blocks of concrete is what I call home, and home is surrounded by tall barbwire fences. Sometimes, when I'm feeling lucky, I hop over those fences. But not today.

I decline swiftly from the trunk and ring the buzzer. I release my shoes from the briefcase to match my apparel once again. An alien in a suit is not an alien without his shoes. I don't know if that makes sense, but whatever. I know it's essential to wear them; besides, wearing them will circumvent the common suspicion of regression among scientists. When the sharp ring of the buzzer cuts off, no one asks who it is. They know it's me. They know it's due to monotonous routines. The charged metal gates creak open to admit. Once again, I drag myself through.

The satin pocket inside my briefcase holds a pass, which I scan at the doors. You ask why I can't scan at the gate. Because when they built this place, they had very little money— and even less common sense to pair with it. The scanner glows green, and I let myself in.

A few scientists, unrelated to Project Opt Homo-Inhabitant, pass by me. I'm sure their heads are filled with the next animal in which to implement consciousness. Maybe a newt.

Dr. Seymore Barberry purses his lips to offer a classic American smile. Though he's not old, he carries himself with a weight that belies youth. I feel like he was kinda cast into this agency to fit the diversity initiative.

He's a nice guy. He's not necessarily sympathetic, but that's almost everyone here. Seymore is a knowledgeable astrobiologist. He is part of the surveillance department to monitor my distress and cortisol levels. When he asks me personal questions, it's in a private setting. Others just approach me like they're ripping sheets off halfway through my fucking REM cycle. And don't get me wrong, I don't care if the scientists are not interpersonal with me and not because I naturally cannot care, which is true, yeah, but also because it's hard to care.

It's hard to get attached to a living thing and watch it suffer, primarily if it was raised among them to walk, speak, behave, attain etiquette, and so on. People are like that with their domesticated creatures and literally fall into an abyss of isolation when they pass. I'm sure when they began as interns here, they probably fell in love with a few animalia experiments. I was raised in an environment of experienced scientists, so I never received that.

I continue down the main hall, passing departmental wings lined with large windows. You can look out, but you can't look in. The floors and walls are slabs of white that interior designers identify as sleek and minimalist. My steps sound professional as they echo throughout the area.

The hall tapers, and I am now at the heart of IRRAB. It's a round-about. In the middle is an empty desk meant for a receptionist, but I suppose we don't need that anymore. Or better yet, I guess we can't afford that anymore. Anywho, I have a choice of pursuing four different routes labeled as "Hall A," "Hall B," "Lab," and "Dining Hall."

I want to eat, but I'm not supposed to. I have to clean myself off before my lab tests, so Hall B it is. I sigh and bend my neck to express a variation in my emotions. The showers are designed in an open layout, reminiscent of a prison—exposed, stark, and stripped of privacy. An assigned scientist waits for my arrival, so technically, I have no choice in which hall I first spend my time in. With a towel, razor, packaged toothbrush, and packaged soap, the scientist greets me half-heartedly. This is definitely just a job to her. "Hello, Lee."

I don't even respond. I just nod and throw a smile her way. She relays the toiletries, and we make contact. I don't know who physically feels more artificial, me or her iced hands wrapped in white latex gloves. Imagine if she's an experiment, too. I pass her, letting the air of my passive aggression confront her stoic expression.

I strip to my thin hair and toss my clothes down the chute. I spray my shoes with antibacterial detergents, take them off, and step underneath the shower head. I'm accustomed to hot water now. The steam builds to deliver privacy. I unwrap the gentle, fragrant-free soap and begin with the soft folds of my face. I use my index fingers to rub my eyes until the comfort of rubbing them turns into a crescendo of burning as the soap slips through. It's worth it.

A generous amount of soap sits in the palm of my hand. I use my pro-vided rag to spread the body wash around my back and arms. I wish someone were here to do this for me. I extend my right arm and shave a portion of it to make it easier for Seymore to draw blood. As much as I'd like to, I try not to rush through my routine because there's a time quota.

The shower turns off as we reach the limit. I can always ask for an extension, but it's not conducive to an eco-friendly facility. Plus, like any other behavior that trespasses regulations, it will somehow reflect poorly on me unless I prove otherwise. I shake off the excess water, and the shower head's rim turns a glowing red to indicate that the heated fan is about to get the job done for me.

I puff up under the rapid breath of this little but efficient fan. If I had a place of my own, I'd want to install this sort of technology. IRAAB is not a dingy agency. It's meticulously lavished with state-of-the-art technology. I suppose when the funding decreased, so did the effort, turning this place into a meretricious opportunity for scientists who couldn't do better. I can't really speak for all of the employees here, though. I don't know why Dr. Alec ended up here.

I read through his file once. He's the leading animal geneticist in the nation and studied at some Ivy League. I wholeheartedly believe he's received better offers but deliberately chose to remain here. I'm not sure why, and I can't be the reason. He joined around the same time I did. Dr. Alec also studied psychology and ethology. If he knows what the fuck he's doing, I wonder why he shoved himself into a world of dismay.

The scientist, who looks like a character from a movie about hyper-realistic AI, hands me my pajamas. They're cotton and hand-woven by children. How sweet! Not only is IRAAB eco-friendly, but they are also child-labor-friendly. I bend the other way so she can get a good look at my backside. I suppose I will journal about this particular instance, too, before turning it in to Dr. Alec or Dr. Barberry, so it can be generated as a weekly report. I think it's a funny situation, and it originates from the feeling of retaliation. I think this could potentially qualify as a great discovery, given that I am retaliating against people for whom I have a slight, left-handed grudge. People like this scientist are automated. But then again, I prefer to be forgiving because some of us are avoiding attachment issues and are maybe even protecting me from separation anxiety.

"Thank you." I lean into her left breast to read the name tag. "Thank you, Doctor…" Jesus, I still can't read it. To my defense, the font is tiny! She must be new here anyway.

"You're welcome, Lee. Follow me."

"Are we headed to the pod room?"

"No." She's a wall with tits. "Dr. Barberry is going to draw your blood for tests."

"Oh." I didn't forget. I was just hoping. I tail her up the hall. She makes a swift left into a room slightly dimmer than the other room. I guess it's suggestive lighting as it *suggests* me to calm the fuck down. For instinctual and logical reasons, I am always afraid of getting my blood drawn. I don't like being pricked, and I don't like knowing that there might be something to worry about after getting pricked. I like to be healthy. Humans don't really appreciate their health until something detrimental transpires, like cancer, a motorcycle accident, or an overdose. Only when something is taken away from you do you value it. It's so awful that they're basically programmed this way. Even in theological literature, civilizations were often regarded as ungrateful. For the *record,* I'm not a hypochondriac. The scientist instructs me to sit on the medical cot using the stepper. She rolls out a sheet of new parchment paper to encompass the mattress. "Is there a new patient I am not aware of?"

"No."

Good, I don't want competition. Is she lying or boring?

I hop up on the cot. "Are you lying?"

This pisses her off. I get that I'm questioning her integrity, but it's as though she was waiting for me to tamper with her last nerve.

"No." She sticks her head out.

Dr. Barberry interrupts by flicking on the other lights. I suddenly feel more seen, and the room opens up as the comforting shadows cooperate to disappear. I squint a little. I feel like all of my expressions are fake. Dr. Barberry pumps two pumps of sanitizer and rubs his hands as he replaces the irritated scientist's position. She steps to the left of Seymore to assist him.

"Hello, Lee," Dr. Barberry greets me amicably. I lift my hand loosely to wave. "I insisted that we replace used equipment to maintain hygiene. That's all," he says softly. Dr. Barberry unwraps the blood pressure cuff. "Besides, what's wrong with adding someone to the picture?" He squats on a stool.

I look up at the female scientist. "Like her?" She glares at me. I like that. Dr. Barberry chuckles as he wraps the cuff around my arm.

"Dr. Cambry has been with us for four years." Damn.

"Well. We haven't acquainted ourselves." Dr. Barberry secures the cuff, then inflates and deflates. He records the blood pressure. I pick at the skin around my nails.

"What—what's my blood pressure?"

"One fifteen over seventy-four." He looks up from his chart. "You're fine."

I exhale. "Okay."

He places his stethoscope against my chest. "Breathe." I do as I am told. He listens to four other points on my chest, abdomen, and back and puts the stethoscope down. "Palpation and percussion through *auscultation* are all in check." I try to pronounce the word in my cute little head. He knows that I need to know meticulously.

I purse my lips and look at his eyes. "I could kiss you." We both laugh.

He spins around to pull a cart of equipment near him, wraps the tourniquet around my limb, and checks for the meatiest vein. "Oh, you shaved," he jokes.

"To your liking, Dr. Barberry."

He cleans the targeted area with an alcohol swab, and I feel the pinch and sore aftermath. I tense up, and Dr. Barberry looks up with that 'you're kidding me' expression. "Sorry," I whisper.

He inserts the cold needle, and for half a second, the pain feels euphoric—thrilling. But it's embarrassing to be *this* proud of myself. The blood loops through tubes and into a test tube. Dr. Barberry releases the tourniquet, and Dr. Cambry covers the prick with a children's bandage. I look closely at it. It's the E.T. from *E.T.* She meets my eyes with a nasty smirk.

Dr. Barberry uses the wheels of his stool to propel himself towards the counter. He uses sanitizer again. "Okay." He puts his hands to his waist like a superhero, "I'm done here. Dr. Cambry, Lee is free to have dinner or rest in the pod room. Just let Dr. Alec know."

"Okay."

I get to my feet and extend my hand to shake hers. "A pleasure." She reaches out to only fulfill social etiquette. I put my hands in the pockets of my pajamas and exit to my pod room in Hall B. Most of the meek interns have dispersed. I look at the glass dome and see the sun has officially set.

The metal doors of my room are open, so someone must have changed the linens of my pod. My technologically advanced abode is furnished as a dorm and constructed like a jail cell. The walls are hard concrete, and the recessed lighting blares white. Every evening, I take two steps into my room, sigh, and flip open the mood controller installed in the place of a light switch next to my door. I balance the lighting to calm my mind and apply eucalyptus lotion. It's kind of like I'm making myself at home.

I scratch my ass and lift my sheets, ready to get into bed, until I hear this jackass's voice barrel through the halls. It's Dr. Alec, and I can tell he's tired and itching to delegate responsibilities without even capturing his expression yet. "Cambry? Where do you think you're going?" I can't hear Dr. Cambry's response, so I'm sure she's frozen, using the weak side of her brain to construct a reasonable excuse. "Don't bullshit me," he says confidently.

Dr. Alec swiftly turns into my room. He scratches his nose and points at me. "No, no. You're not cozying up yet." His gestures are large; he takes up space.

"Fuck," I mumble.

Dr. Alec leans against the door and clicks his tongue. He purses his lips and nods. "Okay." He turns around gracefully, and I know I've fucked up. I obviously can't miss this evaluation, so why am I stalling? Before I open my mouth to plead, he interrupts. "Get on my back," he instructs.

I cock my head to the side. "Did I do something right?"

He's still playfully turned. "No. You're a dick, now get on my back."

By the time Dr. Cambry shows up, I'm already on Dr. Alec's back and headed to Hall A. Perplexed, Dr. Cambry throws a quick glare my way, and I return a half-smile. "Hi," I say to her.

Dr. Alec uses only his voice to locate Dr. Cambry. "Cambry." She responded meekly. "Yes, Dr. Alec?"

"Get ahead of us and set up the lab. Print this week's journal and allocate it as soon as you can. That translates to now, provided your remaining duties are secondary to Project Opt Homo-Inhabitant."

He cranes his neck to wink at me. Smiling, I embrace him like you would a pen pal after a life sentence in prison and whisper in his ear, "So why are you carrying me?"

"I'm in a good mood."

"I appreciate your sympathy, but come on. What's the deal?" We arrive at another room called a lab, but it's primarily used for therapy. Dr. Alec gently sits me on a stool and walks around to the white countertops that split us apart. He pulls a pen out from his breast pocket and assesses the copy of my journal. Dr. Alec presses his glasses down and reads each sentence carefully as I eagerly await his response to my previous curiosity.

"I'm betting on you, Lee," he says casually without looking up. My stomach churns at the thought of disappointing Dr. Alec. He huffs as he reads through the first page and snickers when he gets through the first half of the second. "The chef brought you to climax?"

I shrug.

"So you have a thing for him?"

"Not necessarily." I probably seem fearful of the possibility that I might have disappointed the only guy who's actually rooting for me. "I know that most aliens are bisexual anyway." My shoulders hunch. Dr. Alec sighs and looks through the page.

"Well, I think it's funny anyway, don't you?" I nod enthusiastically. I need to chill out. I don't need to be this fretful. I have time on my hands to redeem myself. "Does attraction matter to you?"

I laugh to myself. "Are you asking if I'm attracted to a fucking lard sweating over my dinner?" Dr. Alec is taken aback by my response, but not in a bad way. I think he wasn't expecting me to shift the dynamic and pursue humor without him initiating any sort of witticism.

He crosses his arms and points at me. "That's insensitive."

I rub my forehead. "What? Are you gonna kill me for that instead?"

Dr. Alec's gaze weakens in mercy. He doesn't need a moment to process the cynicism in my quip. I can tell he's already observed my anxiety and is aware of me picking at the skin of my fingers. He puts his pen down. "Lee." I look up to him. "It's going to be okay." No one tells me this enough, and I feel myself welling up. He holds his earnestness for a moment and then puts the copy of my journal down to investigate the source of my unease. "I know it's hard to be conscious of being conscious."

"Like an expiration date." I look away as the words come out. "That is the first thing I think of."

I sense shame in Dr. Alec's new series of gestures, but he remains composed. He pushes back the stray, golden waves of hair to expose his tense forehead. I've heard that no one can tell if you stare at someone's forehead instead of their eyes. I try it, and he catches me, but at least we have gotten our minds off the tension. Seeing Dr. Alec recalibrate is funny, especially after I attempt to maintain "eye contact." He aligns the sheets of paper, adjusts the thick-framed glasses, and clicks his pen a few times.

I feel like I have to save him. "But we're trying hard," I say hesitantly. I was going to express that *I'm* trying hard, but managed a quick exit to sympathy-land by replacing it with 'we' instead. He nods twice and purses his lips, and I feel heard.

"I'm sorry..." We both souse in his groundbreaking words. I believe he wanted to say, 'I'm sorry for creating you,' but it's best not to say things like that. I suppose it's best for me not to hear things like that because, throughout my development, I've become more in tune with my existence—and it matters more to be perceived, as it validates my existence. It's become more challenging to imagine the world without myself, and I don't mean that in a defensive way to protect and lengthen my shelf life. I just feel like I am more than an eating and shitting creation of procreation. I am a person to some extent.

Anyway, I think Dr. Alec can't do his job right today. He's not off-kilter, he's just off. Dr. Alec is usually off-kilter in a genius way, to say the least. He finds a way to implement the magnitude of his knowledgeable experiences inherited from within and beyond the scientific field to shift the momentum of IRAAB. I'm unsure if the rest of the executives and scientists of Project Opt Homo-Inhabitant appreciate the erudite motions of his epiphanies, but he doesn't care. Dr. Alec cares little about how he is perceived. His efforts and management are expeditious, and I wish I could write a recommendation letter for the guy. Even though we know very little about Dr. Alec, he is somehow very personal yet excessively professional. Today, though, he isn't himself. I think I broke that momentum, and I want to feel sorry. Should I say that?

"Dr. Alec." I almost reach across to tap his shoulder, but that's the wrong social cue. "I want to feel sorry."

He is puzzled and annoyed. "Can you please elaborate?" I place my hands on the counter and look at them. I swivel my opposable thumbs to prove something to myself. I look at his thumbs. "Lee," his urgency intervenes in my thoughtlessness. "What are you trying to say right now?"

I repeat his urgency assertively. "What I'm trying to say is… You want what you can't have." I can tell he's trying so hard to keep his composure that I give him virtually nothing to work off of. This is almost fun, but I cut the crap. "I'd like to feel apologetic, as well as many other things." I pause for drama. "I can't bring myself to. It's not even like I should feel apologetic based on empirical evidence of how the average human feels. I'd like to feel a certain way in correlation to a certain situation, but I don't want to." The storm of my truth passes, and we wait for what will come next.

Dr. Alec looks in and through my eyes to study something my words cannot express, apparently. I can't hear his nose whistle. I look at his nostrils. I don't like this moment. It's not even intimate. It just makes me feel like nothing. His transition into being less Alec and more doctor is unnerving because his assessment by peering into every muscle tension, every gesture, and every expression proves that I cannot just breathe. It's all marked to make a case, and I'm simply making a case that this shit might just qualify as an advancement for Homo-Inhabitant. Dr. Alec has a standard to uphold. Even though he is the head of this project and can shit and eat whenever he wants at work, he does have to answer to a unanimous vote occasionally. Dr. Alec can be voted off, and Dr. Alec's decision to renew my lease can be vetoed.

Most of the time, IRAAB kisses his ass as if some actually dedicate the subject of their theses to him, and it's because he shouldn't be here, but out of some vague, unidentified reason, he chose to linger. He should be somewhere better. I hate that we always find a way to come back to me. It's like a bummer and a reality check. I suppose I should take advantage of this surrender to actuality and look back into his eyes so that he can present valid research. But by the time I look up, he's got his head down and his pen to paper, creating truths that could convert atheists. I try to peek at his notes on what he's observed, but they look like prescriptions for antidepressants. His handwriting is *that* bad. "So you want to *want*?"

"Desperately," I say.

"Skip work one day. Go, go fuckin' do something. Did you ever observe or ask what people do on the weekends?" He mumbles to himself. "Why do you even go to work?"

"Well… I—I go to work because that's the height of assimilation, Dr. Alec." I am a little concerned that I have to remind him.

"You could join the YMCA. That would achieve the same prospect." Oh. I mean, different strokes for different folks. In IRAAB's news-letter, the board publicly released an agency-supported intent of Opt Homo-Inhabitant. So, I think implementing you in the workplace is a lifestyle they want to project, you know? We're appealing to the middle class. That makes sense." He speaks to himself again.

"I read it last week."

"Yeah?"

I push carefully. "So… what do people do on the weekends?"

  BY ZAINAB F. RAZA

"Fuck if I know. Don't ask me," Dr. Alec's laughter hits my inappreciable ethos.

"I mean, I get you can't exactly tell me how to live." I don't mean to draw a line. We both know he can't tell me how to live. I just want to appear comprehensive.

He shoots a severe but fragmented look. "I can't." He shrugs a half-ass apology. I cannot, for my life, ascertain the sullen face Dr. Alec wears in response. Most likely, he is suggesting that he cannot live for me, and I mean, why would someone prefer the vicarious experience? The point is, I think it bothers him that Dr. Alec can't help me. But, if I truly interpret Dr. Alec at this moment, I will discover that he doesn't have an exemplary life to offer in suggestion. He opens his mouth and then glitches. He is about to attest to something. I wonder if he is about to share something private, something no one else at IRAAB will know.

Instead, he shuts the fuck up and leads me out of the room, and we turn left to pursue the main hall. I look back, watching the pod room get smaller and smaller. We take another left for the grand entrance of my personal impersonal hell. Dr. Alec stops in his tracks. "I have to go to my office." I assume I have to wait right here. Imagine if I did exit by myself. Surveillance would go ballistic, and Dr. Alec would personally punish me, and somehow the world would find out, and SNL would do a bit where Dr. Alec has me bent over as he spanks my ass.

He returns with two beers. I'm not surprised. Dr. Alec's tendencies are quite public. We lean into a cold night. Upon my first step out at an unusual hour, I find liberation beneath my numbing complacency. More than liberation, I bear a strong sense of anticipation. So strong that I could go to church or a fortune teller to find an answer. I turn my head like a doll does in a horror flick and smile at Dr. Alec.

"You're so weird." He smirks, but it isn't an insult. Dr. Alec's inherent clemency eclipses all other traits, regardless of their potencies. I follow him as we cross over from cement to terrain. "Come." We forge a trail as we depart further from the facility and land southwest of the fenced location. Dr. Alec instructs me to sit by sitting down. I look up at the speckled night and wonder if the world will one day come to replace the stars with aircraft better than the ones we know and all other advancements that sustain our vices, moving further away from grounded realities. My mind floods with shame against mankind while I nevertheless identify as one of them. How can I say I am against discovery when I am the epitome of it? I smirk at my conceit. Dr. Alec looks over. "What?"

"I think this project and IRAAB's partnership with big pharma is… going to be one hell of a ride, Alec." He doesn't correct me nor flinch at the absence of professional regard. The thing is, I often call him Alec to his face and Dr. Alec when I'm thinking of him.

"What makes you say that?"

"Why question something that is?" I signal him philosophically. "It would be a hell of a ride, and that's a definitive statement, not an opinion." He ignores me. He looks at the sky to avoid generating an iota of thought that collimates my ponderings. He avoids capturing this abrupt conclusion. He opens a beer with his teeth. He spits the cap to litter. "The insistence of tampering with innate behavior is… I have no words, really."

Dr. Alec takes a sip. "It's not an act against nature."

   BY ZAINAB F. RAZA

"Tell that to the public," I toss his comment aside.

He proceeds to take the piss out of me. "It was either you or an ape."

How insulting. "Don't ever put me in the same box as a—no. It wasn't me or some shit- for-brains ape."

"Your species, Lee, if I may remind you, inhabited Earth during the Eocene era! You evolved alongside proto-primates. Look at your mammalian features. You're practically cousins!"

I squint at him. "This isn't about militarizing secondary sentience or big pharma testing. I've read about the old protests. '*Bait Overture.*' I know about it."

"I haven't followed up on the old protests," he says, dumbfounded. "I live under a rock."

"Yet you read IRAAB's newsletter… The people are suspicious; the people are against contact. They know what the government is up to."

Dr. Alec blows me off. "When did you see people in the real world give a shit?" He looks at me unsurprised. "How do you know?"

"Because you didn't choose the ape." Shifting into egocentrism, I raise my brows and lift my nose. "We're the socially apt species anyway."

"Because of your vocal tract," he presses mockingly. If we were colors, I'd be red, and he'd be beige. But then his brow twitches. "Are you making a case against yourself?"

In 1859, Charles Darwin presented the Evolution Theory. In the mid-1900s, it was discovered that the neighboring primates inhabiting Earth since the Eocene are not only more complex than apes, but they are also terrestrially foreign. A scientist by the name of Jay Kindell conducted a study on our species and discovered that we are neurologically and physiologically capable of human-level evolution. After the discovery, more UFO hovercrafts crashed near research facilities. In them were reportedly deceased extraterrestrials.

In the late 1900s, the news leaked after various non-threatening UFO sightings occurred in the span of that century, along with empirical information that my species is less intelligent than homo sapiens.

Popular evolutionary biologists and astrobiologists theorize a more advanced foreign genus chose this planet as a haven for its subordinate species, proving not only is the genus hyper-intelligent, but the genus is not malicious. *They need us.* That was the official slogan for the government-mandated research on us to advance our cognitive ability in hopes of bridging the gap between man and the unseen extraterrestrial vanguard. The U.N. confirmed we've received globally harmless invasions, especially after Kindell's discovery, and expressed that, evidently, the human race is not alone. It's safer to make allies.

Project Opt Homo-Inhabitant and others alike were thrust into existence. Instead of using Kindell's outdated methods, scientists expedited the process of evolution by implementing organoids that were created from progenitor human cells.

Phase Two, "Bait Overture," is about using hyper-sentient opts as bait to advertise the competence of the human race. An attempt to attract the intelligent genus and establish a bond. Phase One is to become sentient. The best way to get sentient opts up to speed regarding human-level evolution is by submerging them into society. There's nothing to hide anyway. We're being watched.

Also, it's true. People did protest against the threatening leap of discovery and were later fed a dull narrative that opt inhabitants are experimented on for Big Pharma or eventual militarization—which hippies were still not okay with. But they all know. And I know, too. Because they didn't pick the ape.

I wish I had declined Project O.H.I., but by the time I could, I couldn't. I *want* to live. "No." I retire my wheels. They're burning rubber. It doesn't matter what the scheme is because I'm here now, consciously, and it needs to stay that way.

"Lee. You won't understand—"

"Why?" I snap. "Because—because I am not you?"

"Well. Yes." He preemptively bites open another bottle, though he hasn't even finished the first. I need to alleviate my temper fast, but for him to even challenge my inability to thicken the thread that I cling to for dear life by being so stupidly short with me is below him. I am baffled above all. "Besides. That's Phase Two." I scoff. "And when do we initiate that?"

"You'll know."

"After Phase One is complete?"

He raises his eyebrows and nods facetiously. "Very good, Lee." I roll my eyes. "Anyway. 'Bait Overture' doesn't mean you're not free.

Let's try to focus on this week, though. How about that?" I shuffle through the relevant portion of topics to introduce an impasse. Dr. Alec looks up at the sky one more time as he prepares to fulfill a discussion that I cannot contribute to. "Why did you even want to apologize?" He looks at me. "Earlier?"

I introspect, "I think it was just that you seemed guilty. Because I haven't done anything to save myself."

"I see." He hands the bottle to me. I look at it, not knowing what to do with it. "Drink," he commands.

"But—"

"I'm the head of the project. If there's anyone you can trust, it's me." I sniff the bottle in lieu of doubting his hand. I hear the force of his words echo through my head again, and I do it. The barley piss sits like a pond on my buds until I find the courage to swallow. I think the first sip can always be interpreted as a placebo because I want to say I'm already buzzed, but absolutely nothing has happened. The world is still orbiting towards another year, the mosquitoes are still traveling through the currents of breeze around us, and I am still fully conscious. "I want you to drink until you can tell the difference."

I sigh. "Okay." I open the hatch of my gullet and drain the bottle, hoping to earn credit where it's due as my obedience outstands me.

"Wow." Nice. "That was enthusiastic of you," he exclaims teasingly.

I wipe my mouth and find my breath. "What's the point of this exactly?"

"You want to want. Right? So, let's get you there." He offers his bottle to me, and suddenly, this feels like peer pressure, and I should be in a fifth-grade drug assembly. "I want you to understand that the pursuit of relative achievement lies in risk."

"As in, risking my life?"

"On some level, yes." Time passes for the alcohol to settle into my blood. "I think the root of evolution is discovery, which, of course, you were unnecessarily negating." He tips against me. "I also think the consciousness that perceives life today involves desire. Same difference, different word. Desire is a mere product of individuality, and I urge you to find yours. This moment is life in a nutshell for you because the risk and the reward are truly, truly gratifying."

"I disagree."

"About?" Dr. Alec allows me to elaborate.

"It's not about discovery. I don't think the point of humans making contact with my parental species is for that reason." I'm trying hard to concentrate on my point, though it's slipping from me.

"It wasn't," Dr. Alec's tone is agreeable. "It's to make allies—"

"Please don't interrupt me, I'll forget." I giggle. But then. I'm distracted by the world around me, and my conjecture almost dissipates into this existential void. Do my theories matter? Does the reason matter? The echo of my giggle is gone, but I can still hear it on a loop. Does anyone think I'm adorable? Should I love myself more? Dr. Alec shifts a little, and it brings me back to the moment. "I don't think it's about discovery—or *safety*. It's about purpose."

"Purpose?" Dr. Alec's tone isn't agreeable anymore.

My head hurts. I lay in the grass and giggle until the giggles crescendo into laughter. I roll onto my belly and rip a fart. Through my heaving, "Did you know that I was taught to say flatulence instead of fart?" Dr. Alec laughs. I yell, "That's so fucking lame!" I get up again. "Alec, I don't remember a fucking word you said."

He looks up at me with soft, gentle eyes. "Very good, Lee." This feels good indeed. I want to dance and listen to music, but the kind of music I am familiar with and can play in my head is either oriental spa music or classical tunes.

"I know what I want," my words stretch and slur. I raise my finger. "I want an apartment."

CHAPTER 2

THE ARCHETYPE

I return to work without knowing how Dr. Alec might have handled the aftermath of breaking regulations. I am not particularly worried, though, at least about myself. What I am worried about is my brewing hangover. I feel like someone grabbed my head and bashed it repeatedly into a wall. However, the drunken memories compensate as they are actually pretty fuckin' delightful, even if I can't remember most of it. I want to share this with someone, so I look left to find Caleb nodding off.

I see Mel walking towards us. His eyes are trying to make out Caleb's strange behavior. I'm sure he thinks the kid is high. I return to the computer to begin the first hour of my nine-to-five shift. Mel knocks on my desk. He swallows a deep breath, expanding the stretchable khakis you pick up at an all-in-one grocery store. He rubs his eyes and lets out a groan. "Hey, Lee."

"Morning, Mel."

"We're going to conduct an evaluation separately for you. Why don't you come on back?" Uhh, what the fuck? Evaluations are rarely one-on-one. Mel's too fucking tired of his life to conduct them.

I stand up and press the wrinkles out of my pants. "Sure. Is everything okay?"

"Yeah, there's nothing to worry about. We have a new HR rep, and she really wants to meet you." Oh, how nice, a fan. I follow Mel through the office, which has a few windows and a stained carpet. Some of the employees look up from their bullshit careers to unusually glare at me. It seems this is not a typical weekday. I must have done something when I was drunk, but that makes no sense. Anxiety flushes my senses, and thoughts begin to rush. I can't imagine I did anything wrong here, but these sons of bitches are staring at me like I chucked soup at the Mona Lisa or some shit.

Mel opens the door to his office. The thick air of processed meat and coffee rests heavily here. I enter first and hate it because I can't watch my back even though I trust Mel won't actually do something, but my paranoia shifts into something else I cannot name now. It doesn't matter; her name is Virginia. She's the new HR rep, and she's standing to the right of Mel's desk, eager and yet sincere. She locks eyes with me and reads my face to understand the phenomenon that I am. Her hands are together, and her shoulders are curved forward. She leans slightly and smiles at me. Her smile is so important that I can't find the words to greet her. Her skin is thin enough to make blue vessels beneath her eyes and wrists visible, and her frizzed locks are summertime and tied into a mess.

She lends an unsure hand. I shake it to prove that, yes, an alien can shake hands. "Hi," her Christmas smile lights up. "I'm Virginia, I'm the new HR rep. You must be Lee." I still haven't found my words. She glances at Mel, not knowing what to do next. Mel circles to his seat and plops down. He looks through my file and gestures for me to take a seat. I rip myself through to reality and take a seat as I avert my eyes from Virginia. I can't imagine what her face might depict. I can't tell what she thinks of me. I need to fucking say something!

"Why am I here?"

Mel sets my file down and places his hands on the table to reveal the big news. I like that his palms are flat on the desk. That means he doesn't have a gun latched underneath. Mel's not really the type to own a gun, though, and that's honestly preferred. "Okay, Lee. We didn't want to share this in front of everyone, but you've earned a promotion." I raise my brows.

"Jesus, Mel… Thanks."

"I think it's best to keep this to yourself. We don't want anyone to get competitive." Ha. I nod in compliance. "Virginia is here because…" He can't even remember.

"I'm here because I wanted to meet you personally, and Mel wants me to familiarize myself with all the employees here. It helps HR mitigate future interactions." I nod again and feel really stupid.

I need to say something to her, too. "The last HR rep died, I think, from an overdose… You seem qualified, so I'm sure you'll be here for a long time." What? *Why?* Why would I fucking say that? Mel purses his lips. Virginia's muscles gradually release her from her smile. I obviously weirded her out.

Mel clears his throat. "Okay, Lee. You can return to your seat. That will be all." I use both armrests to get up and hurry the fuck out. I can hear Melman explain to Virginia that the last HR rep didn't actually die.

On my way back, my head spins. I am actually embarrassed! Honestly, I could vomit because the hangover and social anxiety are kicking in. I find the bathroom instead and storm in. No one is here, thank God. Just me and my self-deprecating thoughts as I push myself through to the toilet. I get on my knees, hunch over, and stick my fingers down my throat to induce everything. Relieving myself brings me to a placid state, and everything feels even, like I am in control again. I love the feeling of control. I give myself the luxury of another minute before I wipe my drool and fix my shit.

The face Virginia held when I blurted out those words, which clearly did not match my tone, flashes through my head. It was like a horror show for no fucking reason! I just met this girl. I can't fault her for my nervousness, even though I prefer to blame everyone who crosses my path for any minor inconvenience. I rest my head against the toilet paper dispenser and sigh. I know I have to get back before Melman revokes my promotion. This gives me a semblance of motivation to return to my feet and leave the reeking bathroom.

Before heading to my seat, I take a glance through the windows of Mel's office. He spots me, and I don't know what to do but wave. "Thank you, Mel." Disappointed in my audible gratitude, he inaudibly groans. Ah, shit. I shrug it off as I get to my seat as fast as I can. I keep my head down, though I hear footsteps tailing me. They're light. It's as if the person behind me is deliberately trying not to spook me but, ironically, is doing the exact opposite. I want to turn around, but if it's Mel, he's going to pull me into the office again, rub his forehead again, and tell me I fucked up. I peek to see I have neared my seat. It's a swivel chair!

I'm sure surveillance back at IRAAB must be curious about the shift in my vitals. They're probably checking and reporting. I'm usually resting at eighty bpm unless someone is speaking to me or I am dealing with a particularly difficult fatass/customer on the phone. I proudly take a seat and swivel towards Caleb, who looks sorta pissed. I rarely ever see him give a shit, so I think I get why Mel wanted to keep this promotion a secret. It's his fault, though. The dumbass gave me a swivel chair. "You got promoted," Caleb notes in a dull tone.

I don't know what to say, "Uh—"

"Lee," I swivel around to see Virgina standing above me. Those were *her* light steps. Makes sense. She's nervous about talking to me, I think. Aw. "Do you mind if I speak to you?" *Speak to me?*

"Separately?"

"No, no. It's not—there's no serious reason. I just wanted to talk." My shoulders release tension. "I just wanted to know if you feel like a part of this company. It's just that you were quite a spectacle… I mean—" I chuckle. She tries to recuperate. "I just wanted to make sure that you feel okay despite everything being normal for you now." I think she used the word 'just' more than the number of times I've been asked how I'm feeling, but I appreciate it. It's not much different from the scientists at home; they only ask how I am to log it into their report. So what's the difference? She's an HR rep, after all.

"Yeah. I'm okay. Thank you."

She nods and looks at the floor as she builds courage, "I don't want to assume your diet, but would you like to grab lunch?" Maybe there is a difference. There are several reasons why people give a fuck about me but rarely is it for the subjectively *right* reason. I sometimes appreciate it when people talk to me nonetheless.

"Yeah, that would be good."

She looks over the employees and opens her mouth. "How about an early dinner? I'm sorry, I just don't think there'd be enough time during lunch." She turns warm, "I'd like to get to know you if that's okay. Is that okay?" I just look into her eyes and nod. "Okay," she smiles. "Sounds good." I don't know how to put it. She's not necessarily afraid of me, but if she is, it's out of respect. I think she's actually afraid of offending me. I know the scientists would have a hoot over this, but I think it's genuinely sweet.

She makes it to her office, and I return to a phone that is apparently ringing. I don't believe either of us noticed. "Cut Theory. We *cut* your weight. How may I assist you?" No one's there. Okay, I guess. I hang up and tap my desk, clean my keyboard, and fix the ruffles of my socks. I don't know how else to utilize this newfound energy.

The second day of the work week is spent in calls, emails, and whatever else until the HR rep comes to gather my attention. After work, Virginia and I walk to a small food cart. She orders a wrap, I order a burger. She carefully watches me unwrap the foil. "You can eat processed foods?"

I talk through my bite. "Yes. I come equipped with a digestive tract that can handle different meals. My body prefers meals and snacks that are endemic to a regular diet, but I'm not too different from you." I want to enforce that last part. We walk to a park nearby and find a picnic table.

Somehow embarrassed, she laughs to herself. "Don't worry. We don't have to meet again."

"What?"

"I just figured this can count as an HR evaluation. I'm sure you have other, more important things to do. Having people always try to figure you out must be tedious."

"Well… You're right about that." I don't even look at her. I release my words, even though I wasn't referring to her. "But I don't mean you, actually." I can see her exhale from my peripherals.

"Can I ask you something?" She squints with innocent wonder. "Shoot."

"… You know what," she takes a bite of her pita. "Never mind. It's weird." I am delighted by this unexpected banter. As far as I've observed, Virginia is not the type to impose any cliffhangers on pur-pose. She is average but thoughtful, and that archetype prefers to refrain from playing with semantics. My face brightens to nudge her toward any interesting divulgence.

"Trust me, I won't feel any way about it," I say. Was that too strong, though? I hope she is disarmed by my tone. I don't know what impression I gave to make her so careful. No one is ever this careful! She shoots me a confused glance but is ready to overlook the bizarre remark.

She lays her wrap down on the wooden table like a rejected bouquet. "Well, I'm sorry. I've seen you on the local news. I know what you are. But why?" I swallow what seems to be my last bite.

I recall a sliver of my previous inebriation when Dr. Alec confirmed Phase Two. "Because billionaires don't want to explore the moon, I suppose." She lets out two huffs of laughter. Does she believe my lie?

"Suppose?" I need to change the topic fast. The naive glimmer of hope in her eye makes me want to release the world upon request, but some things are meant to be contained.

"Why did you take this job?" It's about time I get to know her too and actually give a shit about it as I'm advised to. She slouches like the way Caleb did.

"Why does anyone take this job? I used to work your job until I decided to change careers and actually take care of the people who take complaints for a living. Because I know what it's like. Looking for easy money to fulfill vices that regrettably turn into priorities." Her subdued presence shifts into disdain, but that disdain is against herself. "You're typical vices," she blurts. It appears that after admitting, it's her cue to drag a loosie out of a leather purse that elderlies often are compared to. She bites the butt, releasing the menthol, and lights it with outstanding femininity.

I wouldn't put that specific addiction past her. I mean, it's clear she has a compulsive dependency on something. I guessed heroin, though, but we'll work with vices. "Why?" I ask, even though I can figure her out in seconds. She confesses to antidepressants, and I begin to form a conclusion that subsequently enables my ability to be more honest. The truth is rarely good, and I guess I need to know if she is able to handle it.

Virginia takes her first two drags to ruminate over my interest in her past. "I was depressed." *Insightful.* She rolls her eyes, knowing her response is quite underwhelming. "I'm really no different than the next addict, but I am content with myself, and I hope that doesn't imply complacency." I lock eyes to express that she is heard.

"You know about IRAAB? International Research and Ad—"

"Yeah, that's where you're from."

"Right… So, to answer your question, IRAAB released a public intent for Project Opt

Homo-Inhabitant." I hold my hand up to my mouth to sarcastically indicate a secret. "I'm the subject of Project Opt Homo-Inhabitant." She chuckles. "The intent states that IRAAB had partnered with pharmaceutical companies to employ medicinal processes that enable sentient life to continue without the severe impact of trauma."

"So, depression?"

"Correct. The agency obtains significant volumes of experimental data through this project to acquire all rudimentary patterns and/or correlations to depression. Right now, they want to see if I am able to process human emotion. During Phase Two, the subject, me, is to ingest different doses of different things to interject the release of excessive cortisol and prolong the development of neurons in the hippocampus." I must look like a dork, but I feel like a con. A liar.

"Huh, good to know." Virginia looks away. She takes another drag of her cigarette.

"Essentially, this project is in pursuit of discovering a solution that evades crippling depression." That's how Dr. Alec would falsely put it. "I'm lucky it's not to end up at West Point," I further purport the narrative.

"It's unnatural," she concludes as if we're at a town hall meeting. I'm surprised, though. Is she not a liberal? They don't agree with any of this, and not just because it is immoral to fuck with intelligent beings. It is also obviously fake news.

"I agree—"

"But who are we to define unnatural? I mean, it's not a bad thing. It could be bad because if the project were to malfunction, and you lose the entire ability to process emotions... That would be bad!" She laughs. However, I took that a little personally.

"I see what you're saying," I nod, breathing away the tension. I'll be a free man— emphasizing both words—by Phase Two. I've been telling myself this as an incentive to continue, regardless of how the objective was presented to me.

She looks at me with such earnestness. "Are you afraid?" I want to say 'yes' so fucking badly, but what's the point? I don't want to be her burden. She wouldn't even know where to begin if I were low. I'm usually subjected to several therapeutic options to help me compose the waves of sore thought. Sometimes, I really hate myself for implying that I am still not entirely a person, but the truth is something you have to get used to; otherwise, dissociation is inevitable. I never considered myself one to dissociate, given that it is not my life's objective, but if I were to, I think I'd be able to achieve happiness on some level. That's something IRAAB has not encountered through me yet.

I sheepishly shake my head to indicate that I am just fine. I'm always just fine. She doesn't believe me and continues to look into my eyes as the wind blows, throwing fragmented curls that brush against her supple redness. She's something to marvel at. Have I said that already? My heart rate goes up, and my stomach turns. I quickly glance down at my trousers, hoping to see nothing outside of the norm, but I am grossly wrong… Fuck. A blooming hard-on presses against my pants, and the table shelters its appearance from Virginia's eyes. I push away and yet grip the table. "Hey," she says softly, her oi e a little unsteady. "I didn't mean to upset you." Shit, my heart rate is increasing.

She gets up. I shoot up with her to have her sit back down. *Then.* The severity of shock rips through me in the split-second of a moment, and I fall off the bench, seizing uncontrollably. Virginia's processing turns into shock, too, and her shock actuates imperceivable gestures paired with a lot of shrieking. *A lot of shrieking.* I can only make out her ginger silhouette and the words 'doctor' and 'police.' A vignette forms to impair me visually, and I'm sure the sight of me is as horrible as the feeling of being seized. I'm sure my eyes have rolled to the back of my head, my limbs must be violently flailing, and my torso must be convulsing. I don't know why they didn't just give me a shock collar instead, man. I just hope I haven't jizzed myself…

CHAPTER 3

THE METAPHOR OF A ROOM

I wake up in my pod room, groggy and with a headache worse than my first hangover. I know something bad happened, and I try to gather my blurred recollections by retracting my audial memories. I remember Virginia's voice. I can't forget it because it's something I never expected. The tinge of care was eclipsed by fear in her high-pitched aid. I never meant to put her in this situation or have her witness one of my worst qualities, even though I can't even control that quality. I never meant for any of this, but I know damn well that I'm in trouble. I can only put together a fragmented sentence. Virginia was asking for help, for a doctor, maybe. It's a helpful context clue, but no cigar. No cigar until I really wake up…

I just don't know why I seized and why I'm here, though, because I often have erections. The metal doors fly open almost passive-aggressively. Dr. Cambry steps in and holds up a tablet. She doesn't greet me nor look me in the eye. Her lack of delicacy keeps me uneasy. "I have to go to the bathroom," I speak first. She completely ignores me. Fuckin' bitch.

Without looking up, she reads me IRAAB's regulations. "Any form of intoxication, inebriation, and paraphernalia is prohibited. Smoking any substance is prohibited. You are to record each negative emotional response as an entry. Neurological surveillance devices observe external circumstances to prevent lawsuits and scientific malpractice that could endanger the International Research and Administration of Animalia Biotechnology and Project Opt Homo-Inhabitant." She sets the tablet down mechanically and spreads my limbs to press the back of my neck, triceps, quadriceps, shins, and abdomen. "These implants measure adrenaline, noradrenaline, blood pressure, and body temperature as a bodily indication of physical reaction. The technology also observes the blood that is shunted from guts to muscles. In response, the subject is to be shocked into immediate seizing."

I drop my arms to my side and hang my head in defeat. "Yeah."

Dr. Cambry picks up the tablet and holds it to her side. She pretentiously gestures for me to get up. I don't play. I just abide. "Follow me."

"But I'm in my medical gown."

"Your clothes are in the lab."

"Not to be washed?"

"You ejaculated," she confirms that everyone knows the context in an accusatory tone. I trail behind her. "Where are we going?"

"You are going to the boardroom. Members of Project Opt Homo-Inhabitant and IRAAB's lawyer want to speak with you." Dr. Cambry's petite steps lead me to the double wooden doors of the boardroom. I look up past her bosom to make eye contact. "Go on."

"Why—why am I here?" Her nostrils flare. Instead of responding to what seem to be silly questions, she whips open the boardroom doors to reveal Dr. Alec on the verge of shouting at a hissing project member, Dr. Savea Philips. The chemistry between them, despite their opposing remarks, is… never mind. I probably shouldn't think about that right now. I tune in.

"How could this be any grounds for termination?" Dr. Alec slaps his wad of research papers on the table. Dr. Philips leans into the support of her swivel chair.

"We're not suggesting anything of that nature for Project O.H.I.," she hisses again through her teeth.

Dr. Alec crosses his arms. "Then what, Savea?"

She explodes. "You broke regulation! This is not grounds for termination, but it is a warning!" Dr. Alec huffs. He turns away and scratches his scalp into a mess of unkempt hair. "Fuck off, doctor," he mumbles. No one has noticed me yet. "We're really going to talk about this?" Dr. Alec rolls his eyes.

"It's a project meeting. We should probably discuss all necessary matters. I mean, Dr. Alec, this is already an exorbitant project, and you're tampering with it? With beer?" Dr.

Cambry shoves me in and shuts the door. The heightened tension switches to me, the subject that's the subject of this conversation.

Dr. Alec straightens his jacket and sets his curled strays. He clears his throat and greets me. "Morning, Lee. Take a seat." I choose the middle seat as it best suits me. Felix, our lawyer, who is pretty much my height, uses both doors to provide a grand entrance. No one particularly likes Felix, but we need him.

"Have we begun?" Felix asks as if he is somehow delighted by the current rigidity in the room. He corrects one strand of his fielding gray and assumes the head of the table where Dr. Alec is supposed to sit. I think if Dr. Alec were less excited by Dr. Philips's sheer unwillingness to cooperate, he'd visibly react to Felix's passive disparagement, but Dr. Alec chooses to remain on his feet anyway as he paces back and forth to generate resolution. I look around the room. The classic four have congregated here to decide my fate like gods in white coats.

Dr. Philips and Dr. Barberry sit in front of me and draw their hands to the table as if we are about to shoot for a social studies textbook cover. Dr. Philips answers Felix's question. "We're only twenty minutes in. However," she glances at Dr. Alec and hardens her lips, "you did not miss anything important." Felix plops his vintage leather briefcase onto the table and unlocks it to allocate reports to each project member. I do not receive one, unfortunately.

"This is the state of affairs of the ordeal we have ourselves in. Lee, do you have any questions or comments?" I feel like it's still not my turn to speak... I loosen my throat to prepare for my first question. *What the fuck is going on?* "I hope you know this isn't IRAAB versus Lee. I'm not playing teams," he counters, emphasizing his point. Yeah, you're playing 'who's gonna pay me more?' Besides,

Felix is under contract with IRAAB, so technically, he's not playing teams; I am the property of IRAAB. "I want to keep you alive—

"So do I," I retort eagerly.

Dr. Alec returns for a taste of satisfaction that is often scarce in scenarios much like this one, "I am flabbergasted at the unanimous implications that our subject deliberately wants to negate basic fucking instinct and off himself. The boy makes sure he is doing everything right to meet our fucking prospects! Do you even read his entries?" Felix chuckles and mouths 'boy' to Dr. Philips.

Dr. Barberry chimes in with patent etiquette. "Actually, it's not unanimous. I think he merely reacted. It meant no harm."

Dr. Alec slams his hand on the table. "Thank you! What's your name again?" Dr. Barberry is only slightly insulted by Dr. Alec's lack of recognition of his team. However, I'm sure the overall respect he has for this current asshole surpasses it.

Dr. Barberry re-introduces himself, and Dr. Alec, out of spite, walks over to Dr. Barberry to shake his hand. Felix returns his attention to me. "This discussion can be over now, Lee. Just answer us this. Did you happen to talk to Virginia Byrne about the grounds of extended surveillance and why you seized or were about to seize?" He advertises the adjournment of this meeting, and I am almost his consumer until it dawns on me… *Did I mean to hurt Virginia?*

I look up from the waxy surface of the conference table. "Wait. My chip reacted because I was going to hurt Virginia?" Everyone in the room is surprised that I don't know about the 'state of affairs'. Dr. Alec is pleasantly surprised as he is rooting for me.

"What do you mean, Lee?" Dr. Philips interrogates.

"I vividly remember my thoughts before seizing. I did not want to…" *hurt* her. I suppose you can't blame a machine for recording vitals, and you can't blame doctors for assessing the situation to conclude with the possibility of my body gearing up to react that way, but I'm turning livid. I have to control it. "I didn't want to hurt her," I say through my teeth.

Dr. Philips sighs. "But Lee has not produced emotions that are not solely based on instinct," she smirks, "so this whole thing is pointless. If the subject resorts primarily back to animalistic traits or ceases progress for more than sixty continuous days—"

Felix viciously snaps. "You're telling me I'm doing my job wrong? If in an independent scenario, yeah, then Lee is a shelter case." That's rude, but sure.

"I'm capable of being afraid," I speak for myself. "And I am right now. So can we please reassess?" Felix concurs with a nod, but only to gain approval of his credibility. "I made a friend. At least, that is what Virginia perceives. Dr. Philips is right… But if I could care, I would be A: upset about the reality in which I can commit such a tragedy and over someone who is an ally to my well-being. Or B: I'm frustrated because I'm more than an animal." I look at Felix, "And no. I did not reveal to Virginia why I seized or was about to seize."

Felix purses his lips and writes it on his notepad. "Very well. You may head back to your room." I try to observe the opinions displayed on everyone's faces as fast as I can before scooting away. It appears that the room is paused, waiting for me to exit. So I exit. Outside, Dr. Cambry waits for me. Now I get why she's so grossed out, and I want to connect with her about how putrid I am. I need someone to talk to right now. I wonder how Virginia is doing because I clearly freaked her the fuck out.

Dr. Cambry presses my pod room's code and lets me in. I really feel like a prisoner today of all days. I climb over onto my bed and lay on the sheets. I can't shut my eyes; I just look at the eggshell ceiling without a blink to alleviate the sting of staring, but my mind can only focus on one thing. I was about to hurt someone without my own consent. That really fucking sucks. I feel like everything is taking control over me, and I am left with a small margin of autonomy to save my shitty life. I roll over to face away from the door, and a few tears follow the shift of my new, restless position. My mind is loud with urgency to find a solution and make peace with myself before seeing Virginia again because I would hate meeting her rightfully guiltless eyes.

I can feel the muscle that wraps the vertebrae of my spine tense as I hunch over the conference table. Blood courses through me in preparation for the verbal blows that are to follow after Lee's stupendously noiseless exit. It is merely the quiet before the storm. I don't even loathe the shots each member is about to take. I think what's worse is that I am alone. The dynamic between the members of the project and me is Felix's idea of foreplay. He soaks in all of the drama, proud of himself for landing an opportunity often composed of absolute bickering as he is handsomely paid hourly. Dr. Barberry breaks the ice, "I need to be in surveillance. Email me the notes, Savea?"

Dr. Philips mouths, 'Yeah,' releasing Dr. Barberry. Then there were three.

Felix sighs, "I didn't need to be here to mitigate an appraisal." Felix stands for his grandiose farewell, as most men below 5'6 prefer. He is about to leave us to our barking.

Before pushing both doors, he turns to us with a wicked smirk. "What's the point of this?"

"What's the point of us?" I retort, knowing damn well the rest in this boardroom do not obtain the capacity to resonate with the natural mutuality between this project and human beings. Felix shakes his head and leaves as he implies that I am morbidly out of my mind.

"I do believe there is progress," Dr. Philips inserts. It's not that she's softened; it's that she's unable to dispute further.

I begin to pace again to give momentum to my response. I try to sell her my conclusive theory regarding this official evaluation of our Lee. "It would be absurd to assume he's reached such levels of dissociative intelligence. He can't just put on a show and know we will buy into it. The latter perspective wasn't phrased as 'I *would* feel frustrated.' He *is* actually frustrated. It has nothing to do with his staying alive in this case—"

"Oh, please, Dr. Alec. Do you propose he isn't just communicating upon instinct to save his life?"

I step up to her. "Do you propose that his ability to manipulate and employ the frontal lobe in a complex authority is considered complacent?"

She doesn't retreat. "It's been recorded already. That's what I'm saying."

"Okay." I draw open the stash of hard liquor under the table and flick off the cap of whiskey. Dr. Philips rolls her eyes. I chuckle to myself.

"You shouldn't have let the subject engage in your vices. It's a direct violation, Dr. Alec—"

"Test subject?" It stings. "I'm conducting something real, okay? You guys are treating it like he's a fabrication of discovery! Anyway, I think this is the right time to suggest that Lee should move out."

"What?" Dr. Philips exclaims.

"Think about it. You refer to him as a subject. The only engagement he receives is based on code and evaluation. It's not conducive to our ultimate goal… and it's not healthy. If he stays here, IRAAB is bound to pull the plug. People will lose their jobs, and we'll be the first to go." I don't care about losing my job, but I know she does.

"I don't know," she replies wearily. "We're lucky that neither the President nor C O showed up today."

"It wasn't a serious matter. Only a precaution. Which I don't agree with in the first place because I genuinely believe that Lee wasn't going to hurt anyone."

"Let's not do this," she waves her hands. It's best if I don't propose another counterpoint, given that she is the kind of woman who doesn't budge unless it benefits her in some type of way. She knows that taking Lee's side is risky and would damage her reputation. She isn't a bad person for protecting herself. I know this. But I have to appear disapproving to keep attitudes at bay.

"How about we instill full-fledged circumstances? No support, no reporting back every night, no direct contact… Might as well give it all before it fails." I don't like saying that last part, but convincing everyone to function according to my agenda is fundamental right now. They kinda have to do what I say unless it conflicts with IRAAB. I usually conflict with IRAAB. Dr. Philips un-crosses her arms to accept my proposal. She reaches out to shake my hand and looks at me directly. "Your omplian e isn't required, you know that," I remind her who's in charge.

"It's not me you need to shake hands with," she retorts. Ah, yes. I have to go over this with God. I purse my lips and spin around to exit without a remark, as I am quite sour about the fact that I have to make a case for Lee again. If I did go to therapy, I'm sure I'd be asked about the exhaustion that comes with supporting someone's life at a constant, incessant rate. It's hard to admit the truth because if Dr. Alec is tired, that means it's okay for everyone on our team to be tired. I forget the boardroom to pursue a hall of different air rushing through me as I increase my speed to reach the surveillance lab in time. The atmosphere is warmer as the morning sun heats the a sor ing whiteness of our walls. Getting to surveillance takes a while, but I figure I'll kill two birds. Earning their approval and checking on Lee are my two birds. I figure I should get a green light from surveillance before making my case to Richard. It will be embarrassing to get a yes from the top and no from the bottom. That sounds like a strange euphemism.

I reach the surveillance room. It's the only one that doesn't take a code. You can't just waltz in there because the scientists are virtually emphasizing every twitch and gesture Lee makes. They're monitoring his vitals and neuronal activity. I press the buzzer. The metal doors light up green like it's Christmas, and I step into a dark, muggy room of scientists typing before large computer screens. I cautiously approach Dr. Barberry, who is watching the pod room on a large screen mounted on the wall. I look at what he is looking at, and it appears that Lee is in his room, tossing and turning. In a world that feels nothing, I feel sorry for him. I look down at the matted carpet. Dr. Barberry leans in. "You shouldn't pity him." Dr. Barberry returns to the screen. "It never ends well… Better to keep our distance." The world is right to not give a shit about any apple that falls far from its tree. Lee's not even from my tree. He's not even an apple. When Dr. Barberry suggests that I dissociate, I feel less inclined to turn homicidal.

It appears we're on the same team, and evidently, our party is split into two. My gut feeling also informs me that Dr. Barberry is not inherently a selfish prick, so I just nod at his comment and continue to pity Lee anyway. Lee is staring at the ceiling. He's obviously conflicted with what just happened and what happened yesterday evening. It's a good sign. "We should order an MRI scan," I direct Dr. Barberry.

Dr. Barberry faces me. "I agree. The reports point to development."

"Can I get my hands on his journal?" Dr. Barberry sifts through the desk drawer and pulls out a copy. "Come on, doc. Original." Dr. Barberry's hand pauses and reaches for the original hardback. "Thank you." I skim through the pages while Dr. Barberry returns to his surveillance duties. "Can I ask you something, Dr. Barberry?"

"Yes."

"Do you think we can permit Lee to reside outside of facility bounds? Can he get an apartment?" I catch his attention. He delegates his responsibility of watching Lee to another white-coat.

"How is this productive?"

"Insisting that he should remain in an environment that reminds him of his laboratory origins and purposes is not productive." Dr. Barberry bites the insides of his mouth as he accepts the reality I have brought to light. It's a win-win to assist Lee. In a very non-intrusive way, of course. It is the subject's responsibility to prove the success of Project O.H.I. Dr. Barberry nods to himself, digesting the approach. I feel relief as Dr. Barberry implies an informal approval of subjecting Lee to an independent life, but I'm not wholly relieved because I am in charge, you fucks. And my argument is impervious to alternative options that would override my effort, attitude, and opinion. "Thank you," I whisper and exit the humid room.

The doors slide shut with a mechanical whir, and I'm off to the races, my thoughts racing alongside me as I ride the high of successfully initiating this motion of liberation. I can't afford to pay anyone any mind—not even if a subordinate were to approach me with their inno ent questions. At some point, I will have to make unnecessary discussions and make pleasant with IRAAB's president and CFO to finalize this decision. I just hope I catch the grand president in the middle of his afternoon interests, as leisure is more principal to these mucks. I hope he is rather bothered by my query, expecting me to be the one to call the shots because he delegated this shit to me anyway and for the very reason of increasing afternoon leisure. I have figured out my next task, and it is to read through Lee's journal—which is in my hand. How silly of me to be this scatterbrained!

The signal in my brain reminds me that I, too, need a moment of afternoon leisure that is worth a glass of something hard and burning. My throat hurts every day; it's become as normal as breathing, and yet that too could be hard if I confronted my depressive invocation. But alas, I chose a life of deliberate numbing. It's quite freeing. The dependency on inhibitions is not what I would regard my life as, but I give myself a small but adequate margin to indulge in the act of accepting that I do not have room for inhibitions, which definitely alleviates the tragedy of limitations. I have spent more than half of my marriage confronting, so I plan to spend the rest of my life consciously evading.

I cannot help but admit, luckily to myself, that I am itching to contact Lee to learn about his well-being. Last time I saw him was two minutes ago, but that doesn't concern me. I'm more interested in stepping into his little, unremarkable pod room to look him in the eye and read him like an open book—more open than his half-hearted journal. It is my homework, though. To write a white paper on each entry and shove a wonderful behavioral psychoanalysis in there to make sense of it all to the rest of the members. I expect them to eventually publish my literary conclusions, but they probably want to exploit my abilities as much as they can before doing so. I knew this would be a shit job when I quickly learned that they do not have kombucha on tap. If an agency isn't even trying to be like Google headquarters, you won't exceed in your career. However, I think settling makes for a rewarding personal journey if one is willing to shift perspectives. I chose this job when I was pursuing a life of mindfulness, and everyone can guess why I stayed.

I turn into the lab and slap open the latest entry of Lee's journal. I fix my glasses to reinforce how seriously I take my job in case anyone is watching. Lee is a communicative character. What he expresses is often on the page anyway, so there is less to look into when I am sifting through his transcribed thoughts. I remember the 'should' instance. That's what I like to call it. Lee is now aware that he should feel appropriate—or humorously inappropriate—feelings. I think his rhetoric would make more sense after an MRI scan. At least his claim might be more believable if organoid proliferation is reported. I skim through the entry and find that there is nothing to find.

I feel a deep sense of achievement in this silly moment only because I am a confidant to my creation, and that is indicative of something sincere. Even though I have no paper to type and cannot prove my renowned excellence this week, I still feel satisfied to a noteworthy extent, given that all of the information available in this entry has already been expressed. It is a coveted desire in this relationship—dare I say relationship—to be the first one to know everything that occurs. However, this excitement dissolves quickly into my monotonous state of mind, a static flat line in lieu of much stimulation, as I realize that I am the designated go-to for Lee. The second alarm goes off in my head to remind me that I do indeed need to decompress. I open the drawer of the counter to find mini wine bottles.

I use my teeth to pull the cork and take a gratifying swig like closeted homosexuals do at a bar that only caters draft beer to ugly, judgmental, straight folks. This time, I behave like nobody's watching. I want to be drunk now. I want it to be five here. At the end of every day, I like to imagine that I barge into wherever Lee is and ask him why he treats me like everybody else. He really pisses me off. Not in the way he pisses everyone else off on this team, but he regrettably pisses me off on a very personal level. Of course, I am the easiest to talk to… Right?

Shit. Barberry is probably the easiest to talk to. Lee is obligated to come to me to report iterations of negative feelings, discoveries of newer feelings, and everything in between, right? So why should I be boastful of what seems to be a non-existent relationship? Maybe I am being too forward with myself because it really isn't that serious. I force the journal into the wide pocket of my coat, and of course, it doesn't fit. That's a negating sign against my impulse to get the fuck out of here as early as I possibly can. I continue to collect notes from the journal to support my thesis. Unfortunately, it's not as easy as it looks because it's also as tedious as it looks. I figure this task is better than following up with anyone else on our team, so I should be good to just roam through the pages of this entry. Anyway, I plan to contact the president and CFO on my own time to piss them off a little less. Despite the fact that this regards Project O.H.I., my motion transparently represents only my interest, as there is no coalition supporting my current prospect. So yeah, I'm going to type up my formal suggestion at home.

When I finish my paper on Lee's recognition of appropriate emotions, I pack my thoughts up and prepare to officially clock out. It's finally five here. I exit the room like a Midwestern wannabe thespian emerging from the subway, eager to reach Broadway as soon as possible. Instead of navigating towards the front, all of us scientists head to the back lot. Most of the parked vehicles are company-leased, so most of them are black or white. In the sea of salt and pepper, I see my luxury blue. My conscious choice of automobile is indicative of individuality. It's important to enforce one, and it's also important to have one enforce it. I do enjoy having a personal choice that disrupts the norm, but to depend solely on the display of individuality is bullshit and hollow. Anyway, it's a good car. It's steel blue with a peanut butter interior. I remember my purchase at the dealership as it was recent and relatively uneventful, and though it makes no sense to remember something that isn't memorable, I can't help but hold on to the moment. Maybe it's because I was deliberately choosing something that makes it easier for others to figure me out.

That's the problem with being transparent. Once people get to know you, they feel like you're easier to play. Manipulate would be a better word because that is what people do. That's why walls are an important metaphor; vulnerability is a rare gem. That's why we prefer to remain within a margin of solitude to ensure safety. To contain ourselves stabilizes our identity because it is only dependent on our perception; to have a raw piece of yourself be perceived by another is subjected to judgment. We don't want to be judged. At this point of my life, the second half of my scorned life, I don't really care who thinks what about me. People really don't matter much.

I hop into my coupe. Funny enough, it's actually degrading to enter a car this small. You look like a dumbass, to be honest. It makes me a tad angrier, but I'm going home. Maybe I should rethink that... As I venture through a winding journey to a place that fits the mood, I decide to pass my uphill exit. I don't think going home will give me the solace I need. Rather, the city might do me some good, and by the time I reach there, the sun will be down, and it will feel less inappropriate to get hammered at a pub. I've always witnessed the city at night. I prefer to drive in silence, just like I prefer to eat meals alone.

As I get older, my conventional spark is dying into a smolder—calm and consistent. It's not boring. It's just not youthful. I'm okay with who I am for the most part, and Jesus, I really do want to avoid confronting the parts of me I solemnly disapprove of.

I see the horizon. It's a line of the city. Tall buildings erected beneath a heavy cloud. The sun is away, and the lights illuminate the wisps of cloud. I dedicate speed to reach the pub, hoping to claim the corner seat where I can quietly observe without engaging socially. The exit takes me further until I reach the pothole streets and avenues. A couple of lefts and one right, and I'll be there. I parallel at my usual spot and swiftly push through to enter a very Irish ambiance. It smells like sawdust and ale.

Unfortunately, my stool is taken by a sweaty customer, leaving me to claim the middle. Where I don't belong. I shrug, and my demeanor begins to stick out as the crowd of this pub is slightly more zealous to pregame and participate in karaoke. Am I Irish? Maybe fifteen percent.

I'm a regular here. When I first moved, I used to come to this pub with my ex-wife. We thought it would be fun, but now I simply refuse to entertain new locations because it's pretty exhausting. Once you become a regular at someplace new, you are forced to enter conversations about rudimentary information, and then you are later expected to exchange that interest to learn about your bartender and why they became a bartender. So, no thanks. I don't really mean to be pretentiously curt. I think I am just tired. No, genuinely, I am just tired, and I think that's why most people leave me alone.

The bartender that I am already acquainted with is terribly absent, meaning I will have to make idle chatter with the pourers behind the tap. I purse my lips in an effort to smile. "What can I do for ya, doctor?" The bartender hollers.

"Whiskey. Please," I holler back and flash a smile. The bartender nods. We're cool. There is a group of graduates, it seems, partying together without care of the time. It's an awkward time to party. It's an okay time for us depressed folks to get drunk. One of the kids lays his hand on my shoulder and shouts in my ear.

"Are you singing tonight, Doctor?" The bartender slides the short crystal glass over to me, waiting for an answer, too. I'm sorry. Are we in a musical? I hesitate, unaware of what's going on. The boy leaves me be. I sincerely think he forgot about his abrupt inquiry. I laugh to myself. They look like good ginger kids. The young men board the stage and sing off-key before the song begins. One dives onto a wooden table, causing the legs to collapse as it cannot hold his heavy, heavy weight. The bartender throws the rag over his shoulder and makes his way to the back of the pub to break up the rowdiness.

"Hey!" The bartender yells, using the force of his belly. He stomps over to interrupt the now violent camaraderie. This whole situation is actually quite funny. I chug more courage into my numb system. As soon as I'm tipsy, I stumble without perfect direction towards the commotion. I raise my pointer to check in. "Yes! Hey!" I mimic the bartender. No one really pays attention to me. One guy is still on stage singing a song I've never heard of. The other guys are helping the now crippled "diver" up. Their voices appear to be competing with the loudness of the jolly music. The bartender is snapping his fingers to force them out. I put my hand on his shoulder to interrupt his current and unconvincing fury.

I pull my wallet out for a few strong bills and press them into the bartender's pudgy palm. "For the table." The guys cheer and lift me up like it's my Bar Mitzvah. I quickly polish off someone else's beer before I'm semi-airborne.

For a brief period, I blackout, and then we're squeezed into my car…

The pig-sweating driver with a hundred-watt smile replaces me. I'm sure I'm cursing myself for being unable to drive as I lay flat on a row of men squished into the back seat that's not really supposed to be a back seat. Apparently, I refused to barhop, and instead of putting up a fight, my knees buckled to produce a shameful collapse. That's an engraved story I won't be able to forget, and I refuse to make sense of it. The driver drops me off at the facility. Strange.

I manage to receive entry and fall onto the soft grass. This is as comforting as it gets for tonight. At least, I think it's night. I hear the birds chirping, but the sun is away for now. I close my eyes and doze off into a calm nothingness.

I hear Dr. Philips's crunchy steps as she examines me from a short distance. The dew has accumulated on the grassy lawn, so it's now morning, early morning. She usually gets here around that time because, again, she takes her life extremely seriously. "Alec," she smacks her teeth. Her voice is weirdly sweet. She kneels next to me and carefully picks off my glasses. I groan and turn away from her. "Why are you here?" She gently tugs my arm. "Get up. I'm taking you home."

My eyes pop open. "Where's my car?" She raises her brows in both confusion and concern. I rub my face. "Jesus." I put her in the position of helping me up as I very much need it right now. I lean on her as I make short steps to the backlot. "This is a long walk."

"Walk of shame for a long night."

"And what did you do?"

"Prepare your proposal." She waits for my reaction while trying to subdue her eagerness. I assume that she assumes it will be a good reaction.

I stop in my tracks. I'm afraid of her kindness. "Did you send it?"

She flares her nostrils and rolls her eyes. "Only to you." She forces me to keep going. We don't talk for the rest of the pace.

"I'm very hungover."

She laughs. "You're such a mess."

"I never told you to clean it up for me."

We split paths to sit in our respective seats in her white sedan. "I can only do what I can," she says before ducking in. I rest my head and use the controls to turn the seat into a bed. I lock my hands and leave them on my stomach.

"You think we can get a bacon-egg-and-cheese?" I don't even look at her when I ask. "No."

I sigh. "Is that your favorite word?"

She tries to twist away her growing smile. "…No". I triumphantly rest my head back on the seat and observe her interior for any marks or stains just for my own interest. Dr. Philip's reputation has always appeared pristine. I hope she reaches out to me for a reference letter because, all animosity aside, I appreciate her for her diligence.

Right now, I am looking for a tiny slip-up to reinforce the part of her that I first met. She used to be a person. I also used to be happy. Time changes many things, and neither of us knows what has happened because both of us prefer privacy. Maybe she just prefers to be professional. I can't find one little dash. Just as I suspected, not as I hoped. I rest my eyes and revert back to the tracks that led me to crash on the facility's lawn. "Oh," I remember why I insisted that those amicable buffoons not drop me home. I wanted to check on someone.

"What?" She asks without taking her eyes off the road.

"How's Lee doing?" She rolls her eyes. Of course, the follow-up conversation hosted by yours truly would be about that.

"I was on my way to check in, but I spotted someone ass-up on the ground." I look outside to see that we are now en route to scale the mountains of autumn leafage, where the sun peers through tall trees. The natural light doesn't trumpet; it's soft and running as fast as our speed in the shape of negative space between the leaves and branches. It looks like a miracle outside. "Alec, if I may suggest… You should take a break. Today. I don't even think it's wise to check on Lee. He's processing some trauma, and well, I think giving the both of you a day will be rewarding."

Poor choice of words, Dr. Philips. I don't see how solitude will be rewarding for both of us. "I don't think it would be fitting in this scenario."

"Well. You don't have a choice… If you come back, I'll tell." I'm amused! If I look, I might see the seams of her pants ripping to make way for two massive balls. "I'm serious," she glances over for half a moment.

"Savea—"

"You know, I don't understand. Things are continuing well."

"Really?"

"Yes! Surveillance approved your motion. I'm sure the president will sign off without even glancing at your proposal. It's a breeze. You've been so heavily invested that it's become a repertoire. Maybe even a habit."

"It's not a natural inclination to care, but rather a habit for me?"

"I'm simply afraid that you'll care too much," she waits for me to digest her opinion. I reach into my back pocket for a smushed loosie and a custom silver lighter. She doesn't argue. She just lowers the window like a friend.

"Where do you want to end up vocationally?" I try to figure her out. She uses her peripherals to make out my expression.

"I want to… I don't know." She shakes off her answer. "Why?"

"You have put a lot of effort into this project. Why?"

"I don't want to lose my job," she chuckles.

"So then be complacent. You're not being complacent, though. You're overachieving. Why?"

"Oh, are you threatened?" She raises a brow ironically. I look at her and softly shake my head. I hate to be so prideful, but I do love to be honest… If it's in my favor. "I'd like to be granted the head position on the next project." Oh, her answer hurt. She was playing me. "So yeah… your job."

"I would be happy to write you a referral letter, Savea."

"You'd do that?" She smirks.

"Yes."

"It doesn't piss you off?"

"So long as you don't act like you're the head of this project, we're fine. Because you're not."

"I hope I didn't step on your toes," she expresses gently.

I raise my hand, "now, now, Savea. You shouldn't be afraid of having your referral letter rebuked. Even if you pissed me off, I'd still recommend you."

She laughs, "I'm not afraid of disagreeing with you. Sometimes, you need someone to fulfill that vagrant role."

"The role of an antagonist," I raise my brow. "You need someone to challenge you—"

"Okay, this is what I don't understand about you. I appreciate your maternal need to make sure I am doing fine, but nonetheless, you're still playing a game. Whatever you say or do has this ulterior motive, and I don't know if that sits right with me…"

Savea drives up the exit, a gravel hill that ventures between the classic woods. "Shut up."

"What?"

"I'm serious."

"No."

She smirks and exclaims. "Oh my god! You are just upset that you can't subjugate a conversation. You're upset that every time you figure me out, it's a little too late, and the inability to predict makes you feel small. You care for your grip…" She looks at me. We're at the front of my estate. "I'm not your therapist; I'm your colleague, and sometimes I can play along with you as your friend. You probably shouldn't blame me for that."

I don't miss a beat. I manually unlock her door and slide out. She waits in astonishment for just another moment before reversing to make a very accurate K-turn. I don't watch her leave. I want her to know how easy it is for me to get on with my next task, which is to unlock my front door, walk in, and undress to sheer nudity. But to be honest, I do care a little. I care a little because she has a great way of finding the words that remain like wine on a rug, so as a result of her skill, I do feel vulnerable.

I make it past the verdure lawn that bears a trickling pond of koi and multi-colored stones that forge a path toward double doors. I've already started undressing. The air in my one story is still, and the atmosphere is lifeless and sunless despite the walls being paneled with large windows. I guess that it's only for me to view the isolated greenery.

This is what a good prenup will get you: modern architecture on cherry wood and red tile from Brazil. I'd like to go to Brazil to try top-tier ayahuasca in a rainforest with rainforest natives after I make a consistent seven-figure income. Anyway, until then, I have a memento of my aspiration set in blood-red tiles. I head to the bar to pour another neat and sulk after the first sip, not because of the cunt-like remark Savea spat. Rather, it's a ritual and habitual, and there is certainly comfort in routine, as my father would tell me.

I don't like to mention my parental origins or any nuclear member as it makes me less of myself and more of theirs. But indeed, I had a father. That's all there is to that. I also had a mom. My familial description sounds like an 1800s funeral, but anyway. The liquor stings after last night, but after a few more rounds, I'll be good to go.

Now obliterated, I turn to view grazing deer on my property. I like that my backyard is hospitable to prey, giving them a much-needed break from being hunted.

I crank open the windows for some cross-ventilation and turn on the shower. As I wait for the water to heat up, I examine my body indifferently. I don't care to hype my sex appeal, nor do I care enough to hate my reflection. Before I can even fixate over a certain feature that doesn't suit the idea I have in my head of myself, the mirror indicatively fogs. I step onto the tiles and let the waterfall pour heat over me.

I find the energy and marginal sobriety to wash myself in soap and water. I ensure I have rid myself of bacteria before stepping out because cleanliness matters to me when other things currently matter less.

I wrap myself in a robe and apply some lotion before airing out the steam. The fog subsides to reveal my reflection again, and it looks okay. It's like a reminder that I am okay or that I'm going to be okay. I flick off the lights and head back to the… You guessed it! I pour another at the bar and nap until evening. I like to occupy the center of the house because it makes me feel like my place is less vacant. If I shove myself into my room, it slowly begins to feel like confinement. I watch TV and sip my beverage as I lounge on the sofa. Maybe Savea is right. Maybe I should take a day off because this does feel pretty rewarding. I can't shake the feelings between her and me as we left things a little crooked, more crooked than usual.

I call her. She doesn't answer. My voicemail entails an invitation to my place for dinner because I'd like to review the pre-written proposal with her. "Hey Savea. I have some leftover…" I look to my left to see if there are any leftovers on the kitchen counters, "stroganoff," I lie. "Maybe you should pop by in a few hours, and we can go over this proposal… Thanks." My short gratitude sounds just a wee too soft. Fuck. I rest for an hour and wake up to realize two things: I do not have any stroganoff, and I have not even read the proposal yet. How insulting. I look through my emails on my laptop. The proposal is a little more gorgeous than it should be. It's more Savea and less Alec, but the dumbass of a president probably won't be able to tell the difference, so what does it matter?

I change into casual apparel, start the oven to toss in a ready-made meal, and wait for the doorbell. I guess I'm anxious to see her, and honestly, I don't have a real reason to allocate an invitation. I think the tension between her and me is unusual or worse than usual. And there it is, the doorbell.

I rush to answer, catching a waft of floral scents. She offers a soft smile as if she did not come with the means of business but rather reconciliation. "Hey," I break the silence casually to put our dynamic back in its place. If you're wondering, we have had sex before.

"Hi," she responds.

I step aside, "Well, come on in. It's been drizzling all day." I just realized it has been drizzling since my shower. That's why everything appears so lusciously green, but I can't seem to focus on the beauty of my one-lot plot right now.

She steps in. "Sorry I didn't respond."

"You never respond unless you have to," I smile.

She chuckles. "That's because I'm more busy than you."

I walk to the kitchen, insinuating that she follows me. "And when do I waste my breath?" I ask.

"Whenever someone pisses you off." I laugh. Hearing someone else's voice echo through this wooden junction of intricate and lonely architecture is nice. I place dinner on the table. Savea quits her following and takes a seat. "These are good-looking leftovers." I'm not gonna tell her that I just cooked the damn thing.

"Oh yeah, that's what an oven does… Makes things look appetizing," I reply sarcastically. Her smile drops as she rolls her eyes. I place a plate in front of her and shift the wine glass. I sit across from her and decide not to clink glasses. She takes the first bite and raises her brows.

"Alec, you chef!" She laughs. "This is actually really good." It was my ex-wife's "recipe," but I should refrain from expressing that specific information. I don't want to remind my colleagues that my wife left me. I take a bite, too, and am surprised at the flavor. It's horribly bland. She can't actually like this? I continue to chip away at my boring meal without continuing the conversation because I don't know what else to say. I don't really want to start talking about business, yet I don't have anything interesting to mention. "So, what did you do for the rest of the day?" She interrupts my frantic thoughts as I mentally sift through a questionnaire.

I clear my throat. "Well. I read your proposal," fuck. I guess I've involuntarily made my choice. "It was beautifully written, Savea," I sincerely admit.

"Really?" She chokes for a second on her food.

"I didn't need to make any corrections. The CFO can chart out the costs from this formal request. It should run smoothly."

She appears delighted. "Wow. Thank you." I nod and try to forget about the topic, as there isn't much to elaborate on. It's good, and that's great, I suppose. All that's left is keeping up appearances with the dickheads at IRAAB who claim they run this godforsaken agency. At least, that's what their titles claim.

"And what did you do?"

She wipes her mouth with a napkin. "Nothing, really. We filed a few malfunction reports. It's like any other day at work." She smirks. "Had lunch. Checked in on Lee and let Dr. Barberry know he's looking a little green around the gills. It's obviously anxiety—"

"Why? He knows he's in the clear." It makes very little sense that Lee is feeling anxious because all of the potential reasons that would induce such a state have been nullified. I wonder what he is worried about. I get out of my seat to retrieve his journal.

She puffs her chest as I skim through the journal. "I don't see any other indication of stress. I know that his colleagues were acting strange the other day, but it's no reason to dramatically build worry." I ponder with a sudden cigarette lit between my middle and index.

"Could you put that out?" She requests. I don't understand. She allows me to smoke in her car, but not in my house?

"No," my voice trails to imply how lost I indeed am. I can target a reason for this sort of behavior. "Maybe I should head back there," I say as I finally acknowledge Savea's request to put out the cigarette. I toss the thing into my glass of wine.

"Alec, I really don't think it's wise of you to show up at weird hours. You're going to get yourself in trouble." I don't want to provoke her, but what does she care? Hell, maybe she does care.

"As much as I want to heed your advice, I don't believe in sitting idly by as the things you care for… suffer." I hate that I admitted my first iota of care, especially for the fucking alien. Jesus. Now she knows I'm in too deep. "I mean, it's just unethical behavior to practice negligence, especially when tensions are high. So, if you'll excuse me—"

"No!" Savea stands up, letting the wine glass tumble and roll to the floor. She doesn't even flinch when it shatters. I want to respect the summon of courage. "This project is an investment. If you keep poking and prodding, there will be no room for qualifiable progress because you will have fucked with the entire thing! Let it go. Seriously, let it the fuck go."

"I think that he needs the push that I provide. I think that you and every other asshole on this team makes him feel more and more synthesized. And I have to sit there and first watch, and then clean up your fucking messes."

"Shut up, Alec. You're just fulfilling a void."

I clench my jaw. "Better that you leave." She grits her teeth.

"No." I watch her stand her ground, and I burst into maniacal laughter over the absurdity that's taking place. I want to give her persistence a chance, but how can I trust someone like her? Tears suddenly well up in her eyes.

I throw my hands in the air, still laughing, "why are you crying?"

"Because I'm worried for you… I'm scared of you." I know I will have to let Lee go for a second. Savea quickly wipes her tears and makes her way around the table to evacuate. I follow her and gently grab her wrist. She jerks it away but quits her stride.

"What?" she sniffles. I bend down to hug her.

"Thank you," I whisper in her ear. When we pull away, I involuntarily kiss her lips. She closes her eyes, but I don't. Savea puts her hand on my head to keep me. I eventually close my eyes, too, and lift her. She holds me tight and does not repel the journey to my room, where I feel comfortable enough to enter for the first time in a long time. She just nuzzles her face into my neck. I want to say that I've always loved her. I can't tell if she would say it back, but why should that stop me?

I lay her down on the white sheets and watch her thin strands tangle on the pillow. Her arms are still looped over my neck. I let myself go, "I love you…" She thinks to herself as she keeps her eyes locked in mine.

"I love you too, Alec." I kiss her forehead.

***

This can only go one of two ways. When I open my eyes, she'll either be here, resting soundly, or she won't. Before opening my eyes to see, I slip back into sleep. When I wake up and find her absence, it will make sense as it is late in the day, and she is a busy woman. I think anyone could paint this picture easily, anyone besides me.

In the most manipulative attempt, I had sex with my supposed antagonist. But even in that wretched scenario, I find I am not the worst, and she is still a little shittier than me. I hate to say it, so much so I could wince like a delusional victim to reality, but I have no plot in favorable motion. I think I like Savea.

My eyes open to reveal that she has, in fact, left me, and I am free to roll to her side because I have the simple privilege to do so. It's hard not to catch her scent and hold it to remember. Everything about the aftermath is embarrassing, so I get up to continue a routine I find comfortable.

Lee

The return to normality is rather a dwindling journey. I haven't heard from anyone. I am currently unaware of what's to happen to me, but I assume I'm off the hook. I hate to render such an assumption as it reflects poorly on my character, but I'd rather ignorantly gamble because, if I'm right, it'll reflect well on my acumen. I've learned quite a bit about the functionality of this place, as most have become tediously predictable, but I suppose things are changing for the worse. While it's unwise to predict optimistically, I don't see why I shouldn't. Existentially, I think I should be hopeful because what is there left to lose? Even if the members decide otherwise, at least I ended my story with a semblance of hope. In my coincidental favor, I receive a signal as the gears shift in the doors of my "cell." It's like everything in my life is sequenced, constructed, and written more than recorded. So, like everything, my golden gates open on cue.

My instinct is flight right now, not fight.

I don't want to fight this shell of a scientist. Anyway, there's no reason to. She doesn't have a syringe. I think I was right; I'm not going to be put down. I open my mouth to encourage myself to speak up. I should do this for myself to rid myself of the pain of the nerves that are so high-strung. "What's going on?" I try my best to sound content with fate. The scientist purses her lips and gestures for me to follow her. I hate everything. I have acquired a painful rage begotten of betrayal because, come on, I think I'm about to die. Have I said enough? I hop off and follow her like a degenerate in serious trouble.

We are going to the cafeteria. Her demeanor is passive-aggressive, which is unfairly valid given there is a mess that needs cleaning and

I am not the appointed custodian. She turns to me stoically, and I immediately look down at my feet. I become hyper-aware of how inorganic everything is between us, and I somehow blame myself for it. I think my arms are too long, and they shouldn't be hanging the way they are. I think I look oafish, and it's obvious from my body language that I'm extremely embarrassed to be myself. I feel bad for those who study my entries as I dwell on self-inflicted criticism. It's not even productive criticism. "Why don't you grab lunch? Dr. Alec should be with you in a minute." The scientist suggests.

"Thank you," I breathe a phrase of gratitude as if I'm thanking her for saving my life or some shit. Her eyes dart in any direction that avoids locking contact with me. I take little steps to the lunch line and grab a damp tray. I lay parchment on it to act as a visor from any bacteria because I'm just not in the mood to take risks on account of jaded laziness. I follow through the line and involuntarily ignore the entrees as they are never that enticing. I don't pick up a fruit like a jackass. Instead… I just give up because I'm not interested in eating. I'm interested in the results of my evaluation, and no, Dr. Alec doesn't show up in "just a minute." It takes him twenty minutes.

I sit alone at a round table with my chest caving in because that's how I feel as a whole. I can't even turn my head to watch the groups of interns become pedestrians to the scientists's right-of-way. I can't observe the thickets behind the lot through the windows. I just use my eyes to navigate and construct thought. It's like a shame for me to be thoughtless, you know? My hollow sight catches a frame of Dr. Alec, and my body straightens itself like I'm about to go live on camera in five seconds. Dr. Alec doesn't want to see me. He looks perturbed. I want to run away from everything, so I position my feet gradually to prepare myself for the worst-case scenario. Dr. Alec sits across from me with his hands folded on the table. He looks me in the eye, and suddenly, I feel like a fool for misinterpreting him. He's not disinterested, he's *human*, and this particular human does give a shit about me. "It's good to see you," he nods.

"Likewise," I project. I watch Dr. Alec swat the table to rid the surface of crumbs. He lifts his briefcase to pull out a file that apparently further reinforces his supervision.

"This is a proposal," his eyes flicker up to mine. "You're free," he scoffs, "well, not technically free, but you don't have to live here anymore, Lee… I want you to be happy, and I'm sorry this time has been anything but. It's just preliminarily bullshit, but I promise you—"

"I know," I reassure him. I know he's doing his best. "Thank you," I whisper. It's good to know that Dr. Alec is still concerned with my well-being, but I have to say, something feels off. "I heard you didn't come to work yesterday," I leave the words for him to mull over.

Dr. Alec's expression lightens from guilt to relief as there is something else to think about other than what's triggering those distinct wrinkles. I'm gonna continue with my lucky streak of good judgment and assume he is guilty about something. Anyway, he opens his dry mouth and then tilts his head. "You knew?" He rolls his eyes, "Figures."

"I didn't mean to upset you," I shrug. "No one directly told me because I'm guessing most are weary of my reactions given how shitty the circumstances are right now." Dr. Alec waves his hand almost politely to cut me off.

"I'm not upset. I was drunk."

"Figures," I repeat him jokingly. I look back. "I know it's not something to laugh about. It's never been, and I know that. I'm sorry."

"You don't have to be sorry."

I cock my head to the side, "I'm sorry for you. I don't know what prompted you to— to…" I feel like I'm losing control for a second. I don't know what to say to him. "I don't know why you got that hammered." *Hammered.* I shouldn't know that word. Dr. Alec smirks.

"Why? I've got nothing to celebrate?"

My body grows rigid again, but I am not an ignorant wall, rather a brittle thing that could shatter at any retort. "No." Dr. Alec pauses at my abrupt response, and a subtle smile forms across his face. He chuckles with his signature humility like he's accepted some foreign, unidentified defeat.

"I've been wanting to discuss something else with the members of Project O.H.I. I think you'd naturally be indifferent to it," he chides. I can tell he's attempting to change the subject, but he's also realizing that he's doing an unsuccessful job at it. His incompetence relieves me from the dominating grip of this conversation. "Your chips," he points at me and then to his neck, "they should be replaced with something durable. I hate to remind you of what's happened, but they're bound to fry." He shoots his honesty at me. He's short and brutal. "I was thinking of teaming up with some people and redesigning a replacement, maybe something more comfortable for you… I think that's something to consider when you enter Phase Two."

"Okay," I am in no mood to fall into his trap.

"Okay." He gets up from his seat. "Best of luck to you, Lee," Dr. Alec circles the table to put his hand on my shoulder. When Dr. Alec passes me to continue his life, I have to force myself to refocus on mine. Everything is still the same. Some people are eating, and others are socializing.

I shift away from the setting to return to my room. There, I will pick out my outfit, premeditate discussions, and maybe journal some more. The halls are less populated, but in my head, the echoes of loafers coursing through still maintain a rhythm. I can hear the busyness like it never left its post.

I retreat into my pod, seeking solace like an introvert on the edge. I haven't socialized much today, but most of my socialization has been particularly significant; therefore, I feel drained. I should probably exercise this in the near future, as communication is a tool.

The first person I can think of talking to is Virginia. I wonder what she took away from this, and I wonder if she's insightful enough to catch on to the narrative that broke into heavy consequences that night. I don't think her finger-pointing will lead to a mirror. I hope she can never guess it is her fault, and to be morally honest, it wasn't. Technically, though, it was. She's pretty, her tits are even, and her curls are as loose as most men wish her to be. The way she looks at anybody is intricate, gentle, and unassuming. If I were any more of a man, I'd fall in love with Virginia. But it's not her fault. It's not my fault either. Maybe they should replace my chips...

Anyway, she must be thinking about me. At the very least, she must be wondering. At most, she's worried. I don't know what I'll say to her. Probably that I had an anxiety attack because I'm not used to talking about myself or talking to people that much. As I rearrange my thoughts, I pick out a belt and loafers first, which must precisely match. Something chestnut to take the attention off of the face I will most likely wear tomorrow.

I know I'll be jaded. I know the whites of my eyes will be evident at the bottom rim, proving my exhaustion. I picked a gray on gray on gray. Gray jacket, gray khakis, gray shirt. This palette should speak on my behalf, right? I think I have enough time to polish my shoes and iron my articles. I buzz the interns like they are subjects to me. Another power move to thrive off of. I hang my outfit and place my shoes next to it. It's fine. They applied for the opportunity.

The intern enters in the frame of a minute to collect my outfit. I purse my lips. "Thank you." The intern bravely looks up at me. He knows not to tamper with the subject. He attempts a nod that looks more like a twitch and backs out. The young man is like forbidden fruit, and I want to chase the instinct of further acquainting myself with him. After all, no one is physically watching me. Before the doors shut, I slip out.

I slip out only to find that the kid has disappeared. I wanted to make a friend. I don't want to ponder on the random interest, though I consider it thoughtful as he has nothing to do with me. He is of no benefit. He does not have the privilege of reporting information. It's like exiting a psych ward. This shit feels like a psych ward, prison, and lab all at once, and it's miraculously detrimental. That's the case I had to make for myself in order to flee this barbwire hell. I suppose that's one sentiment everyone shares when you reach a certain age. This shit's a mini hell, and that's life in a nutshell. I come back to my pod.

CHAPTER 4

EMBARRASSED

I am back in business, assholes. Fuck you. That is exactly how I feel today. A big 'fuck you' for no reason. As much as I want to turn to a dipshit pedestrian and blurt that at their face, I probably should refrain. This is my first day free. It's good to be back, and somehow, the energy beneath my feet, below the metropolitan concrete, channels against it almost mechanically. Like it's pushing back on me, and all of my nerves and intuitions are blaring to warn me. I'd like to rationalize this.

I reach my floor. IRAAB has already informed my boss that I am returning to work. They're handling this better than I thought, as I was anticipating a necessary discussion regarding my whereabouts. I spent last night practicing my words very carefully. It's more than words, you know? It's about the dramatic beats and building tension to enforce significance. The most crucial part of delivering critical information is subtlety. You have to give room to allow the audience to figure out what's going on here. Show, not tell. That's showbiz. I think I've had this existential battle before and will not give in to it now. I'll let you figure out why I should go to therapy.

I watch my chestnut loafers step into the office. I don't want to look up. I don't want to be noticed right now, but if some people haven't noticed my absence, I think I will be disappointed. Maybe not the meth-head department, but yeah. My jaw is locking, and the white noise increases by leaping decibels. I can't feel my fingertips, but hell, I need to take a leap of faith. I look up.

Upon my glance, I meet a pair of eyes intrigued by my return. It's Caleb. I nod my head like we're in a Western classic, as if we belong to some enemies-to-friends trope. Caleb swivels back. My chair swivels too, bitch. Those aren't the eyes I wanted to meet, so I begin to search. My search forces mobility, and I suppose function follows form as my curiosity leads me to the hall where HR is. HR and management. I can hear her glowing voice. Can I even describe a voice as glowing? I can't make out the words, but I can hear her light footsteps travel round and round in my boss's office. It all sounds urgent.

It's all happening in slow motion again. Virginia strides out of the office. Startled, she does a double take. So many emotions wash over her. She smiles. Everything is bright. I'm sure IRAAB had a conversation about whether they should send me back to this job as another mistake could happen again. This time, it would be obvious.

She comes to me in her coat shoes to greet me like it's personal. "I'm really happy you're okay!"

I have to say something. "Me too." I really mean it. She looks back to check for something. I try to check, too, but she leans to obstruct my view.

"Let's get out of here," she wildly suggests.

What the fuck is this? Some red-pill, blue-pill type of shit? "Why?"

Virginia pushes me out of the hall and holds out her hand so I can grab it. "No. I—"

"Trust me," she says with so much honesty she could sing the words. Virginia gestures to Mel's office. "He's not going to notice. Besides, he wanted you to spend a day with HR." She rolls her eyes. "Classic move."

I grab her hand and let her lead. I hope surveillance is giving me the benefit of the doubt here, as I am merely attempting to conjure a new collection of feelings…

Virginia unties her bouquet of ringlets in the elevator. With a sour face, she wraps her hair in a more practical style. And a few strands let go like dying rose petals. She smacks her teeth. I don't know if she's inviting me to make conversation about hair loss, but I decide to work with the social cues I have been brought up with and ignore her mild irritation. The silence is strong. I look up at her. I can smell her lavender-esque, homey perfume. "You should brush your hair at night… You know. Before going to bed."

She raises a brow to respond to my comment, "I like my curls. I don't really mind paying the price of a few strands. So long as it doesn't make a difference," she shrugs. The elevator opens to let us move forward in a very literal and yet conversational sense.

We head out of the building and into the mellow street. I've never seen it so calm. I suppose those of the middle class occupy cubicles and other workplaces lit by fluorescents at this hour. Those who are privileged litter the streets with elitism as they tour and weave through classist brands that are plated with white gold. I like how the world works at this hour. It doesn't overstimulate. The world I witness is not to the extent of distraction, so I can actually hear myself think, for fucks sake! "My mom would tell me to brush my hair before bed," Virginia says without looking at me. She just employs her peripherals to monitor me. I find it interesting that she continues the conversation regardless of how little spirit it has. I thought we were just blowing air to mitigate an awkward elevator silence.

I chuckle. "Are you implying something Freudian between us?" I regret everything that comes out of my mouth, but it sticks the landing. She bursts out laughing.

"You're funny, Lee. I didn't know you were programmed to be funny."

"I wasn't," I look down at my shoes. She squints her eyes, wondering what I meant. "So, what's the plan for today?"

She shrugs. "What do you wanna do? We can do anything you want today."

"I don't really know what to do. I usually go to work and then go back to the facility. I haven't really had the chance to explore, you know? I mean, I've visited take-out places local to us."

"Wanna start there?"

"Where?"

"You have a favorite place to eat?"

     BY ZAINAB F. RAZA

I smirk, "it's only my favorite because I'm not antagonized as much. Less attention, less probing." This makes me realize something quite troubling. I may like the comfort of the facility due to similar intentions. Shit. People are people, and they still look and say mean things. Other aliens are physically protected, and people naturally have more respect for important brands, companies, organizations, etc. IRAAB is definitely ambitious to let me roam with a lot more liberty than the other lab subjects, right?

"Lee?" She actually turns to look at me this time around. "You there?"

I rub my face. "Shit. Sorry," I think this is the first time I've cursed in front of her. My attitude takes her aback, though it's evident that I didn't direct it toward her. It's as though she is pleased by my casual vernacular. "I guess we could eat."

She scrunches her face, "I don't think we're hungry right now. How about we just walk around, and maybe something fun will find us." Her face lights up. "Let's go to the pier Have you been there?"

I smile. "Nope."

"Awesome! We can explore. Are you cool with riding rides—like— do you have motion sickness?" She begins to ramble basically to herself. "No. How would you know? I guess we can try kiddy rides, then work up to it." She looks at me. "Sounds good?"

"Sounds great," I force a smile.

Before taking a subway that drops us near the ferry, we stop at a food cart for gyros and rice bowls. I don't know what Mediterranean food is, but I assume it's rice and shaved meat. And yogurt?

The turn of events isn't riveting, sure, but it tells of Virginia's nature, which counts as riveting to me. I've never had the privilege to study someone based on interest. Most of the time, I just sleep with one eye, forcing myself to remain conscious of what each gesture of each judge in those white labs suggests. Anyway, when did she get hungry?

I linger behind while she exchanges change. She picks up the room-temperature water bottles from the bin next to the smoking cart and tosses them into the yellow plastic bag of two meals. She comes back to me with a gripping smile and eyes that are even brighter. Her beauty competes with her, and it's hard to decide what to love most about the composition of her complexion. "I'm sorry," she says without gearing up to explain her random apology. What could she possibly be apologizing for? We start walking to the subway.

I grab the bag as we go down the steps. "Did I say something to make you feel sorry?"

She twists her face. "No. No, it wasn't you. I just kinda overlooked the fact that you might be hungry." She fidgets with the skin around her oval nails, which are at corporate length. "I just wanted to let the fun begin, you know? I realize that no two are alike." What the fuck? I hold my breath to refrain from laughing. Does she want to relate to some ugly-ass opt? I cannot ascertain the point of her thought process, which throws me through a fucking loop. And honestly, as much as I don't want to, I was thinking the worst things about her. I don't think she's a crackhead. I just think that she is so lonely that it's brought her to a point where she is sheerly out of touch. "Your idea of fun might be different from mine. And," she looks at me to gather my absolute undivided attention. "And I just want to make sure you enjoy your day." We pause at the subway platform.

Virginia slaps her forehead. "Do you even like this kind of food?"

I smile softly and maintain an intimate volume to calm her. "Yes," I lie.

She sighs in relief and flaps her hand to rid herself of the embarrassment. The subway rushes in, throwing those loose curls in the air. I try to collect myself as we board. Maybe I should have asked for my own car instead of an apartment… I sit next to Virginia, and we asynchronously open the styrofoam box of gyro shit.

Anyway, I fill my spork to take a heaping bite to prove that the meal is actually fucking enticing. She watches closely, so I know I have to bring my A-game. She smirks. "You don't like it, do you?" Defeated, I rest the box on my lap. She looks on ahead like we're in a drama. "I thought so." I carefully put the box back into the yellow bag by her feet. I mouth an apology while looking down, but to be honest, should I be so sorry? I don't really owe Virginia my joy. I just owe her my honesty.

"If it makes you feel any better, food is food to me. I'm okay so long as I get fed," I say as I nudge her arm. She responds with another wave of concern.

Her face twitches. "You don't like anything?" She bites the peeling skin on her lips. "I don't want to come off—I don't know if this will sound really insulting, but don't aliens even have dietary preferences?"

I shrug and sway my head from side to side. "I don't really like alpaca meal," I chuckle. I only like what I'm used to. "So think of me like this… The current state that IRAAB and I have achieved is different from being an alien. I'm like a neutral being, not a new-born. I don't really have likes or dislikes, and that's the fundamental challenge of Phase One. While that's the intended starting point of the subject, it's not okay to be in this perpetual state." I shake my head ever so subtly. "Like it's definitely not okay."

"…Have you experienced happiness?"

"Maybe," I pause—maybe not for drama, but simply because I don't know where I am going with this. I don't think I've particularly experienced that emotion. "I mean, I go into a lab where they scan my brain for activity, you know?" I point to my cranium. "In the lobes. The reports help them identify which emotions I claim to have experienced. So far, the closest thing to happiness that I've experienced is relief. Happiness is subjective, though. I think. Some find it in activity or triumph or hobbies or people…"

Virginia grunts. "So you lead a life of indifference?"

"Not entirely. I really have made some good progress." I hate saying that. The act of convincing is degrading regardless of whether it's true. I think more than anything, it's exhausting to relive the process because that's the routine of my life. She smiles and stands up to indicate that it's our stop. We step off the subway. I look around to consciously process my unfamiliar surroundings for the first time since we've left the office. I suppose being next to her pulls me out of the phenomenon of my shitty existence, and therefore, I don't imme-diately notice any heads turning. At least no one has approached me, but that may be because I don't appear approachable.

Anyway, we don't talk. We are both hyper-aware… for my sake. My whole world is watching me, and even those outside of my world are watching me. Glancing at the very least. We scoot up to the kiosk to purchase tickets. Virginia unzips her purse, and I put my pink hand over hers. "Can I?" What am I? A child? "Shit," I mumble to myself, but she hears me.

Where's a wall to slam my head on repeatedly? Why did I say that? Little does she know that I am screaming at myself in my head. "No," she says, but I laugh, to which she raises a brow. I slap filthy cash on the counter to pay for our boat ride or whatever the fuck you call it. It's so goddamn pretentious to refer to everything by its specific title, name, or— you get the point. Virginia surrenders to my surge of decency as she raises her hands to insinuate that she's backing away.

"I didn't know you could talk," the baffled cashier points out. Does he live under a rock?

Virginia crosses her arms, "I didn't know he cussed either."

I rub the abashment off my face and try to get through that brief moment of utterly poor communication by continuing to laugh. She laughs with me, and the guy at the kiosk tips his cap on me like we're in some insurance commercial. Honest to God, I never thought I would be caught in a moment like this. I'm about to touch water, something most science experiments in flopping sci-fi movies can't do, and among this, with a new friend, surrounded by people who are now gawking.

The boat is rickety and smells like piss and fungus, but it is a pleasant time. I watch the tumbling waves glisten as we cut through them. A family of four politely introduces themselves like we are B-list celebrities. They take a few pictures and offer to mail a copy to

IRAAB. How fun would it be to receive fan mail? Ah, yes, but how awful would it be to receive hate mail?

"Why did we take a day off, Virginia?" I state her name to make it clear that I need an honest answer because, again, I didn't expect things to transpire this way.

Virginia's facial muscles relax. "Well," she purses her lips. She looks at the crashing waves. "Mel wanted me to take a day to ensure you're doing okay."

I clench my jaw. Not because I'm agitated, but instead, I am, again, withholding a burst of painful laughter… Fuck it. I laugh again but harder. I snort. Virginia's eyebrows wiggle, playing along with her perplexity. She isn't sure if she wants to laugh, too, but I know she wants to. So she does. Is she searching for relief, or are we both laughing at Mel's bullshit? "Oh God," Virginia's laughter subsides into a chuckle. She has nothing to follow up with.

"So—so, is there a list? Is there a list of questions I am obligated to answer?"

Virginia huffs. "Let's try and improvise. Keep it casual." I have to be honest with her, but I hope this doesn't compromise our time together.

I scratch my head. "I'm okay with this, I guess. I'm okay with it," it's obvious that I said that twice to only reassure myself. "But, I mean, it's just that I've been through a whole process of questions. I mean back at home—at IRAAB. I really don't want to sit here and—" and lie some more! Lie until I'm caught, and yes, there are some great moments where my utterances align with reality. That's when I'm truly speaking for myself, and it's, of course, liberating. Right? "Is that okay?"

Virginia raises her brow, "I know," she laughs. "We're going to keep it casual." I forgot that she said that. How silly, how redundant of me. It's clear that she didn't really catch my drift. Now, we're both biding time, wondering what the first question will be. She knows that I know that the next topic will have some relevance to the bland list Mel printed out from his withering, ugly desktop. Neither of us wants to be this aware. It is written on both of our faces. Good thing the ferry is docking. I guess that's what you call it.

We sit in the back and courteously wait for the families to pour out. They spread out to various jingling attractions with their fat sons. Virginia smiles softly at the sight of the kids. "You have kids?" I attempt to change the conversation.

"No," she positions herself to get up as her eyes follow the last family on their way out. Virginia and I walk off the boat. "I'd like to have kids at some point. It all depends on readiness; some people are ready earlier than others." I don't know why she's always comparing herself. "I'd like to have two kids. A boy and a girl. I'd like to have a girl first so I can be a mom like my mom was. I had good parents, you know? I had a great upbringing, too. Most people would imagine that the source of my downfall has all to do with my familial background, but that's actually not the case." Good to know.

We assess our surroundings on the sun-bleached dock. She puts her hand to her brows to see better. I also experiment with the gesture and to my delight, I find it's a good way to produce shade. She looks for fun things to do while I look for practical resources. I see a kitschy gift shop full of explicit knick-knacks like shot glasses with tits on them and a shirt that reads, 'Fuck you, you fuckin' fuck'. Against my practicality, I do want that shirt, so I trail off.

As I cut through crowds that are most likely formed to ogle me, a kid taps my shoulder. His mom holds the kid back with obvious fear. I think it's time I actually make an effort to appear less threatening. This is what celebrityhood must feel like. It's a constant war between two realities that all fit into one. Celebrities sign off on this intangible contract that compromises their personal bubble and yet have to submit to the people to convince them that they are deserving of the notoriety. "Hi," I say very nicely.

"Hi," the kid exclaims. He reaches out to yank a handful of my loose skin. He's probably seen my kind behind stained glass. I'm more afraid of myself than the kid. The mom pulls the boy away, watchful people hold their breath, waiting for me to react. Some pull out their phones to record as they expect something to become of this little stunt. I make sure that my heart rate remains steady.

"It's okay. He's fine, I'm fine," I wave to everyone. These classic Americans pause for a second and then start whooping, throwing their hands together to produce a roar of clapping. I'm not about to be thrown in the air, but they celebrate me, and it's a weird but nice moment. The mom takes a picture of me posing next to her son.

"Are you… Which inhabitant are you? You know they should stop toying around—I'm—I'm siding with you!" She speaks to the crowd. "It's fishy." Then looks at me with nauseating pity. "It's not ethical."

"IRAAB's, ma'am," I respond cordially, knowing that I'm being watched. She looks at me dumbfounded. "International Research and Administration of Animalia Biotechnology." She opens her mouth and nods. Virginia's hand reaches through the crowd and gently tugs me out of the now shrinking circle.

"Okay, okay," she projects. "Thank you everyone. I'm sure Lee appreciates all of the attention, but we're just normal civilians like you, and we're just here to enjoy the area." I follow Virginia out. She leans in for a second, "I thought I lost you there for a second. Are you okay?"

"Yeah, no. I'm definitely okay." I look back at the gift shop as we walk farther away from it.

"So I was thinking. Since you are indifferent to most cuisines, let's try some carnival food. You might like it!" Fuck it, yeah. I'm in a good mood right now, and I've successfully handled a situation that should have riddled me with discomfort. Virginia gets me to the side of the boardwalk that smells like sugar and fried batter. "You like berries?"

"Yeah. It's part of my diet."

Virginia parks it at a food truck and points at the menu next to the rattling cash register to nonverbally place her order. The cashier returns with a plate of fried batter dusted with powdered sugar. On top of the dessert is a lump of red syrup and glistening berries. Something about it wants me to take a quick picture, slap an indigo filter on it, and upload it on every social media platform IRAAB permits. Funny thing is, I don't really manage those accounts, and I don't have access to them. "So, do I just eat the berries?" I remind her that I am foreign to the culture.

"Well," she laughs. "You eat the whole thing! Well. You don't *have* to eat the whole thing, but you have to have it like this." Virginia demonstrates this by ripping a piece of the sugary dough and dipping it into the syrup. "See. It's funnel cake!" I can see why Americans find this appetizing. It's pretty. She feeds me a bite like fuckin' Jane Goodall would. I work the muscles of my face to express comprehensiveness as if I'm actually anticipating amusement. It's literally just bread and sugar. I find that my processing abilities are much like a brain experiencing clinical depression.

Albeit, most depressed people have fantastic taste, ironically, in everything else. When you're in a good mood, any song on the radio sounds fair. But they're looking for something to make them feel something, and oftentimes, depression seeks gems— diamonds in the rough. I force the indifference down my throat and follow with a smile that is led by eyes first to imprint amusement. I have no words, but I just nod with that sort of delight intact. She raises her brows with innocent hope, "you like it?"

"Yeah," I force.

"Good," she blinks away. I like that she doesn't hover to acquire honest feedback. She lets me do what I will with this plate. The more I look at it, the more I feel this is a simulation. When Virginia turns around to search for the next fun thing to do, I vacuum the flimsy paper plate. Nothing left but edible, white dust that couldn't get you high unless you're a kid with a bedtime. Virginia glances at me and then double-takes at the plate. "You finished it?"

"Was I not supposed to?"

She chuckles. "You could've saved some for me." I wish I had. Anyway, Virginia points at a school of poorly engineered rides huddled carnival-style. "You wanna try a ride? We don't have to go on a rollercoaster.

"The roller coaster…" My voice is meek.

"Yes, but there are other rides, too, so we don't have to start with the ride that's one loose screw away from collapsing." Good, good. On the way there, I see the shirt again.

I tug on Virginia's soft cotton sleeve. "Hey, can we stop for a sec?" I look over at the shirt, and she does, too. Her forehead wrinkles in playful disapproval. I laugh, moving forward. We step into the sweltering hut, barely cooled by the sluggish air conditioning, crammed with souvenirs. I go directly to the cashier. I want to disregard his curiosity and the eyes that light up at the sight of me. "Hey, can I have the 'Fuck you, you fuckin' fuck' shirt?"

The guy behind the counter has his mouth agape. I sigh to make him realize that this shit is getting old, I'm old news. The cashier's expression rests a little, and his mouth closes before responding. "What size do you need?"

"It's hot as balls outside, so nothing too restrictive," I look at the cashier. It's weird because it really feels like a human interacting with a social animal. The cashier manually blinks and then searches through cardboard boxes for my size. I look back at Virginia and nod. She nods back.

I pay with cash, rip the tag, and change in front of everyone. I guess I can get away with this sort of behavior because assumptions against my lack of social cues render a level of pardon.

We course through crowds. People look at me, then at my shirt, then at me again to make sense of things. Virginia holds my hand protectively as we get in line for a kid-friendly ride. Ponytail moms with their press-on nails comfort their kids as they're jerked around in bumper cars. The tan dads don't seem to give a fuck. They effortlessly smoke cigars and effortlessly look away from the kid they created. Strange. We're in line for a children's roller coaster, and the head of the cart is a dragon or a frog, I don't fuckin' know. Virginia pulls me out of the line and whispers, "I have an idea."

She cuts everyone and goes to the entrance of the ride. "Hi, I am with the property of IRAAB," ouch. "That's the International Research and Administration of Animalia Biotechnology. We are conducting a social experiment. Could you help me expedite this process as we are trying to keep the subject, Lee, within a certain level of comfort?" She asks with such assertiveness that the guy counting tickets has no choice but to let us on. I reach my hand out to shake his.

"Wait," the guy says with immense hesitation in his voice. He points to the animated board that measures little kids. Oh, okay. I look at Virginia, and she rolls her eyes. We're clearly on the same team here. I stand against the board and strain my neck in hopes of meeting the mark, and I do.

"Prick," Virginia says to the guy under her breath, but I don't think he meant any harm. She picks the rickety first row and scoots over to give me room. The guy circles around to push the lap bar down. "You ready?"

"How fast does this thing go?" Then it starts to go. The cart wobbles aggressively, and the tracks veer left and right; however, the rusted coaster is not threatening. It's a little awkward because there's not

     BY ZAINAB F. RAZA

much thrill, and it's hard to acknowledge the ride as an enjoyable experience when kids are screeching. This would be the time to deliberate between the pros and cons of this day just to measure the legitimacy of all the good things that happened. The existential perspective typically obstructs my optimistic foresight as I am often lost in the awareness of who I am, why I'm here, and how fucking weird it is that I exist, and today, I'm riding a roller coaster with the HR rep of my job. The fact that I even have a job is crazy.

Everything about this is crazy! This shit is fucking crazy! I turn to Virginia to smile. She smiles back as we are jerked around in this animated cart. I want her to know what I'm thinking because it's kind of hilarious how life works out. Shifting into a positive, optimistic, rainbows-and-fuckin'-butterflies type of outlook needs effort. It begins with a dose of hilarity. Laughter is reconciliation with yourself. It reminds you that either life is not that serious or that it's okay to indulge in whatever is funny regardless of the bleak conditions. Nothing truly makes sense. The why-factor of everything always and fucking inevitably ventures into a pitiful, pseudo-scientific conversation that most don't want to even participate in, but the absence of their rumination is later internalized as they are now left alone to think—or rather not think—about the meaning of everything. When you look at life that way, sure, it can be funny for a minute, and yeah, it'll function as a stepping stone for the course of remaining positive, but then it just feels blank. Like you're staring at something frozen and inanimate for the rest of time. Not believing in God is a brave thing.

Anyway, I'm supposed to be having fun. On that hefty note, the tangential point is that nothing about everything matters, and it's fun and sad at the same time, and it's kind of up to us which one we'd rather resonate with. I think I want to have fun. I want to also put Virginia at ease because she's been nothing but kind.

The ride comes to a terribly abrupt stop. And the bar that Virginia pulled down… I push into it. The force of the ride stopping causes me to lurch forward, pushing me into the *fucking* bar. It doesn't even take a second—the bits and chunks of funnel cake travel through me like a speeding car on a deserted freeway. I bite my lips to hold everything in, but there's no point. I'm not swallowing that shit twice.

I spray cake all over the cart's head. Jam and batter wash over the dragon's dead eyes. Parents gasp; Virginia hops out without looking back. After puking, I look up at everyone as they eagerly wait, wondering if I'm about to go berserk. I think I look motherless.

The neediness in my eyes and the embarrassment paint my expression with detail. I can't hide it. I don't want to be embarrassed, but it's good to feel this in retrospect. Inadvertently, this is a good experience. I have to tell myself this over and over again while breathing in the stench of my customized vomit.

I look to my left to see Virginia standing there, unsure and afraid. Maybe she's scared that I'll seize again. Maybe she, like probably everyone else, is afraid that I'll become animalistically violent. I crawl out of the cart and try to avoid catching sight of my puke or anyone else. I look up, sidestepping the waning intrigue, to find the bathroom. Should I go to the men's or family stall? I realize that I have to lose the new shirt. Without hesitating and with immense mental exhaustion, I strip from the waist up.

Virginia catches up to me with a stack of paper towels. She gently rests her hand on my shoulder and squats halfway to clean up my

　　　　　BY ZAINAB F. RAZA

messes. Every facet of me softens as she pats the thick sheets of paper towel on my chest. I take over. "Thank you," I whisper.

She sighs and pushes her flyaways back, revealing the outline of her face. "I'm sorry. I shouldn't have put you in such an unfamiliar environment. I just wanted you to have a good time."

"I don't think I'm having fun," I say as I meet her eyes, "but I think this shit is so… strange that it's funny. You know?" I experienced humiliation. It can count as something But my embarrassment couldn't last because the hope of progressing assumed control. I throw my hands in the air. "I mean. You're hanging out with an alien who can talk, and we just went on a roller coaster together. Did you ever think that would occur in your life?" Virginia shakes her head and smiles a little. "I vomited," I point to the clumps of saliva on my chest. "I, an alien, and you're fucking colleague, vomited on a kid's ride that's shaped like a dragon," I do a double take at the coaster being serviced by janitors, " or a fuckin' frog! I don't know!" Virginia starts to laugh. We both laugh until there's no air in our lungs.

"Come on," she says as she rubs my head. "Let's find a bathroom to get you cleaned up."

I enter with a motive as I carefully step over the shallow puddles of yellow and watered- down soap. The faucet is already running, and I dive in with four pumps of soap to scrub off the drying funnel cake residue.

To maintain an optimistic attitude, I think of who is waiting for me outside of the bathroom. I'm excited to find more situations to laugh at together. I put my face and neck through another round of scrubbing and stand under the dryer instead of opting for paper towels to save the planet. I then retrace my steps to hop around the puddles and fling open the door. Virginia is standing there with a large cup of lemonade. "You good?"

"Yeah," I return to my embarrassment.

"I'd offer some lemonade, but I think it's wise that we bypass my suggestions…" She smirks to herself. "Did you just wanna go home? I mean—how do you feel?"

"Oh. No, no. I'm okay. I just want to get out of this area. Maybe we can hang the boardwalk," we do as I recommend. I think Virginia's ashamed of herself. "You know it's not your fault." Her face twists so subtly that if I hadn't known her typically expressive pattern, I wouldn't have noticed the slight discomfort.

I peek over at the shitty dragon ride. The custodians have cleaned up my mess, and not to my surprise, the front cart is already in use. I chuckle as I enjoy the heat of the sun. We reach the part of the boardwalk that is lined with carnival games. Balloons are popping, kids are screaming, and ringers are ringing. My curiosity peruses through isles of five- dollar, five-minute slots of entertainment. The boardwalk creaks, and the whimsical carnie music blares. "My senses are so overstimulated," I say out loud.

"What?" Virginia asks with apprehension. Clearly, she's had enough of me and my alien business.

"Nothing's gonna happen," I try to subdue my irritation. Can every-one just stop freaking out for a second? "I'm just saying that it's kind of loud."

Virginia doesn't stop, but she grabs my shoulder gently with her cool hands. "I guess I want to make sure…" She looks down at the boardwalk as she squints her eyes to shield herself from the sun's reflection bouncing off the rotting wood. "I just want you to be okay under my watch." Her hand slips off my shoulder.

"You really don't have to worry about a thing, I promise. I know when I'm about to have a seizure. I'm aware of the things I have to avoid," I falsely reassure her. "Morality is not my largest concern." And she stays quiet. "Virginia, you have to let it go. IRAAB would probably withdraw me from this job if it were your fault." Virginia's eyes widen, letting her lids isolate the ponds of green that happen to compliment her ginger.

"We can try the beach," Virginia says. Strangely enough, the words come out hoarse. She and I both look at the gripped lemonade. Virginia takes a sip as if I asked her to do so, and then she presses her eyes shut and slowly opens them. What the fuck was that? That was suspicious, right? I'm not even high-strung—and I should probably mention that to Dr. Alec. I'm just frustrated that the good feeling is slipping away. Weren't we just laughing like ten minutes ago? Shit, it's starting to feel like a figment of my imagination. I'm tired of explaining myself. I just walk past Virginia and follow the crashing noise of the shore. Thing is, Virginia doesn't follow!

Where I make a left to hop off the boardwalk and into the sand, she makes a right, cutting and storming through people until she reaches the end of an alley. She swerves behind a dumpster. I mutter profanities as I chase her free fucking spirit, leaving the beach, and eventually smell her free fucking spirit too. It smells like everything that smells like weed. It's obviously weed. I peek over to find Virginia taking a hit of a small joint. She looks over at me, and honestly,

I think she's going to cross her arms and say, "It takes the edge off." But thank God, she doesn't. "It's legal," she starts with a defensive attitude. "But I didn't want to do it in front of kids."

"So I'm a kid?" I ask.

She rolls her eyes. "No. But I want to care for you. I just don't know how to."

I change the subject fast, as I don't want to get caught up in another lengthy conversation where I have to divulge the intricacies of my psychological functionality and emotional processing. All I know is that Virginia and I get along in a way where I don't have to change most of myself because it doesn't feel like home, and it almost feels like what home should be. She's pretty accepting of the truth, and I don't think Virginia alters it to make things more digestible for her. "I think all you have to do is ask how I'm feeling. That's usually enough for me to know that you care," because you're not the one keeping track of any sentient progress. You're not the one deciding if it's worth attaching another two months to my name.

Virginia looks at her joint cross-eyed and then refers back to me. Virginia smokes, exhales upwards, breathes air, and tucks her flyaways behind her ear. "How do you feel?" She giggles, "You know? After throwing up?"

I follow up with laughter on my end. "I feel—I feel empty," oh god. The wordplay was not intentional, and it's killing me that she might have interpreted it as such.

"Hmm. I'm glad you threw up," Virginia admits through a wind-chime-like laugh. My eyes light up as I resonate with her truth. "I had a good feeling you were not into that pile of—" She gestures a pile with her hands, "a pile of lard—a turd of lard," Virginia and I laugh even harder because she said 'turd' and she's also pretty high, I think. Virginia, almost out of breath, uses the last of her air. "A pile of turd…Shit!" We have both lost it. It isn't even that funny. Virginia wipes building tears from her reddening face and sniffles a couple of times to wind down from riding her dopamine.

I lean against the dumpster, enjoying the distracting smell of marijuana. "I didn't hate it, I promise."

Virginia purses her lips, "okay."

I chuckle, "I have some preferences, but it's interesting, opts have more opinions regarding food than I do,"

Virginia's mouth forms an 'o', and she nods repeatedly, almost thoughtlessly. "Why?"

"I don't know," I look down at my feet.

"It can't be limited to food, then… right?" Virginia asks with this implied tone of defeat. "Correct," I confess to my vulnerability. "But I'm trying to not be indifferent." Virginia's weaves in and out of focus. "How can you try?"

"Well. It's not like describing color to a person who's been blind their whole life. It's possible to experience emotions, but there are a lot of variables that come into play to track the accuracy and variety. Some feelings are iterated, and our scientists are constantly searching for new emotions to compare them to scans of the average human brain." I suppose I don't need Xanax. I haven't ever been rendered emotionless on account of voluntary disinterest.

Virginia tries for a warm, meaningful smile, but she's blazed, so it just looks weird. "I want to help you." And I don't want to ask why. Neither of us would like the answer, I assume.

I change the subject to something relatively more intriguing than my inabilities. "What does being high feel like?" Virginia looks at the wet lipstick stain on her joint as she twirls it between her index and thumb.

"It's fun. You're a bit numb, but I don't mean numb from all of the pain," she zones out and then wanders back to her description. "It's like your brain actually feels numb. Your eyes are warm. It's like the feeling right after laughing hard with someone, and everything you do is funny to you. Like you're constantly part of an inside joke. It's tingly. But to be honest, the feeling is what you make it. If you are prone to anxiety or are currently anxious, you could just trip yourself out. I'd say good company really makes a difference." Virginia holds out the joint for me. "Wanna try?" Fearful, I lurch back, and she recedes too.

I shake my head. "What if it's too strong?" I point to my chest. "Vitals." Virginia takes a lengthy drag and points at me. I'm a deer in headlights again. She signals for me to come closer, so I do.

She blows the smoke in my face. "Just say that it was an accident." She takes another drag and blows it in my face. Then we wait. "I don't think I want to hang around a dumpster the whole day. We should go to the beach." We walk out of the alley. "Let's go to the beach." I'm waiting for the high to kick in, but I don't know what I should be looking for other than what Virginia said.

"Hey," I say, following it with a long pause. Both of us stop in the middle of the boardwalk. People walk around us. Yeah. I think I'm high. This could be psychosomatic. Virginia's smile could wrap around her face as she tunes in. "So," I carefully calculate my next set of words. "What was it like the first time you were high?"

Virginia and I cross over to the beach. We jump into the heated sand and fight over mounds of it to make it to the shore. Every step is a hill worth dying on, literally. The sand slips, and it doesn't make sense why each step is so difficult, but my focus is on every step. "I think it's different for every person." She answers too late. I look up and realize we are near the waves that are inching closer and closer. Virginia takes off her shoes and steps past the border onto the sand that is soaked in sea. She doesn't really take in the moment as if it is something to remember. She just continues with one foot after the other for me to follow. I don't think I am ready, though. The sea breeze amplifies my senses as I feel the tickling movement of my strands swaying in the direction of the air— whichever way it blows. I confront the temperature in preparation for what it might be like in the water. I think of the syllables in the word 'hypothermia.'

"Nothing's gonna happen," Virginia calls out. She waves over to leave me with no option. I'm obligated to follow. I try to focus on the things I like, such as the sound of the waves. I used to select this sort of ambiance in my pod.

I focus on the good before it gets ugly because, knowing the pattern of my life, it's no smiling metronome. The pattern of my life is hormonal and ever-changing life. I take my first step to stay within the bounds of Virginia's circle. I don't want her too far and me wading behind.

Interestingly enough, my high is beginning to subside. Is the ride over? Shit, it's only been about… I don't really remember how long it's been, but I assume it's ten minutes. That's pretty weak.

"Virginia," I call out with my voice shaking. Virginia hears my voice tremble, too. Something's wrong. Panic ensues down each nerve, and I can feel every converging atom break into the code red. I am definitely on the verge. Virginia is trudging through water, leaping over short waves. Her hands get to me first, grabbing both of my shoulders. I'm frozen and thoughtless, yet it feels like a stream of thoughts is flossing villainously through my mind.

I physically feel my panic pulling through the tissue of my brain. This might be a reasonably helpful distraction until sweet Virginia intervenes with her impulsive worry, "Lee! What's going on? Are you seizing?" I snap out of it and snap back to the matter.

The shift is heavy in a sense. "What's gonna happen when IRAAB realizes that I got high?"

Virginia's eyes widen as she shakes her head. "It was an accident." I pant in frustration, my lips wrapping around my teeth. *That's not the point.*

"What if my brain is no longer compatible with the procedures and experiments?" I look around conscientiously to learn that envy is something attainable. Families get to exist and let their children make mistakes like swim one wave too far or get sand on the towel, and they get to live. The unfairness of it all does not even need to be

   BY ZAINAB F. RAZA

mentioned. I suppose I've always felt like someone on the outside looking in. "I'm scared," I say breathlessly. I yawn shortly after. Is my body attempting to cooperate with the state I'm in?

"I honestly think you're going to be fine—"

"Oh, you think it's going to be fine?" I interrupt her with this new-found tinge of aggression. I've never really spoken to anyone this way. Both of us are surprised at my tone, but I can't just stop there. I can't even stop myself. "It's your fault!" I look around, and people are noticing. My heart rate is not as high as I thought it would be. Is this a breakdown? "I'm just as human as you!" Kind of. "What if they decide against Project Opt *fucking*—" I hate the title of this godforsaken project, Jesus. I chuckle to myself. "Oh god," I groan. "I don't want to seize," I speak to the chip under my shirt, though it can't hear me. "Don't fucking press any buttons, I don't need to seize."

Virginia behaves with accountability. "Do you want me to come with you to the facility? I'll admit that it's my fault," I look up at her with awe.

Maybe I'm still high, and I'm projecting a distorted expression based on previous sentiments of encumbering fear. "You'd do that for me?"

"I'm sorry for putting you through probably the most anxiety-in-duced day of your life. This is an utter shit show, and I just want you to be happy. I want you to be happy with your life," her charge increases, and so does her voice over the cathartic waves. "I want to be part of your life. Let me at least take you home. Get you there safely." Virginia hasn't let go of my shoulders. Everyone's a selfish animal. This has to be her redemption story: failing, then becoming an HR rep to exploit compassion, and finally finding me to fulfill the humane purpose of her job rather than its monetary goal.

The stress has me drained. "No," I say, defeated by an unfortunate perceptiveness. And walk past her. She knows not to come after me. She's afraid. I know what I said, and letting her ruminate over it alone is another mistake I am fully committing to, but I need to be alone. Maybe even say goodbye to myself. I retrace my steps to the dock, where the water taxi floats. A line of people who are waiting to embark notice my demeanor. That's probably because of how I appear. I must look upset. It's important that my physiognomy displays a neutral appeal to disarm the potentiality of an uncomfortable situation. A bleach-blonde wife eyes me up and down and whispers to her sunburnt husband. I force the curve of my mouth, pulling me out of my head.

Knowing that I have to submit to comforting others and assuring them that they are safe around me is a degrading, draining, and isolating achievement. The line starts to stir and move forward as families enter the water taxi. I look over to find the sun setting. Has the day already gone by? It must be the egregious unease filtering in and out of my head that lets the day fly by, but I don't think I'm ready to go home yet. Better yet, I'm not ready to face my potential consequences; however, it would give me time with Dr. Alec. I'm not sure, but I think he and Virginia are quite dissimilar even though they both put in interest and harbor real concern for me. I think Virginia does it from a transparent place of redemption, and Dr. Alec… It's unexplainably different.

Reluctance is the game's name as I rethink and overthink the decision to move out, as I know how strangely lonely it would be without

Dr. Alec. And yes, it has been recorded that I am capable of feeling lonely, but it's amazingly limited. Maybe that's the wrong word, but I recall Dr. Philips claiming this verbatim; however, it isn't as though she's marveling at my extent. It's rather with disdain that she observes me. I don't really mind because Dr. Philips is rarely at the forefront of my thoughts, given that her capacity does not regard any decision-making. She is a vote, not an executive. Anyway, I will suffer in the absence of Dr. Alec as I thoroughly recognize his voluntary effort to brood over me. The very point is that I know that my eventual suffering in this newfound seclusion—a.k.a my studio apartment—will not be met with some bright realization that I can emotionally reciprocate. I can't love Dr. Alec even if I wanted to.

I find my place at the end of the row, and many people avoid me. When I'm out in public, most are indifferent; some approach, others scatter, and usually, it takes one person to dictate the crowd's energy. A few passengers "bravely" sit in the row ahead or behind me. Heads turn to continue their staring. Not one person on this boat puts in the effort to conceal their reactions or judgment. It's just a fucking free-for-all. Today, I choose to care less as I look past the wondering eyes and let my sights rest upon rippling waves. The engine burns through the chatter, and we are off, setting sail or whatever. I'm actually really proud of myself that I can preview my disinterest to be amicable without regarding what people might think in return. I think I'm just trying to care for myself and the odd turmoil I've been put through.

Virginia. Where do I begin? Does she actually care for me more than herself? Should I be expecting that from her? I just feel like, in this case, it makes sense to prioritize me just a little bit more. She shouldn't have gotten me high, and I guess I shouldn't have…

breathed. Wow, double entendre, am I right? Score one for the self-depreciative. I laugh to myself, and passengers flinch as they listen conspicuously. Anyway, I think it's wise to let everyone leave the boat first just so I don't really give them a reason to dislike me more than they already do. I don't want to be mean to anyone for my own good, but it would be such a dream to be a more honest version of myself.

I think what I'm really asking for is the absence of the burden of complying. I have to make sure my emotions are in control and manage any triggers that could get me physically in trouble just from the press of a button. If I didn't have that responsibility, an obligation looming over my head, I think I wouldn't be much different. I'd probably be more verbally profane and sarcastic. I think I'd just be more expressive of the lack of feelings. Maybe I come off as sociopathic.

We return to the dock, and clusters form to exit as fast as they can within the civil boundaries of etiquette. I think some would prefer there be an emergency just to have a reason to push and shove off the boat. The woman glaring at me in line approaches the captain with fury, jaw tight. "Excuse me," she projects with shrill entitlement. The captain shrugs and looks at me because he knows what's fueling her tone. "How are you ensuring our safety on this boat when you let an unsupervised—"

"Actually, I can assure you," I, to my genuine surprise, intervene. "I'm a product of IRAAB," I step forward to the front of the boat. The woman steps back. I mean, even if I am an angry, unadulterated opt, how bad can it get? You can simply jump off the boat if I start pulling punches. "I physically cannot hurt you because the facility is monitoring me. If they even remotely assume that my body is gearing up for a physical reaction, they shock me so badly that I seize and pass out…" I let the words settle until they rot. I can tell that she's embarrassed that she basically treated someone, or I don't know, *something*, poorly. "If you don't believe me, just look it up," I throw my last words in her face as I step off the boat directionless. Reminding myself of IRAAB's semi-cruelty makes me reluctant to go home. I decide to tour the city because I rarely do. I only go to work and come back to the facility.

The sun is down, which implies two things: less attention if I hang around the dimly lit streets and an increased state of vulnerability, as that is when the sadists come out. I definitely shouldn't be out and about, but considering this might be my last day, I'd rather spend it through will. The sky is in afterglow. I make sure the groups of passengers are far behind. I'd like to wander safely. It occurs to me that I am actually shirtless and should probably pull out my button-down that's jumbled up in my back pocket, but it feels really nice not to have a shirt on. Am I regressing? Do I like being an animal? I think people also like hanging around without a shirt or pants, for that matter.

I am itching to know about my death sentence. Maybe I should just go home because it will be pretty hard to enjoy my day. Is enjoying your day really that crucial anyway? Why do people strive for delight when it's not supposed to be consistent? Life consists of variation; sometimes, you shouldn't bend the truth to comfort yourself. It's weakening. Sure, for the fuck of it, remain positive, but what if I told you that positivity is merely a mechanism, at least a majority of the time. If you were to perceive life through an honest lens, you would find that the most appropriate thing you'd feel is indifference as the colors of triumph and tragedy balance out into the absence of color. I haven't studied color theory.

Remaining neutral has its benefits in a fairly disappointing world. I cross the busy street to venture into the city. On my left is a strip club with tinted windows and red curtains in lieu of doors. A typical, large bouncer guards the entrance. If I simply disregard any eye contact, there's a lot to notice. Like the smell of baked goods next to the strip club. A row of aromatic pastry shops. The city street is peppered with liquor and vape stores. A lot of pedestrians have dogs. It's a fairly easy subject to psychoanalyze, but I think I'd just like to enjoy my day without any comparisons.

Something sweet that IRAAB does every week is provide me with an allowance. I'm starting to think it's just my salary, though. So I visit one of the pastry shops, and I know I can't just go up to the counter and place my order like everyone else. I have lines. When I think about the lines too much or just the introductory scene in which I am compelled to read the reciprocating expression of the person I'm talking to, it puts me in an overwrought state. I turn into one of the small bakeries. The bells hanging on the hinge jingle like an announcement.

I look up from the dirty linoleum to meet the startled, puzzled cashier who's clearly covering for a parent, as this appears to be one of your ma-and-pop shops. She's a kid. A scared and extremely confused high schooler. "Hi."

"Uh," she responds.

"My name is Lee. I am a product of IRAAB, International Research and Administration of Animalia Biotechnology. My vitals are constantly monitored," I grouse. "So I cannot harm you. They shock me if the lab senses any change that might indicate physical harm. I'm just here to purchase a pastry," I nod as I put my hands in my pockets.

"Um. Sure," she agrees with a shaking voice. Her chest is rising and deflating faster and faster. I can't imagine how uncomfortable it must be to accept the stipulations.

"Do you have a gun?"

Her eyes shoot to the cash register.

"No, don't worry. I'm just saying, if you have one," could you shoot me? "You can keep it near you if you feel unsafe."

"Oh… It's okay. I mean, I do have one. I know how to aim. So…" She looks me in the eye, "don't hurt me." Most are indifferent, some approach, some scatter…

I sigh as I move forward to the pastry display case and look through the ones that appear the least greasy and sugary. I don't want a repeat of today, and I should stick to the general ingredients of my diet. I spot a date pastry stuffed with chopped pecans. I put my finger on the glass to point, leaving my fingerprint there like graffiti artists who sign public property. "This one. The date one."

The girl quickly whips out parchment paper and collects the pastry. She throws it into a bag and rings me up. "Thanks," I get the bright idea of tormenting her more by finishing the pastry here, but kids are kids. That much I understand.

I exit, sweeping the street to find something interesting to do. I see a bar glowing neon in the distance and a cathedral next to it. I don't really have much of an option. Ha! I guess the cathedral it is. The cathedral is composed of Gothic architecture pointed high towards heaven, stained by years of changing weather. I walk towards it to better see the Rose windows depicting Mary and Jesus and possibly his disciples. A homeless beggar kneels by the tall cathedral doors, whispering prayers to himself, hoping the god he talks to is agreeing more than listening. The homeless man has a tattered hat next to a cup of lukewarm coffee. The hat is flipped upside down, and a few quarters and singles are in it. I don't want to disturb him, so I silently slip my change from the bakery into his hat.

Watching the bearded and broken man plead is entertaining. His hands are clasped together so tight that you can see his knuckles lose blood and transition to a thinning white. Praying is soulful to the needy and soulless to those who have a bed to return to because when you are well, and you don't really need much help, you have the leisurely time to consider religion as propaganda. You question not only God but His existence. Privilege does that to you. I look at this man and make sense of his brick-in-the-wall scenario as it entails a life of either poor decisions or bad luck. Regardless of what cards he was dealt and whether he did it to himself, he is homeless, and he has no one to turn to.

I take a step forward to greet the man, but he doesn't even notice. The wind blows between us, and he shrinks further into his kneeling position. I think I wish I could do more for him, but I'm not one to give the shirt off my back or out of my pocket. Best of luck to him, though. After a few depressing seconds, I switch over to the doors that are probably locked at this hour. I don't particularly agree with religion, but going to church is something I think I should encounter once. Instead of bothering the homeless man, I carefully try the large handle of the door, like I'm decisively pulling a trigger. The lever twists all the way through, letting me into a warm shelter. I leave the door cracked in case the old man needs a place to rest from his worries. The ambiance is not homely, but it communicates a home, and it's transparent, and it might come off as tactical, but I think religious people mean well, and they probably don't realize that issuing a reform is not actually respectful. The attempt to convince people that their truth is the only truth is implemented in every facet of religion's face.

Regardless of the obvious attempt, being here, in the comfortable silence, can even make an opt inhabitant believe. I sit in the front row, looking at a sculpture of Jesus in the arms of Mary under a shower of light. The door creaks open, and I turn around to find the old man poking through, minding his own business as he mumbles to himself. I let him do his thing as I am delightfully concerned with mine. If I were a fool, I would think that God is among us both at this moment, giving us a place to catch our breath. I want to be thoughtful and mindful at the same time. The warm lighting is something I rarely experience.

Whether it be the job or the facility, I am typically met with harsh fluorescents that could honestly trigger a migraine. I can change the scheme in my pod room, though. I will miss that room. I'm not sure if I'm dying tonight or if I've moved out. Whichever it is, I will miss my room. My room is in the heart of motion; scientists dashing up and down the halls. Those participating in Project O.H.I often visit to check up on me, and Dr. Alec stops by to say hello. At least I was never alone, even if I felt lonely, and I guess if all goes well and I make it out alive, I will be alone and lonely!

"God, I don't want to die," I audibly pray. I don't even check to see if the man heard me. We have bigger concerns than each other. I wonder if I had more things to say out loud. I think it would be a silly thing to voice whatever upset me. Voicing it to an entity your parents told you about growing up is kind of embarrassing. I won't make fun of religious folks, but I have my own theory. In my early stages of development, Dr. Alec and I would study different faiths. He would refrain from expressing his views or biased opinions, but I found it difficult to assume Dr. Alec permits theological fallacies to pollute his judgment.

I think the introduction to religion is an interesting route to pursue as it collects many enamored people through divinity and holiness. It could invoke sentience. I can only go as far as understanding it, though. I'm sure believing that life's grand scheme of hierarchy has a limit that you can fathom by labeling it as utmost perfection is… relieving. I learned from Dr. Alec that one must be kind by listening to such fragile vehemence, as believers are mainly composed of hope in an unfortunate world that has little room for said hope. Kindness is not agreeing to what is being said or preached. It is the act of allowing one to preach. I genuinely wonder if I am heard today.

I feel the benevolence everyone's been talking about here in this church. I think about what it must be like to congregate and hope together for a better life, maybe for yourself or for your loved ones. I know that passing the threshold of mercy is a materiality of deterioration. The reality opposes mercy, but some people remain before the barrier. It's a matter of picking the truth. I want to stay here for a while, and it's funny, but I cannot ascertain the origins of my comfort. Is it because of religious propaganda that leads us to believe that God is love, or is it this pseudoscientific, undetected energy that we call God that beguiles me? Spellbound or high, I want to stay.

After deciphering, I quickly realize there isn't much more to consider. No ponderings to chew on; silent epiphanies are gone definitely unheard. I am itching to get the hell out. So I do. I return back to the harsh reality with a prejudice for aimlessness. It makes sense to meet my fate by taking the subway, then the train, and then the road to walk to the facility.

On the way to my first stop, I count the homeless littering the streets over unfriendly architecture designed to prevent any rest. I find a man rummaging through the trash can like an animal would; like he has already resorted to instinct—surviving. He catches me observing and mirrors my stare. I flinch. But not him. He departs from any curiosity for what I am, and even I forget my occult.

I leave to entertain the perspective I have, which is almost celebratory as this could be the last time I recycle my routine. This could be the last time I board the subway, and it's an opportunity to take everything in with gratitude. Dr. Alec was right. I should have lived. I should have lived before leaving, and yet, with all this regret, I can still recall rationality.

The lights flicker in a pattern, and the cart trembles over every third unit of the track we're traveling on. I lean into my dirtied seat in an attempt to stabilize my heart. My penitence hollers the same message in my head but through various phrasing. How could I have messed up this badly? Knowing you're going to die is chilling. I mean, I pretty much know I'm going to die, and then all of me will be narrated through Dr. Alec or Virginia. I wish the last thing I said to Virginia was more thoughtful.

I review my experiences in their entirety, the point of my existence, and the advancements that inched me closer to Phase Two. I have understood complex humor, physical attraction, fear, relief, guilt, and, recently, embarrassment. What if that new emotion counts? It's confirmed, based on previous evidence, that Dr. Alec is going to defend me against all odds. It will be the boner situation all over again, and I'm not even sure if all of this defending will be of any service if my brain is actually damaged. It's not fun, but it is engaging to think critically and tackle all possibilities in hopes of acquiring hope. I recall the evening when Dr. Alec and I shared a couple of beers. Shouldn't that have affected me neurologically to a permanent extent? Do I sound innocent? …Am I cute?

The subway reaches my stop, and I collect myself, dragging my feet over the short carpet. The stagnant air of the station is dense, settling deep into the tension of my shoulders. It's almost like I have to carry myself to the finish line. It's been a marathon, and by 'it,' I mean everything, and no one's really there to run it for me for even just a second. How isolating? I feel bitter. Off to the train station, I guess! Reaching this part of the city, you find it more populated.

Outside the subway station, you can hear the hum of tourists as they snap photos and comment on the glimmering lights advertising the next Broadway show or fashion icon. Someone's always promoting a sketchy comedy club. To be able to mindlessly indulge in materialism is such a privilege. To be happy is… I know it's not something handed to you. It comes with effort. It's something you seek through studying yourself and various sources that cause your synapses to fire. I suppose happiness, to the average person, is like a cancer cell waiting to be triggered. But it's something I have to proliferate.

I try to stay near the stores and away from the crowds. I'm already nauseous from anticipating the literal fucking worst, you know? I count the stars on the concrete sidewalk to get my mind off the over-stimulating environment. Every example is an example of the big bang in the sense that the glitter embedded into a slab of ground resembles the incandescent body of our night. Fruits, cut in half, look like the tree of life or whatever the fuck. They look like our nervous system, and everything looks like everything. Orchids look like vaginas. It's good to know that I am a part of it, and I was allowed to be conscious enough to acknowledge that I am part of a greater picture—a picture that happens to speak a thousand words that possibly mean the same thing. I follow the glitter concrete to the train station and entrain.

I have my eyes glued onto the floor and do my best not to look around as that obstructs the speed of occurring thoughts. Dr. Barberry actually taught me that trick. When I would get my physical and bloodwork done, I'd often ranted about accumulating fears. I remember him taking out his stethoscope from his ears—a classic doctor gesture—to listen to me express every little worry. Dr. Barberry's kind to me, and sometimes I can say more to him than I can to Dr. Alec; however, I know that my loss will be taken harder by Dr. Alec. Jeez, I can't even imagine how he'll carry himself afterward. Not to toot my own horn, but I think he'll become a full-blown alcoholic. I should probably stop him before it all unravels.

Anyway, I remember Dr. Barberry handed me my clothes to change into. I untied my robe and undressed in front of him. Can't sexualize an inhabitant. I kept babbling about how weird my coworkers were with me. I used to have this fear that I would come off as illiterate, which would then get me fired. This was back when I started working at Cut Theory. I had completed my English course and acquired grade school education, and I was just scared that I wouldn't be as competent as my coworkers, even if they were just snot-nosed burnouts. "When you have these thoughts, do me a favor and just stare at an inanimate object. Stare as long as you can, and try not to blink. When you feed your brain minimal information, it is harder to produce thoughts, calming your anxiety," Dr. Barberry advised. He pointed to a fun little chart of the brain and cues in on the amygdala. "You've had a lot of development, which is relatively good because, well, this portion of your brain manages emotional processing and integrating. But. It's developing because of the recurring anxiety you feel. It's also generally produced in this part. Let's try to control it to make room for different emotional patterns to form," he smiled, "sounds good?"

I looked into his eyes as they communicated the same smile. "Yeah, Dr. Barberry," I nodded.

Those were easier times to endure, though. Scientists were drinking more often because I was advancing faster than most laboratory aliens. We were headlining. Dr. Philips and Dr. Alec would get along to a point where they'd even subtly refer to each other as friends. The executives rarely would butt in, and Felix visited once in a rarity to establish legal regulations as I was gearing up to be independently released into the real world. I remember my feelings from then. I had heard a lot about people, and I wanted to study other aliens and even communicate with them to inquire about their experiences with strangers. Still, none of the agencies permitted any sort of interaction. They, in a sense, issued restraining orders against me and each other because the intervention of other aliens could disrupt our respective developmental journeys. It was a mutual agreement, so shortly afterward, it never again occurred to me that other aliens might be living happier, healthier lives. It never occurred to me up until recently.

Scientists then magically discerned that their research might backfire on their reputations and that IRAAB was financially tanking. They bit off more than they could chew. I felt like a burden to my world. No matter how hard Dr. Alec tried to keep me from the debilitating jargon that was often held right in front of me, I became more and more emotionally regressive.

In school, I would read literature that endorsed romance, culture, friendship, and loss. I read about lives of nothingness by Thoreau. I read about heartbreak, too. I even listened to music, including the song '*Cat's in the Cradle*.' That's so fucking stupid. I mean, honestly, does it look like I had a daddy?

When I reach my destination, my dry eyes pull away from the vibrating floor. I need to get to the facility as fast as possible. I take the chance and run until I reach the barbed wire fence. I do my best to keep myself in a meditative state so as not to reflect on the wrong implications. That would suck ass. I can hear my breath. I can even hear my heart. Before I know it, I'm using all four of my limbs to run, forcing every muscle to propel me forward.

Shit, I'm not even running anymore, I'm leaping. I'm competing against myself instead of fighting the urge to express every morsel of betrayal. To maintain one consistent and safe emotion of neutrality is lost on me because of the overpowering sense of freedom. Freedom is where my rare tranquility belongs. It's a shame that I barely come across moments of true peace, and the fear keeps on assembling with heft. I am pitiful, yet no one really takes pity.

I think about Virginia one more time before getting to the entrance of the facility. I picture the look on her face when she processed the last few segments of honesty I threw at her. She's probably figured it all out by now. I think it's good that she finds a reason to stay away from me because I don't think her friendship was beneficial anyway. I don't know; I could be wrong, but it felt transactional and not just on my end.

I wonder if I hate her. I wonder about the fine line between love and hate. The facility's doors unlock, and a crowd of scientists from Project O.H.I wait just a few paces behind the door. No one is about to yell, 'Surprise.' They actually look surprised, and I look tired, withered, and worn out. I probably look like a drawing a fourth grader made based on a simple description. An alien who works a corporate job is about to be put down. Clumps of wispy hair are standing in different directions, depending on which way the wind hits me. They appear bewildered. Dr. Philips just rubs her forehead. Dr. Barberry purses his lips with disappointment.

And I don't see Dr. Alec. I sense another surge of worry cross my chest like a strike, and my nostrils flare to exhale faster. Dr. Barberry extends himself from the mild crowd, "Lee. Where is your shirt? Your shoes? Where's your briefcase?" I don't like that his questions are loud enough for everyone else to hear. It seems intentional. If I didn't know better, I'd think he's trying to exemplify my incapability like I'm some wasteful sycophant.

I swallow, "I was running home and must have lost them." He sighs, "Why were you running that fast?"

"Can we talk about this in private?" I whisper the request, making sure that no one can hear and potentially object to it.

Dr. Barberry looks back and shakes his head. Dr. Philips rolls her eyes as a response. "No, Lee. We should probably go to the lab and… drug test you," Dr. Barberry says softly. However, his tone held a detectable tinge of dismay. I want to cry. I step aside to address the entire team.

"It was an accident," my own octave startles me. I rarely hear myself being this loud, especially in the context of repercussions. "I really didn't mean to get high, and I didn't know that contact high is a thing." I feel like a president on TV apologizing for receiving a blowjob. My fingertips are trembling. The world feels ten degrees colder. I think I'm breaking out into a sweat.

"Please," Dr. Philips smirks. "I honestly don't know which is worse, Seymour. Him," she accuses me, "jeopardizing our jobs or IRAAB jeopardizing our reputations by investing in a void experiment," she crosses her arms to enforce her point. Dr. Barberry looks down, trying not to visibly agree with her, but I get a damn good feeling that he does, in fact, resonate with the sentiment. I'm really tired of feeling small.

"Lee. Would it make you feel any better knowing that Dr. Alec is waiting for you in the lab? Maybe you can discuss the circumstances of this particular situation with him. I understand it wasn't your intention, but it doesn't matter if it was your fault. We cannot continue to experiment on damaged—"

"Goods?" I give him sarcasm as I interrupt Dr. Barberry's repetition of protocol. I see my way out of this dynamic. I see the scorn settling on Dr. Cambry's face. I snap my fingers and point at her. "My briefcase is outside." Dr. Cambry's jaw drops. I mean, I have nothing to lose, and I always thought of her as a cunt. Dr. Cambry looks around for approval to confirm that she is not a low-ranking scientist who was hired to execute petty tasks such as picking up after me. No one offers her confirmation.

Regret in the middle of the day is a different type of nausea. I reach the laboratory, and Dr. Barberry was right. Dr. Alec is waiting for me. He isn't as cool and collected as he usually is. His rigidity implies the severity of the situation. Dr. Alec doesn't even acknowledge me as he paces back and forth. He returns to the counter to retrieve a cup with a label on it. Dr. Alec tosses the cup to me. "Bathroom," he says shortly. I wait for him, hoping he might spare some sympathy. He grits his teeth, "what?" he yells. I reactively jump, and my eyes widen as I feel my world disintegrating. Am I losing Dr. Alec, too? All I can do is circumvent my grieving. Who needs this drunkard anyway, right? I unzip my pants and pull out my penis. Dr. Alec rushes to me, "No, not here! It's going to overflow!"

"Why won't you look me in the eye?" I say to him with my flaccid penis out. Now, he has no choice but to look me in the eye. Dr. Barberry strolls in and abruptly stops at the sight of my intimate moment with Dr. Alec.

"Don't ask," Dr. Alec shrugs defeatedly. Dr. Barberry steps back out without a word. It seems as though no one knows how to act accordingly, considering the absurdity of the issue. I shove my dick back into my pants and zip. "What do you want me to say?" Dr. Alec returns to me. "I'm not ever going to give up on you, but sometimes I wonder if you're even trying." His words throw me in for a loop. I've been breaking my back to renew my counted days, but maybe I'm losing the will to live.

"It wasn't on purpose," I say through my teeth. "I know when you're lying."

I purse my lips out of embarrassment, "sorry."

"Everyone else believes you. You're not still high, right?" I shake my head. "Yeah, I mean. I don't think it's going to do any real damage. Your cells will regenerate… To be honest, I'm in a little trouble too. IRAAB knows I got you drunk. They needed a clean experiment, and I fucked it up. *I* thought it would expedite the process—that was my intention," he huffs. "I'm sorry. This incident really puts us both on thin ice," Dr. Alec ironically pulls out a mini bottle of hard liquor. It's peach-flavored, and it's clearly from the gas station. "Quite honestly, it's just an intentional scare from the committee. But this should not be repeated," he points at me. "Recording everything has its faults," Dr. Alec chugs the liquor. He wipes his mouth like a child. "They want to sell your records to various industries, but how can IRAAB prove validity when the test subject was inebriated at a fuckin' point?"

"So we're just going to have to wait?" I ask.

Dr. Alec shrugs. "For a little. It's most likely going to be alright. I'm sure Felix will find a loophole. Maybe claim discrepancy. Anyway, this is just a blip. We'll treat it as one." Dr. Alec loosens up. "So. What was it like?"

I know what he is inquiring about. "I could physically feel my thoughts not being a straight, coherent line. It literally tickled my brain until I was paranoid."

"Yeah, that happens. I'm glad it scared you," his voice dies down like he's lost an audience. "It's better that these things leave a bad taste in your mouth. Does that make sense?"

"I don't know. How's your peach…thing?"

Dr. Alec chuckles. "Let's move on to a different topic… So, you got fired." My face flushes, and heat travels through my body at a nause-ating speed. My blood pressure! My reaction is almost cartoonish as I'm met with one stress after another. "Good news is, we have your apartment set up. You're going to have to pay rent, though. Your life is primarily going to be your responsibility now." Then his tone softens, "If you ever need help, just ask me." I can see two of him.

"Alec," I barely say.

"Virginia emailed me at the beginning of the day. Unfortunately, it was starting to piss people off that an opt was outperforming them. On the bright side, you're competent!" Dr. Alec pushes with a pitiful smile. It made sense why Virginia was acting so strange.

"I need help."

He nods. "And I will help you. But I can't pay your rent. IRAAB expects you to succeed independently. If you rely on my help, you're not advancing. So just… work harder, okay?" His last words break me. I cannot conjure a response. "It's going to be okay." How many times have I heard that?

"Why are you telling me this now?"

He stiffens. "I'm obliged to. Maybe it's a wake-up call." He bites the inside of his mouth, tongues the crater he's just dug. All I can think of is the relief he'll feel when he returns home and lays in bed. In his luxury, he'll soon realize that my life is not his life.

Whether it be alcoholism, overdose on prescriptions, or reckless driving, Dr. Alec and anybody else doesn't get to choose their judgment day, let alone fight it. I feel envy again. I feel like my life was not supposed to be written to corporeal fruition but rather for an opera. I'm supposed to be fictional. I know Dr. Alec's eyes, and right now, they're commiserative, holding on to the agony he's put me through, but I am so jealous of him. Where will I be soon? The journey to save my life is like a beacon breaking over a bleak landscape of challenges, boundaries, limitations, and burdensome expectations.

I hope for a time in my life when I can laugh and not believe it to be medicinal like I need it to cure the troubles I didn't ask for. I'm not an adolescent, but is this what every teenager feels? All of this bullshit they didn't ask for, and yet their parents never asked for an accident, so now both parties have to accept the matters at hand across from each other at a generational chestnut dining set. How many more demographics am I going to study before I get a PhD in sociology? I should have goals, shouldn't I? "Can I journal before I leave?" That's going to buy me some time here at the facility.

Fuck. I'm not ready to move out, and now I'm unemployed!

IRAAB is really putting its reputation on the line. Other scientific agencies are most definitely going to make horrible fun of us for sending me off in this condition. Maybe the press will rephrase the situational decision as an intended extension of this experiment. Should I help them? I think of that stupid bitch, Dr. Cambry. I recall the potency of my sentiments towards her when I felt like I had nothing to lose. Nothing to lose, really.

"You have something to write about?" Dr. Alec asks. I reluctantly recall the splatter of vomit on the head of the coaster.

"I do," I hope I don't look unsure. I need the extra time, and to be honest, this could actually be a qualified emotion. The criteria for receiving approval doesn't only entail journal review. I know I'll need an MRI scan. They'll measure the proliferation of cells in the targeted lobes to prove that this emotion was actually experienced and is enforcing development. I'm not very comfortable, albeit willing, to share my first recognition of humiliation.

CHAPTER 5

TO BE BATHED IS TO BE LOVED

My eyes open gradually to another four walls like a drunkard's would. Only this time, the walls are paper thin as most apartments are in the city. I'm not sure what woke me up. Maybe the sudden roar of the air conditioner blaring the most underwhelming temperature, maybe it was the momentary sirens of an ambulance passing my street, or maybe it was the anticipation that sits restlessly at the pit of my stomach. I don't need the AC. We're bordering winter. The spell of the all-American grogginess needs time to wear off. Yet, I need myself intact to comprehend the finely printed criteria of jobs listed and certainly circled in the local newspaper.

Yeah, I guess I read the paper now, and that's only because I have to. The short command 'have to'… Having to do something makes you an infidel eventually, and it's often tempting to fantasize about a life that is emancipated. I lift myself off a mattress that has no frame. My place isn't very decent right now.

I drag myself to the calendar to mark another day towards extermination. I'm a month and a half away from it, which is fairly decent, but I cannot develop any scenarios that will help me achieve yet another breakthrough. When my brain is fully developed, it's like my balls have dropped. I can't wait for that. Dr. Alec and Dr. Barberry went over my scans before my departure to a new lifestyle. I'm living the dream of a post-grad girl in her twenties who is trying to "figure herself out." I vibe with it, though. Dr. Barberry said that I'm not too far away from my goal, but it's vital that I maintain a social life in order to stimulate that part of the brain and shift my emotional trajectory. So, I guess I have to put myself in situations that evoke care?

I'd like to care. I can imagine what care feels like. I've noticed it in movies like *Sleepless in Seattle and 10 Things I Hate About You*, and I think people get a kick out of my taste in films. However, it has nothing to do with liking the movies. I don't fucking care if Tom Hanks ever meets her. It's just easier to understand what care looks like when the story is only somewhat dimensional. The members of this project and I have gone round and round like children in regard to my ability to comprehend. I feel very little, but I understand pretty much everything that I am subjected to.

There's definitely comfort in subjecting yourself to routine, as most fathers who prefer their hair short would say, so I yawn, stretch, and walk to the bathroom—which isn't much of a walk. It's almost hilarious and slightly disgusting because I can still smell the shit I took last night from where I sleep. I rinse my mouth with something that nine out of ten dentists recommend, look at my dead eyes in the mirror, and use baby wipes to sanitize my ass and armpits. I don't want to increase the water bill.

I walk around the crumbs of my dwindling groceries from IRAAB to retrieve my intended yellowish button-down and gray slacks. The acid in my stomach crashes against my lining, reminding me of my aching hunger. Every step I take creaks to produce a poor man's harmony. I can hear my neighbor turn on his TV. I can literally fucking hear him press the buttons.

I bet he can hear me creep into my apartment every afternoon, as I call it quits because the job hunt was absolute shit. It's my time to *creep* out of my studio now, so I pack my briefcase with a couple of snacks, my newspaper, and my laminated card. The card states that IRAAB is legally obligated to monitor every emotional and physical trace that is linked to violent urges in order to protect others from physical harm. The card also elaborates on the lengths IRAAB goes to to avoid harm and a lawsuit.

I hope my neighbor doesn't feel the need to give me a warm welcome. But as Dr. Barberry described, I need to put myself out there to grow. To humans, this sort of phrasing might be interpreted as dating. Because growth is not taken literally. To people, growth is pseudo, disingenuous, and stupidly proclaimed, as it's inevitable whether you like it or not—it's quite literally just about change. Change is merely an adjustment based on empirical knowledge of trauma and whatnot. Growth is a marketing term.

Whatever. I figure it's worth subscribing—even unfaithfully—to the ideology and trusting the process. So, my footsteps echo down the hallway, the sound grounding me as I move forward, ready to remind my neighbor that I exist.

But door number four doesn't open… thankfully. Should I get a therapist? This aversion to social interaction feels a bit extreme—almost uncomfortably introverted. I mean, isn't it natural to want to understand why I am the way I am? Maybe I'm my own therapist, and that's perfectly fine. Ever think you don't *need* a therapist?

My real struggle with making connections might come from the desire to be "okay." I know why I try to make friends. So maybe that's why the effort rarely feels sincere.

It always occurs to me that I should feel bad. It's like the applause sign in a talk show, and it goes off in my head like a determined indication. I'm always on camera, performing. Jesus.

Speaking of Jesus, I think I'm going to pick a god to believe in. That's how most people of this generation do it, right? When they have the time, they'll believe. I can't hate on it, though; I was literally turned conscience in a lab full of white-coat atheists. Dr. Barberry is a… what's the word? Fuck, I should pick up a dictionary along the way. And a thesaurus. I'd like to better my vocabulary as communication is a subject that has little to do with content and all to do with presentation. Etiquette should be studied. It's not about the point. It's rarely about the point. It's about your vernacular. Your identity chooses your peers. People recognize how you butter your bread and where you place your silverware. Dr. Barberry is agnostic, by the way. He's the weakest link. If I met him outside this project's parameters, I think I'd want to make him my friend. It would benefit my cause at a quicker rate. And Dr. Alec is about to take a hiatus, I think, and it's frightening.

My hallway is short, dim, and colorless. I would assume I'm colorblind, but the piss I took earlier was too vivid to avoid. I think, if all fails today, I should probably hydrate and maybe, just maybe, take care of myself.

The first interview on my list is for a receptionist job at a start-up research facility. It's really just a floor in a mediocre building that provides studies on branded pesticides. The corporate side of agriculture. How ironic. I think this company is low-key and wants to do business with IRAAB. They'll cut me a favor by handing me a cushy job and, in return, receive a discounted alien to play with.

Gives them clout, more importantly. I think the president would like to further acquaint himself to acquire evidence of my functionality. He'll want to assess me and see if it's worth buying a conscious thing that technically has no real value because it's not human.

The reality is not as offensive as it used to be. I know the game. But I feel bad for the next guy, as in, I feel bad for the next opt. Being bought would be fairly alright if the level of sentience would be that of a rat, but another animal that walks and talks and thinks like me, whose only purpose is to serve, regardless of the industry, is imprisoning. Honestly, I think I'd rather go to jail.

The wind collects my attention as I push the apartment building's door halfway open to squeeze by. If I had a top hat, it would fly off. If I had an umbrella, I'd fly away. Imagine if I did have such accessories, though. I'd be the punchline of every joke, and I think it would be kind of nice, as it would be this inclusive thing that everyone finds camaraderie in. The only other scenarios I've thought to be "inclusive" have to do with my applied effort at work or the facility.

Man, sometimes girls just wanna have fun. I'm a boy, though. Again, I wish that I could ditch all of my responsibilities. I think I'd go line dancing and hit a museum to look at Egyptian artifacts, letting my fascination associate with humans and their gradual history of advancements.

After a few blocks, I arrive. I'm not even that nervous anymore because I think I have the advantage. They want me. That's hot. I hop on the elevator that actually has no elevator music and reach the second floor. The girl at the front desk greets me with respect and averts her eyes quickly as if I'm going to turn her to stone. She asks me for my laminated card and identification. Mesmerized by the apparent authenticity, she lets the phone ring multiple times. I know that feeling.

I sit and wait patiently while the receptionist steps out to retrieve the manager of this janky operation. I think I'm about to ace this interview. "Lee," she says. She doesn't look me in the eye but rather my forehead. "Unfortunately, Leslie cannot meet with you at this time." She doesn't seem entirely truthful about it.

I just wait for her to explain. To confess. She is inanimate at our juncture, so I shrug and pick up my briefcase. I walk to her to collect my paperwork. Then, the manager I was supposed to interview with enters the underwhelming scene with incredible drama.

"Lee!" Leslie exclaims. He's delightfully young. With my eyes wide, I look him up and down. He extends his arm to shake my hand. "Listen, I'm sorry for today." He thinks for a second. "I think we will move on to the next candidate… I don't think I could hire you in good conscience." He appears soulfully dejected.

Leslie, I don't care about your conscience; however, I asked him why.

"I think you understand why we want to engage with you and IRAAB. It's not a very fun reason."

I feel myself sulking. "But. It doesn't affect me," I know I probably shouldn't have said that. It reflects poorly on my character. Well, now he knows that I'm a selfish prick, but if we're being fair, I'm kind of incapable of concern for another's well-being as of right now.

Leslie squirms. "You're very interesting, Lee. But I'm sorry," he looks at the door, referring me to it. I cut my newfound losses without another word. Quite honestly, I admire Leslie. He made a political choice that didn't benefit him. Normally, I'd consider it a mere weakness, but deep down, I also resonate with the cruelty he bravely obviated. This and other facilities that create us are in it for the innovation and good pay.

It's how the world works, but life takes after the inside scoop on a famous chocolate brand. On the one hand, commercial children are whooping with joy because fuck, I don't know, the company dropped a new candy filling that tastes like your mother's breast-milk—and on the flip side—child labor. Minimal pay succumbing to a child's starvation.

Leslie gets it. This guy. I chuckle as I step out of the office. We both made a difference in each other's lives today, but it doesn't matter. None of the meaningful shit ever matters when you're unemployed. In this economy? Forget about it! I need to scream at someone so bad right now. Kicking and screaming, in my head at least, I drag myself to a diner nearby for a meal I can't really afford. The diner is retro, but the waitresses disappointingly walk their orders instead of breezing past customers on skates. *Lame.*

Whatever, I just need a soda and protein. I do the whole verification routine with my laminated card before I'm seated.

The waitress, with a raspy voice, takes me to a booth. I open the menu and look at the prices before deciding what I'm in the mood for and then debating its nutritional value. Everything is worth more than a fat bill. Hopelessness is kicking in. It's not fear, panic, or any of the emotions that keep me constantly on edge.

How am I going to get through this? I realize that my whole body has been aching as it is slowly becoming accustomed to the shitty apartment temperatures and the miles of walking I have to do for every disgusting interview. It makes you question your worth and feel pity for simultaneously. "Can I get you something to drink?" I like this waitress. She doesn't acknowledge my species. She actually looks at me with the intent of solely wanting to know what I want to order.

"Can I have a water?" My voice trembles. She doesn't know that I'm going to leave.

She flips her notepad. "You got it." I carefully position my legs first to slide out. My back rubs against the plastic seat, making a squeaking noise. Life is either a comedy or a tragedy. It's about to get tragic.

Anyway, what did I expect? People to go about their conversations, chewing mid- sentence, and not fuckin' notice me? If I had less hair on my legs, a sexy, slender, sexy waist, and the face for Vogue, this would be much less of a pitiful nightmare, you know?

Instead of heading up the street, I go down to the alley. I remember the homeless man I saw the night I met God as I approach a dumpster that smells as rotten as it looks. It's stained and graffitied, the lid open to display remnants of bread in various stages of decomposition. Should I pray?

I don't think mold is listed in my diet. I can smell shrimp and rancid cocktail sauce. I see an entire grilled cheese—well, almost entire. It has a bite taken out of it. I wonder why anyone would ever reject such a beauty. Suddenly, I don't feel as shitty about myself. It's not that the lack of pride has been replaced by the validation of necessity. I've never been a prideful person, but seeing literal trash as both a blessing and a meal doesn't is a strange feeling.

In fact, I feel more sure about myself, and it's worrisome. I *am* taking care of myself. I am doing the essentials. I never had a meal meant to be discarded, and while exploring my nature is interesting, I know it cannot be suitable for me. It's the most animal thing I've actually done, and nothing in the past counts in my books. Sure, it's embarrassing if I wasn't so fucking hungry. On the basis of instinct, I have no shame because getting dirty has its fair reasons. Starving really tells you about a man. I open the grilled cheese to inspect for any rat shit or green splotches.

I hork it down and continue to look for more perfectly unexpired food. I find a tart that's too sour, a pungent smoked salmon, wet carrot cake, and scattered hash browns. After the fat fucking meal, I wind down at the edge of the curb and undo my belt. The whipping air of the passing cars feels melancholic, and I'm fighting back all the rejections I've faced this month. It's insane. I'm unemployed. Do unemployed people worry as much as I do? If so, that must suck.

It blows to wake up in the morning to a chest that hurts so bad because your steady heart rate has recently increased by leaps. Your back hurts, and your mind cannot afford to pay attention to all other priorities because they seem so menial. All of your energy is burned, and you're running on an empty tank. My feet hurt, too. I need someone to look me in my eyes and feel my pain and just fucking be a hero for me.

Leslie was my last shot at a job where I could successfully pay the rent. The careers left to consider are starting to describe my worth, too. When I had the time to fuck around, I should have secured a passion so I could avoid feeling this aimless.

A pomeranian across the street barks at me at the most ballistic decimal. Literally, what if I bark back? Stupid little shit. I get up and keep moving. When I return home, the lights in my hallways are off, but I'm not too sketched out. I'm preoccupied with my dwindling options for survival.

I know what I should do next, and though it may appear to be a last resort, it's not. I pull out my cell phone and dial for her. I've been thinking about Virginia every day since I met her. The last day she and I spoke, I knew we had breached a rift.

When the phone rings, I pull it away from my ear. I don't like to hear it. It keeps ringing.

Then, at the very last ring, "Hello," she says. I think we're both stunned to be in contact again.

"Hey, Virginia. It's Lee."

"I know… What's up? Why are you calling?" Is she upset? It's not insulting. It's just interesting.

"I need your help." God, I hate being so direct.

"Why? What's going on?" Her questions aren't coming from a place of concern, but I need her to worry. It's good for my journal entries. Virginia's lack of enthusiasm to remain gentle with me is off-putting.

"You have a few minutes?" She doesn't say anything, so I begin. I update her on everything that's happened since we last spoke, and when I finish, she doesn't have anything to say. I hate not being able to read her. "I also figured you might want to know what happened after smoking me out," I smirk. She still doesn't say anything. Is she stupid?

"Hello?"

"So you're looking for a job?"

I sigh, "Virginia. Why did you answer?"

She makes a weird noise with her mouth as if she has an immediate retort lined up to fire. "Lee, things got strange that day. I'm sorry for getting you high. It was my mistake. Trust me, I felt guilty, but I really can't let these feelings fester. It's not good for me," she says, revealing how much she cared. Is she selfless? For me?

"I'm sorry," I say as my voice trails.

"Yeah," Virginia responds. She doesn't even need to ask what I'm sorry for. We both just know how much I put her through. It's my second offense, right? And while people get a third chance, I find it wise for her to be weary of me. I don't deserve another chance. "So, what kind of job are you looking for?" I have the urge to ask why she even gives a shit. Maybe she just doesn't want to be around me anymore, and I wonder if this is all about her safety. What changed? What occurred to her?

"I've been interviewing for any and every job, and nothing's sticking."

"Hmm," she genuinely wonders. "How bad do you need a job?"

"Bad," I say. That's all I have to say.

"Well. Do you know much about taxes?" Ha! You have to be shitting me. I mean, you really have to be shitting me. Taxes have to be the most rudimentary facet of civilization that every fucker has to learn about. It was emphasized so much before moving out that it's literally become a joke. *Taxes*, Jesus.

"I actually do," I chuckle. She's not responsive to how humored I am.

"Well, I might know some people looking for a diversity hire. They're interested in employing opts. But they haven't heard of IRAAB, Shapiro something," she mumbles.

"Anyway, I searched before Mel asked me to fire you. It's a temp job. Should that sound good to you, I will let them know when you're available." What?

"I'm confused," turned off, I say. "A temp job?"

"I mean, it's all I got. Honestly, it seems to me that no one wants to hire you," she assumes sharply. Virginia's never been one to *not* sugarcoat things.

"So is this job like—"

"You can maybe land a real job there," she interrupts. "They don't get a lot of business, though. However, that shouldn't be a problem for you. You'll be paid hourly, less since it's a temp position. But you should really know a good deal about taxes."

"Why a temp position? Is there an actual way I could work there permanently?" Virginia sighs as I kind of ask an inevitable question. "I'm not sure if that helps," she sighs again and follows it with a groan.

"Why would clients trust an inexperienced alien with their taxes? You know what, I can't help you. I can't help you, Lee! It's too much…" I can hear her pull the phone away as if she's ready to hang up on me. Neither of us hang up yet.

"Virginia, I'm scared. That's not anything new, yeah. But every day is so fucking painful.

Every day is a silence from every stupid thing I've had hope in. And I'm getting tired, and you were the only person that made me feel good… I'm losing."

"What's that supposed to mean?" I don't answer her; instead, I let her think for a minute.

Let her come to her own conclusion. "Oh," she voices gravely, connecting the points. She was rooting for me, it seems.

"I'm okay enough to hold a job and be good at it," I say with minimal conviction.

"You don't need to sell yourself to me," Virginia speaks softly for the first time in this conversation. "I just want to know how you're feeling. Isolate yourself for a second from all the things you have to do, and tell me how you're feeling?" Her HR is showing.

I want to answer her because I know she's not writing this down to materialize into data.

This isn't a transaction or an ulterior motive; rather, she genuinely wants to know, and I genuinely care to answer her. Virginia patiently waits. "I don't know where to begin. It's just that when I really think about everything, I feel afraid for my future, but that doesn't put me in the position of discovering anything new. I guess I feel numb, tired, and sometimes angry. Most of the time, I feel nothing, and you know that."

"I know that. I do. I'm sorry about that, but maybe you should try to worry less about making a discovery and live in the moment," she kindly suggests.

"Why would I want to live in a moment like this?"

She laughs, "I suppose you're right… but why do you confide? Doesn't that work as a lead? If you called me to tell me something or whatever, ask for a favor, you ended up expressing yourself. Shouldn't that stand for something?"

"Being social doesn't break the threshold of the monotony of survival. I want to be more like you, so I'm not in a shelter case. I'm just protecting myself. I'm surprised you still care, to be honest," my throat swells. I'll always be grateful for Virginia's mercy.

"What happened that day?" She isn't referencing the day we got high. I don't think she needs to further specify what day she is thinking of. I can hear her panicked, hollering for help the evening I seized. "Why were you shocked?" I know Virginia wants to make sure of her safety before she continues to be of aid, and it's completely fucking valid. I couldn't stop her even if I wanted to.

"I didn't want to hurt you…" My voice is trembling. "Then why?" She asks.

"I didn't make the rules—"

"But what are the rules? Under what circumstances? Because you ended up flailing in a park due to the *circumstances*. And I couldn't even do anything about it. Was it my fault?"

"Okay," my voice turns concrete. "You're throwing too much at me—"

"But it's a weight I've been carrying, so I need you to answer… Please."

"I never wanted to hurt you, but the scientists who were monitoring me detected a change in my vitals—they're just precautionary measures."

"What were they anticipating?"

"Virginia," my perseverance fails me as I sigh her name. "Can we at least talk about it in person?"

"I—" her voice breaks. She clears her throat, "I will let the tax preparers know that you're stopping by. Does next Monday sound okay? In fact, take their number. Just do it yourself, please."

I give up. "…Yeah." She tells me the phone number, and I scramble to write it down.

"Great. Goodbye." She hangs up curtly, leaving me in the dust. My heart sinks. That sounded like a forever kind of goodbye. Desperate, I try calling back, but upon the first ring, it goes straight to voice-mail. I bang my fist on the counter.

Something inside me unravels. I've been clinging to every rule and expectation like it's the only thing keeping me alive. I told myself that if I proved my worth here, if I made the project succeed, I'd find a way out, maybe even a reason to keep going. And it's not that she knew me, not really, but she saw me, even if only in passing. And that made me feel—if only for a moment—like I wasn't just part of this machine.

Without her, it's as if Project Opt Homo-Inhabitant is closing in on me, walls pressing tighter. It's all so empty again, just numbers, wires, routines, and an endless cycle of demands. I realize I'm not even trying to survive anymore—I'm just trying to feel like I exist. And if even she couldn't give me that… what's the point of holding on?

I let out my regrets, "Fuck!" I sound like an adult male, drunk and probably hopeless. Not even the potentiality of being employed can lift my spirits. I lost someone today. It's not her responsibility, but does she know what she's putting me through? Does anyone ever feel remorse?

Because it's tragic to be left alone constantly. To endure every hour alone, wondering if the end will come for me soon or if it will wait until natural causes intervene. Even living at the facility, I felt alone. Even hanging with Dr. Alec, I felt alone. "Alec?" I call for him. I feel crazy.

It's like praying, and I fall to my knees, heaving and actually weeping. The tears are heavy and land on the hardwood audibly before it becomes a stream that burns my sensitive skin. "I hate this!" I yell out on behalf of the constant misery.

I bring my hands up to my head and let my fingers run through parts of my scalp that are the most sensitive. And I pull. I pull my already thin fur until chunks follow. I keep ripping. I rip the dry chips of skin off my face and scream in obvious agony. Even through the film of tears, I can see small amounts of blood staining my hands.

I touch my face cautiously to source the wound. I don't even want to look at the mess. I don't want to give myself time to process the sting. Instead, I open my suitcase and pull out a beanie, messing up the order of neatly folded dress shirts that Dr. Cambry contributed to. I force the beanie over my head, barely leaving room for my eyes. Wrap a scarf around my face so that no one can differentiate me from any other dirty fuck—so a person—and evacuate my apartment without bothering to lock the fuckin' door.

It's drizzling outside, casting people to the nearest pavilions. Heading down the sidewalk, I realize that none of my official identification permits me to purchase… liquor. I revise my impulsive plan by locking eyes with pedestrians who are without interest in legally protecting themselves. It's not hard to find who I'm looking for, provided the city fosters such sorts due to whatever fucking economic climate we're in right now. It's hard to keep track of the economy when you're poor. Ironically.

Anyway, I see someone who's basically dressed like me, someone who is freckled with scabs like mine—well, mine are currently healing. Actually, mine are pretty fucking fresh, and I am, to my surprise, to my delightful surprise, pretty proud of my wounds as they are all sponsored by triggered rage that I find quite healthy in retrospect.

Funny thing is, this was one of the first emotions I've ever felt. I vaguely remember when it was recorded. I think, at the time, I was more concerned with why I felt that way. On my way to approaching my twin of a wayfarer, I think of my subjugated introduction. Should I begin with what I am or just completely method act as a person and hope they'll buy into it? "Excuse me." The guy looks left and right. His right eye squints, forcing his left to note my presence. He doesn't look very malleable. "I don't have my ID on me," I begin shakily. Don't you just know you will fail right after making the first move? This is the start of another failure as I clear my throat to make my urgent point. "I'm trying to buy some… booze. And I don't have my wallet on me," I rush through the excuse. When did I get so bad at lying? Maybe I haven't been exercising my skill enough. I can tell because of the look on the short man's face; it's full of scorn and disgust. But, like bitch? We look alike.

The guy makes a weird noise, almost a grunt. "Forget it, kid." No one wants to go to jail these days. However, it doesn't sound like a bad idea if you're inept, right? Free food, a bed to sleep in. I accept his decline and move on to the bigger picture: the liquor store. This is the teenage dream, isn't it? Your nerves are the first to enter, and you look up at the world of wines and all other intoxicants. Am I a wine girl, or should I go for the fireball shots Dr. Alec stashes in every drawer of every room pertinent to him? I feel my chest open in excitement and understand the meaning of the word "possibilities." The choices are endless fun, but I don't have time to indulge. I need to duck and weave through aisles.

Upon ducking and weaving, I find a mirror secured to the top of the back wall, serving as a cheap method of security. You'd think they'd invest in cameras if the windows are barred. My inconspicuous modality is on the verge of backfiring when the cashier approaches me. A bloated man with hyperpigmentation and sun spots and thinning hair that's been bleached at least five times suggests something I cannot understand. "Can I interest you in something dry? Some are on sale." I realize I am at the darker end of the wine aisle's hombre. I'm delighted by the question because, well, I'm in, baby. I don't want to flash my moon of a face. Shit could get weird really fast. I'm assuming the folds of my skin that rest on my cheekbones imitate age, and my apparel covers those features deemed inhuman.

"I actually would prefer some liquor… Are your mixers on sale?" The man leads, and I follow. He picks up a more expensive liquor. It's clear I don't know what it is. He then picks up a colored mixer, catching my child's eye. It's so vivid that any baby would want to toy with it. He scans the two bottles—one glass and the other plastic—and places them in a brown paper bag. "Sir," he says haltingly. Ah, fuck. The jig is up. "We charge for paper bags. And plastic bags, for that matter," he chuckles.

"I don't care. I'll take two." I keep my eyes on the bags so my head can remain at an angle where he can't make out the features of my face and compare it to a normal customer. I can tell he is confused because his hands don't do anything yet. After computing my request, he takes the mixer out of the first bag and puts it in the second. I don't know why I even asked for two. It just seemed to be a gesture of charity. Whatever, I'm nervous. He rings me up, and I pay in cash.

On my way home, I smell the familiar scent of marijuana again. I follow the strength of its pungency to not an alley but an adjacent street. I mean, no one really has a reason to hide it. There is a young woman smoking; it doesn't seem like she's had it hard. Her skin glows, her hair is neat, and her outfit is tastefully colorful and appropriate to the weather. She has headphones in. I don't think, I just tap her shoulder and back away to not intimidate her, but hell, I know I will. "I don't have cash," she says in a nasty tone.

I wave cash at her from my pockets. "I want your pen."

"It's like thirty-five bucks," she responds by swatting me away.

"I'll give you a hundred." I impractically slip out the cash and hand it to her as she rolls her eyes, knowing that she'll have to accept the wild bargain. She hands over the pen that's three-quarters full. "I like your outfit, by the way," I sincerely comment before moving on, uninterested in her reciprocated gratitude. After the come-down of my tantrum, it's become immediately easier to note the people around me as not a benefactor but just as what it is. It doesn't really matter anymore; I just can't care enough, so it inadvertently makes things a little nicer.

I hit my pen. It's *mine*. It's flowery—hibiscus. I wouldn't put it past the girl who seemed to have attended any fashion institute at random. I take another hit without caution, and it doesn't ring me like a bell. I have enough time to get to my apartment before peaking. Of course, the anticipation of getting high has me in this dopamine chokehold. One minute, I feel high; the next minute, I feel like a fool of assumption.

By the time I reach the steps of my apartment, I feel the muscles of my legs tickle and twist like they're some indication of where my

     BY ZAINAB F. RAZA

mind is. I grin warmly to myself and return to the day at the beach with Virginia as I enter my disappointment of a fetid apartment. It doesn't matter to note the clumps of dead hair glazed by blood. My sensory deficiency relies on better times to lull the unfamiliar numb, and what I mean by this is I don't like to be subjected routinely to poor sights, temperatures that barely accommodate, and whatever else that I'm met with on the basis of luck. I have chosen to run away and give in because nostalgia is as sweet as it is melancholic.

I can hear the white noise of crashing waves, how my head would absorb the kindness of the afternoon sun. Virginia accompanying me. I should have just trusted her.

I flick open the cap of liquor and chug, not minding the burn as it slides down my throat. I cough out the pain and drink until the alarms of my senses dull. Drink until I'm drunk, finding my steps incoherently as I dance from one corner to another. I'm not sure, but I must be singing at this point. I can hear my voice, but it doesn't sound like me. I stop singing, so I start laughing. I smoke more without realizing what I'm doing.

What's interesting about inebriation and intoxication and being absolutely fucking crossfaded is that you can hear what's going on around you, but that doesn't mean you can make sense of it. I hear footsteps, quick and heavy ones. I hear banging on my door, and in my head, I'm blasting music dramatically. The banging on the door becomes more rapid, interrupting my swaying and overall indulgence. I wince at the noise and drink a little more to drown out everything I didn't ask for until the doorknob twists. I hear the faint jingling of keys through the hole. The door whips open to reveal my middle-aged landlord, upset and already hollering. He throws his hands in the air as he sniffs out the weed, "What the hell, man?"

I don't even look at him. I'm humming deliberately. I focus on the small window leading to a fire escape. The landlord looks around and notes splotches of blood, and his eyes widen like funny circles. "What's going on? I'm calling the police!"

"There's no need to," says a familiar voice. My hero? It's like bait and hook. Visceral. Piercing me everywhere vital.

I should have known the aftermath would result in this: a Texas shootout between us three. My fucking neighbor probably complained about the mediocre, at best, singing. IRAAB must've recorded my BAL, causing this motherfucker to show up. I can hear them bickering about rent and the rustling of cash. It makes me nauseous. I leap to that window and blow chunks outside. I know both of them are looking at me right now, and fuck, I can't even care. This is the second time I've vomited, right? This is also the second time I've been high, and this is the second time I've been drunk. I don't know what it signifies. Maybe that I don't learn from my mistakes. I hang my head and take in the fresh air. A warmth pulls up next to me. A hairy wrist wrapped in a blue-silver watch pulls me away from the window. I try to fight him off. "Lee." I'm a devolved, tantrum- throwing child.

"He's late on rent, and the whole hallway reeks of pot," the landlord waves at Dr. Alec.

I raise my finger, still trying to find my way out of Dr. Alec's grip. "Actually, landlord," I never learned his name. "No one calls it pot anyway, so you sound ridiculous," I mention without a giggle.

"Jesus, Lee." Dr. Alec groans. Dr. Alec snaps his fingers at the landlord, "Rent's been handled. If that wasn't your problem, you wouldn't be here."

"Someone complained," the landlord retorts.

"That bitch!" I motion to the wall that's left of Dr. Alec and me, insinuating that my fucking neighbor is a stone-cold stranger and has nothing to do with being "thy neighbor."

"You need to calm down," Dr. Alec says to me. He then refers to the landlord. "And you need to leave. I don't think you're in any position to complain…" His voice trails off, implying the lack of necessity of the landlord's presence. The smallish man steps back while still watching over my glazed expression and my enervated body hanging in Dr. Alec's arms. His head tilts, and I'm sure he's wondering whether he should report this scenario. The landlord eventually backs out of my apartment. He doesn't even bother to shut the door.

Dr. Alec extends his neck to smell my breath as he cradles me in his arms. His nose scrunches. "Fuck," he dismisses my choice of courage. "It smells of straight liquor."

I move my head around, searching for that other brown paper bag. "My mixer. It's green apples." I wiggle my arm out of his hold and try to reach for it, proving that my depth perception is way off. I laugh, "I think now is a good time to get behind the wheel." He doesn't seem to find that funny. I drop my lifeless arm and look around the apartment with wonder. My eyes are large, and I'm observing the room like a newborn would, like everything is new to me. Dr. Alec just takes the back seat as he gently releases me from the wrap of his forearm. I feel like a recently disciplined child. But I'm more than that, aren't I? I'm a delinquent. I laugh out loud at my own jokes and look at Dr. Alec, hoping his face gives away even an inkling of wonder.

Dr. Alec picks me up and takes me to the bathroom. He turns on the shower and keeps his hand under the water as he waits for it to warm up. "Tell me if this is too hot," he directs me to put my hand under the water. I shake my head. "You have a first aid kit?"

"I don't want to shower," I whine.

"Stop it," he cuts the gentleness with severity. Dr. Alec carefully slips me out of my sweater, ensuring the neckline doesn't scrape against my abrasions. I independently squirm out of my pants. Dr. Alec turns around for privacy and gives me instructions. "Use the body wash we administered. It's on your rack—don't look at your chest, you're not funny. Pour a generous amount and start with your chest, shoulders, and neck. Add more to your palm and clean your back and bottom. Add more and clean your limbs. Take the face wash, use one pump, and gently scrub your face. Be careful not to irritate your cuts." I try to follow his orders a quarter of the way through. He checks his watch, "are you done?" Is he stupid?

"Dr. Alec, I'm drunk," my slurring echoes through the grime-tiled bathroom.

"I was being optimistic," he turns around, only looking upwards to avoid any awkward encounter. Dr. Alec then goes over every step slowly. He insists that I get myself clean before changing because it appears that I'm filthy, and that will increase the likelihood of contracting a nasty infection. Fair. After the shower, he hands me a towel, lowers the toilet lid, and sets me down on it. My legs dangle. "Wait here. Literally, Lee, don't move," he says with his hand raised like he's training me. I cross my arms and slouch back. Dr. Alec rustles through my bags, groaning and incoherently mumbling to himself. When he returns, he has a few bandaids in his hand

and alcohol spray. He bends over to meet my height and carefully observes the open wounds on my head and face. The dried- up blood sits heavy on my cheeks. "I'm going to treat these, and it's going to burn," he sprays as soon as I close my eyes.

"What the fuck, man?" I exclaim. "It burns—"

"I said it would burn. It shouldn't be a surprise to you," Dr. Alec puts on a few skin color bandaids after letting the stinging settle to patch the holes on my face. "Are you better?" I'm still drunk, and he knows that, but I do feel better. He tosses some pajamas my way, expecting me to have the coordination to wear them. I put the right leg in the wrong pant leg and stumble over the fabric. "Just quit while you're ahead," Dr. Alec motions for me to stop. He helps me get in the pajamas and flattens the rest of my hair. I step out of the bathroom and crash on my mattress.

"You know what you remind me of?" I slur. "Like a mother of a son who hasn't moved out yet. Like a mom. You remind me of a mother, Alec."

He chuckles. "Okay, Lee. I'm not here to do your laundry, so don't bet on it."

I roll over on my mattress, "I wasn't." I'm in a silly, goofy mood. Not a thought coherent enough to make use of. "Watcha doin'?" I can see what Dr. Alec is doing, but I can't understand it, which happens to be my life and my perception in a nutshell, which sucks. But now it doesn't suck anymore! Dr. Alec is sliding items into my fridge. He pulls out bread, butters like five slices, and offers them to me on a paper towel.

"You have to eat it."

My neck lets go, and I drop my head onto my dimensionless pillow. "But I'm tired."

"You can't be drunk. Eat." I doubtfully tilt my head to the side until he admits. "It slows down the metabolic process of absorbing the shitty liquor you chugged from your gut to your blood—which we've been recording, dumbass."

I reluctantly bite half the first toast and chew it without it ever sitting on my tongue for too long, as I'm afraid I'll throw up again. I see Dr. Alec in my peripherals; he's watching me, and I know I can't obstinately shove bread under my mattress. He's looking at my every move. I do as he says, downing another slice, and glance over at him, only to find that his eyes aren't fixated on monitoring me. No, he's just lost in awe. "What?" I asked with a mouth full of buttered carbs.

His eyes flick away from me. "Nothing… When did you start eating so sloppily?" I shrug. "We didn't teach you to behave like this." I let the comment of random solidarity with IRAAB pass me.

I swallow the last of it and lay back down. "Alec, I'm tired."

"I know. You can sleep," he says with a hushed tone. Dr. Alec climbs out of the window and onto the fire escape. I don't have the strength to ask him to stay, but hopefully he will anyway. I hear the faint zip of a lighter burning the end of a cigarette, and I imagine him remaining there for the entirety of the night, helping me drift off.

CHAPTER 6

YOU ARE A MATCH, MATCHLESS AT ITS WORST. ON FIRE AT ITS BEST

I'm not sure what wakes me, the pitter-pattering of the rain meeting the metal of my haven of a balcony where, to my relief, Dr. Alec remains. Has he been there all night? Dr. Alec is drenched. He must be cold. The more I gain consciousness, the more I am reminded that the future holds a violent hangover, ready to comprehend any inhibition I have to compensate for what I've done. However, I know that redemption is not contingent on anything. I don't know what I can do to help it, to help anything that's happened so far.

The ache travels to my forearms, quads, and even my ankles. They hurt as I twist them to ensure my nervous system functions like a car engine would after a storm or a desperate winter. I can use this imagery as a metaphorical comparison to my recent charade, but it serves no purpose anymore. Firstly, metaphors are really fucking dumb; secondly, the whole point is not to acknowledge what's become of me on behalf of the witness. I soon realize that I am in cotton pajamas. I can't remember the last time I wore pajamas. They feel nice, and it makes me sad. I know why Dr. Alec is still here. I think I broke him.

Dr. Alec climbs back in with no rush in particular. "How's your head?" He asks dryly. He barely keeps an eye in my direction. He's composed of disappointment.

"It hurts worse when I speak." He squats on the edge of my bed, his back facing me. "What are you doing?"

"Waiting," he says. "I need answers." Dr. Alec's tonality has proven me right. He is indeed broken and obviously upset with me, too.

"I'm sorry," I whisper. He scoffs under his breath and shakes his head. He doesn't move much after the short remark sponsored by some deep severity. The fact that he's just sitting there is a strategy because I know he's forcing me to make a choice. Either wait in agonizing silence or speak at the cost of my scarce ease. "Alec," I choose to speak. "What do you want to know more about?"

"I feel like I know nothing." And then he turns. "I don't think I know a thing about you, but I fear my hypothesis," he rolls his eyes at the word, "is correct… And Lee, I'm not ready to be right." He pierces me with a misunderstood glance. "How could you do this?"

"I'm depressed."

"You can't just pull a fast one on me and hope that this will save you," he trudges on, "you—you can't just say that like it's going to protect you." His palms are open, gesturing with dramatics to communicate how wrong I am for this. He gets up and faces me. "Depression is not a mile marker. It's an animalistic behavior, and lately… it just seems like you've been regressing," Dr. Alec rambles. "Your hygiene is one thing, but to barely eat is strange. You used to have somewhat of an appetite. You were interested in," he stops himself. "You at least knew what you don't like."

"You're describing clinical depression," I say blankly.

His voice builds from the depths as he forces himself to keep it below level, but he can't. Dr. Alec yells at me. "Do you fucking want benzodiazepines?" He extends the suggestions like it's supposed to scare me. "What the fuck do you want?"

I chuckle. Dr. Alec's jaw locks. "You want to hit something, don't you? I know you won't do it." He huffs at my remark because he's aware that a point is being made. I'm not just challenging him. "Imagine being penalized for something you cannot control."

"You want me to remove the chips? I can at least motion for it, but they won't *trust* you. I'm sorry, you and I both know that," he winces. The fear in his words reminds me of when *I* was young, and the only person who'd stay in class as I learned my ABCs was Dr. Alec. He'd use flashcards with me. Granted, Dr. Barberry would take over on his off days, but he was always there during every advancement. He'd let me pick electives, study them with me, and subsequently teach me his perspective because I listened. I was almost his child. He'd read me the tribulations of philosophers, and we'd laugh about Diogenes pissing in the streets and whether the egg came first or the chicken, only to conclude with the utmost idea that some knowledge shouldn't be sought because the reason for the answer isn't far from the question.

"I know that. It puts a damper on things."

"It's a restrictive life, but how could it conquer your instinct to survive? Something so intrinsic, so innate, was compromised because you're *sad*? Lee, what do you want?" How can I tell him that I'm done?

The consequences of IRAAB for an offense such as this are as engraved as the Ten Commandments. "Come on, Alec. This wasn't a cry for help, it's obvious. This was a decision," I say with heaviness. His eyes open to realize that maybe his insinuations were wrong and his deepest ruminations over the course of yesterday were right.

Surely, he's not stupid, and he's aware that my stupidity is only so limited, as this was a choice, not a mistake to be made twice. I know I'm hurting him, but there's only so much I can offer. Besides, it will be okay for everyone, even me, because no one is saying goodbye to me. It is my turn to say so. I am also confronting my decision in real time because last night wasn't of linear thought. It was impaired by so much that I just can't regard it as a heightened or, God forbid, exaggerated reaction. Everything that happened from my mind to my function was honest.

It seems like he doesn't know what to do with himself. I can sense his nausea and the weakening of his body. "You're not a failure," I tell him to honor his fragility.

"…Was I enough? I'll do more. I thought that maybe if I took a step back, it would make things better for you because you wanted this!"

He expels a hysterical laugh. "You wanted to move out. Maybe that's what put you in this position. You can come home. You know that, right? You can come live with me." I can't bear to ruin him. I've never heard him beg before.

"You have to let me come to terms," I demand.

"You don't have time!" He grips my arm and tugs me out of bed. "Let's go."

"Alec, I don't want to seize. Please," I try to keep myself calm. I know if I don't, I'll have no choice but to wake up at the facility. His tenacity fails, softening his grip. We both synchronously seat ourselves at the edge of the bed. Both of us wait a moment, unsure of the value of keeping this conversation alive. "You know. I've been trying to believe in God," I change the subject.

He finally lets go. "Is that so?" He doesn't face me, but I see thin tears leading to his stubbled chin. "Which god?"

"I went to church, " I say without remorse for what transpired fifty seconds ago. "Monotheism is a Silk Road tale."

"Don't bring your narrative into this," I hiss. "I think it's real," I don't. "Well, part of me believes it's real—something has to keep nudging us along. Too many coincidences that defy the subject of coincidence."

"There's an explanation behind everything," he snaps at me.

"And that reason can be part of the definition, too. I just think it's nice to personify the idea of everything into oneness," I respond with an openness that Jesus-loving Christians put forth.

"So you're aware of the game at play."

"Whatever."

There's nothing left for us to chat about, as the art of "giving in" serves an unsettling command. Dr. Alec rubs his palms on his thighs as if he is gearing up to say farewell, but his breathing is audible from a distance. It's controlled, and I'm sure he's aware of it, but he's undoubtedly unaware of my awareness. "I don't want to talk about the better days we had, but I feel it is a requirement certainly more than a desire... Remember when you were loved?" *Loved.* "They loved you over at IRAAB," he hesitates, "in the beginning. They wanted to see you grow and had hopes for you. They still care whether it's evident or not," his honesty doesn't help much.

I clench my jaw, "fuck off." I like hurting him. Maybe it's the comfort of having someone that won't leave.

"Okay," he chuckles. Dr. Alec stands up, appearing many units taller than usual. I swear to God, if he even tries to enforce this sudden optimism for IRAAB, I will literally apply for a gun license, purchase a pistol, and off myself in front of him. "You think a lot of things, and I let you. But this isn't gonna happen," he puts his hands in his pockets.

It burns me how much I hate having him here because I know Dr. Alec will be the guy to change my ways. He knows it, too, and regardless of what I want, he'll always get his way. Something about this suicidal tribulation blooms into newness. It also stops raining, and while I want to throw a tantrum over Dr. Alec, this stupid fuck, intercepting my grand attempt to save myself from the tragic monotony, I let him go. We don't exchange goodbyes.

Fuck, I feel like an imbecile for regretting my choices, but this must all be part of the process. What is Dr. Alec is going to say to them? I try to locate the missing pieces by making sense of my drunken recollections of his remarks, but I can only visualize him rather than remember any inquisition. He wore a face full of not only confusion but awe. Eventually, the darkness of the night allayed into day to debut grave expressions.

My body hurts. The aching, burning, and itching become more prevalent. I don't even know what to do with myself. I reach for my phone and dial for Virginia, though I'm unsure why. It rings four times. "Hello?" She answers.

"How are you?" I don't really hesitate.

"What do you need?" Virginia doesn't want to pursue a friendship with me anymore. I don't think I particularly need anything. "What do you want, Lee?" Her irritability offends me, and while I can give her a pass, sometimes I wish someone would give me a pass. "Lee," she's impatient again.

My mouth is agape as I compute a reply, "I just want to make sure you're well."

"You don't—I'm really not your concern," I suppose she's partially, only partially, moved on. If she rejected me nicely, then I'd believe she's absolutely moved on. Do I harbor toxic masculinity? I listen to *Florence and the Machine*, though.

Her bitter apprehensions are reasonable, and my garrulous attempts to rekindle things repeatedly are proven moot because she's right. It isn't my place to cement a bond between two unlikely companies.

We're different. It doesn't make much logical but emotional sense to call her at this time. I sigh and just hang up. She doesn't need to know about anything that's happened.

I change out of my fresh pajamas into corduroys and a sweater. Brush my teeth, wash my face. I put on a beanie and wrap my face with a scarf. Before leaving, I note the window in my peripherals. That's where Dr. Alec sat maybe all night—I'm not sure, I don't know. But I climb out to the fire escape to trace the light traffic and pedestrians with my eyes. The bright morning bothers me but not enough to discourage the newfound inclination to get out.

I climb back into my apartment, where the warmth is still. Where I am unable to be cut by the winds. But I have an impulse. A good one, a healthy one. Without a process or any rumination, I leave my apartment. I do the responsible thing, lock it, and then knock on the neighbor's door. I hear a man behind the door grunting as he reluctantly crosses his living room to answer me. It's not hard to predict people superficially. It seems everyone has average tendencies. Surely, he spends his time doing the most normal thing—having a microwave lunch with beer and watching something most people recommend on a popular streaming platform.

The neighbor opens his door to reveal himself as a burly man with his construction vest on. He must be on his lunch break. "Hello," he says with a kindness that I think might be necessary to him. "You just moved in, right? Well, not just," he rolls his eyes at himself. He stares at my features to comprehend the situation.

"Hi, no, yeah, it still feels kinda new. I'm Lee," I intently wait for his next move. Every interaction feels alienated because you don't know what to expect. Each interaction is unique for me, and while that can serve as an obstacle, I strangely feel very little fear. He reaches out his hand after eyeing me up and down like most do. I shake it, knowing that this gesture will be a clue to help him understand or even second guess what I am. If I were in his shoes, I'd be baffled. He doesn't flinch his hand away. He looks at it for a second. I use my other hand to pull out the introductory, laminated card administered by IRAAB. "You should probably read this," I chuckle with sudden charisma. I like this version of me.

He takes half a step back, trying so hard not to make me uncomfortable. He grabs the edge of the card, avoiding more contact. He reads it and flips over the card to locate more information. "Hm," he raises his brows and purses his lips. "And you're allowed to live here?"

"It was my idea, but the decision is up to them. So yeah," I shrug.

"How do you like it?" His friendliness reminds me of the people I almost interviewed for.

"I don't like it very much," I randomly confide and then laugh. "It's a studio and even a studio's rent is crazy." The casualness is pleasant rather than draining.

"So you're from," he looks at the card again, "International Research Administration of Animalia Biotechnology?" He hands the card back. I nod my head. "Never heard of them, but it's not so much of a surprise. I don't really read about science," he poorly puts it. "I know that Wall Street let one intern for like a month, right? It was in the Times. Not everyone was happy about it."

"Yeah, another's at NASA. Doing big things," I feel like shit for a second.

"I think your story is more interesting. I used to want to be a journalist. I think I'd pick you as my subject… among other aliens. Can I call you that?"

His etiquette is delightful! I won't tell him that it's sort of considered a slur. "It's all good. I am still an alien."

He looks at the scabs and patches of hair missing. I want to cover them so badly to avoid any suspicions that might interrupt introductions. I am in a good place right now. "So, are you transitioning? What's the motive? If you don't mind me asking." It feels awkward to continue chatting at the doorway when it's not really chatting anymore.

"No, the goal is to see if I can reach a humane level of sentience, to put it simply." I've become good at explaining myself.

"How far are you?" He tilts his head and asks. How unpredictable. Alas, he meant well, I'm sure. "I can't measure."

"Oh…" He scratches his head, "Did they not teach you to count?"

I laugh again! "No, no, I can do basic math," I slow down to remember that time again. "I can't really tell how far along I am," my voice increases in pitch. "I think I can say, without confidence, that I'm more than halfway through."

"Hm," he kinda grunts. "Well, enjoy the rest of your day then. Let me know if you need anything." He's nice. I know he was the one to call the landlord, though.

I smile honestly. "Thanks. See ya." I go forward in the direction of the street with an ever-changing inclination to release reservations but in a way that isn't spiteful or full of anything other than positivity. Positivity is such a brining word, but it's encompassing, which I'm trying to get at. I'm optimistic, as I've said. I'm optimistic right now, at least.

And while these feelings, yearnings, and hopes might vary and are contingent on environmental circumstances, the sudden openness is something worth chasing, even if the chase isn't lengthy. Upon pushing the door open, the wind backs into me with a force that blows my scarf off. Shame ensues as I scatter on the chilled concrete in search of the scarf, my eyes clocking the glances of each pedestrian within proximity. I wrap myself with a commitment similar to returning to a horse after falling. I continue toward populated municipalities. I like that no one is watching me unless they're near.

I make a stop beforehand at a store that sells novelty keychains and profane shirts that poke fun at big corporations. Like the one I went to by the beach. I need a snack, so I purchase a plain bagel. I should still be wise with my money. You never know. I buy juice for myself, too, the kind with the pulp, and get back on foot.

To my left is a group of monks promoting their practices by handing out "handcrafted" bracelets. I don't say anything to them; they're okay with it, which feels intuitively pleasant. Their brochure illustrates open land and greenery to stimulate the connotation of meditative lifestyles that monks commonly adhere to. The existential detachment, the nirvana of it all, is profoundly relevant but not a prospect. I take the brochure and the bracelet, wear the bracelet, and trash the brochure a block ahead. A block ahead, there's a museum of natural history, which seems enticing; however, I know I will be skipping the Neanderthal exhibit to avoid a child possibly tugging on her mommy's skirt and pointing at me—something from a newspaper comic, I imagine.

I walk up the grand steps to the golden-plated doors of the museum and find myself already at the end of the line. It's a weekday, it's early, and it seems many have considered, like me, to begin their day educationally. Why? I won't lie. It makes me a little excited to think that I might be able to relate to a crowd. As I inch closer to the desk, I realize there is a fee, and that totally blows because I only want to afford food. I politely step out of line and walk out of the building. I can have fun for free. I'm just going to have to ask around.

I walk straight to the park, where people are picnicking already. Did I get the time wrong? It must be my morning and everyone's afternoon. I see a few performers, one painted silver and another dressed as a cartoon. They are getting paid by the tourists for pictures, and it's not a bad gig, depending on the competition. I need fifty bucks, but I don't have it in me to advertise verbally.

A person who appears local looks down at me to verify that I am indeed an inhabitant. "Oh shit," he mouths and switches his farmer's market tote to the other hand. He reaches into his pocket to find a crumpled ten. "Do you have change?"

"Two pictures are better than one," I quickly reply, accepting the random vocation.

He agrees. "What pose?" The fuck? Literally, just stand tall next to me and smile. "Wait, who's taking the picture?"

"Maybe we'll ask someone… Could you ask someone?" The kid waves to a randomly spawned passerby and asks him.

The stranger agrees to waste his seconds taking our picture, which garners a little more attention. "Thanks," the fan nods and hands me hard cash.

"Yeah," I speak over a looming silence, anticipating further questioning of my origins, but nothing occurs.

I meet a following family of four. Twins for kids. They're actually kind of cute, and their voices are high-pitched as they convey necessary curiosity. The mother's eyes are warm, she has smile lines, and the husband encourages her. "So you're an alien?" The wife asks jokingly. Her chuckle is tossed at her husband. "It's a good costume. My kids really want a picture."

Should I explain myself? I'm not sure. "Of course, I can do two for ten or three for fifteen." I learned math, not business.

"Two is fine," she says conclusively.

"I actually am an alien, by the way," I tell her as I make the definitive choice of revelation. My honesty could help as an advertisement.

Spending my money makes me so happy. The cliché is true. I've learned over the years that originality has little to do with straying from commonality and more to do with one's personal truth. Clichés are generational wisdom sourced by experience; we're all experiencing the same little life. There's comfort in routine, my Dr. Alec would tell me. Anyway, the cliché I've subscribed to is that money you earn is more gratifying to spend than the kind that's lent. I'm spending on the little things I want, and I don't feel bad about it either.

Much easier to enjoy the little things when there isn't a fucking deadline over your head, inundating you with bullshit expectations.

I have no expectations from Dr. Alec rescuing me; I think I've found peace in letting go. If Project O.H.I. is terminated, if *I'm* exterminated, at least I know that it was because of my conscientious decision. Anyway, it's easier to talk to people, and people are quite pleasant when you let them remain unassuming.

I make enough money to hit the museum, but part of me wants to start a business. Make a living off this, and then use that money to travel the world. I could buy a timeshare. I should ask the guy painted in silver if he knows of any.

The idea of doing something with my life is nice. The attempt to negate all melancholic residues of the aftermath of last night is impressive. To my wonderful surprise, I don't think I'm sad. Goodbyes used to scare me to the point of visceral anxiety. Now it feels like rest.

I've made enough money not only to afford a ticket but also lunch. I wave to the crowd, thank them generously, wrap my scarf around my face, and escape. The line is still tragically long. I just wanna tour and look at all of the fundamental art and natural history and all the defining records of information and whatever else. When I reach the kiosk, I spread my cash to purchase one mighty ticket.

I follow some families out of line and marvel at this giant archaeological emblem. I don't know. I'm trying to put it in a way that expresses the magnanimity of this planet's past, but it's just the skeleton of a dinosaur. Well, not "just". But you know, it's not an emblem.

I release myself to the art exhibit to get the boring shit out of the way. No, I don't really like art. It reminds me of all of those Rorschach tests.

I don't enjoy the suggestion of glorifying a particular piece, as it is placed under optimal lighting and mounted on a blank wall to amplify vibrancy and intricacy. An art museum should be viewed as a tribute to the chronic expression of human emotion throughout history—so much so that it has created singular roles of artistry. Therefore, to marvel at a piece is not my cup of tea because it is not an efforted depiction, and its value cannot be gauged. It is an expression. The architecture of a museum enforces false glorification, but how can you glorify something that cannot be valued?

I travel to the next room to find a ranging tourist, taking her steps lightly as she merely glances at the art. It's like she wants to look insightful but barely cares about the pieces on the perfectly lit walls. She's mumbling things to herself that I can't hear. I check her apparel to confirm her economic status as she just might be a crackhead who snuck in, which I respect. I think I could equate to that. I used to be judgmental. Regardless, it is apparent that she is not from here because she's wearing a fanny pack.

"Hi," I say. She checks me the way I checked her, and I'm sure she's also trying to confirm whether I'm a crackhead.

She purses her lips. "Hello," she says, now indifferent to who I am and how I look.

I look at the splatter-painted piece that's garnished with violent brushstrokes. "What do you think of this piece?"

She looks around, wondering if anyone has noted our interaction. "I find it jarring."

Jarring. The kind of word that is for impression's sake. She's imparted a specious interpretation, and I bet it's in hopes of ridding herself of me. Maybe I still am judgmental.

Then, I wonder if she's maybe just afraid. I forget that I'm not the only one who's often scared because the terror I've received as reciprocity usually translates to some sort of violence or maybe verbal abuse. I don't think she means to be rude, but I do think she wants me to know that she is taking evident precautions.

Obviously, I cannot outright ask her if she's afraid of me because that's going to come off creepy, and I don't think I can even comfort her. The skin I wear is a monstrosity like those pitiful tales later turned into children's movies. I give her a soft smile, soft enough to disarm her caution, large enough to peek out of my binding scarf. She smiles back out of policy.

I forgive her. And then I walk away like it never happened. Hopefully, that relieves her. Hopefully, I won't bump into her again.

I think I'm biding my time in this corner of the museum because I just don't get artists. It's kind of weird. At most, I only understand music and literature, but the expression of art is embarrassing and boring. It's hard to leave, though, not because of the girl but because I don't know where to go, and I don't think I could stand being disappointed again.

Maybe the room with all the whales will do it for me. Do you want to know what's weird? Marveling at animals like they're beneath you. That's weird. I feel like a city block that's been renewed, restored, and regarded as gentrified. The nerve, really, right? I should be scolded for my insolence. I mean, it's not like I feel above it because

I am, unfortunately, bound to be studied, observed, monitored, and tracked.

I have an end that is worse than the animal because it has little to do with liberty and all to do with hands; hands that'll soon be covered with blood. It's fair to be this dramatic. As the hour goes by, in fact, as the day goes by, my attitude shifts into normalcy. I wrote a poem once. It went something like:

> *What has become of me but the match And sparkless.*
> *Nothing of friction,*
> *As if the opposing force has in itself found eternal demise*
> *so grave and dissident, sheerly objectified as a weakness.*
> *It requests instead,*
> *And where there is harmony, there is little life*
> *Where there is peace, it is beneath the world we tour, rest-*
> *ful. Lightless and six feet deeper.*
> *The spark never belonged but borrowed, mine and yours.*
> *You are a match, matchless at its worst*
> *On fire at its best.*

It's my take on the lack of tribulation and how impossible complete peace is because it would cause insanity. The feeling of not ever being challenged is primitively unnatural. Therefore, you become hollow, and even though it is regarded as peace, the absence of challenge will inevitably drive you crazy. Total peace is an imbalance. That's how I can differentiate between me and actual animals.

I follow the signs that lead me to the whale exhibit, and I'm a little excited to see the blue whale hanging from the ceiling. There's nothing more to it. It's just really fucking big. I've seen a whale penis before and accidentally left it in my search history. Dr. Savea had to assess me to find out if there was some sort of neurological damage I'd undergone. She then told me it was out of line to search these things, but I just did it out of sheer curiosity, and isn't that the human spirit?

After last night, I've been looking at humans from an appreciative lens because I think I feel released. The human spirit is curious and growing. Look at how many people are here today; how many parents are holding little hands, pointing at displays to capture their young's attention. I think looking up whale penises is the human spirit, and I believe that rebellion is also another testament.

As much as I'd like to continue humoring myself, I force a halt to trace my location on the extensive directory screwed into the wall. I place my finger where it says, "YOU ARE HERE," and then I route myself to the marine life exhibit. Straight down and a couple of left and right turns, and I should get there in one piece.

An uncle taps my shoulder. He's smiling cautiously. "You think we could get a picture with you?" He politely asks as he points to his wife and his teenage daughter. They all appeared excited, trespassing into a singular depth of hope.

"I wish I could," my face contorts, "but unfortunately, my agency is not permitting any photos at this time. I'm very sorry." I should have started using this excuse when I stepped into the limelight—except when making money from them. The old father nods and lets me go, and I let go of him, but the feeling of regret weighs heavier than I anticipated. Regardless, I don't want to service every person here. I'd instead participate in small talk.

I cross many streams of people looking at different historical memorabilia, people poking in and out of rooms. Museums are so surreal. Maybe the art exhibit left a bad taste in my mouth, but I don't think that I will rescind my opinions so soon. I realize that the mark of civilization is so prominent that those who contribute to it feel a vast need to study its origins.

I think it's important to know your history. I think it's important for a historical museum to exist, but the rhetorical meaning of life has little to do with generational themes. Rather, it has all to do with the personal loss you experience. I step into a hall that I know will lead me to the whale exhibition.

I know I'm in the whale exhibit or the ocean exhibit or whatever you wanna call it because the floor is blue and the walls are blue, and I look up, and there is this gigantic fucking blue whale hanging above me. Great placement. I'm pretty astonished at the size of this massive whale but also slightly disappointed that this is the actual length of thirteen school buses. Like, that's it? Not everyone is looking up. They're looking at the giant squid hidden in the shadows of the corner.

This world possesses sublime measures, and yet to be able to fathom the ratio of yourself next to magnanimity is unprecedented, so when you find that some things can be defined and measured transiently, it puts you back on Earth. Knowledge has turned everything mundane, and even God has a definition. It's not some magical air equated to a spiritualist's energy. Even as the—apparently—God-fearing creation I am, I find that the coalescence of information regarding everything holy paints a picture anyone can easily visualize. Every era speaks of this God; some historically entertain his wrath, others his judgment, and white people consider his love the most.

I think about Muslims and Jews and how they are ordered to avoid certain meats. While there may be a canonical reason, I often wonder why these harms were created in the first place. Why was a shit-eating pig created in the first place? To avoid it? It's usually interpreted the other way around: Why can't you eat pork? Because pigs eat shit.

I like to think that all entities of tangible creation serve a lesson one way or another, and their interpretation will generate redundant themes, however necessary. I'm neither Jewish nor Muslim… nor Christian, for that matter. I'm a modern-day agnostic, possibly.

When I look at this whale, I think of God looking over us in grandeur. The only difference is that we have counted the whale in size, and God has counted us. What if I became a Jehovah's witness? What if I became a Jehova's witness who also sells Girl Scout cookies? What a business venture that would be. I laugh to myself in a room large enough to echo ambient chattering as it nearly parallels the sound of a running faucet, ironically… because we're in an ocean exhibit. Imagine if they played music in a museum. It would be taken much, much less seriously! I do a twirl to get a good look at everything, but I refuse to twirl in the center as I am afraid the lights will dim, and only a twinkling spotlight will shine on me, and I'll be on my toes suddenly, solemnly dancing in a contemporary rhythm, with my hands dramatically draped over my face. I think I'll also be wearing a tutu.

When I do leave, I enter an Amazonian room. There still isn't any music; instead, there is the fabricated noise of bugs and crickets. It also sounds wet. I can count the seconds between the drops of rain playing through hidden speakers. It does have an effect. It feels like a journey of time travel as I rush through each hall decorated with faded artifacts, sculptures, scriptures, fun things, and taxidermy animals.

When I am almost home-free, I see that uncle again. He's forgotten about me, and so have his wife and daughter. I hate to be reminded as I'm on the verge of moving on. I can imagine the weight in my chest as I picture my life shortly after, how I'd feel on the subway, how I'd think about his kind eyes and the graying mustache tipping over his top lip. His smile was so humane, and so was his acceptance when I lied in rejection. I come to an abrupt stop. The thoughts in my head are passengers, confused because we are currently en route. We are en route, right?

I've almost felt this way with Dr. Alec once. It's guilt, isn't it? Unless it's long-term, it doesn't qualify as progress. I barely feel remorse for the uncle, but something prevents me from continuing my day.

I don't know what to do with this information besides the right thing. I walk up to the old man and tap his softened shoulder. "Hi. I hope I didn't interrupt," I pull my hand out of my pocket and gesture toward the towering exit doors. "I was heading out and saw you guys. Did you still want that photo?" I offer warmly.

He barely looks back at his family, this time to reach a consensus. "We'd love to! Thank you!" I take out the laminated card to verify for his convenience so they can live the total thrill and never doubt whether this was all a sham. "Honey," he says to his wife with emphasis. She knows she's been summoned to enjoy this moment with him, and they look at my identification with amazement, their eyes following IRAAB's official statement on the back. The wife glances up at me with wonder.

"Can I touch your head?" She asks softly, the paper-thin skin creasing around her mouth.

I bow in her presence but leave the beanie and scarf on. "Of course," I say quickly. She glances at her husband for unspoken approval before reaching out, letting the tips of wrinkled fingers land. She rests more of her hand to ensure I feel her, and she pets two times.

"Okay," she whispers. And then she fixes the pleats of her shirt, tucks her flyaways behind her ear, and stands next to me. The uncle takes my right side, and the daughter is on her mother's left. We realize no one is there to take a photo, so we all laugh together.

"Excuse me," I say to two girls about to leave. Their eyes dart to me, tracing my outline with their perceptiveness. "Do you mind taking a picture of us?" The father pulls out his cell and hands it to the girls.

They haven't responded yet. I'm hoping they don't ask for a picture too. "Uh, sure." A sister takes the phone, her eyes still outlining my features. She takes a couple of photos while the family quietly poses. Their energy is calm and surprisingly hospitable as the mom tries again to pet me. Is it evident that I am suffering "emotionally"?

The girl returns the phone, "I'm not sure what to ask…" She looks at her sister, teasing telepathic thoughts. "Can I ask what the reason for this picture is?"

I protect her courtesy with pleasantry. "I am Lee, the alien. One of many aliens who are undergoing experimentation. I am a product of the International Research Administration of Animalia Biotechnology." They aren't skeptical, so I leave my card in my pocket.

Both of the sisters raise their brows with surprise. "Can we also get a photo?"

I don't miss a beat. "Unfortunately, I cannot take any more photos as I am obligated to follow my itinerary. Sorry, but it was a pleasure meeting you." I feel like I'm reading off a script, a script that I wrote. I look back at the family and wink.

"Bye," the family of three says in unison. The sisters are speechless, but they'll recover.

I push the door and enter the free world at my whim's disposal. I am excited about whatever I do next, although the anticipation of IRAAB reaching out dawns on me. Before I can worry anymore, I see a food cart at the end of the street and a few people standing before it. The menu is plastered on the cart, and suddenly, I'm craving shawarma. I hate to, but I remember the last time I bought cart food, and it's really difficult not to go down the path of review, but I can't help myself as I prophetically eye the cart from where I am. I've never wanted to hurt anyone. Why would IRAAB let me ever think that I could?

I don't care if it was for precaution's sake; they shouldn't have communicated it, and they shouldn't have allowed me to internalize a possibility that I know couldn't be possible. I hate that Virginia has an idea of things because they're untrue. It's worse when you have to convince someone because then it just looks like a lie. I don't think anything between us is salvageable, which blows, but that's what anyone would think, and anyone would suggest that there's no need to contemplate it.

It feels like trauma to the head. Well, back to a cart that reminds me of the worst day of my life. It was the beginning of my descent. Maybe it's the nature of every sentient thing to blame and relieve oneself of regret, but man, I wish Virginia had never decided to get her life straight and take a job for Mel. I wish I had never met her. Lining up at the shawarma cart, I feel like I'm facing my trauma in a way that is not instinctive but a product of therapy. I recall this procedure in a handbook, though. If the experiment is undergoing severe mental distress, the experiment is then subjected to therapy. Where's my goddamn therapist? I notice the employee in the smoky cart pause before taking my order but I don't care to acknowledge it. "What can I get you?" He says with a foreign depth.

"I'll take chicken over rice. Less oil. More salad." What? I care about gut health. "Okay," he punches it in. "Seven dollars."

I fumble through the cash I just earned. "Here you go." I give him a tip, "I don't need cash back."

I stalk to the end of the cart where the pick-up window is. It doesn't take longer than five minutes to receive my lunch. "Thanks!" I say confidently and waddle to the bench, giddy to eat a hot meal. When I dig in, I do it with haste, as the best meals begin with spoonfuls of greed. I lowkey remember disliking this meal… All flavors are sitting on top of each other. It doesn't really taste good, but it feels good to eat. I cannot stand etiquette when hungry. "Fuck," I moan. I feel heat permeate through my body. I hope no one heard me moan.

I am dressed as an introvert who leaves his apartment once every month to feed pigeons, and I again hope no one heard me utter to myself because it just looks more perverted than it really is. I finish more than half of my plate quicker than I imagine, making me pity myself, as I did not know how hungry I was until I ate. The meat and the rice sit warm in my belly, and I can feel my blood pumping through my back, shoulders, and temples. Health is glory, I think.

I don't think today is reaching catharsis, but it is headed in the right direction as it parallels the sun. It's almost going to set, and I'm craving something sweet. I envision a moment that should be one for the books if I give in to my cravings. I imagine a styrofoam cup held by my opposable thumb, index, middle, and fore. I can hear the plastic spoon, tainted by microscopic orbs of salvia, scraping the inside of the styrofoam cup for more. I think it's ice cream, and I imagine it's strawberry.

I hop off the bench and dispose of the meal. Right before I drop it into the trash, I picture the homeless man I once saw at church. I could aid someone like him with my leftovers, but I comfort myself with the reality of selfishness, as it is sometimes an example of sub-jugation. I believe that kindness is often a privilege.

When I am on my way to nowhere, I attempt to note my surround-ings to generate thoughts worth counting. It's the way I'm wired over years spent on fleeing. When I say the word "goddamn," I think about Henry David Thoreau and Jack London, and I also think about chewing on straw. I remember reading certain fiction and understanding the civilized attempt to cut social fetters and embrace man's burning, isolated nature. I usually note my surroundings when I'm going somewhere, but I don't know where I'm going, and my visualization of past literature is blinding me.

When I come up for air, I see an ice cream shop across the street. I thank God for His lead. I'm so excited by the convenience of its location that I want to run like a dog to it. I enter an ice cream shop that smells stale but sweet from the hot waffle cones. The temperature is off-putting, as it is warm here, and the colors of the tiles are faded yet multi. I keep my head somewhat down but use my eyes to convey intent, proving that I am not a penniless vagabond… with cash instead of card. A few people are working behind the ice cream bar, straining their thin forearms to pull scoops of rocky road and cookie dough from large frozen bins. "Strawberry," I say without looking. "Strawberry cone," okay, Elvis.

"Any toppings?" I note without looking up that it's a young boy, probably a freshman in high school, asking me.

"No." I don't want to say 'no' because it feels rude. "Actually, yeah, nuts." No, but I actually am craving nuts. It's been a while since I've taken care of myself by eating nutritional content.

"Anything else?"

I barely glance at it and nod. Oddly enough, I notice him more than my sweet treat. "That's good, kid." Kid? I wonder how all the people I've met so far are doing. My strangely friendly neighbor, Caleb, the people who rejected me when I applied to their company, the girl who let me buy her cart, the girl who was afraid of me at the art museum, Dr. Barberry, Savea, the teenage girl at that other dessert shop. Oh my god, Miss Tangerine from my favorite Thai spot. Not too bad for an introvert.

"Okay," the kid is also weirded out that I called him a kid. "Okay," I mirror.

He points to the end of the counter where the register sits. "I can ring you—"

"Oh! Right." I scooch down to that register.

He punches in my order. "Six dollars."

"Six dollars?" I exclaim. Suddenly, I'm not so introverted. "How did we get to six dollars?" I'm gonna also remember this interaction.

"The nuts."

I sigh. Why am I so annoyed, though? "Take them off."

"What?" The kid says, outraged.

"Yeah. Pick them off."

"I can't do that, sir."

I look baffled, though I'm aware that it isn't my place to be. Rather, I should be rightfully abashed by my instigation. I must be setting a horrible impression of laboratory aliens. I bet it irritates him to imagine how much worse my temper could get. "Okay. Throw it away and get me a scoop without."

The kid shrugs. Aw fuck, it's so unfair. How unfortunate for him to be met with a customer who is borderline a sociopath, unable to resonate with his defeat. My lips quiver to convey a change of heart, but the kid listens.

The employee picks each halved peanut off the plentiful scoop. I think he's nudging holes into the scoop on purpose, and I think it's kind of funny because some retaliations never result in change. People find satisfaction to be such a tangible option. It's almost silly. His pettiness is silliness to me. He slides it over and reduces the price. "Thank you." I give him a bill, and he gives me change.

"Yeah," he says. Our eyes dart to the tip jar. No.

I take my ice cream and eat it too. "Have a nice day," I say maliciously. But it's just simple fun. It shouldn't make him want to do something drastic, like look up videos of people who jumped off the San Fran bridge and lived.

I use my change to pay a quick fare to the nearest bridge.

The taxi driver doesn't look at me, and I don't look at him. "You live here?" He barely catches a peek in the side-view mirror.

"I thought I'd enjoy my ice cream on the bridge," I speak up.

The man nods. I can smell his cologne and body odor after every gesture. "Going through something?"

"I'm doing okay, thanks for asking."

"I want to get you in time for the sunset. It's beautiful. It'll make you happy." I already said I'm okay. We bear silence for the next ten minutes. I don't touch my ice cream. I'm rigid and rightfully hung up on the idea that watching the sunset and having ice cream on the bridge will be very cathartic. I'd like to look over the city, right above the glistening body of water.

The taxi driver pulls over with his hazards on, and I give him what I owe. "Take care," he says. I feel like he meant it, but I try my best not to show face.

"Thank you," I say shortly. The shutting of the door interrupts my deferential gratitude. My ice cream is down to half—half a cream, half intact but quickly softening. I lick it because I left my spoon in the car, but I find myself to be a creature of resource. I'm afraid to look up at the view. The sun is setting. The sun is setting faster than my ice cream is melting, and if I don't catch it, I will only rely on stupid imagination. I look up and am met with movement. It's not disappointing. This is beautiful because the windows of each tower, which people undermine by calling them buildings, sparkle from the orange rays.

Alec

What's worse is that the temperature is cooler than my already verbalized preference in this godforsaken boardroom. I think the decision has been made, and no longer is my leadership regarded. I want to be proactive, but I have no legs to run with or arms for defense. My mouth is my mouth, but my voice does not produce. I am the center, but nothing revolves. I did it this time, didn't I? Dr. Barberry, Cambry, and Savea are here. Felix is here, too. His hair is fine and freshly trimmed, which speaks to my unkemptness. My appearance is precisely that of a scientist. Savea meets me with disgust written at the bend of her mouth. She rolls her eyes as many times as possible. I'm just looking to check if she's anemic because of how her eyes flutter. The room smells like toxic lemon, and I really hate that the air is cool. It's threatening. Someone decided today I won't be in charge anymore, so it's okay for the air to run at a nice sixty-seven. It isn't even a "fuck you" number. It's professional. It's serious.

I can think of everything but the ramifications, and certainly, I can feel the amplitude of each seismic wave bordering my failure. I am not regretful. There is no shame to be implied, so even if everyone's arms are crossed, and their heads are shaking with such agonizing disappointment, it does not play a role. I did what I simply had to do. "Dr. Alec…" Savea looks at the party first to retrieve the green light to speak. Everyone's silence is a unanimous decision. "What do you expect out of this conversation?"

I take a seat, charting my gravity as the rest follow my instinct. "I do not want to give anyone the gratification, I assure you, but it seems that I have indeed put myself in a position of debt," I carefully put it.

She smirks at my Shakespearean delusion. "Just—just," Savea has already lost her patience with me. "Eat shit, Alec." She slaps her hands on the table.

"I know. I'm about to."

Dr. Barberry puts a gentle hand on her left shoulder. "We're simply just trying to say that things have gone wrong despite your guarantee. In all fairness, you were wrong, Dr. Alec, and it's hard to say this," his voice sorta trembles, "because I know, theoretically, your approach was the most eligible. I know you were endorsing the subject's capacity to be sentient through unlimited experience, but his freedom was more than Lee could chew, frankly—"

"Actually, no. It's still because of his limitations that he did flip." Fuck all of this. I push back the table as I realize where this conversation might go. "Are you fucking putting him down?"

"Do you ever understand the consequences?" Dr. Savea hollers back.

I jeer with intense hatred. "I will slap the shit out of you." My finger warns her. Aghast, her lips tighten, and she takes a step back. I hope she is afraid of me when she drives back to her place tonight. I feel a rush of unfairness on behalf of Lee and for myself, too, a painful gush of pity I once found to be underwhelming. Felix is about to interrupt. "You all are fucking it up!" I smash my old glass of dried liquor against the whiteboard behind me. "I gave him a shower, I wiped his blood, I carried, fed, and fucking raised him!"

No one regards my outrage. "You paid for his rent, implying he cannot care for himself. Lee damaged his brain—"

"Nothing neuroplasticity can't fix," I quickly give my rebuttals.

"Those are not the rules. Why can you not accept that?" Felix says, laughing at me. "Why can you not see how unfair it is?"

"Alec. Stop bringing yourself into this," Felix says, looking down.

I want to cry like a child. My brain feels like it's suffering from electrical damage, and it's crackling, and I wonder if I will foam from the mouth. These are things I used to visualize when my parents would hate me. Every man in their midlife goes through a time when they remember what their fathers have done to them without reason. This was that chapter in my life. The employees at this facility treat me like a dementia patient whenever I open my mouth to any of them. I cannot let Felix win, but he makes me want to just break the fuck down. Savea is my Achilles heal, and the sad thing is, I cannot respect Dr. Barberry, the one man who agrees with me.

I twist my neck. "Why haven't I received any reports of him today? Where is he?"

"Surveillance labs are still doing their jobs," Dr. Barberry chimes. "He seems to be okay today, and his vitals are average. If that makes you feel better."

It does. "Okay. What does that indicate?"

Savea steps forward, dropping the grudge of being physically threatened. "Don't make a point out of this, Alec, because there are legal ways to induce progress. Legal."

"Oh really? He was suicidal, Doctor. He went against all instinctual and survival ethics to preserve residual peace because of, in fact, the limitations imposed by IRAAB. You," I laugh, "are all wrong! You are all so, so wrong; it's lost on you all because I planted a rebellious seed." I press my finger violently against my head. "Freedom is not in the equation. It was never the influence."

"Then why was he under the influence?" Felix practices wordplay like a complete asshole. Clearly, this ordeal is not bigger than his ego. "If you were not the head, if Lee were less sentient—let's say a rat or a creature of lesser potential—wouldn't you agree with us if the scenario's variables remained the same? The most prominent variable is inebriation. And let's say your reputation, along with your colleagues', is still on the line, and *let's say* this project is still as expensive. Wouldn't you agree with us?"

"The only thing I understand is that you see him as a lab rat."

"Just say you're sorry," Felix doubles down.

"Could you, Felix, just shut the fuck up?"

"Dr. Alec, I will not let you speak to me that way!"

"Why are you acting like there's a stenographer by your side?" I exclaim. "You talk how you fucking look."

"Are you being homophobic?" Savea demands. "So you know what I'm saying?" I ask.

"So you're implying I'm gay?" Felix huffs.

Dr. Barberry pats his head to relieve his headache. The situation is definitely out of hand at this point, and no one is truly tired of it yet. They want me to give in. I feel itchy in my skin, but I keep my feet planted. "No," I continue. "Felix, you're just being a dick. The way you're talking—the way anyone is talking in this room is so confusing," I say the last word while rubbing my face. The tears are flooding. I know if I look down, it'll push heavy ones out to land on the conference table. It'll be noticeable.

"We know that Lee's attempt to commit self-harm is a touchy subject, and while that may indicate some level of emotional independence, do you not feel bad that you brought him here? Where there is more, you realize you have less, and we all believe that is what stressed Lee," Felix returns.

"It's not his fault?" I whisper, surrendering. One of us has to be wrong, right? I don't know why I phrased it as a question, though. I am definitely to blame as my chicanery is out of flame. It is my fault. I brought myself into this, and now most scientists can't even tell if Lee is behaving like me or if I'm becoming Lee. The act of every-thing coming together full circle is the most jarring, hair-raising realization one could ever encounter. I see why Lee went to church now. I'm not quite sure who to look at when I say this, so I look down and forget, but the tear spills. The room is tense and possibly in disbelief. "I'm sorry."

Felix looks out the window shortly after the pressure subsides to a degree where we can physically move a tad. "Alec, Richard will be coming in soon. You should go home. We will decide what to do next that is best for IRAAB."

Savea pleads, "Alec." I don't wait for her. I push through the next set of doors to exit the facility. "I just have one more thing to say."

"Why are you not afraid of me?" I twitch from her persistence.

"You act so painfully righteous, but Alec, I think you should save yourself the agony and admit, even to yourself, that you care about him just as much as the next scientist here."

I'm sure she thinks that by uttering those words, I'll want to hit her. I don't feel very sorry for threatening Savea, but not out of spite. It's that, by not commenting on it, she forgivingly overlooked my remark. Feeling comforted, I overlook, too. "I'm really tired, Savea."

Before anything tangential can occur, I step out. I'm sure the bastards pacing the conference room feel accomplished but not celebratory. My hovering perspective switches like surveillance would, and now I'm seeing the world through my lens. I don't think I've ever noticed how white the walls of this facility are. Very sterile or barren. I think of my son.

I get to my unlocked car; the heat resting in the leather has already accumulated. My ass feels like a bundle of love, but my back is beginning to sweat. It's hard to be in tune with myself, so my conscience is more so leading preemptively. What should I do now that I've broken down in front of my antagonists? What should I do now that I'm on the brink of losing a job that I think I loved and now that I've thought about seeing my son after an uncomfortable amount of time? I open my mouth, wondering if Dr. Alec Masklig will scream. This gesture extends for many seconds and subsides into a yawn instead.

I start my car and back out without caution. I drive out of the facility, not sure if I should speed with petty rage as everyone is probably watching me like a bunch of round-belly, thumb-twiddling dumbasses. I choose the speed limit until I hit the highway and pick the nearest exit. I am in the pockets of a town where shabby motels reside. There's a washed- out diner and an off-duty stripper planted next to it. Her skin is leather. I see an on-duty officer. Neither of them pays attention to each other. It's not a harmonious place for low- class locals. It's just what depression assumes about the world. No one cares, and everyone is dirty.

I know I don't belong, but if only. What a simple life it would be. I would be forced to worry about trivial things like taxes and rent. I think rich people cultivated the hippie archetype and pawned it off to people who couldn't afford it. Hippies don't care about taxes. Neither do the rich.

I park my car at the front of the diner so I can keep watch of it as I have my breakfast on a cracked plate. The booth is sticky, as expected, and my glass has lipstick stains. I feel sick, but I think it's because of something other than this C-rated diner. With a voice resembling a duffle bag's zipper, the waitress asks me what I need. Booze. "I'll take a water," I mumble. I must appear aloof. It's true. I'm not too concerned with what I'll have to eat because I've reasonably lost my appetite, and in its stead, I'm simply trying to figure out if admitting is the first step in AA or grieving. The waitress doesn't write it down.

"Our griddle isn't working. You can order…" her eyes fixate on my car, and then she looks at my apparel. "That's your car out there?"

"You want to take a ride?"

"My husband works here, you know?" She carefully gestures at the territorial ex-con glaring at us. His nostrils flare, and it reminds me that we were all once animals. I push myself out of the booth, and this bitch doesn't budge. I'm like an inch away from tits that remind me less of their pleasure and more of their anatomical purpose.

"Excuse me," I say politely, knowing damn well her husband is watching us. "Sure, honey." She finally moves! Jesus, the tension.

"I think I forgot my wallet in the car. I'm sorry." As I rush out to leave, it occurs to me that I want to go home. But not my home.

My ex lives fifteen minutes from me. At the time, I wanted to be on good terms with my ex and stay nearby if she and Joseph needed anything more than money. I never intruded, and that's because I moved on gracefully. There's a bitterness with how easy I made the divorce, but I think I'm owed some gratitude.

When I get there, I realize it's a weekday, and my kid is probably in school. I know that when I pull up, she'll notice. I never had the chance to give a dramatic, unexpected entrance into her life by knocking on the door, revealing her past. So yes, she's most likely already seen me and deciding whether to answer.

I park in the driveway of a three-bedroom, two-story home. Magazine-esque shrubbery surrounds the house, and pink wildflowers accent the shrubs. She did an excellent job at making a home.

She opens the door, and her belly is the first thing to exit. She's carrying. That's real sweet. I feel a wash of relief over me, and it's chased with faith that maybe she's finally found the love she deserves.

Her hair is blonder but still a dirty blonde, and her layers loop through each other. Her skin is softer now, and she has lines. But the way her eyebrows are naturally arched, she still looks sexy. She's wearing a green paisley shirt, making me wonder if she's gone holistic. It's funny, I hate paisley.

She doesn't have shoes on but proceeds to scamper down the hot cobblestone trail to meet me. Her face is perplexed and maybe even slightly annoyed. "Alec?" Her tone is calmer than expected, which means her heightened emotions from the past have abated. "Alec," she knocks on the window that's already rolling down.

We both look at each other in silence, trying to solve each other. The birds are chirping, and I can hear wind chimes. "What's going on? Joseph isn't home, you know."

"Who's Payton?" Not a solid way to kick things off. Clearly, she doesn't like that I've stalked her new family online.

She puts her hands to her hips and huffs, blowing her soft hair out of her face. "Why are you here? Do you wanna meet the guy?"

"No. No, I don't care to meet him." I chuckle. She squints. "What?"

I groan in misery and put my head against the steering wheel. After a quarter of a minute, she rubs my head. "Why don't you come in?"

"Why are you so nice to me?"

She chuckles, "I have tea brewing. You know Payton dries the herbs out himself. I grow them." She sways like a palm as she walks up into her home.

"You make a good team—tea." I don't project enough for her to hear. She continues into what seems to be a reconstructed home. Everything about her place appears customized, and that's something she would do. It's part of her personality. I remember everything she'd buy displayed some essence of originality that I believe she was trying to convince me of. I wonder if she thinks that I didn't assume highly of her and that I thought of her as any other tolerable, average young woman. I don't really blame the fact that she moved on fairly quickly. During my divorce, I was the one who was overtly nonchalant. Now look at her, she just fucking patted my head.

Upon entering her home, I notice that the chandelier does not match the architecture of her house, but it does match the decor. Old-timey crystals hang next to floral wallpaper; she probably put all of this up and uttered to herself that she's turned into her mother. The windows are open, letting in soft melodies of the wind. The wood only slightly creeks as you move further into the home. The couches are new, a beige felt with a teal blanket draped over to match the excessive tones of cream and sage. Her personality permeates this home, and I don't think I miss her. I just think that if I had still had this life, I would've learned to appreciate it.

We get to a kitchen that is sitting on slightly aged tiles. It smells like organic lemons, and there are plants growing on the windowsill under the rays of conveniently located sunlight. She takes homemade iced tea out of the fridge and swiftly turns to me. "Iced is fine?"

"Yes," I reply quickly.

"Iced it is." She pours three glasses of tea and sets it on the wooden table. I chug the tea without paying any mind to how cold it is and how sensitive my teeth have become.

She shifts her weight. "Fess up, Alec."

I point at the tea. "Actually, can I have it hot?"

"I'm serious."

I smirk. "You don't want me around when Payton comes home, right?"

"It's not that. I think it's fair I ask why you visited without warning." I scoff at her remark. "Don't try to make me the bad guy here. I mean, I'm not trying to say that you were the bad guy. But certainly, *I'm* not at fault for saying how I feel—"

"What does Payton do for a living?"

She crosses her arms, knowing that Payton cannot compete with me. "He's a contractor."

"Oh, that's fun," I poke.

She aggressively withdraws the tea from my hand and puts it in the sink. "You have no right to show up arbitrarily, expressing your thoughts and opinions."

I put my hands up to surrender, "I didn't mean to." I did mean to. "I'm sorry… I lost my job."

She sighs. "Well, I'm sorry to hear that. Why'd they fire you?"

"It's going to be much more than firing, I fear." My attention immediately switches to the undoing of the front door. I hear rustling and lighter footsteps. It's Joseph. Based on those timid steps—compared to those of a fifty-year-old contractor—it's definitely Joseph. Is Payton fifty? Or worse. Is he younger?

"Mom," his voice echoes toward the kitchen. She's frozen, shooting a glance at me. He steps forward. "Can you sit next to me while I drive? Payton dropped me home early, and I wanted lunch at that deli." He keeps shuffling. "Also, what's with the midlife crisis parked in our driveway?" I smirk. Joseph finds us, and the room is tense enough to raise body temperatures. "Dad?" At least he still calls me that.

I get up, press my shirt straight, and greet him with half a smile. It is a solemn moment for our family, but I feel important. It's been a long time since someone has put me on the pedestal. "…You're big now." He has stubble, and he's maybe half an inch taller than me.

His chest is concave, shoulders hung over, glasses sitting right before his eyes. He looks like a good boy, my Joseph. I swiftly joke with my ex, "Is he even ours?"

"What—what brings you to town?" He doesn't look at me when he asks this. He looks at his mom.

And Mom answers. "Alec heard you just scored your permit and wanted you to try out that blue midlife crisis parked up front." She doesn't look at me when she lies, and I don't like that.

My face drops, "Your mom is lying."

"Alec," she hisses. "Joey, go—"

"No." I interrupt.

"Yes!" She pushes back.

"You're such bullshit, Nancy—" I haven't said her name in years.

"You can't have that language in here," she warns me. "How come you act so warm, but when—"

"It's because I know you want something. That's why you're here, aren't you?" Nancy's voice breaks a little.

Joseph sits, "I think I'm old enough to decide… What's going on, Dad?" It's not a question of concern. Rather, it's obvious that he wants to make me feel like a burden.

"I'm sorry I haven't been around as much. I figured you're better off without me, and I don't know how you'd turn out under my influence. Your mom and I both thought it'd be better for you." Find my words on a greeting card.

"That doesn't answer my question."

"Joey." Pause for dramatics. "I know an alien named Lee. He was a scientific experiment, and my company wanted to see if he could reach human-level sentience. I don't know how much your mom told you about me, but I basically raised him… I was the head of a big scientific project. Talking aliens is not an innovation, I know, but he had feelings," I look down, "my efforts got me in trouble, and I got fired. I broke the rules, and I got fired. And I have this feeling that no one cares enough to want me around. Ever…" I look up at him, "I think I'm going to lose everything."

He doesn't waste time to respond. "So now you need us?"

He traps me with such a question. "I've always needed you, Joseph." Truth is, I didn't think of my son when I was with Lee.

"You replaced me with an alien. You—" he raises his voice, "you are such a joke. Get out, I want you out!"

"Joseph." Nancy presses his arm to calm him. But I agree with him and accept my loss.

LEE

Silence fills the air. It's been this way for a while, though I haven't kept track of the days. When you stop counting, freedom doesn't come in rebellion or anger. Instead, it emerges in a state of mind you'd likely have while vacationing at a timeshare. It's been very restful. Of course, I don't like that IRAAB hasn't reached out. What else could they be occupied with other than deciding my fate? Are they still deciding? When is my next check-up?

But on the other hand, I've been enjoying my grave resignation by touring the city and embarking on aimless retreats at the local park. It's become routine to watch the sunset before returning home.

When I reach my door, I spot a notice slapped on it, wrapped in an orange plastic bag. Fuck. "Fuck," I mutter as my eyes land on the ugly word: "EVICTION." I'm not sure what I need to do next, but my fingers tremble. My body tries to advertently calm itself down. Knots twist in my stomach. It's like I have to shit immediately.

The letter confirms my suspicions. That fuck ass landlord is tired of my shit, and he wants me out. It's all my fault, and I don't want to go back to IRAAB with this news. I unlock my door and run to the bathroom. My mind is swarming with ideas of what I want to do next.

More importantly, what should I do next? This is a very "existential" moment for me. What is it that I want from this life? I no longer have a choice to be complacent. I rip ass and blow up my toilet.

My head is heavy, and I let it rest in my palms. I press my eyebrows to relieve what I want to call a migraine. I'm about to run out of toilet paper, and there clearly isn't enough for the shit I've taken. I use the last of it to wipe about eighty percent of my butthole, but I know I'm not done. My towel is too far to reach for. I know it's disgusting, but it often occurs to me that many constructs don't matter as long as I'm not breaking the sustainable ones consistently. I use the back of my hand to wipe the last bit of my crack. My foot flushes the toilet, and I run to the sink to rinse off the wet shit clustered in the wrinkles of my hand. My poo disintegrates under the hot water and lather of soap. Yes, I do wash my hands with soap. It doesn't save me from what happened, but oh well.

I refuse to look at myself in the mirror to curb any double entendre of the term "reflection." I am in no mood to reflect on me wiping my ass with my hand. I can hear my own judgment. I think I'm protective of myself, but I am not myself; I am always just watching myself the way scientists watch me. Should I call IRAAB? Should I just go to them before it's too late?

I close my eyes to let my heart guide me. There isn't much my heart wants to say. I haven't had a check-up in so long, so I'm not sure if I need to be on Adderal. When I said I watch myself, I wasn't lying. It's true. I see myself with a surge of pity because I am looking at myself through the lens of Dr. Alec.

Then, I look at myself with rationality and I remember Dr. Barberry. And then I feel a labor of disgust, haste, and downcast, and I know I am watching myself through the lens of everyone else at that agency. I don't have a home.

While my eyes are still closed, I just think of who will help me and who will help me feel comfort, but this doesn't seem to be a motive of the heart, right? What is love to humans? For fucks sake, why am I being penalized for reviewing things the way people do? Do people love more than this? I think the whole "unconditional love" notion is bullshit because there were conditions that led you to love them this much in the first place.

Unconditional, infinite, and immortal are measurements people cannot calculate because these are incalculable facets. We cannot own them by soul; we can only watch them as foreigners to such beliefs. People can't commit to these things, so what is the point of holding *me* to such a standard? It irritates me to the grave, I swear. What am I supposed to do in a world that does not offer any conclusive response to love?

Love is a construct, and I know that any agency tampering with the evolutionary potential that creatures like me possess does not expect love. They should not pursue that, as love is only true to its beholder and nobody else. I wish it was not forbidden to reach out to other lab experiments; there is a high likelihood that I would be much more socialized if aliens beget of scientific testing were brought together. There's a chance I would understand myself better if I were to look into another alien's eyes. How many times have I felt this way before? It's been too long since I've journaled.

I know what I was born for. Service. My service was created for bargain. By now, my eyes are open, even metaphorically. I will visit Virginia, and I will not call her beforehand to announce my visit. I twist the rusting knob of my mildewy shower and let the first wave of stale, chilled water wash out. I am used to the amount of time it takes for the warmth to flood the shower floors. When it's ready, I step in. The last time I bathed, it was by Dr. Alec.

Such a nice man. I hear the voice of a seventy-year-old widow in my head complimenting Dr. Alec, unassuming and unknowing of his typical insensitivity to things. I wish Dr. Alec and I talked more when we last met. I didn't have much to say after seeing that look on his face.

Everything was dim that night, like I had just been delivered in the arms of a doula at a home birth. His hands were gentler than you think, and I try to imitate his presence by lathering the shampoo into my fur. The pitter-pattering of the water sounds like music if I don't focus too much. My palms smoothen out the shampoo to cover my head and neck. I get behind my ears. I think Dr. Alec would remind me to wash my ears.

The warm water washes through me, cascading through eroded routes of skin. I have little rivers running through me. I'm not sure what time it is. It's probably late. I wonder if I should be appropriate and visit Virginia in the morning or just say fuck it and head her way now. Maybe it's better to save the theatrics for later. I'm not playing the role of a hero anyway, so gallivanting to Virginia's apartment and knocking on her door won't be met with open arms.

The best I can do is propose etiquette when I see her. It's like an ex trying to win their ex back. The rollercoaster I've put her through makes me feel awful, but it doesn't compare to the rollercoaster we've experienced together. Ha.

It's been this constant push and pull. I remember when I found Virginia to be this meretricious force of kindness, and I would think it was all bullshit because there was no viable reason as to why she wanted to be my friend. It bothered me. I used to think of her as a one-dimensional human who chose to associate with me in hopes of redemption.

Now I wonder if that truth is actually that distasteful. It's not her fault for wanting to feel important to herself, and I happened to be a convenient opportunity at that time because it's not like Virginia didn't want to help me. I can't pretend that she arbitrarily got up and left me, and maybe I shouldn't even put it that way. Maybe she didn't leave me. You know? Maybe she just distanced herself because the consequences of helping me—who isn't yet a person of caliber—are too costly for her self-esteem. Maybe I compromised her morality as she slowly realized that there is no saving my state. That I'm no good.

My wet feet slap the cold tiles, forcing my nipples to poke from the chilling discomfort.

My arms and chest are more sensitive to the studio air as the shower's humidity dissipates. I tug on the hanging towel and take the knob with me. I wasn't even that aggressive, Jesus. I look at the recent hole in the wall. The silver knob rolls out of my thinning towel and clatters on the floor. It's spinning on the porcelain and looks alive for a second. It even looks afraid.

Thrashing, feeling out of place, it looks like the collision against wet tiles has woken the knob up. Odd of me to think so metaphorically, but it conveniently slows everything down. The knob eventually surrenders to potential energy. It is as still as a child whose energy was spent in a piercing tantrum. I'd like to write a poem…

I decide to let the knob rot on the floor. My towel soaks in most of the water, and I use the remaining patches of dry cloth to wipe my face in a massaging fashion. This isn't one of those self-care nights. I'm still under a lot of stress and still need to consider what exactly I will say to Miss Virginia.

Through small piles of used clothes, I pick out a casual outfit. A polo and jeans. And sneakers, white sneakers. Country club sneakers. Instead of wearing pajamas, I lay naked on my mattress. Soaking in my animality in a sense. It's definitely cold, so I wrap the blanket around my body and let my temperature adjust.

My hesitations oscillate between intros and dialogue with Virginia. For obvious starters, how will I begin my conversation with her? Should I knock on the door and step aside, so she doesn't see me and think I'm just the mailman or something? If she sees me, she might be more likely to turn me away. No. That's stupid. My battery slips into preservation mode as I exhaust myself with options for approaching her.

CHAPTER 7

THE PEN IS MIGHTIER

It's a quarter to six in the evening. You can tell from the color of the sun when it hits the pavement. Also, the air gets a tad cooler. The humidity descends, and the atmosphere is more "open," if that makes any sense; I just feel like humidity clings to you. One of the more effective meditative practices was noting my surroundings without paranoia. Being observant supposedly gets your mind off the source of anxiety, and it's worked for me in the past when I was scheduled for MRI scans or medical checkups.

I notice people first. People in lightweight coats, the fashionable loafers. Most of the loafers are accented with metallic buckles. Cheap. The sky is getting dimmer, and it's getting dimmer fast. I think I'll shed soon. I quickly check my arm hair to see if there's any difference. My arm does not denote any signs of thinning. I used to take vitamins and rub oils to keep my hair nice and rich. I used to be a particular person, especially with my health.

The next thing I notice are the post lamps, bright and tall. The lamps, the telephone poles, and electrical boxes either bear a taped poster for an open-mic thing or a missing dog. The missing dog posters are funny because they always look like they're ready to run away or will pee soon. I try to read the graffiti as if they are some modern-age hieroglyphics, but I can't, and my failure brings me to the source I am working to avoid. It's closer to six in the evening, and I'm standing before the glass door of her building.

It looks like she affords herself a nice place, something I've been craving ever since I gained the ability to earn a living. The walls and lighting are warm, and there's a centerpiece, a cozy lounge, large flowing curtains, and a guard waiting to open the doors. The guard is observing me. I go to open the door, not breaking eye contact with the security guard, but to my embarrassment, the door is locked. Evidently confused, I look around to see if there are visiting hours, as if Virginia is locked in an asylum, and then I see a small pad of numbers. It requires a code. I push the microphone button, and the receptionist answers. "Hi. I'm visiting apartment four twenty-one".

The guard is still watching me. "Can I have the first and last name of the person you're visiting, please?" Shit. "Virginia Byrne." I do not get a response after stating her name. I just have to wait for Virginia's approval.

The door buzzes miraculously. Virginia wants to see me! Virginia wants to see me! Give me a fuckin' top hat and a cane to do one of those heel taps in the air. I open the door and pass by the guard with a smug attitude, and the receptionist holds out a clipboard for my sign-in.

I find the elevator, press the button, get in, and press four. The elevator creaks with fatigue. When the doors open, I smell the asbestos almost instantly. Maybe she can't afford the best. I calmly knock three times and put my hands together to wait patiently. I hear her door unlock, and she opens it halfway. It's been a while since I've seen her, and she looks a little less like herself. I wonder what's causing this. There is a purplish hollowness under her tired eyes, and the pores around her nose are somewhat larger than before. She's lucky to have freckles that distract you from them, though. Her lips are tightly pressed, taking the blood and color away from them. "Hey," she reluctantly opens her mouth.

"Hey." I greet her back. "I'm sorry I didn't call first." She looks me up and down as I explain myself, making me feel small and even intimidated. "I figured it's best if I just show up." I smile awkwardly. She scoffs, her chest caves inward.

She opens the door, leaving space to come in. She turns around to head inside, and I follow her. "Is it an emergency?"

"No…" The image of the eviction notice encased in orange plastic materializes in my head.

"I mean, things are getting progressively worse," I chuckle. Virginia doesn't respond to any signal. She doesn't throw any lifeline. She opens the fridge and pours herself a glass of water from the pitcher, allowing me to take her lifestyle into account. Maybe if her life is visibly in shambles, it would make sense why she's ignoring me even more than I'd think, considering how long it's been.

I look up at the recessed lighting and pine cupboards. Below them are counters iced with pale granite. Flowers on the island. A double sink and a running dishwasher. She has neat and sturdy fixtures—lucky.

Looks like her way of living does not reflect her attitude. "Can you say something else?" she demands, agitated.

I peer out the large sliding doors by the living room. It opens to a balcony. "Sorry," I sigh.

"Really? You're sorry about what? About being quiet for an inconvenient amount of time? Or are you deeply sorry for showing up here unannounced? You realize I don't want anything to do with you, right?" She says sharply. I physically recede as her voice continues to rise. "Right, Lee?" She is breathing heavily, shaking even. "Answer me!"

"I lost my job. I don't have anyone to go to except for IRAAB, but I didn't go there because it looks *really* bad." I'm not going to tell her that I tried ending the project. "I didn't have a choice."

She groans, "I don't want you here."

I'm not too sure how this makes me feel. Fear? If she can't help me, what's going to happen? It's as though her rejection makes me want to fight for my life again. Weird how if my fate is in the hands of any other power, the anxiety kicks in. But if I am the culprit of my own demise, with enough intention, I'm okay. "I didn't mean to impose—"

"Oh yes, you did."

"Okay, Virginia. Can you at least tell me why?"

"What does it matter to you? When I look at you as a person, I loathe you." She looks away. "When I look at you as an animal, I fear you."

"You feel safe enough to admit your vulnerability," I retort. "You should leave," she points at the door.

"Why don't you like that I know you?"

"Because that's all you do! Find a way to get your way. Read into things just so you can grasp anyone's weakness and use it to your fucking advantage. You're the closest thing to sociopathy."

"Why are you so emotional?" I groan. "Why does it hurt you that I don't care about you?

It's not personal," I laugh. "Jesus Christ, I'm literally drowning, and you are too caught up in being betrayed. It's embarrassing and stupid, and you're just like everyone else."

"I tried to be good to you," she says with a muted look on her face.

"If I could worry more for you, I would. Virginia, please. I know I'm about to feel something, but I'm not quite there yet. You *are* a friend."

"Friend?" Virginia belittles me. "You wanted to hurt me that night…" She forces herself to look me in my eyes, making me conscious of how monstrous I, at least physically, am. My eyes are black, which probably makes her stomach twist. "Admit it."

"No," I whisper. "Why did you seize?"

"A miscalculation."

"Bullshit!" Her voice hits the walls of the apartment. "You wanted to do something to me. What was it?" I scoot back as she inches closer. Her fists look like they hold violent intentions. Her scraggly hair lifts from the gusts of her increased shouting.

"It's really not what you think."

"You seize when you're about to hurt someone. I tried believing anything else, but the truth couldn't be more obvious, right?" She moves with force and pushes my chest. The blow increases my heart rate, but I commit to restraint. She pushes me again. "If you want to fight back, they'll know. It'll record you. Make you hit the floor, right?"

"Virginia," I plead. My eyes widen out of fear. I'm not afraid of her hurting me. I'm afraid of proving her right. She slaps me across the face, and my head bounces off the wall. My scab flies off. The sting deepens.

"Please," she sobs.

"I don't want to hurt you."

"You did! Fuck you! I hate you!"

"Why?" I scream back. "Why does it matter so much? It doesn't make sense to me, Virginia." I approach her. "And Virginia, you're a cunt." *Wow*. I surprise myself. "You loved me to forgive yourself for fucking up your shitty life. It's why you're HR! I hate you for trying to be so important in my life! You're a horrible friend!" The words chip away at her. She crumbles—softens even. She looks sorry as I try to catch my breath, and then she twists away from me. Her shoulders tremble while weeping. I watch her spine stick out of her shirt like brail. It moves at each sob. It's hard to decide whether to tap her or wait until she asks me to leave. The minutes get longer, and her cries are stifled to a silence. "Virginia?"

I can't hear her breath anymore. She swiftly turns back with a stupid ballpoint pen and stabs my right arm with enough strength to break the skin. The tip of the pen sinks into my flesh, and everything feels hot again. It's blurry. I try to push her off, and I'm about to use my nails to claw her, but it happens. I'm wrong, and in a sense, I suppose she's right. She is right.

I am gasping for air, and though I can only see figures and can no longer express myself, I can tell that she is merely standing above me. She isn't worried anymore. She's watching me suffer without remorse, yet I don't want to bet on it. I want to keep telling her I'm sorry for what I've done, yet am I? Horrible or not, Virginia is still my friend, and I know that she does not relish the fact that she is the reason I'm flopping on the floor. My body is burning, and I can feel nerves flare and muscles tense up like a death grip. It's hard to remember anything after that...

I wake up to a synthetic warmth beneath me, alleviating my sore back. It doesn't take long to remember why my back feels blown out, and it reminds me to keep my eyes shut for a while longer. I have been returned like a shipment and put into my pod. It's nice to be back, but it's never good to be back. One of the doctors might have turned up the bed heaters and amplified the soothing ambiance. It's an awkward mix of percussion and rain.

I open my eyes to a thankfully dim room. The lights don't hurt my eyes, so that's one part of my anatomy that isn't in grieving pain. Every other part of me is in a state that is similar to a hangover. My head is throbbing like a babbling child that knows no words to explain the source of discomfort. My arms ache, my legs, my bones. It's pleasing to be tucked in a mattress that consumes my body welcomingly as opposed to the dingy thing lying diagonally in the middle of a damp but cold studio. The lights above me are warm instead of a sterile fluorescent.

I squeeze my eyes shut for another minute to rid myself of the flighty sensation pulsing through me suddenly. I realize that as of yesterday, I don't have a home. I wish I would have caught that emotions-less son of a bitch. I'm talking about my landlord, whose last memory of him is distorted by alcohol. I can just remember Dr. Alec whispering unintelligible words that are supposed to be yelled or expressed as a beggar. I'm not sure. I hope the first person to greet me is Dr. Alec.

In order to *feel* ready, I listen for the footsteps nearing my pod. It's hard to hear over the bullshit rain. Granted, the effort does achieve some relief, but come on. I'm not a dipshit.

You'd have to put me in your lap, kiss me on the forehead, and tell me everything is going to be okay to convince me. I hear not footsteps but beeping. Someone taps a familiar pattern—a scramble of numbers—on the pad outside to unlock the gray sheets we call 'doors.' When the doors slide open for a grand entrance, they reveal the simple, almost saccharine Dr. Barberry. It feels staged, like a scene in a play; if it were, he'd take a bow for polite applause from an adoring audience. He'd be the fan favorite. I sit up, letting my legs dangle off the egg-shaped, egg-like bed.

He is polite. "Good morning, Lee. We didn't think you'd be up so soon."

"Good to see you, Doctor." Why isn't Dr. Alec here?

Dr. Barberry steps into the pod and taps the pad on the side of the door to brighten the lights back to its factory setting. "Hate to do this to you."

"I'll live," I pass a melancholic joke down for the both of us to sit with. He doesn't laugh.

"I'm sorry for what happened last night. On the bright side, it gives us the opportunity to have a conversation, do your blood work, and have a checkup. Sounds good?"

I have no choice but to nod. "Are we going to the lab?"

He points at a robe at the foot of the bed, and I follow the directions. "Why don't you put these on? We'll get you cleaned up first."

I hastily jump into the apparel so he doesn't leave me behind. Dr. Barberry leads me to the lab down the other hall. Many scientists notice me for a change. Some smile, some even wave. I guess everyone knows I tried to off myself…

When we get to the shower room, Dr. Barberry opens the door to let me in. I try to shut it, but Dr. Barberry prevents me. "It's best if we don't keep everything private," he sticks one foot in.

"Upon whose decision?"

"The CEO," Dr. Barberry scratches his head. "I'll be in the lab next door."

I need prayer, a prayer that someone has already spoken into existence about those who have no backing. I just feel very alone. As a tall drink of surrender, I step into the shower room.

Medical-grade soaps line the shower floor, each one designed for flea-ridden aliens, but I think I'm better than those opts. I don't have fleas. I have dandruff. Buy me some medical-grade dandruff shampoo. It's hard to waste time idling under warm water when I know I'm being watched. Has it come to the point where the literal CEO gives a fuck about Project O.H.I.? It makes sense, but to see that I've rung his bell does not sit still at the pit of my belly.

"Are ya done?" Dr. Barberry calls out. I don't think he's looking, though. "Do I need to use soap?"

"Yes, Lee. Yes, you do," he answers with a tinge of confusion and disappointment. We both understand that I once had better standards. Maybe I had mistaken his tone. It could be that he is concerned that I have changed. Regardless, the fact remains that I have changed. After my shower, I pick up my robe from the floor. "Don't wear that," Dr. Barberry directs me. His hand only enters with neatly folded pajamas sitting on his palm.

"Thanks," I whisper as the water drips loudly from my chin to the tile. I wear the pajamas.

They're looser on me now.

"Take these," he hands me plush slippers to match my dark pajamas. I do take them with gratitude.

My slippers slap the tile as I walk out and make the floor of the hallway wet. I look up at Dr. Barberry, "I'm sorry." Dr. Barberry hasn't relieved my anxieties very much. He hasn't commented on them either. He just rushes into the lab and sits on the stool near a bed that's dressed with parchment. I climb on it as usual. "How've you been?"

"I feel I should be asking you that question first," he responds but doesn't look up from the chart. I don't surrender to his implication. "Things are good in my life. My wife is pregnant. We're at the end of our first trimester."

"How exciting." I try to be genuine. He doesn't care to read my expression, and it's probably because he has already anticipated a fabricated emotion. I feel like he's upset with me.

"Where's Alec?"

He finally looks up from the chart. "He's out today." He puts the chart down and begins the show. "Okay, why don't you hop up on the scale."

I don't "hop up."

"Dr. Barberry, can we talk for a second?"

"What's up?"

"Are you okay?"

He chuckles with false confusion. "Yeah, I'm well, Lee. Thank you for asking."

"I feel like you're evading something. Like, are you okay with me?"

"Yes," he says confidently.

"Is anyone not okay with me?"

"Lee. I'm not in charge of answering on behalf of other people…"

"That's such a weird way of avoiding my question," I persist. "You have to stop—"

"Why? Like seriously, Barberry, you're acting weird."

Firm lines elongate between his brows. "Please don't try to start anything right now.

You've done enough," he says harshly. "I can't—I'm in no position to fix any messes. I'm just here to support the project," he looks me in the eye. Did they brainwash him? He's lying! He's clearly lying and wants to tell me he's lying.

"Barberry. You're acting different," I say gently.

"Let me just do my job," his palms flex as a reaction to stress. "Okay," and I let him.

"Actually, stay put on the bed." I stay put on the bed. The parchment rustles beneath me.

He flips over the page on the checklist and begins with a lick of his lips. "Any form of intoxication or inebriation is prohibited. Smoking any substance is prohibited. You are to record each negative emotional response as an entry. Neurological surveillance devices actively observe external circumstances to prevent lawsuits and scientific malpractice that could endanger the International Research and Administration of Animalia Biotechnology and Project Opt Homo-Inhabitant." He sets the checklist down mechanically and spreads my limbs to press the back of my neck, triceps, quadriceps, shins, and abdomen. "These implants measure adrenaline, noradrenaline, blood pressure, and body temperature as these are bodily indications of a physical reaction. The technology also observes the blood that is shunted from guts to muscles. In response, the subject is to be shocked into immediate seizing."

He takes a long breath after reciting. Dr. Barberry's mendacious replies cause distrust of course, but it's obviously not his fault. Someone else is puppeteering him, and it's most likely the CEO. Funny, I don't think I've ever met him. Maybe I've seen him when I was a wee lad. I want to continue pestering Dr. Barberry, but he can't even digest his own reticent behavior. "Okay, now the scale," he says. I listen to him, performing an act of obedience to soften him. He moves the units around and pens down my weight. "You're lighter," he purses his lips.

"How's my figure?" I stand with my belly out and my shoulders hunched over.

It's a tough crowd. I mosey around to the bed to let him take my blood pressure. Dr. Barberry wraps the Velcro and squeezes until he gets a read. Then he carefully undoes the sleeve, making sure my hair doesn't get caught. He uses his cold stethoscope and asks me to breathe. He writes all of these vitals down and then taps my abdomen. He checks my reflexes, my mouth, and my ears. "I'll have to take your urine sample later," he gets up and stretches. "Let's get you to the other lab."

"Why?"

"It's about time we take your MRI scans."

"Oh." Oh. They're going to measure growth.

"We can talk about your feelings afterward," he says without comfort.

I know that this has all to do with protocol and Project O.H.I., and nothing to do with how I'm feeling. Maybe because of the redundant opinions and emotions I've been producing, no one cares to listen. I follow him to the lab just up the hall. It's been a while since I've been here. MRI scans are typically conducted after receiving information that may suggest cerebral development, so that's a good sign. I try to think about the previous events that might have forced an increase in emotional intelligence.

- Virginia stabbing me with a pen
- Suicide attempt
- Eviction notice

Yeah… They're not reasons worth celebrating, but maybe it's cause for action. I step into a barely lit room where the machine rests. Behind it is a large window where I can look into a room. That's where the doctors will be, observing my wrinkly—hopefully—brain. I wouldn't be surprised if what's in my head is smoother than my ass.

"Lay on that and try to focus on the new emotions you experienced," Dr. Barberry points at another bed, but this one will go onto the glowing microwave. When I lay down, I feel like the look on my face is the same as anyone else. I'm staring at the ceiling, implying a million thoughts running through my head. "You're good?"

"Why are we doing this?" I say with my finger pointed up like a star pupil. "We can talk after," he strides into the other room.

"It's going to take a while. I'd like to be in peace while conducting," I try and try to get him to talk to me.

"Quite honestly, Lee, I don't want to acknowledge the reasons because we both know what they are. You should just be patient."

I sit up. "You're being a dick."

"I have to finish!" Dr. Barberry finally pops. "The CEO and Felix are waiting for you. Why are you like this? It's no wonder—never mind."

"What? What do you need to say? It's no wonder you all treat me like a lost cause. Fuck you! Fuck everyone!" I remember how Virginia cursed me out. I can feel her rage living through me. "You show no remorse—"

"Enough!" The room drops all force. Nothing matters after he raises his voice. It's weird how much power Dr. Barberry holds at this moment.

"Fine." I pout.

The MRI scan commences once Dr. Barberry leaves for the other room, slamming the door shut. When I lay in the hollow cylinder, all I can think of is his perspective. What is he seeing right now? Damage to the brain? Yeah, that makes the most sense.

Time is moving awfully slow in this bitch. Dr. Barberry is being such a bitch. It's not hard to stray from thoughts that regard my environment because last night was pretty eventful, but obviously not in a good way, making it easier to worry about. I can feel my concerns slip away into a blurred memory of Virginia watching over me as I convulsed on her kitchen floor. It was like an alien, being her, probing a human.

It was scary to see her not express any sorrow or fear. She was the equivalent of a child flushing a dead goldfish. I don't know what happened after the "stabbing," but I imagine help was on its gradual way.

The bed is serving me out of the machine. I fix my clothes, pat the hair on the back of my head, and step off the bed. "I said we can talk after, so let's do that," Dr. Barberry offers me a petty conversation as he exits the other room—gently this time.

"Okay," I sit back down, desperate to have someone listen.

He finds his chart again and flips a page to ask premeditated questions. So, it's a questionnaire, not a conversation. Where have I seen this before? "The night Dr. Alec visited you, your landlord was there. Correct?"

"Shouldn't our dear Felix ask me that?"

"I am just trying to understand your emotional intake that night. Wouldn't it be harder to answer a vague question about how you felt? Or why you drank?" He doesn't wait for me to respond. "What did Dr. Alec say to the landlord? Or what did he say to you about his conversation with the landlord?" Dr. Barberry reads off the chart.

Here's the distinction: I'm not a rat; I'm a *lab* rat, so I admit nothing. " I don't remember." I grit my teeth, "I was too drunk."

"Do you recall any symptoms?" He asks me, surrendering to my game-play. His eyes flicker to the next question.

"I think it's just hard to keep going when whatever direction I choose is wrong," I answer him with a reply that felt practiced. But it is the perfect truth. Dr. Barberry writes this down.

"You have development in the limbic system, Lee. It counts," he kindly tells me as he's writing. A rush of consolation flows through me.

"How?"

"Control on your feelings, surprisingly. Ironically," he smirks. I don't want to believe he's being mean right now. "Do you think it's possibly a sign of maturity after receiving exposure from living independently?"

"I think it's just a sign of aging."

"You think you'd have achieved control if you resided here?"

"Yes. So long as I can still be in contact with the people I'm used to," I submit my response even though I'm not sure if I'm right. I just want to negate Dr. Barberry because his stupid questionnaire is pissing me off.

"Does development in this cortex make sense to you, and if so, how?"

"I think the aftermath forced a will to live without fear. I attempted… It didn't work that night, so I waited for IRAAB's consensus for the next few days. And no one contacted me!" I laugh. "You know how messed up that is? And I had to make peace with my fate. I had ice cream, watched the sunset, and went to a museum. I just lived because there wasn't much I could do about the problem."

"Hm," he scribbles down my confessions out of greed. "I should have had a recorder on me," he nervously jokes. "Why did you go to Virginia?"

"She's my only friend."

"How can you decipher between an acquaintance and a friend?"

"She's done a lot for me, even worried for me when I haven't done much for her. You know?" I chuckle, "I used to think very poorly of her. I never disliked her. I just found her kindness to be so much less complicated than the people I know and, therefore, found her transparency to lack sincerity. Like it's because she needs to desperately redeem herself, but that's not true. She quickly figured out that I wanted to hurt her—on some level—and still stood by me. She was hurt by the truth. That's a friend." Dr. Barberry doesn't look me in the eye after professing all of this. It's suddenly hot in this room; my cheeks are flaring red, and I'm not too sure why.

"How does that make you feel? Knowing that Virginia is one of your friends?" Dr. Barberry tilts his head and squints. That heat spreads to the back of my neck and shoulders. I shrug, trying to remain calm. Technically, I'm not really in a bad position, provided that I passed the MRI scan. There is an evident amount of development; however, out of tendency, I worry that passing the test may not entirely equate to sentience. Should I lie?

Would it be best for me to admit that I do not feel any sense of reciprocity in poor Virginia's direction, and that no matter how much she has proven herself to be this maternal, caring, concerned figure in my life, I will remain involuntarily unrequitable despite the quintessential negligence I've unfortunately gifted her? Or should I

     BY ZAINAB F. RAZA

lie halfheartedly? "The best I can do is understand what emotion I should feel," I say with grief overflowing in me.

"What emotion do you feel for Virginia?" Dr. Barberry asks as he pens down my thoughts into permanence.

"Regarding her, it is important to feel guilt for the confusion I've caused her. You can't ask so much from someone and keep them in the dark. Right? I hope to know the feeling of appreciation for who she is and not for what she's done for me. It's hard to make sense of because I know what to be grateful for, but there's nothing more to say on the matter," I say my last words with a sigh of failure. "She knew how to treat me."

"She stabbed you."

"With a pen," I defend her.

Dr. Barberry doesn't write the last of it down. We hear a knock at the door, and Dr. Barberry's head snaps in the direction of disruption. I turn my head, too, hoping it's Dr. Alec rescuing me from this torturous conversation.

It's not Dr. Alec, for fuck's sake. It's Felix. Felix is like a recurring character on a show because he wears the same shit, parts his hair the same way, and always holds the same briefcase in his left hand. He looks like the work of a devil, but the devil is playing jokes on him. Man's nearly my height.

"Didn't mean to interrupt anything important," he did mean to do that, albeit I'm not upset. "Rich is itching to meet you," Felix says as he looks at me.

I look at Dr. Barberry to find answers. "The CEO, Lee," Dr. Barberry says. "Oh. Should I change?" I ask Felix.

He judges my attire. "We don't have time, unfortunately," he writes me off. "Shall we?"

I nod without turning back to Dr. Barberry. Fuck him. I trail Felix across the facility. At the very back is a room I've never actually seen before. Two large glass doors generously offer a view of the chief's office. It's larger than a room. It's like a living room. "What's his name again?"

"Richard Kaminsky," Felix whispers to me.

"They named the dining hall after him," I suddenly realize. Felix swiftly opens the door without implying any weight. The door is so fucking big, I can't imagine a guy that small even attempting.

Richard is busy behind a computer. His desk is crafted as an L. It's dense and polished.

His whole room is glass, and all of the blinds are raised. A couple of lounge chairs, a loveseat, and a custom coffee table sit in the middle of his office. There's a bar on the right. I wonder if Dr. Alec ever stole from here. Richard pops his head and notes me.

He hospitably rises from his desk. Richard is in his forties. He's very tall, very slender—a definite runner. "Lee!" He walks around his desk and tosses an empty bottle of green smoothie into an electric bin. He puts his hand on Felix's shoulder and shakes my hand, gleaming ever so beautifully. "My goodness," his voice is soft for a man but not thin. "It's a pure pleasure to finally meet you in person.

I've heard so many things about you. How are you doing? How was your checkup today?"

I shake his hand in return. "It was good. It's nice to meet you too," I smile and look down from his peering eyes. I don't think he's fucking blinked!

Richard lets go of my hand and puts it in his pocket. He glances at Felix to exchange some sort of discrete information. "And," he tries to figure out what to say next. I feel like this guy can only make conversation with extroverted people. "Have you eaten anything? We can order in." He looks at Felix again.

I want to tell him that it won't be necessary as there is a high likelihood that I will regurgitate everything. His shampooed carpet would be a mess, the room would stink, and I would no longer cause him to produce feelings of personal indifference but rather disgust.

"I think I'm okay," I tell Rich kindly.

"Well, okay!" He scratches his lip and looks around, and his eyes dart to the two chairs. The room is suddenly really quiet. We can practically hear each other think. "Why don't you have a seat, Lee? I have a few questions to ask." He makes this clicking noise with his mouth, and I assume he's filtering his curiosity. "That Virginia girl. She's caused a lot of trouble."

"Yes." I don't want to defend her again because that would imply where I stand. I don't believe I was as wrong as she made me out to be, and even if she was motivated by fear, she acted on betrayal— something I never intended.

"Tell me more," he asks without insisting again to be seated.

I admit, "I don't have a reason to elaborate. I've thought a lot about her, but nothing conclusive."

"If things hadn't gone wrong, I'd suggest you consider keeping her in your life. I am not an *emotional* person and that's a good thing depending on your prospects," he smirks with an indulgence in his obvious pride. "There are two things I see. Benefit and loss. There are losses with this Virginia, but ultimately, she is a benefit… Maybe I shouldn't introduce my ethics to you, but it is something to think about." He spins around at the bar. "That is if things had not gone wrong. In this case, you are forbidden from seeing her. Wanna drink?"

My face and heart fall. "Um."

He points at me with an unnerving grin. "All jokes here!" He sits down, and the gears shift. This nepo-jackass—not even sure if that's true—shifts his demeanor so drastically you can't even tell if he's capable of making jokes. I take a seat next to him and feel uncomfortably close.

Felix walks over to his desk and opens the briefcase. He pulls out a file and hands it to Rich. Richard flips through, reading classified notes and medical reports. I even see a few copies of my journal entries. "You're bisexual?" he asks. I think he's reading the report about the cook at the Thai restaurant.

"It's not a choice." I'm not kidding. It's a common inclination within my species. "What choices do you think you have?"

That's actually an insightful way to begin a conversation. It makes me respect Richard more. "I know I am allowed and even encouraged to socialize with my peers, have a job, and live independently."

He grunts as I list these points. "Throughout Project Opt Homo-Inhabitant—Is it?" He looks at Felix for confirmation. "I have been informed of multiple infractions, which made me want to review you and your influences. Ultimately, Lee, I have accepted that in order to have this company progress, I have to learn that no one is on the same page. Not everyone has the same idea of bringing this project to fruition. The priorities, definitions, and motives differ… The point of saying all this is to understand *you*. It might appear ingenuine as this is our first time meeting. And I'm sorry for that."

"Rich," I almost scoff. "I don't see you as a negligent father."

"Is it because you can't produce those emotions or—"

"Well, yeah, but even if I did, just because you were not interested in my development does not mean I necessarily think you're a bad person. I can observe, judge, and come up with these conclusions just fine."

"How do you judge me?"

"I think you are what most people dislike, and I mean this respectfully. I'm just being candid. You have a company to run." I realize what I must say while speaking without navigation. "You need something from me. Don't you? Either it's that, or you're here to tell me that my time is up."

He adjusts his seat, "I do need something from you." I'm not sure if he's insulted. He shoots a look at Felix, and Felix hands him a letter and a pen. "Going back to what I was saying. Everyone has a different motive. I want to protect this company and my reputation. The members of Project O.H.I want to expand their careers, Felix wants to make money, and you want to live… Is that right?"

"Dr. Alec didn't do it for his career; he doesn't need me," I hate to sound like his minion.

"Dr. Alec's been fired, unfortunately." Richard's confession knocks the air out of my lungs.

I gasp audibly, involuntarily. "What?"

"You don't need to ask. We all know why. He was not a good influence on you—"

"Yes! Yes, he was. He wasn't doing it for himself. He did it because he had mercy for me. He saw me as more than an animal to test on. How could you? For the sake of your company, you fired your best scientist?" I am hyperventilating at this solemn point.

"Lee." Richard scolds me. "You were going to end your life, right?" I freeze at his question. "Right? You think you would've reached this level of despair if you hadn't known the options you have. Dr. Alec revealed what's better before you were even ready to handle it."

"He meant well," I pout.

"He broke protocol. He hurt you and maybe even used you. I'm sorry you fail to see that," Richard ends this conversation by tapering the strength of his voice.

Dr. Alec is gone. So much rushes through my mind. I wonder where he is and if I'll find a way to see him again. Does he still want to care for me? I wonder if Dr. Alec left without a fight. Maybe he is resolving something with himself through me and is okay with moving on. That fear manifests as perspiration, and a lot of it. I wonder if I'll leave a sweat stain that outlines my ass on his pretty couch.

"What do you need from me?" I say from my teeth.

He holds out the pen and paper. "This contract ensures that you want to live independently. We are asking you to remain at IRAAB, though the only drawback is that there is a high likelihood that you will not progress as much as you have been outside of the premises. *However.* The public is relentless and believes this company has neglected you, but it was Dr. Alec's fault, not ours. I don't really care if you believe that statement. If you live independently, we are risking your safety, quite frankly. You've seen life outside of this place, and it's been rough. You look rough. Signing this contract proves to the public that you happily live independently. There is no other ulterior motive… I've laid out my intention flatly," his lips wrap around the last word.

I take the papers and sign them immediately. "Will I be able to meet Alec again?"

"It's illegal for him to see you," Felix intervenes.

Poor choice of words.

CHAPTER 8

GOING TO TOWN

The tough part isn't leaving the facility. It's returning to my life and accepting that I compromised. The reward of compromise is worth it all. I know where Dr. Alec lives. I read it in a file somewhere. He's described his home to me before to paint his isolative picture. A one-story home, black on the outside, with wood flooring, a lawn graced with stone pathways, and trimmed shrubbery. A koi pond. I am sure that his place is a lavish haven, a getaway for those above the tax bracket. He has a three-car garage, and apparently, his wife took two of his cars and sold them because she didn't like the lifestyle he "enforced."

I know too much about Dr. Alec without him even admitting every detail, and maybe he's the first person I have observed, so the illusion of knowing him like the back of my alien hand keeps me grounded. It keeps me attached. Again. Very Oedipus, unfortunately.

But yes, the journey of returning serves little purpose because there's nothing to return to. I'm not even sure if there's a point in collecting my things because I don't want to pull around a bag of random shit.

I'd hate to feel more weight on my shoulders as they already hang heavy, you know? I am in the middle of my dissension. Worrying about what will happen next is becoming louder and louder, and for fucks sake, what will I do when I'm hungry? I wonder if I have it in me to remain hopeful because the idea of coercing myself into being optimistic makes me kinda nauseous. I remember the day I watched the sunset. I felt sick, and none of my efforts were proven effective. It wasn't real.

I consider the library, the church nearby, praying, or purchasing a night at a motel ridden with bedbugs and/or cum. I could maybe afford a few days, and some change at that kind of motel, and it's tempting, but perhaps I should save that money for a security deposit. Maybe I should apply for a few jobs, so yeah, *maybe* I should go to the library. The problem is I don't want to use this day to better my situation. I signed that contract for a reason. I want to visit Dr. Alec.

I don't take the subway to the city. I wait until we reach the suburbs, and then I wait a little longer to reach his town. Upon stepping out, I find the municipality to consist of woods, tall and old trees mostly. There are only two-way streets up in the hills, and I walk on the thin shoulder like a hitchhiker. The area smells natural, less like piss or pollution and more like pine. Pine needles are scattered everywhere. The houses I pass as I enter the more residential side of Dr. Alec's town are grand. Each house boasts unique architecture. The front doors are enormous, and the windows above the front doors are just as large, giving a sneak peek at these gorgeous crystal chandeliers. I'm used to feeling like a pariah, but now that presumption is ampli-fied by subconsciously comparing myself through the economic lens. Strolling through Dr. Alec's neighborhood reminds me that I belong in the bottom rank, and while this does strike me with discomfort, it's not my problem right now.

Sure, I'd like to make money. Eventually, I think I'd like to make even more money to afford the capitalistic luxuries most capitalistic people chase after, like a seven-thousand- square-foot home among pines. Did I ever mention that I fundamentally don't believe in socialism? I think socialism would benefit my life, but not in the long run. In the long run, it doesn't make sense, and I think it would put everyone on an equal platform, and from that, equal expectations are presented. I'd like to digress some more as I get closer to where Dr. Alec resides.

My opinions of socialism remind me of Richard when he was babbling on about choosing what benefits you and what doesn't. Maybe he's right, but I am not inclined to return to Virginia now. Partly because she would kick my ass, mainly because I don't want my ass kicked. That doesn't make any sense. I think it's wise to avoid conflict.

That would benefit me more. Still, though, I believe that having her in my life would make a difference, and I mean that in a good way. I miss her goofiness and her frizzy hair. She is never afraid to admit what she doesn't know. That probably means her transparency is legitimate, especially when expressing what she doesn't like. Virginia does not like me. Not very much so. If I could just get it through her stubborn head that I have no feelings for her and that I sadly don't even have feelings for her as a friend, maybe things would begin to look up for us. It's just frustrating to know that, on some level, she's right, even if she's got it all wrong. Thinking about her again makes my head numb.

I'm finally at his street. My paces lengthen to the point where I lose balance and stumble over the rounded, eroded pebbles of pavement that were swept to the side by the wind of speeding luxury cars. I bet I could ace the driving test if given the opportunity. But Felix, with his inch-dick, would piss all over my dreams.

I see Dr. Alec's home at the end of the street. Indeed, it is black and one story. The square footage must be like five thousand. His house looks like it owns the peaceful land it sits on. No lights are on, and I notice that the curtains do not obstruct the view from his windows. And though I'm still quite far away, I can already tell that dust is collecting in his empty home. Did his wife take most of the furniture, too? Ha. I wonder if he's already seen me. His car isn't here, but then again, what is a three-car garage for, right? I'm checking for any indications that may prove his absence. This is making me loathe everything. If I don't see Dr. Alec today, what should I do?

I walk up the stone path, the one that Dr. Alec told me about. He picked the features of his dominating lawn. The grass is soft. Deer must roam here. I would like to know if tics affect aliens and how headliner it would be to be the first sentient alien to have Lyme disease. Never mind, that's fucked up. When I reach the door, I ring that damn doorbell, and I ring it twice.

After a few beats, I knock on the door. I don't feel this need to perform formalities. Doubts settle as I slowly realize that the house is quite possibly vacant. *Shit.* He's not home.

What if he's actively avoiding me? It's hard to believe that Dr. Alec would miss the opportunity of seeing me in person. My shoulders wilt, and my chest caves as I surrender to his inconvenience. It might be implied that I should not be visiting him, but going against

IRAAB is not my fault. Unless it was specifically stated that I am not permitted to visit Dr. Alec, I can technically get away with staying here. The only issue is he might not be back later today or tomorrow. He might be away, taking a brief hiatus from the messes that have been made.

But if I wait for Dr. Alec, I could also be waiting for Richard or Felix or any other fucker from that godforsaken facility too. I drag myself across his lawn, deliberately avoiding the path.

I guess I have the luxury of reflection, especially since seeing Dr. Alec is unpredictable. Perhaps therapy would help me make sense of things. Psychology could even be worth studying. With Project Opt Homo-Inhabitant nearing its end, an education seems out of reach. Still, it was satisfying to learn about politics, history, and sociology, all for my own growth. I've even heard there's a class called Personal Development.

From these compelling subjects, I conjured epiphanies that were synchronous to nihilism, but it's like striking an oil that can't be fuel. I was soon disconnected from information that would lather into derealization.

If I were a person, I would be innocent at first—learning emotions, the names of colors, and what happens when you subtract, add, or multiply. 'Please eat my dear Aunt Sally,' I think that's the phrase. I would then have my phases. Studious, rebellious, depressed, mature, funny, and then old. Feeling old is a phase, and I find that those who are actually old believe themselves to be adolescents stuck in a wrinkled corpse. Feeling old is an act of doubling down on the insecurity of being immature. It's silly.

If I don't have Dr. Alec listening to me, then I think I might actually need a therapist. Right? As I return to the station, I kick gravel a few paces further from me. I have to keep journaling, but talking to a void doesn't seem productive. I wish someone else were genuinely interested in listening to the arbitrary threads of curiosity I use to keep myself occupied.

Boy, I'd love to sit in Dr. Alec's lap and tell him how much of a bitch Dr. Barberry's been. He and I would probably have a good laugh about all of this. Instead, I have to deal with these freshly cut shortcomings independently. The issue is, where do I deal with them? The day is pretty much past me, and since it's too darn late to be productive, I don't think I have a reason to return to the city. I've never seen suburban life before. Dr. Alec surely must live near a small town. I envision the roads to be partially cobblestone and the stores to be renovated, but their bones are antique. The charm of this imagined town must lie in its antiquity. I bet there is an elementary school nearby, and the kids don't stray far from it because every-thing is where it needs to be; it's all within a radius.

The small bagel shop, boutiques, a grocery store, and a gas station. There are probably cafes that turn into restaurants by night. I pass the train station in search of a town. I could eat.

I don't have the means, but I could find a way to eat. Technically, I do have the means, but not the kind I could waste on satisfying dinners. Relying on my instincts is freeing in a sense, and though there are regressive consequences to such behaviors, I think my opt instincts come in handy. I haven't made an alien joke and genuinely laughed at it in ages. I don't remember the last time I truly laughed at some-thing. It's been far too long, and quite honestly, I miss socializing.

I also can't hold my piss any longer. I slip into the woods. I am walking alongside, and I use the shoulder of the road as a sidewalk. It's not very ladylike of me to pee out in the wilderness, but it doesn't make me an animal. People do this, too, when desperate. So I quickly zip down and release. I look down at the earth soaking in my puddle when I'm done. The birds chirp in the distance, and I can hear a plane passing over. Yes, I want to travel, but it's highly unsafe as I cannot be surveilled in the air due to a weak connection.

I love how nonviolent I am. That's the first thing my agency made me doubt, and everything else tumbled with it. I use the front of my shoe to cover my piss in more dirt. I can't imagine the satisfaction a dog may receive from marking its territory, but hopefully, I will seize a life that reminds me of ownership. Being proud of myself is not news to the scientists leading Project O.H.I. I think, though, that if I were to be proud of something I did selflessly, it might be one for the books.

Emerging out of the woods, I continue to the coveted town yet to be discovered. I am okay with being incorrect about its existence, as there is no routine to tend to, no emergency to report to, and no one to answer to currently. I would not like to piss Richard off, but to be candid, ever since I tried to off myself, I've been a little more lenient with leisurely indulgences. I'd really like to tell someone about my redundant feelings because even if the lab doesn't consider them valuable, I do. These emotions are already carefully examined and, unfortunately, determined as a constituent of sociability. I am naturally a social creature. With or without any public assimilation, I will always have needs that communication can potentially solve.

My stomach rumbles, echoing its emptiness. What am I supposed to do? Climb a tree and attack its vines for nuts and berries? I look to the woods accompanying my stroll and note that there are no vines, and I am misinformed to the point of idiocy. Although, I feel more pampered than stupid.

I grew up on lunch trays and Thai food. That was the beautiful yet high-strung life that I took for granted, and the acceptance of it churned in my stomach because I had just now become a little more acquainted with the reality of Dr. Alec not being as proficient as he claimed to be. He just listened to what I wanted and didn't think about what I needed. Or maybe he did think.

The fact of the matter is he was wrong. Dr. fucking Alec miscalculated and was so painfully wrong, and now I've lost my libido, some of the fur off my face, and my fucking studio apartment.

CHAPTER 9

WHO NEEDS WHO?

I've given it a week. Without minding just how pathetic it may be, I stand on a stale "welcome" mat, ringing the bashful doorbell of Dr. Alec's residence. I remember the last time I was here, the rejection felt like a quick jab to the abdomen. I can't say I've healed. I'm just desperate.

Lately, nothing has been authentic with other people, and I'm starting to believe it's my fault. That's the way the facility makes me feel anyway, and they're probably not wrong because, let's face it, I've built relationships before. I lost one relationship. I cannot lose Dr. Alec. I see the light on in his bedroom.

The door opens swiftly. His lips are tight, but his charm consumes the glint of reluctance I briefly witnessed. I don't know if I should step back or buy into his pensive eyes. A smile stretches to greet me, and it feels like Christmas and Judgment Day all at once. I think I hear music… It's finally happening. I'm with Christ. "You're not supposed to be here," he informs me of the evident. The music stops.

I'm stunned to see him despite my anticipation. His smile settles, and the worry returns. I think it returns on both of our faces because I can feel my forehead muscles. "I know," I reply in dejection.

Grief brushes his face. "How are you doing?"

"Don't look at me like that. It makes me sad for you."

"It does?" he subtly raises his brows.

"Can I eat something?" I tilt to the get a look at the inside of his home.

Dr. Alec hesitates, shifting his energy one way and another—debating, dithering, deciphering. He sighs and waves me in. I follow into a home that smells like the pine outside. Only this scent is artificial. Still, it's nice. His house is mostly empty, but everything that inhabits his place indeed looks expensive. It's hard to think that he has opinions on decor.

I walk into the kitchen and turn to him like he bought me this house. He lifts his hand to acknowledge the sleek refrigerator. "I'm not much of a cook, but help yourself." He looks at the front door, "I don't know how much time we have. Let's just be realistic."

"Will you get in trouble?"

He shakes his head sacrificially. I can't care because I need him. I need to hear from him regardless of how IRAAB wants to deal with it.

I open the fridge and assess his groceries. Mostly jams, cheeses, and deli meat. I pull out the bag of bread, which shouldn't be stored in the refrigerator. Before I begin to build a sandwich for myself, I look at Dr. Alec, who is now sitting at the dining table, writing something frantically. "I'm really happy," I tell him. I've never visited his home before, but I'm here today, rummaging through his fridge with an unnecessary amount of comfort.

He looks up, his concern melting away to give room for invitation. "Why don't you take a bag and put as much as you can in it." I laugh at what I assume is sarcasm. "I'm not kidding."

"Are you serious?" My voice leaps a pitch from the excitement.

He gets up, but with intent, and in his hand is that piece of paper. He's gripping it tightly. I realize that it's meant for me. He gives me the note. It's just a scribbled address with a date and time underlined. Next month at three a.m. "You're homeless, right?"

I shamelessly nod, phased by curiosity. "What's going on?"

"I am not allowed to see you, Lee. Not anymore." His eyes keep darting at the front door. "Do you remember when you wanted to move out? It was a big dilemma. They accused me of being this ambivalent asshole who's incapable of seeing the big fucking picture." Dr. Alec's desperation is jarring, and it makes me flighty. My gut twists as he speaks. "You seized for the first time in a long time, and I researched different chips, better implants. I suggested it and even ordered samples. And *Richard* fucking rejected them since they were more expensive! Jesus Christ!" He takes a breath, calibrating. "They were afraid you'd do something to make you seize again. When you said you wanted to move out, I knew there would be a slim chance. So, I found other chips from the same manufacturer. Sync's with the account set up in surveillance. I ordered them."

"What—What kind of chip?"

He chuckles, "I ordered a set of seizing chips because I know how much the ones you have hurt you. They're unnecessary and degrading. Fear is confinement. I'm the only one who trusts you." It doesn't feel good to hear that. I know he means well, but it doesn't feel good. "When I bought them… I thought I could maybe extract your tracking chip. We can manipulate the system."

"Okay?"

"I signed off on it, I paid for it, and I have the account password, so it's not that fucking hard to sync them. I can't replace the entire set because that'll call for a reboot. I have to physically be there to do that. I know this is a lot of information for you, but the point is… you need me. I found someone who can do the surgery, and that way, we can be together again. It won't be scary, and I'm not rushing you into this, but I don't see why you would decline…The only issue is—"

"This doesn't seem right. What if they catch us?"

"Then I'll be the one in trouble. They won't, though! We don't need a system reboot, just a silent, inconspicuous replacement that will go unnoticed. A brief glitch in their room at most. It's not going to be hard, Lee. I promise you."

"Which chip are you not replacing?"

"Your vitals. You can't technically turn off tracking, but you can leave your chip somewhere safe and go wherever you're prohibited. The lab is going to assume you fell asleep or are just hanging out. You're just going to have to keep your vitals calm." His nostrils flare from excitement. "Do you get the point? I'll be able to take care of you, Lee."

That's when it clicks. I found my haven. "Okay. Can I think about it? I just passed an MRI."

He wilts in disappointment. "Sure. Sure, yeah. If you're ready, meet me there in a month from now at that exact time." He points at the note.

Dr. Alec's face is tilted downward to meet my eyes, but he flashes his sight towards the front door, reminding me that we are not held in eternal privacy and at any moment, our significant discovery of digression, call it even an opportunity, if you will, is to be interrupted by men in white. "Thank you for the food, Alec. I hope to not miss you for long." Even for me, it's hard to gauge what I have meant by that, but my intention is to communicate that I will think about the surgery and I'll see him again…

My walk to the station is monotonous. I'm not ready to contemplate my option of liberty as the concept of liberty was persuasively redefined. I force myself to remain numb, blocking obsessions of Dr. Alec's proposition to avoid mishaps with IRAAB. Robotically, I buy my ticket and wait for the train and board...

Upon arrival at my neck of the concrete woods, I allow myself to spend the following hours processing every exchange between Dr. Alec and me. I guess *now's* a good time to think about it. Weighing the pros and cons of my decision turns into a performance of coercion.

I'm sitting at the edge of the sidewalk of an empty street, convincing myself that my life will end sooner than later if I choose to live in obedience to IRAAB's expectations. So far, there's been minimal reward. They've tormented me to the point where I wholeheartedly consider trading lives with a zoo opt. The surgery will bode well, and Dr. Alec is not an idiot. What worries me, though, is his desperation. I don't like the idea of someone needing me more than I need them. It's unnatural. Though it is quite insulting to myself to admit how unnatural that may be, I know what I am, and I prefer to be realistic. Dr. Alec's not okay. I'm not worried for him; I am only ever looking out for myself—in case that point hasn't been communicated enough. If I do go through with the replacement—no, not with the zoo opt—it's imperative to devise a plan.

I need to expand my horizons. It'll be conducive for me to clean up my act and get a job. I don't have a proud mother to celebrate my transition from being a bum, but having someone in the stands is not really a priority. Having someone emotionally near me and developing a bond might not even serve as content for progress, so in that regard as well, the priority in my life should be to steer myself to normality. The plan is pretty basic:

Get a job.

I need to find a place to stay, and I need to save. I do want to live a good life. I feel an almost manic burst of motivation, which lifts me to my feet as I seek a nearby library. The day is almost over, but it's worth churning out every bit of inspiration.

I reach the moderately sophisticated public library. Someone has scratched off the 'L' in 'public.'

Calmly, I weave through the tall isles of alphabetically displayed books. At the far end of the building rests an island of unoccupied desktops, ready to use. I cannot remember the phone number, but I can remember the first half of the company's name that Virginia suggested when I asked her to help me find a job. It's Shapiro something—small business.

What a shame I can no longer call her up and ask again. I understand that labeling wrongdoers as enemies will not get me far, burning bridges will make me stagnant, and I should not waste my time hating Richard for keeping me from the two people who nurtured me.

While undeniably disheartening, the real loss is the precious time slipping away—time that could be devoted to forging ahead. Embracing the art of cutting my losses has unexpectedly rekindled a sense of optimism within me. Maybe it's because I'm tired of stinking and sleeping on the cold pavement—I can barely call it sleep as the footsteps and laughter of pedestrians keep me available for spare fucking change. I've thought about shelters, but I've been in a room full of junkies before, and this time I'm not getting paid for it.

I am less sentient than ever. I scavenge from garbage cans, relieve myself wherever the police won't see, and survive purely on instinct. I have become animalistic. I hope the executives and scientists rot in hell for what they've done. I miss the tenderness of Dr. Alec and Virginia—it's a goddamn tragedy. I'm fighting to hold onto my composure, but why did Richard have to cross that line? Just because she stabbed me, just because he got me drunk, doesn't mean they didn't mean well.

The conversation I had with Dr. Alec haunts me again. It could potentially have been our last conversation. I've been given a divine intervention of choice. Dr. Alec would want me to call it an opportunity, but I think it's a choice, and I've been deliberating. How will the surgery go? What if they catch me? What would IRAAB do to me? Most importantly, do I need this?

It's getting dark out, and I forget I'm sitting before a dusty desktop at a library. I'm biting my nails. It's become a terrible habit. I look for a 'Shapiro Tax Preparer near me.' Luckily, there's only one, and I assume it's the one Virginia told me about. I immediately send my resume and designated information from IRAAB. This will be interesting. Taxes must be the most mundane attribute of every citizen's life. It's tedious but mandatory, and everyone knows about it, but no one talks about it until after April.

It's very sociological, and being part of this practice makes me feel human somehow. I should probably journal this newfound sense of inclusivity. I think the idea sounds nice but in the "American Dream" way. I'm not halfway there, but I'm somewhere. When I worked for Mel, I think I was just a kid. Mentally, at least. I was just a kid, and I had parents—if you consider the scientists at the facility as parents. I had a home, and now I've moved out. I went through a brief period of depression, tried some drugs, met different people, and hit rock bottom. Not so much the American Dream, but it's definitely American.

And now I'm cleaning up my act and getting my life together.

After hitting send, I rush out of the library to catch the next train back home. The sidewalks are fortunately not as crowded as the streets are since they are filled with clocked-out employees who desperately need to get home. I will be that person someday, except I'll still travel on sidewalks.

There is a crowd at the station, and it takes a while to buy a ticket. Punching in the info to purchase a train ticket is muscle memory since I did it every day back when I worked at that bullshit weight loss company. I wonder how they're doing now. It doesn't matter.

Thinking about Mel twice a day is gross. I rip my ticket from the machine and hurry to my designated platform—just like the good old days when routine was part of my life, and I didn't have to imagine how the next day would be.

When I board, I can hear someone playing music at the end of the train. I don't think it's a flute. It's a clarinet, and it's piercing. If I were not a domesticated alien, I think I would have a massive breakdown and possibly go viral since there would be a high likelihood of me ripping the musician's jugular out...

Merely on the precipice of violent inclinations, I am at my stop.

I walk like a schoolboy to the facility and imagine what my life would be like if I turned hostile on the way there. They're expecting me now because of my tracking chip, but what if I lose my mind one day? What if I leave my chip somewhere and sneak up on them with homicidal intent? That is, if I go through with the surgery.

Conveniently, to my surprise, the gate is open. The doors are unlocked, and there is no need for me to punch the code to have the security system recognize its bait. Sometimes, I feel like bait or as if they are taking advantage of me. That's the reality I have to live with, but I don't know how much longer I can take it. If I continue, I will require someone sincere to me. The feeling of starting over with someone is nauseating, but there are, of course, plenty of fish in the sea to befriend.

I see Dr. Cambry notice me because I'm short, I'm wearing a lot of weird articles of clothing, and I probably stink. She presses her clipboard to her chest, "Lee. Hi," she says warmly. I sense pity.

"Hi, Dr. Cambry." Clearly, she hasn't been promoted, so she cannot keep track of my whereabouts while under surveillance.

I want to fuck with her, though. "You didn't know I was coming?"

Her smile drops. "No." She's callous. "Where would you like me to take you?"

"I think I'm here to see Richard." I kind of just made that up. I'm not sure who I should see, but I need to report to someone about the job I applied for.

"Richard?" She raises her brows. "He's not in… usually. Is it urgent? Did something happen?"

"If not Richard, I guess I'll go to Barberry." I evade her guidance by walking past her. After all, I don't need to hold her hand.

She tags along anyway, "Dr. Barberry is—"

"I know where he is."

"Can you please not interrupt me?" She mumbles.

I waltz into the lab, where Dr. Barberry attacks a sub with his left hand. He's taking notes in the other. Obviously, he's expecting me because the creak of the door does not cause him to lift his head and check who's there. I don't really want to chat with Dr. Barberry. I merely need to update him with my goals. "Hey," I pull up a chair and sit near his desk.

"Sorry. Late lunch," he looks up. "You look like you haven't had lunch. In a while." He presses his lips together in disapproval.

"You look like you don't care."

He tilts his head to the side. "Would you like me to?"

"Not in a way that's worth reporting," I respond curtly.

He leans back in his seat and wipes his mouth with a thin napkin. "We saw that you visited Dr. Alec multiple times. You seriously can't do that anymore, and I don't want an explanation… What are you in for?"

It feels good to hold a secret. "I applied for a job that Virginia suggested a while back." He takes note of it. "What kind of job?"

"Tax intern." Dr. Barberry shoots me a confused look. "It's a tax preparer shop. Paid internship."

"Well, that's news. And how does that make you feel?"

"I actually am looking forward to achieving a better life for myself. I don't know if this introduces a newfound idea of competition, but I know I am searching for a status. Not necessarily for authority but for convenience. I want a good life. An income that can afford me a sexy coffee machine or a memory foam mattress. And when people visit me, they are met with the smell of pine or artificial aromatics." His brows furrow. "That's all I got… Also, what you guys have done to me is pretty messed up, by the way.

Stopping me from meeting the only two people with whom I've developed a bond. It's fucked up."

"It wasn't my decision," Dr. Barberry admits. "I'm sure you didn't speak up for me."

"I'm not Dr. Alec, Lee. I'm sorry." I let his remark sink in.

"I know you tried to get on his good side, though, and you almost understood the lens he saw me through. Why are you acting like this? And don't even ask me what the hell that means because you know exactly what it means."

"Do you need me?"

"It's hard to trust you."

"Is that what you're looking for?" The shallowness of his questions deter me from conversing with him because I know it's all part of the assessment.

"What can you admit that would redeem yourself?" I ask with a tinge of hope.

"I also raised you. I used to change your diapers and feed you when Dr. Alec was busy. We used to learn about different philosophers, and it was fascinating to see how quickly your cognizance developed. You'd begun to pick apart schools of thought and make a persona for yourself. I was part of your growth, and I'm sorry for backing out at the worst time of your life, but quite honestly, Dr. Alec was beginning to frighten us. We were told to avoid building a real relationship with you, and you know what? They were kind of right. Look what it's done to Dr. Alec. It'll be hard to see you suffer and love you at the same time. It's already difficult to watch you roam the streets helplessly. I promise you, it hurts me. It probably hurts Savea, too. At the very least, it makes everyone uncomfortable because we've brought you to sentience, and it's not necessarily backfiring, but it's definitely not pretty."

"Hm," I grunt. "I always knew you weren't awful. It just sucked when you changed. It seemed like you made a conscious decision, which means you processed my experience and decided against reconciliation."

"I didn't want it that way… Do you think it'll get better between us, Lee? Would you allow that?"

I look at his unfinished notes. It's hard to read upside down, especially when I am technically not supposed to have my nose in his book. The pressure of silence forces me to reconsider, "I'll think about it."

CHAPTER 10

THE GYM MEMBERSHIP

A month is almost up, can you believe it? I've been visiting the library more often as it reminds me of a period of my life that was more refined. I was entering a chapter of stability and identity when Dr. Alec and Dr. Barberry sat on my head with stacks of homework. I didn't attend Socratic seminars but watched them online and formed loose conjectures of ethics and morality. I used to be interesting, but nostalgia is another symptom of regret, and regretting everything wastes my time. Time is a currency that is earned, bought, and sold. In the legal terms of this shallow and scientific existence, it's a transaction. Unless, of course, you make use of your burning regret.

This is the part of the story where things are looking up. I've decided to make a routine despite my current homelessness. I find it fascinating that there is a balance between utilizing opt inhabitant instinct and sapien curiosity to create a fruitful life. I want a good life.

I have plenty of things to look forward to ever since I've been granted another set of time—even though I've used about half of those days. I've been wondering whether I need Dr. Alec. If I get this job, I can start fresh. Besides, there's no point being on his good side. Since IRAAB unrelentingly dangles my existence before my eyes, it would be best to appease them.

This is one hell of an evolutionary conundrum as it just continues to bloom. If I cut Dr. Alec off, I'm cutting off the only source of therapeutic release. He's the only one who's ever humanized me. What will become of me once I've suffered that loss? Admittedly, it has been lonely. Sure, I'm approached daily, but I'm yesterday's news. IRAAB rarely appoints media, and I can see why. I'm not exactly the healthiest alien on display, and I've heard rumors of another agency's bitch-ass alien roaming my streets. Apparently, he's a 'scholar.' If people believe they're partaking in a rat race, then what the hell am I? And no, I haven't been frequenting the public library out of competitiveness. At least, I don't think so.

I have read up on the other woman. The rival agency's alien is a male; apparently, he's majoring in history. Given his privileges, I envy his leisure as there must be an abundance of it. He can just get up and go to school. I'm here, picking up my own pieces to summon grace. I think I just want a life that's as good as his. I'm done with giving up. It's too hard to give up, and endless consequences compliment failure, which I clearly cannot handle. I'm tired of reeking of shit. I'm also tired of scavenging for leftovers. Though I am a fucking alien, I really despise the sight of roaches.

I've considered investing in a gym membership. Free showers, a sauna, and, of course, I can work out. It might add definition to my canvas and bring out the undertones of my humble beginnings. The other aliens never had to endure such treacherous conditions.

They probably harbor their own version of trauma; however, there's always controversy on the subject of trauma. One party might disagree that mishaps can equate to trauma, provided that party might have encountered severe measures of abuse, financial destitution, etc. And then there's the other party. They believe that any negative experience that may affect the course of perception negatively can be considered trauma. It's a very legal way to put it, yet it is the most emotionally intelligent perspective. I have not yet been recorded for emotional intelligence, so I stand with the first party, especially since it's been a bitch of a ride. I'm waiting out the library's last hour because I don't want to stagger into the mildly threatening city.

When the library's fluorescent lights flicker to alert fellow bookworms of its closing time, I log out of my email. I waited practically all day for a reply from that job I applied to and, unfortunately, have not heard back. I am in good faith, but I pray that it does not dwindle as I have very little patience to be generous with. I hate to be pushed out into the wind with a musty scarf covering my drying nostrils.

The library's doors do not slide open. Rather, the librarian uses her keys to unlock and pry them open. A procedure we've witnessed many times. I wave in gratitude. She doesn't respond. There's nothing to be noted, as it was neither awkward nor insulting. Even if that's what she wanted to get across. I don't mind being a burden because considering other people's comfort has not been essential lately. Normally, I'd dwell on how awkward an exchange might be, given the stakes tied to my sociability. But the stakes—and the course of things—have shifted. It's not about making another friend. It's about surviving.

Speaking of which, the night of survival now commences as I take my first step outside the toasty building. The cold relieves me briefly as it airs out my sweaty tufts of hair, but eventually, my cheeks burn. It's not painfully freezing, just uncomfortably chilly. Wandering the streets while bearing loneliness only the suicidal can resonate with will either be the last straw or the reason to turn the page. Doing all of it on your own without shelter makes your hearing sensitive. I'm always listening for threats because it's too late when you see them. I've already been good at reading expressions and rooms, and I've become excellent at picking up energy. Maybe I should try yoga. I mean, I'm certainly not the type because I believe I was raised to scrutinize hippies and classify them as burnouts instead. Those who make peace with what they have come off as are horribly complacent. Right?

I was not raised to be all-accepting; I am not God, and I am not composed of benevolence in any sense of the word. Interactions with people feel like a computer game, where you assess a conversation and choose the most appropriate response. The only thing I've genuinely felt is guilt for not feeling; that's the only level of "benevolence" I could conquer. Anyway, maybe yoga or meditation can be an option for me because I don't have anything better to do other than prey on dumpsters. I look up at the night sky. You can never map stars from here. I can see my breath push through the wool scarf. My nostrils flare as they send heat to the material, warming me up. I put my hands up above me, palms facing outwards, as I do not intend to make a prayer. I just observe my opposable thumbs. They've helped me become a skillful manipulator of various objects such as door knobs, jars, and other finger-friendly gadgets.

I look at the overgrown set of nails. I need to prepare for the interview if I ever score one. I'll need to trim my "beard" and establish a little skincare regime. I'll have to purchase a new wardrobe or

    BY ZAINAB F. RAZA

resurrect the suits I graced the office with at my old job. I think it would somewhat affect my mood positively.

That positivity is not substantial because the real me is going crazy. I just know I have to pull myself out of this godforsaken situation. Then I can cry because at least I'll be crying in my own apartment on my bed instead of the public bus bench. It's always bubbling inside of me. The insanity. It is always there, waiting for me to lose control only to relieve every stress my body has endured since the day my parental-like scientists brought me to relative consciousness. How fun must it be for animals to be forgiven as they are only animals. When a wild animal overreacts, the self-proclaimed, learned, educated, and intelligent defend the animal with claims of instinct. They blame themselves for antagonizing the thing, shielding them from apprehension. Rather valiantly, I shake away the thoughts.

My tummy rumbles in reminder. What do I want? What am I in the mood for?

I think I'm in the mood for Thai. Man, here come the tragic flashbacks. I wonder how that lady is doing? She would film me nearly every time I stopped by. She would be so devastated if she saw me in this condition. Regardless of the potentially awkward encounter, I'm still in the mood for Thai.

On the way there, I see a strip club down the street. Normally, I don't notice surrounding venues unless I really need to, but the bouncer's impeccably large and their wine-colored curtains in lieu of doors catch anyone's curiosity. I don't think I've had an erection in a very long time, and no one has had a healthy conversation about sexual urges with me. Maybe engaging in such a conversation inadvertently promotes beastiality, and so many refrain from discussing the topic, assuming I am preserved in unassuming innocence. Nah, I'm just kidding. All the scientists know I've had a boner at least once. Not to touch on that topic again. I just want to touch on the fact that I have not touched myself in a minute. Here's the thing, though: if Dr.Barberry had the decency to bring this subject to my attention, he would quickly learn where I stand on the matter. It is fair to openly accept urges provided that I was raised with their beauty standards; therefore, I cannot look at another alien and think of fucking it. Hell, I can't imagine *actually* planning to fuck a person either. It's just the concept that incites hormonal flares. It's something that clicks in my head, but an orgasm for me only feels good. It's not really about having sex with someone.

I'm a few blocks away from the restaurant, and more than anything, I think of eating. The idea of hitting the gym is not a distraction to make this journey quicker, even though I've nearly arrived, to my surprise. I pray I find a fortune cookie at the bottom of a forgotten bag of takeout. I'm not the racist one here. The manager throws in a couple for every entrée.

I see the manager outside! Oh my god, it's been ages. She's cut her hair shorter, and it's blacker than usual. She looks healthy. "Thank you," she walks out an elderly couple. A few seconds later, I see her remember something. "Wait!"

She holds up a hefty bag of food. *Fuck.* My observation pans to the side of the road where the couple is parallel parked. The wife of the elderly man steps out of the luxury car to retrieve the bag. "Thank you," poise, the lady waves. The wife unties the bag and peeks through. "Do you have chopsticks?"

"They're in there," Miss Tangerine verifies cheerfully.

There that couple goes… driving away with my food. It's nice to see Miss Tangerine, though. Before she catches a glimpse of me, I scurry to the alley like a rat would and scan for any familiar employees out back.

I use the grip of my shoe to hoist myself up by pressing it against the textured dumpster. At this point, half of my body is leaning over. I'm forced to smell the rotted waste closely, making it harder to remember how desperately hungry I really am. I dig through until the tips of my wrinkled fingers detect warmth radiating from a greasy styrofoam box. I carefully pull it out from the garbage piles, ensuring I don't break it open through the fault of haste. Once the box reaches my sights, I open it to find garlic noodles. My mouth waters as the smell entertains me. Garlic noodles, sliced eggplants, and broccoli coated in sauce. It isn't a large portion, but it is enough to keep me grateful.

Normally, I'd appreciate a scenic spot for dinner, but I am past the range of normality. I use the same tainted fingers and feed myself in large bites. It takes four attempts to finish the entire thing. I lick the remaining chili oil at the corners of the box and dive for more, but I only locate uncooked veggies this time around. Pretty soon, I'm full enough to endure the night, so I shift my weight and climb out of the dumpster skillfully.

The back door swings open, and a large splash of mop water follows. "You have a lighter?"

"Yup," an employee hollers from inside. He tosses it to the other guy. I take a peek and see a chef light his cigarette. Both of us feel relief as he inhales. I don't recognize this guy, but the recognition of any employee here doesn't pay shit, so what does it matter? I watch him smoke the entire thing. He shrugs more and more after each drag, as if his chubby body is giving out. The guy is clearly a man—not a boy in his twenties still figuring things out. This chef, in his mid-thirties, has a neatly trimmed beard, a greasy complexion, and a face that perpetually wears an expression of disappointment. This is it. This is his life.

I'm quite eager for him to finish his smoke, but a server steps out. "You got another?" The server asks.

The chef doesn't look at him to answer. "Yeah," he reaches into his pocket, prolonging my stay, and grabs a loose one. He lights the smoke for him, claiming ownership over the server's lighter. Kind of a weird power move if you ask me. "How much you earn in tips today?"

"Nothing. She's been keeping it for herself." The chef smirks. "You're not from here?"

The server steps back as he chokes on the smoke, and his eyebrows raise with concern. "No one's supposed to know."

"It's okay. She does that. It seems fair to you, doesn't it? In some way? She hired you. She should keep the tips."

It changes my opinion of Miss Tangerine. Kind of a shitty thing to do, and trust me, I want to defend her because I knew her, but it's hard to evade facts. What a shame.

"It's fair. I think," the server ashes his cigarette. "You take home any of the food?"

"I take home the free lunch for my kid."

"Resourceful," the chef grunts. "I'll see what I can do." I smile at the kindness of the chef. How special is it to witness something you need for yourself?

"Oh," the server waves his hand. "You don't have to do that."

"Okay, fine." The chef flicks his cigarette and turns to head back inside. I almost laugh at the sudden carelessness.

The server gives it a second thought, "I just don't want to get caught," he twists his fingers. Worry painted on his face. I subsequently feel nauseous, but not because of the garbage food.

"Why would I run that risk?"

The server tilts his head, unable to understand. "I don't understand," he says, proving my observation to be true.

The chef chuckles and pats the inferior on his back. "Don't worry." The server's feelings pour into a frail smile.

"Thank you," he whispers.

When the two officially tend to closing responsibilities inside. I exit the scene, again, like a rat would.

I find a vacated bus stop and take shelter for the night. That doesn't require much preparation. I sit down for a little while and watch for any threats before deciding to drift off, and when I do, the hours pass like minutes.

Before I know it, the sun is up, and people flood the streets. I lie there, turning the ruckus into a sleep-inducing ambiance. A screeching car snaps me conscious. Nothing happened, no accident or anything. I believe my brain is just looking for a reason to wake up. I feel a jolt run through me as I digest the abrupt noise, but pretty soon, the tension in my muscles release, and I'm okay. I sit up, rip ass, and stretch to encourage blood flow. Usually, it's chilly in the morning, so half the day must have gone by considering the temperature. I feel a little dingier than usual. I think the dirt and grime on my skin and underneath my nails have exceeded their stay because I can only smell rot. It's time to get a gym membership and then hit the library. I guess that's what's on the ol' agenda today. So I can get myself up and running. It's a local gymnasium, meaning the owner might be in. It'll make this process a whole lot easier.

I open the door of the gym, and in front of me is a flight of stairs. A board is bolted into the walls, and the board tells me that the gym is on the second floor. I wonder if there's an elevator. I bounce up the steps and open that door, which leads me to a small place occupied by equipment and a few middle-aged moms in ponytails. I first wonder if their kids all go to the same school. Seems like they all know each other, and maybe that's the reason. "Hi," a hesitant employee steps out from behind the desk. "The shelter is, I think, further down. Would you like me to give you their number or…" She waits for me to answer.

"No. Can I speak to your owner?"

"Um. Okay. One minute."

I nod and immediately reach for my laminated card for introductory purposes. After a minute or so, the sculpted manager reaches me. His features are uncanny… "Hi, I'm Blake. How can I help?"

"Hi. My name is Lee." I hand him my card, but he doesn't want to break eye contact with me. I think he's also trying to figure out what he's dealing with. "You should read that first."

He blinks away as he skims through. His eyebrows hit the top of his forehead. "My goodness," he whispers to himself. "Wow," he looks at me. "How can I help?"

"Yeah, I mean. I just need a gym membership. I wanted to take care of myself and, if possible," how do I put this? "Use your facilities." He looks me up and down with dissatisfaction, then he looks back again at the curious moms. "Would you prefer we talk in private?" The guy walks to his office, expecting me to follow.

When I enter, it's like a spa, except there's a desk. He's playing weird binaural music. If you call that music. There are candles lit everywhere, and I feel like this guy commits crimes in his leisure. He's too handsome to be this off-putting. "You seem homeless," he says as he sits behind the desk. That's forward.

"I am. I signed a contract that proves I voluntarily chose to live independently despite the option of remaining at the facility." Are you happy, Richard?

"Interesting. A lot of homeless people have tried to sign up, and you know, we have a reputation to keep," he tells me in a sorry-ass tone.

"No, I get it," I back up from his desk.

His tone switches to keep me in his office. "Oh no, but your case is different." Now I know where he's going with this. "I think it would be an interesting look for us. Is that something you're comfortable with?"

"No, not particularly. But beggars can't be choosers," I joke.

The muscles on his face rearrange themselves to fashion pity. "Who takes care of you?"

"If you're looking for attention, I suppose I can endure it in exchange for a membership. Unless you'd like me to pay."

"Don't worry about it," he's already begun creating a document. "Do you have a last name by chance?"

By chance? "No," I respond. "Do you need maybe some further authorization from IRAAB?"

"Is that necessary?" He reverses the question, and I shrug in reply. "Best if you come in the mornings or early evenings. I'm sure a lot of people would want to meet you."

"Okay. Sure," his kindness makes it easy for me to be cooperative, and I think I yearn for his approval, making me more and more self-conscious of my current condition.

He purses his lips and shifts his weight to notice me just when I don't want to be seen. "I'm going to need a picture of you. You don't have a different set of clothes now, do you? Maybe athletic wear?"

"Nah, not on me right now," I tell him honestly.

"Hm," he thinks. "Kinda wanted a picture to put up on the website for tomorrow. That way, people will know what to look forward to." He fidgets with the toys on his desk. "Felicia!" He calls for someone abruptly, and I'm already dreading the situation I've put myself in. Anything for a hot shower, I suppose. I wonder if he'll let me sleep here, too.

Felicia, the girl from up front, comes by with a weary smile on her young face. "What's up, Blake?"

"Can you lead Lee to our lost and found?"

Felicia looks hilariously confused. "He lost something? Here?"

"No, no. This is Lee. He is a lab alien from a science agency. Unfortunately, Lee is homeless, but luckily, he's become a new member of our gym! Why don't you help him find a new outfit so that we can upload a picture of him online, yeah?"

"Yeah, totally," she says with a warm smile. Felicia doesn't have to say much, but I can feel the charitable energy permeate through the room, mingling with the good—or perhaps bullshit—vibrations of these weird shaman candles. "You ready, Lee?" She thins her voice sweetly.

"Mhm." I follow her out. Looking back, I see Blake typing away on his computer. He's not the worst of the bloodsuckers I've ever met, so I let myself make sense of his needs. Of course, he wants more people to occupy his gym, and I'm an opportunity that happened to waltz through the door. Why shouldn't he make use of me? Would that make him such a bad person?

Look at me. I'm making excuses already for the guy who's given me elementary tiers of compassion. "You're gonna like it here," she pushes her kinky curls to the side to take a better look at me. "People here are pretty accepting, and we have nice showers," Felicia's out here reading my mind.

"What are the showers like?"

"I'll show you after!" She opens a door with her key that hangs on an orange lanyard.

There's a room with a bunch of storage boxes and scattered clothes. "We need to organize this stuff, but at the end of the month, Blake lets us take whatever we like home," she winks at me. She measures my emaciated waist with her eyes. "You're definitely a small."

"Yeah, I suppose," defeated, I concur.

She steps over small mounds of athleisure. Felicia picks up a women's pair of blue shorts and a white tee. "How's this?" She tosses it my way.

I hold up the shirt in the light. "Yeah. This is good. The shorts are actually kinda cute." She laughs, but I meant what I said. "You think I could grab track pants and a jacket? It gets cold."

"Here," she folds a tracksuit for me. "Actually, I'll go ahead and wash them for you. You can come back later for the picture. Sounds good?"

"I do need to shower, though," I'm already worried about being a burden. "Yeah, do you have soap? We don't really have anything."

"That's okay. I'll figure something out and then come back. You're open—"

"All day, all night. Come back whenever."

I smile with relief. "Thanks, Felicia. Tell Blake it was great to meet him. I'm really grateful," I say earnestly. She copies it with a nod, and we take it our separate ways.

I can't believe it. This is my first win in a very long time, and though exchanges were made and both parties benefited from the decision to accept me as a member, it feels great to be treated with respect. I hope that never goes away.

I guess the next thing on my agenda is the library. Time to try my luck there and see if I've received any informational emails that will point me in a more productive direction. When I get there, the place is nearly empty. It sounds silly, but I've grown fond of this place and understand the people who frequent it. It's pointless to explain the value as we all know why people who love reading love libraries. Apart from the free internet, I like the fact that I can explore nearly any genre or topic I'm in the mood for.

After locating a computer in the back and logging in, I browse the health section, an aisle I've been avoiding for some time now. It turns out that there is some decent content that can help me revamp my lifestyle; for instance, if I stretch just fifteen minutes a day, I can increase my lifespan. That sounds like bullshit, but it also seems kinda obvious. Anywho, I'm looking forward to putting my life on track by taking showers routinely, dressing better, and even hitting the elliptical once or twice a week. It feels better than dragging myself through the streets, hoping to discover sustenance. I ate to live, but I didn't even know what to live for. I think I have a better idea of what I want out of life, and I hate to admit this, but if it hadn't been for Rich kicking me out, I wouldn't have found my spark.

Now that I'm on this path to a better life, perusing this part of the library makes sense.

There's even a book on the male libido, and the cover of it is a shirtless male crushing a blue pill. Nice.

I look left and right before swiping the book and hurrying back to the computer. My emails have loaded, and I see an emboldened reply. I sit down, letting the book fall off my lap. "Holy fuck," I whisper. The tax preparer company emailed me back! They're asking for an interview! I reread the email several times before replying with gratitude and selecting a time they've provided. I look through the resume I had attached to surmise what stood out. Maybe it's what I am that stood out, but whatever the reason, I'm blessed for this chance. Anyway, today is Tuesday, and I have my interview on Thursday. It's in person. That's a rarity, but it will be more beneficial for them to meet me in the flesh to evaluate my capacity.

I pick up the book from the floor and aimlessly flip through it, trying to conceal my excitement. I wouldn't know what to do with my joy if I let it run loose. I decide to channel my energy elsewhere. Maybe I should try… You know? As I skim through various tips on how to treat erectile dysfunction, I wonder what's the harm in searching up some classic internet porn. I mean, I won't crank one out here in public. No, that would be atrocious.

I do a quick scan of my environment and type away. Immediately, the bells in my head ring as I see several nude people loading—and unloading—on the screen. I know I'm not supposed to be doing this, but it feels good. Not even in a sexual way. It makes me want to explore that feeling even more so. I think I'm less horny and more inquisitive of my nature. I wonder if animal porn would get me off.

I open a new tab real quick and find too much content on the subject, and it's rather disturbing. So I click back and just cram every megapixel of every rack and peepee. At the first sound of footsteps, I click away and dash to the bathroom, where I attempt to masturbate in a barely locked stall. I squeeze my eyes shut and try to think of the thumbnail I saw, but I'm going blank. Is it the anxiety? Maybe it's because I'm not supposed to be doing that kind of thing here. I used to be able to! I poke my head out of the stall, hoping no one heard me rubbing one.

Before leaving, I grab the half-empty soap bottle by the sink and stuff it in my oversized pants. When I return to the computer, I see a librarian thumping. Her arms are crossed.

I see the screen. It's animal porn. I laugh to myself. "Oh my god." She points to the exit. "You have to go."

"I'm so sorry, " I realize she probably saw the libido book, too, and laugh even harder. "Go!" She steps forward.

I run away like a hyena would. "Sorry!"

"Don't come back!" Don't come back? I don't even look back as I run down several blocks, far away from the library.

As I flee, I come closer to that glowing, curtained place down the street. The strip club. It's almost a snap decision; I go for it. Even on the way, I don't let my mind ponder over the decision.

I am not really in the mood, but I think I need newer experiences as they would serve as material to write about. Besides, I have nothing better to do at this point. My overall plan for the days leading up to my interview has all to do with maintaining leisure. Like many, I socialize best when I'm not under any pressure. The only thing left on my list is to visit the facility to pick up a suit.

The bouncer doesn't look at me when I reach the strip club. I must look old or older due to my disheveled appearance. I imagine that my height would cause some line of questioning, and the discovery of my inhumane existence would be perceived as a decent reason for rejection. But alas, he doesn't note that I'm an opt, and I suppose they don't hold back on homeless folks. Every dollar counts, I guess. When the curtains move aside, my eyes adjust to the dim room. I've only caught the silhouettes of nudity so far. The neon, purplish lights backlight the bodies. The music is blaring, but there isn't enough chatter to balance the ambiance.

It's depressing here. I can see why men of recent divorce want to drink their troubles away rather than enjoy themselves in the Americanized indulgence of lust. Not a shocker, really. I watch my steps more than I watch the strippers become more apparent under the lights because I seriously do not want to trip and cause a little scene. I touch my face to ensure there is a scarf wrapped around it to keep my identity hidden and find myself a booth to sneak into. It's near the stage. I look across to find any other men lingering, but I count a few just scattered across the room. They're not paying attention to the women anyway.

Once I summon the courage to notice the strippers, I find they are not alike. They come in different shapes and sizes, and while that is admirable, it is certainly unconventional— something men who often visit strip clubs typically do not appreciate.

It isn't that these ladies don't meet popular beauty standards. I'm just not interested in ogling them. I think I'm observing, and since the setting is made to shield identities, I feel comfortable watching as much as I like. So I suppose seeing porn pop up on the screen at the library made me uncomfortable because I wasn't supposed to be doing it, not because of the nudity.

I feel smaller waves of lust, though. I worry that maybe I am trained to sexualize a certain type of body, and while that doesn't have much to do with the act of sex, the unfortunate characteristic is often associated with shitty and annoying men. I care about how I am perceived because how I am perceived dictates the longevity of my life. It's easy to find the source of my personality when the source is pretty consistent across the board. That's the goal. I am led to believe that that's not far from how humans function, though. They're probably in survival mode, too, one way or another.

I see a near-naked stripper making rounds, crawling into booths to whisper something in someone's ear. Since there aren't a lot of people, she is orbiting faster than you'd think, and I'm reluctant to speak to her. Her hair is matted, and she wears a thong you can barely notice. Two booths away, and I'm debating whether to hide or leave, but I think that would look rude, and she doesn't need to feel shitty about herself. "What's that scarf doing around your face?" She asks in a sultry tone as she leans against the table, putting her chest in my face. Yeah. I feel it.

"I—I… I have a cold," the words rush out, "I have a cold and—and besides, I can't really see *your* face," I triumphantly say as I confuse argumentative banter with flirting.

"I don't think that's what you came here to see," she puts one knee on the table and arches her back to push her chest farther out. It gives me anxiety, so I scoot away. I feel the phantom memory of seizing throughout my body, and I remember Virginia screaming in the park. I'm afraid surveillance will assume the worst of me. The stripper takes her knee off the table and comes to me. She puts her lips near my ear. I can smell her sweat. Or is that cheap perfume? "One fifty for the whole night," she offers.

"I'm not so sure. I have a wife and kids. One is four, and the other one is about to go to college." What the fuck?

"I don't see them here," she pushes. Yeah, why would you? "Honestly, you're lovely. I just came here to enjoy. Thank you."

"You're telling me you're not interested?" She chuckles.

"I'm telling you something different."

"And I'm not buying it," surprisingly, her tone hasn't changed.

"Tell you what. How about I give you some free money? Would that satisfy you?"

"It gets the job done," she backs away.

"Good," I reach into my pocket, guilty of betraying my own needs to fulfill another's. I pull two bills and awkwardly slip them into her underwear.

"Thanks, love," she stands.

"Mhm," I nod. I hang back for a few hours, watching and forming my own thesis on the nuances of socialization. I have faith in Freudian thinking because the behaviors that most exhibit are with the intention of being acknowledged, and the highest acknowledgment, again to most, is lineage, procreation, and sex. I wonder if the prioritization of having children and making them the center of one's life is a social construct. When many lose hope in themselves, oftentimes, the will to live is fueled by their children, and I don't know if it's part of nature. I mean, I know it's part of nature, and I am also nature, but the magnitude children have is something I cannot fathom.

Maybe it's because I lead a quasi-existence between a conscientious man and animal, stuck in an emotional limbo. I know I don't want children, and it's not like I sneer at the sight of them. I just am comfortable with having a singular existence that ends with no legacy. Lineage can be so dramatic. I can't say it's for no reason, but when people describe the topic of lineage in relation to their own, the way it's expressed is overly important.

Anyway, I haven't imagined having my own, and maybe that's how I was created. I was not raised to consider the matter, so it never really occurred to me. Even my primitive tendencies are limited. They were possibly interrupted by scientific manipulation.

It's kind of awkward thinking about all of this, but I pretty much forgot that I'm rotting in the booth of one. If I were to have a child, I don't believe I would care very much to protect it. I hope that isn't too sociopathic of me. I remember I used to be described by my enneagram, political beliefs, and whatever else, but I wonder where I stand now. If I were to redo my monologue, I would redress my take on who I am because I've become a little more pessimistic. I've also become too comfortable in my bath water. I've become complacent. I don't want that to morph into laziness, but my point isn't about laziness unless it somehow references the sole concern for my well- being. I'm trying to say that I've become too comfortable with being a tad selfish.

Maybe I've been let down with my hands tied behind me, unable to reach for those who were sincere. Maybe I haven't entirely healed from my past, but part of me has given up on people helping me become one of them. That prospect is selfish in itself, isn't it?

I don't want to be a sociopath, but the goal to escape that sort of psychological evaluation is difficult when the goal is self-serving. I have to prove I can love, connect, or care, but how can I achieve such humanity when it's for the approval of extending my existence? Fucking how? It's an unsolved equation, and the only person I know who can do that math is anticipating my arrival at three a.m. soon. He was right. I needed to break the rules and find myself first before anything. Identifying emotions will always be different from feeling them for someone. If I had to describe myself, I'd say I am still a Democrat, I am agnostic, I subscribe to hedonism currently, and my enneagram is still a five.

I scoot out of the booth, exhausted with myself. I need to kill time because it's clearly too late to travel back to the facility to collect my suit for the interview. Oh my god, I'm so excited again. "Leaving so soon?" The same stripper comments sarcastically as she makes another round.

Before responding, I look for the glowing exit sign, but the bar catches my eye. Of course, I can't drink anymore, but free water

BY ZAINAB F. RAZA

sounds good to me. "Better now than never," I tell the stripper. I should have learned her name because I don't want to keep referring to her by her job, not that I find her job immoral.

I slip to the bar, ask for water, and then make my Irish exit. I don't realize how humid the club is until I step out, and I certainly don't realize how much I stink until now. I wonder how others can talk to me. Maybe they do it for the money, like the folks at the gym. Maybe it's unwise of me to shower at this hour, but I've reached my limit. After my last dumpster dive, I physically cannot stand myself. I let the brisk air cool my sweaty body by taking large strides.

When I get to the gym, Felicia is still manning the desk. "Hey," I wave. Her face lights up to my delight.

"Hey! Got soap?" She places a large paper bag on the countertop. "I washed them for you as soon as you left." I'm touched.

"Wow. Thank you, that's so kind," I pull out the hand soap from my pants like a weirdo, "Yeah. I have soap."

"Uh," she's a little taken aback but quickly covers it with etiquette. "Let me show you the showers!" She gestures to me to follow her. "People come and go, but don't mind them. If they have a problem, they can take it up with me. But don't tell Blake."

"Okay." I worry about the burden I could become.

She opens the door to the men's locker room, which is divided into sections. First, there are rows of tall lockers, then there's the bathroom, and behind the stalls are the showers. I take the one that's all the way at the end. "Don't worry," I hear Felicia's voice behind me. She sets down the brown bag. "We'll notify our members so they won't be surprised by you joining us. You shouldn't have to expect any—"

"Hostility?"

She looks at me, meeting my call for pity. "Don't worry, Lee," she offers a soft smile, leaving me with my privacy. Once I hear the door shut, I peel off the dirtied and soiled articles of dead clothing and toss them in the bin. It's pointless to even wash such tattered clothes.

It's been a while since I've toyed with a shower. Each is different, but luckily, I don't have to ask for any assistance. It's just a pull and twist in the hottest direction. I wait until the water boils, observing myself in a mirror that is rapidly collecting steam. I put my hand under the water's pattering stream and enter the small shower with peace and thankfulness. The water runs through my knotted hair, forging streams that cheap suds of hand soap will soon occupy.

I pump soap into my palm and first wash my hands before allowing myself to touch my face. I intend to be perfectly clean. Then I pour a generous amount on my scalp and neck, and use the remainder to scrub my face. Instead of aggressively washing away the collection of grime, which is expectedly caught in several folds, I employ a gentle hand to maintain thoroughness. Indeed I wash my pits, back, ass, legs, and everything, so that when I do step out of the shower, it will feel like an achievement, and I will measure that achievement with how much soap I've used. It took me half the amount, but it was worth every guilt of stealing it from the library.

Before I'm done, I let myself have a drink of free water here too. Maybe I should fill my bottles here or just be normal and use the water fountain like everyone else. I truly wonder if people would be disgusted at the sight of me, but Felicia gave me her word. I shouldn't worry. Yeah, fuck that, I have more important things to worry about. Like the interview. My stomach turns with anticipation and fear, and my heart skips a beat. I am half full of optimism so long as I present myself well and justify my previous termination. Maybe I should have acquired a recommendation letter…

I do not want to be gluttonous with the shower. I rinse myself one last time and turn the knob to its original position. The cool air saturates my body, so I quickly wear the slightly effeminate tracksuit and then consider slipping on my gross sneakers, but that would ruin the whole point of getting clean. Maybe that's a tad illogical, but I do not want to interrupt this tranquil feeling of cleanliness. "Hey, Felicia?" I holler. Maybe that's too extroverted of me. I can hear her jogging in my direction.

"Yes?" I hear her, but I don't see her. "I'm in the locker room. Is everything okay?"

"Yeah, sorry," I laugh a little. "Do you have sneakers? In the lost-and-found?"

"Oh… I don't think so—"

"You can come in," I say as I zip up my jacket.

She pokes her head in timidly before entering. "Even if we were holding a pair, I don't think they'd be in your size." She looks down at my nasty, dirt-stained sneakers.

"You don't have to make me feel self-conscious about my size," I joke. "Oh." She begins to ramble. "Oh my gosh, I'm super sorry. I—"

I laugh, "I'm just being sassy. Do you have socks?"

"Yes! Mismatched is fine?"

"Any." I purse my lips.

Her muscles loosen. "Okay, cool. I'll go look." She runs back to the room in search. I can't believe I've found such nice people. It almost makes me want to go to church again. She returns with an ankle sock and a compression sock. Weird, but ok. "It's all we got," she tosses the pair to me.

I quickly put them on. "Not a problem at all. Thank you so, so much. You guys have been severely hospitable. I didn't even expect all of this." She humbly waves off the gratitude. "How do I look?"

"Outstanding. You're ready for the picture?"

"Mhm," I pick up my bag, put on my shoes, and follow her out. When we get to the manager's office, Felicia quickly logs on to the computer and turns the camera clipped onto the top of the computer to face me.

"Strike a pose, Lee," she says as she looks at the computer, not me. I stand straight and smile. "Nice." She clicks and types for a second. "Now try one with your hand up, like you're waving."

I obey with a wider smile. "How's that?"

Her face twists with criticism. "Good, not great. Same smile, hand down." I listen, and she gleams. "Perfect." After a few clicks of the mouse, she uploads the picture. "Wanna see?"

I happily walk around the desk. It's a good look. "I love it."

"Cool. Get ready to meet a lot of friendly faces soon, Lee. I'll give you a tour around the place so you can familiarize yourself with all the equipment here. Did you want to put on more muscle by chance?"

Actually, Felicia, I'm here to use the bathroom. That's the only real reason I asked to become a member, but I think providing this level of honesty would not be good for me. "I think I want to maintain. So I might do some light work for about an hour. Twice a week." That should be enough.

"Perfect. See you soon then," she lifts her cheeks to give one more smile and glances at the door, hinting that I've overstayed.

"See you soon, Felicia." I leave her to work on the company website. On my way out, I think of places to stay for the night. I'd prefer a spot that won't get me dirty.

It's pretty empty outside. The roads are nearly vacant, making it easy to walk or even cross without looking both ways. And then it hits me. The church! Fuck, thank the lord for manipulating the masses into building charitable places of worship. I should have been using the church for sanctuary, both metaphorically and literally, ever since I was allowed to leave the facility. I'm sure someone will kick me out eventually, but I'm also confident I'll manage to score a few days there first. Anyway, it's a nice, quiet, and dry place. Plus, there are an infinite number of benches from which to choose. If I like, I can sleep near Jesus. The only drawback is that it's far, and I'm already tired from the detailed shower I took.

I look up at supposedly God for guidance, and as I let my sights target the sky, I notice the tall buildings obstructing my view. What if I used the fire escape to sneak into someone's apartment for the night? That would be pretty wild, right? No. I shouldn't consider trouble for myself. Tempted, I look through nearly every window of an apartment building to see which studios are occupied and which are most likely not. It's best not to take a risk, but I still search until I reach the top row of windows. Above it is the rooftop, and I can see a garden. A few pots of wilted flowers that rest near the ledge indicate a garden, which makes me curious about what other things grow there. My stomach turns sentient on behalf of its emptiness.

I climb the building using the fire escapes and window ledges. Hopefully, no one will capture this strange behavior and upload it online. The only social media presence I wish to receive traction from is the picture Felicia uploaded online about an hour ago. As stealthily as an alien would, I make it to the top, discovering my version of heaven. It's undoubtedly humble, but I am standing before a garden of radishes and spinach.

I don't let myself wait. I pick and pull from the soil. The sensational crunch fills me, and I am again grateful. I haven't been this thankful in a very long time, but I believe that this ongoing approach to life is a virtue that is greater than patience. Just one more radish and it's time for me to rub my belly to sleep. The delicate night lets me drift away until early sunrise.

When the birds begin to chirp in unison, my eyes open fast. I can't say I didn't sleep well. It's just that I never get enough sleep. I wake up to a half-eaten radish in my hand, and it makes me wonder how the tenants prevent wildlife from picking on their food. Shit. Maybe they use pesticides.

My body stretches itself to get the blood flowing. I yawn a couple of times, thinking it will reset my brain and flush out the thumping headache. I can't even tell if it's from lack of sleep, food, or water anymore. I make my way down the apartment building, and to my surprise, someone is on the balcony doing yoga. You gotta be fucking kidding me. There's not much I can do—I wouldn't survive a valiant jump from this height—so I step onto their balcony, where they're in the downward dog position. The dude notices my bottom half as he looks between his legs. I look between his legs, too. I can only see the profane outline of his balls. He is indeed wearing leggings. He chokes as he falls out of position. "What the fuck?"

I don't rush; I hop under the cheap balcony to hop onto the next. "Please wear underwear, sir." He looks down at me as I continue to descend.

"I'm calling the police! I voted against you fuckers." He hollers.

I don't have time for this. "And say what? An opt was on your balcony?" I smirk. They might actually believe him.

"That is a violation of my privacy—were you on the rooftop?"

"Yes," I admit.

"Oh my god. My radishes!" The guy scrambles to check on his garden, but it'll be too late. I'll be off and laughing away with freedom.

"Sorry!" When I reach the ground, I book it to the train station. People notice me, and it's not just because I'm running manically; it's that I don't have a fat fucking dirty scarf wrapped around my face to shield me from onlookers. I even hear someone shout my name, but I refuse to look back. Now's not the time.

When I reach the subway, I catch my breath. Some people have their phones out to record me, but no one is interested enough in talking to me, which is good. I pay for my ticket like an average civilian and wait on the platform. I bet everyone here has thought about throwing themselves onto the tracks at least once.

I'm not really thinking about suicide anymore. Sometimes, it's hard to keep track of how well one is doing, but a good way to measure well-being is by counting the frequency of suicidal thoughts. I remember my life back in the day when I wanted to end it. I wonder what's different. Technically, my situation is far worse as I no longer have a roof over my head. I cannot complain, though, because I now rarely descend to such levels of depression, and that's something to be proud of. My train is here, and I don't shove. I let the ones ahead do the work of paving a clear opening. Luckily, I find a seat. I pray for no pregnant women or elderly to steal the privilege.

At my stop, I exit without waving goodbye to anyone watching. The air is warmer out here. It's nice. My walk to the facility is more of a stroll because IRAAB isn't expecting me. There isn't much sightseeing when you're walking toward the facility; there is just a whole lot of barren land and an old road leading to IRAAB. I focus on the trees in the distance and the artificial ponds that smell like sewage.

It's not much to look at, but I find it pretty in contrast to the gray city. I enjoy the greenery, I guess? It calms my nerves, so I stop and stretch for a moment, letting the sunlight fulfill any vitamin D deficiency I might harbor. I let the fairly unpolluted air sink deep into my lungs, raising my serotonin.

On the way, I daydream about my life. Once I get the job, I'll invest in a new apartment.

I'll start looking at furniture catalogs and pick out rugs and throw blankets. How exciting. I'll get to stock and restock my pantry, and I'll go to the laundromat to change my sheets. How fun will that be? My dreams lead me to the tall barb-wire gates. I stand there, hopeful. I'm entering the premises without guilt for the first time in a very long time. Before pressing the buzzer, I look at the yard where Dr. Alec and I once sat, putting a few beers away and contemplating the kind of life I should lead.

It takes a second, but the gates open. I casually walk up to the doors that are conveniently unlocked. "Knock knock," I mumble jokingly to myself. Hopefully, someone will note the optimistic shift in my energy.

Dr. Barberry passes by and does a double take. "Lee!"

"Dr. Barberry, good to see you."

He notices my feminine tracksuit. "Are you due for a check-up? It hasn't been long since the last… Is everything okay?" His expression grows into clear disquietude.

"Nah. We're still on track with the timeline. Actually," I look up with a prideful smile, "I have a job interview tomorrow. I'm here to pick up a suit."

He puts his hands on his hips and huffs. "An interview? Wow, look at that. That's great to hear."

I angle my feet toward the direction of my pod. "Is everything as is? Or did you guys turn my pod into an exercise room?"

He laughs. "Not at all. Come on." We walk together down the hall, and the smell of the place infiltrates my nostalgia. I miss the days when Dr. Alec would carry me on his back to my pod. "Nice track-suit," Dr. Barberry says with sarcastic judgment.

He snaps me out of fond memories. "Huh?"

"Did you purchase it?"

"Are you asking if I stole?"

He sighs as he punches a new code into the system, opening the room. "I'm not even sure, Lee. Anyway, welcome back. I'll leave you to browse, and then you can meet me in the cafeteria. Sounds good?"

Whatever. I walk past him, taking in my former scent on the unwashed sheets. I sit on my bed first, watching the doors close to encase me in beautiful privacy. The lights turn on automatically, and the sterile shine casting on my walls makes me feel more like an experiment, so I hop on over to the touchpad to switch to warmer hues. I turn on ambient noise to make myself feel more at home even though there isn't much time. This pod is no longer my home, and these people are not really my family.

I slide my closet open, and the hangers shift a little, giving life to my skeletal collection of neutral business-casuals. My fingers select which material is finer, which button-down is of better quality, and whether a blazer should be paired with it. I choose a gray shirt. Best if I keep my apparel boring. I think I have already hit the unique factor, so going into my interview donning teal or lavender will cost more than amplify. In fact, it might just be too imposing, and I don't want to give an egotistical impression. Gray it is. A light gray button down, a gunmetal blue tie, socks to match the tie, and charcoal slacks. That should be good. I lay my clothes on the bed and picture myself wearing the outfit. "Hi. Thank you for taking the time to meet with me," I whisper in practice. I clear my voice and repeat the line over and over again, followed by an explanation of my previous experience with customer service and the reason for termination. "I had just received a promotion, but due to…" I can't find my excuse. How do I explain that I was so good it got me fired? That's such a prick thing to say! My nerves sharpen as I repeat myself until a knock interrupts me.

"Can I come in?" To my delight, Dr. Barberry's muffled inquiry travels as comfort.

Interviewing myself can appropriately be described as debilitating. Jesus, I'm so dramatic.

"Yes. Yeah," I say, wishing I had a cigarette in my hand.

The doors slide open once again, and Dr. Barberry enters without hesitation. Sometimes, he's more comfortable than he should be, but I believe he's just compensating for our last conversation. He absorbs the energy in the room. "You ready?"

"What do you think?" I shift to the side to let him make an opinion of my outfit.

"Nice choice. Did you need a garment bag, maybe?" He scratches the back of his head, unable to provide a real bias.

"Yeah, I was gonna ask."

"Yeah, I'll see if we have one…" Dr. Barberry doesn't follow up with another question.

I actually begin to worry that he might not have a garment bag for me to borrow. What will I do if my suit, God forbid, wrinkles? I picture myself putting my hands to my face like a damsel in distress, like a comical alien who hears no evil, sees no evil, and speaks no evil. "Barberry." I prepare myself to make a bold request.

"Yes, Lee?"

"Do you think I can stay the night here? I just don't want to mess up my suit or risk looking unkempt before the interview." Dr. Barberry sighs. I keep going. "We don't—we don't have to tell anyone. I'll leave early, in fact."

"Lee. I'd love to have you, but you know that's not part of the deal. I'm sorry. I like my job. I'd like to keep it." It's hard to understand why he likes his job if it has less to do with my well-being. "I'm sorry. You signed the papers."

I smirk. "It's fine."

"Would you want to eat something?"

My glutton prevails over my pride. "Okay." I swallow my hot blood as I walk behind him to the cafeteria.

A few other scientists notice me from the corner of my eye, but they don't really turn their heads to greet me. In fact, I think they're avoiding me. Maybe it's good that I'm not spending the night here. The morale would compromise my enthusiasm, and besides, it's a good feeling when you get things done independently.

Dr. Barberry and I collect two trays and get in line. He picks up a salad; I grab a side of Greek. I also grab some grilled chicken, a turkey sub, chips and guac, jello, and a brownie. Dr. Barberry looks over, letting his judgment linger all over my tray. His eyes speak of detestation as well as guilt. "Hungry?"

"Yup," I say in a dry tone.

Dr. Barberry scans his badge at the register. "Why don't you find a place for us to sit?"

I pick a secluded table by the large windows that give us a view of the vast field. A field which solemnly ends by the punctuation of a barbed fence. I glance at the woods in the background. I wonder if the sight of it ever served meaning to me when I was a little younger, but I cannot recall if it did, as I was too immersed in the efforts of becoming assimilated into society. "I brought you some juice. Maybe you need some sugar in your system."

And what if I just took the juice from his hand and just chucked it? Walk off as if he commented on my weight? "Thanks." I'm not too sure where that intrusive thought came from. I hold my breath to refrain from laughing at the thought because I don't want to explain myself.

First, I take a bite out of the brownie and then sip on cran-apple. The uncommon mix doesn't bother me. "I'm sorry," Dr. Barberry spits out again.

I swallow my food before speaking, careless of the sting of silence. "You're good. Richard's pretty adamant, isn't he?"

"Everyone is," Barberry admits, reinforcing my suspicions. "They don't like me, do they?" I can't help but feel embarrassed. "How does that make you feel?"

"Don't do that. Doesn't start evaluating me—"

"It's part of my job."

"Your job is to treat me like a human," my voice grows louder for emphasis.

"They do care for you, I care for you…" he let the words stain. "You're not just an opt inhabitant." Why does that hurt? "I just wanted to track your responses for your own good."

"Fair," I pick on my meal. I think I'm about to lose my appetite. "I know I haven't made this easy on you all."

"It's not your fault. You weren't always in the right hands."

"Dr. Alec was doing a fine job."

"Alec did what we warned him against."

I roll my eyes. "So we had a few beers. So what?"

Dr. Barberry sets his bite of dry lettuce down. "I meant that on other levels. You think we hate you, but it's a choice. Come on. We're glorified vets, for fucks sake. The bonds we choose are the ones we have to become responsible for. It's a dangerous game." He presses his lips together; his face is twisted with final.

"So what I'm getting here is you choose not to love me. Unlike Alec did."

"Yes and no."

I'm not sure if I need to hear more of this, so I take a break from the conversation to eat.

Many chews and swallows go by until I can form anything coherent. 'Yes and no.' The fuck does that mean? "Alec loves me, and I know that took a lot from him, which is probably why none of you have the guts to feel the same."

"You're right," Dr. Barberry tells me, but with a tone of surrender. He's given up on the conversation, maybe even the point, or us.

I shake my head. "Say something. Say something significant, Barberry," I push aggressively with only my words. My nostrils are open, my forearms are tense, but I'm in no mood to be violent. I think I'm just begging him. "Be someone in my life."

"That's enough. Alec needed you more than you needed him."

His words sink into my chest. I don't want to believe him because Dr. Alec is more complicated than the average person. I don't want to connect the dots of his past to render such a bullshit truth of reality and reduce him to something more two-dimensional than me. It would kill me. It would fucking kill me. "Okay," I whisper. In just a few seconds, I feel orphaned by the strike of Dr. Barberry's confession.

"How's the food?" He changes the conversation fast, putting our soulless dynamic in its place.

"You're not good at your job either, even if you're still employed."

I can tell I'm pressing his buttons, hitting his nerves, pushing him to the edge. "I used to be Dr. Alec's right hand and believed in his cause until he started experimenting with you. He risked your life, Lee. You were going to kill yourself."

"Jesus. Could you be more insensitive? That's not his fault!"

"His idea of saving you almost cost your life."

"Newsflash, Barberry! Everyone's idea of saving me is fucking costing me my life. Ask me how that makes me feel!" I take the juice and chuck it before storming out of the cafeteria.

Instead of requesting a fuckin' garment bag, I pick up my shit quickly to avoid any follow-up feedback on the lame interaction Dr. Barberry and I just exchanged. I'm obviously not concerned about how I'll make it through the night at this point, so when I leave, I don't look back.

I hurry to the station and catch my train. I slump into the overly used seat on the train and rest my eyes. I guess I'll catch up on sleep in intervals before the interview, even if it's just for an hour. By the time I arrive, the sun is high, burning my already burning eyes. The heat radiates through the window, and for some reason, it activates my hunger. The regret of abandoning my meal occupies me, but I grip my dignity tighter, and with that, I step off the train. My pretty suit in hand.

To my convenience, there's a park nearby, and I don't need to scope out places to rest because I've been there before. Mainly college students filter in and out of that particular block. I venture in the opposite direction to find myself some sustenance. There's a line of food carts serving cheap plates of meat and rice. How familiar.

I'm really in no position to spend the money I need for emergencies and train rides, so I politely approach a customer in line. I pray Richard doesn't hear about my attempts to unintentionally defame the agency by appearing as an abandoned beggar on the streets. "Excuse me, sir."

He looks up to locate the source of my voice within his small proximity, and once he looks down, he gives me a nauseatingly familiar reaction. His brows are raised, his lips are a little parted. "Oh my god. You're Lee!"

I nod, pursing my lips. At least we can skip the intro. "I'm so sorry to bother you. Can you spare me a few bucks to buy myself a meal?"

He's sorry. "Oh. Sure. Of course, I'll just purchase you a plate. Do you mind if I get a picture with you?" Is this a bargain?

"Sure," I shrug and shift near him. He neglects my body language and takes a quick selfie anyway.

"My wife's going to freak," he doesn't look at me. He looks at his phone to text his wife the picture. We then stand in awkward silence after he shoves his phone into his back pocket.

"Thank you, by the way."

"Oh sure, sure."

"I forgot my wallet. Can I pay you back?" It's an obvious lie, but it doesn't have to be a lie forever.

"It's my pleasure, and to actually meet you is really cool," he chuckles. "At my uni, there used to be protests against opt experimentation. Good people, really," he focuses on my hollowed features and adds in guilt, "I thought it was a cool discovery."

A woman in front of us turns around like it's her cue. She gasps. I wave casually, making it known that I'm used to the attention. She laughs, "I thought it was some D-lister celebrity behind me. I didn't know it was Lee, the alien!"

My face squirms with discomfort. "Yeah."

She catches my drift and lowers her voice. "Sorry," she whispers. "I'm sure you're tired of all the attention." She also checks to see if anyone notices. I find that women are kinder.

"The attention comes and goes, " I fabricate a laugh. "Did you also want a picture?"

"Oh no, it's okay. You look hungry," she smiles. "Best you worry about what you're gonna have for lunch than a few annoying fans," she giggles. "Nice to meet you!"

I grin at her politeness and scoot up the line. When the man places his order, he asks for two plates instead of one. "Need a drink?"

"Water's fine, thank you."

He plunges his hand into a cooler full of drinks and melted ice and tosses the water to me. "There ya go." The dude working in the food truck wraps our plates in tinfoil. "Would you like to eat lunch with us?"

"Actually, I kind of have to go back to the agency to retrieve my wallet," I lie again, but I do it effortlessly this time.

"Okay," he chirps. "Nice meeting you, Lee!"

"Nice meeting you," I stretch my hand out for him to shake it. "Brad."

"Brad," I smile. "Take care. And thank you again."

I remove myself from the public's line of sight and find an open patio of a coffee shop.

The first thing I do is chug my water, and then I rip off the foil. As much as I try, ridding myself of the idea that Dr. Barberry was pushing about Dr. Alec isn't an easy feat. Does he really need me more than I need him? How unfair is it to be paired with someone who isn't as genuine as I believed? That's kind of what it's like with kids who realize their parents aren't heroes. Their parents are actually people who weren't ready to have kids. It's weird to think that I served as a replacement for certain connections Dr. Alec lost throughout his life, but at the end of the day, he's a better man than me, I suppose. At the end of the day, he's a man, and I'm not.

My whole life, I've been as bitter as the people who've spent their lives working or, better yet, spent their lives working in the city.

That's the vibe I give. I don't feel much, but I judge a whole lot. In my head, I think you need to fuel emotion with logic. Feelings make more sense once you source them. Dr. Alec is someone grander than the people who choose to reduce him. He knows that himself, and I'm sure he's aware of his weaknesses as well. My food tastes better when I think more positively. I look up and enjoy the view of passersby.

At the end of my meal, I walk the bloating off, letting the hours die because I can't find a better way to kill them. How much more can I prepare for the interview? I realize that I did not bring any paper-work with me other than my laminated card. I guess when—not if—I get the job, I'll bring in legal documents regarding my ability to work. My stroll takes me to the park.

There's plenty of sunlight to keep me warm. I lay by a tree. It's actually quite serene. People graze the vast park, and trailing behind them is their echoing laughter. It's obvious that today is better than most. The window of time left for me to find an actual spot to rest is getting smaller, but it doesn't stop me from getting shut-eye…

I wake up, and the first thing I look for is my suit, which thankfully isn't missing. It's propped up against the tree. "Shit," I look up to clock the sun. I think we're at seven a.m.

I race to the gym for a quick shower as I only have a few hours left. On the way there, I dodge the early crowds and j-walk when I can. Upon arrival, I push open the door and fly up the stairs. "Felicia," I wave at her and press my palms into my knees to catch my breath.

She looks up from the computer with confusion. "Oh hey!"

"Hey," I say back, still breathless.

"Everything okay?" She gets up from her seat. "Yeah," I point down the hall. "I need to shower."

"Okay. You left your soap. I'll go get it."

I walk behind her to the storage room. She grabs the used bottle and tosses it to me. "Thanks. I have an interview."

I don't wait for her response; I scram to the showers. "Good luck!" She says. I smile at her well wishes as I enter the locker room to drop off my suit.

In the shower, I rub the soap into my crevices. When the water rinses off all the suds, I turn the faucet off and let myself drip dry for several minutes. Instead of ultimately waiting out the progress of evaporation, I repurpose my old clothes into a towel and dry myself off productively. Oh fuck… I forgot my loafers. Fuck me.

I know there isn't a chance Felicia will have a lost pair in storage, so my only option is the raggedy pair I've been wearing. I put them on halfway to avoid stepping on the dirty bathroom floors and make my way into the locker room.

I jump into the suit pants first. It takes a few frustrating tries to get the fucking buttons of my shirt to align. Then comes the tie. I'm wearing this with sneakers, I mean, for fucks sake. I look like a douchebag or a big-time director… This would only pass on the red carpet—in theory. I see myself in the mirror with complete dis-appointment and slap my thighs with as much force as possible. Before my anger further transpires, I take a few breaths and begin practicing my interview.

Hi, Lee. I say in my head.

"Hi, Thomas," I reply to myself with the name signed at the bottom of the email.

Thank you for coming in. What experience do you have with tax preparation?

"Well. I have done my taxes recently and was referred to you by Virginia, an HR manager at my former job. While I do not have experience in the particular field, I make up for it by being a fast learner and have great attention to detail." I read online that that's how you're supposed to respond when you lack bullshit experience.

It says on your resume that you worked in customer service. What made you leave?

"Unfortunately, I was terminated. It seems I was not the best fit, but it was not due to my work ethic. I earned a promotion before being terminated, actually." Should I elaborate further? I give myself a few more seconds to get used to my elevated heartbeat. "You're a bad bitch," I say to myself and turn around to see a middle-aged man staring at me from behind. "Oh my god," I let out a dry chuckle.

"I read about you! They told us you'd be in from time to time. I didn't think I'd be lucky enough to run into you!"

"Hi," I grin. "It's nice to meet you." I step forward to shake his hand. "Sorry, you had to catch that interaction. I have an interview."

"Wow. Impressive." Is it? "Thank you."

"Well. I won't take up any more of your time. Hope to see you again."

"Hope to see you again," I walk past him with my clothes balled up in my hands.

I hurry to Felicia. Luckily, she's not dealing with anyone. "Hey," I go behind her desk and crouch to hide from members.

"Hey," she looks down at me, still confused. "Everything okay?"

I smile at her kindness. "Yeah, everything's fine. Is it okay if I leave this with you?" I hold up the dirty clothes.

"Yeah. Do you want me to wash them?"

"No, you don't have to do that. I don't want to trouble you anymore."

"It's fine. My boss was just saying that you can use the facilities. Just try to use the gym too," she scrunches her face as she makes the request. "Sorry. It's part of the deal. Brings in more customers."

"Oh, I totally get that," I wave off her apology. "Don't worry, I'll be in. I actually just met someone in the locker room. He's real nice."

"Okay, good, good. When's your interview?"

I look up at her computer to check the time. An hour has already passed. "It's at ten thirty. Not too far from here. Just have to take the subway."

"You nervous?"

I look up at her. "Can you tell?"

Felicia spots someone coming to the desk. "Hide." I duck and wait. "Okay, you're good."

"Thanks," I pop up a few inches. There's a moment of silence to remember what we were discussing. "Oh yeah! Yeah, I guess I'm nervous. I'm also excited too. I have a feeling I'll land it."

"I hope you're right," she smiles earnestly. I tap her desk, "I should get going."

"Yeah," she resumes her work.

"Thank you again for everything."

"Hurry. Before anyone else sees you."

I gracefully slip out. "Wait!" Felicia listens to my command by turning her head. I point to my shoes. "Obnoxious?"

She purses her lips. "It's not noticeable," Not noticeable, among other things, I presume.

I twist my fingers to form half of a heart. "Thanks, girl," and then I dash to the station. I look forward to the temperature change as I leave the gym. The cool wind prevents excessive perspiration. I don't want to stink. Just in case, though, I smell my pits— nothing. Good enough for me.

It takes about an hour, but we get to my stop on time. I carry myself with the crowd instead of pushing through, and once the flood of people disperses at the station, I find my path upstairs. The city smells different over here. It smells like trash and fried food from a short distance. I'm definitely hungry again. Luckily, my soon-to-be job is just around the corner, so I pause for a moment, using my predatory instincts to smell the source of such aromas. I've gotten used to identifying trash as food, even if it does disgust me deep down. My scanning comes to a halt when I notice a diner halfway down the block. The place boasts a bright red awning with a neon sign hanging from it that claims it is open.

I assume the fried scent I'm getting a hint of is home fries, a breakfast delicacy in this godforsaken country. I take a step in the direction of the diner but stop myself, shaking my head. If I don't focus now, all the joy I'm aching for will go to waste. Now's also not a good time to be poetic. I continue towards the office. Heads turn, but the energy I radiate protects me from being approached. This must be some kind of power people profit off of by writing about it several times as a "law" and then publishing it at some local bookstore.

When I reach the office, I find that it is a thin building squished between other buildings. The window of the door is smudged, but I can read the sign. The tax preparation office is on the second floor. I open the heavy door, and without making much noise, I lightly move towards the elevator. When the doors open, it dings, jump-starting my heart. I hope there's no one in there.

Luck favors me as the doors reveal a barren and creaking box. I push the button and let my brain fry into numbness because I am about to change my destiny, and there's not much left to revise regarding how I expect the interview to pan out. I pick the skin on my thumbs that protrude like thorns.

No one notices the habit, not even Dr. Alec, which surprises me because it is an obvious indication of anxiety. I suppose there are other indicators of anxiety, such as my meltdowns, panic attacks, and excessive drinking—that one night. Yeah, there's plenty of evidence.

I bite the dead skin off quickly while the doors open to an empty hallway that's painted baby blue. The carpets are dark blue, but I can still see the coffee stains that trail to the office door. Someone must have been rushing, but I can't imagine why.

I follow the stains to the door and peer inside. I can only see a receptionist who is busy on his computer. Carefully, I open the door, and the receptionist looks up. The muscles around his eyes loosen as he adjusts from the brightness of the computer to the image of an alien in a suit. Baffled, he gasps. "Oh my gosh," he walks around his desk. "You must be Lee."

"No, I'm Ryan…" I let the joke sink in. Clearly, it was a miss.

Confused, he laughs awkwardly at my joke. "Very funny. Did you want water while you wait?"

I let the embarrassment wash over me quickly and snap back into the conversation. "I'm okay, thank you." There's an old loveseat and a mismatched coffee table covered in napkins and magazines.

"Okay, great! I'll grab Thomas. Please take a seat anywhere." I'm tempted to make another joke about the seating, as I don't have many options.

Before I can sit down, Thomas pokes out of the office. "Lee!" His voice storms through the office. I turn and look up to meet my new boss's hazel and tired eyes. He already stretches out his hand and walks to me. "Pleasure to meet you."

We shake hands. "Likewise. Thank you for taking the time to meet with me," I smile weakly at the brawny man. He doesn't look mean, but he certainly doesn't look sympathetic either. His face is droopy, and his build is quite large. A tall man. Tall men tend to be less sympathetic, based on my experience.

"Of course. Come on into my office. Did Marcel offer you water?"

"Yes, he did. Thank you," my gratitude emerges timidly. Clearly, he's an overpowering guy, but it's hard to believe he enjoys his authority, given that it's over employees who do people's fucking taxes. He's just Mel with perhaps a bigger penis.

"Good," he opens his office door. The room is warmer than the rest of the office, which makes me feel comforted, oddly enough. He doesn't have much, just a desk and a swivel chair—the same kind at my old job, surprisingly. He plops down and types on his computer. I notice how thin Thomas's hair is under the blaring, bluish fluorescent lighting. "I'm just going through your resume." He looks up with agitation. "Sorry. I should have had Marcel grab you a chair. This won't take long, though." He hums as he reads through. "Interesting that you have to attach paperwork with the resume."

Where is my mind? I forgot that I sent them via email. At least I don't have to bring a physical copy. "I do have my government-issued card, though. Would you like to take a look?"

"Just out of curiosity, sure. I get the gist of all this. You're basically approved to work and withstand work-related environments... Let me see the card. What is it?"

I pull the card from my pocket and hand it to him. "It's a confirmation of safety regulations."

He reads it over and grunts. "So, did all other employers turn you down?"

"Well—"

"I can't imagine why this job would be your first pick."

"I was referred to this position by someone." I'm unsure about mentioning Virginia as my former HR manager.

"Are you interested in taxes?"

"Yes. I believe it is a good career to pursue, and I have experience filing my taxes."

"Okay, nice. I have to be honest, I am skeptical about hiring you. You are certainly considered a citizen, but I fear we are going against the grain. I hope you understand. You haven't had a job for some time, and I assume you need one, so I assume you've interviewed elsewhere and have been rejected, which leads me to believe that it is unwise to hire you." The room falls silent, and we sit for a moment while Thomas's gaze lingers on my features.

"It is true," I swallow, "that I applied to other jobs, and I cannot give you a solid reason why I was turned away. Maybe it reflected poorly on the businesses I was applying to, but I excelled at my previous job. I can tell you this: the company I worked for was simple, but ever since I joined, it has received a lot of attention. Eventually, that attention shifted to focus on the business and what they are selling. I would imagine that it would be the same if I were to be an employee here." I sit back in my seat after placing a hefty declaration before him without factual evidence.

He purses his lips. "Not bad." He sighs and looks at the computer screen. "You didn't list references."

"I can provide them if you'd like."

"I'll find them myself," he raises his hand.

Oh god, what if he speaks with Mel instead of Virginia? Regardless of where we stand, I know Virginia wouldn't say anything bad about me. "I should also disclose…"

His eyes aggressively flashback to me. I wonder if he's already made his decision based on his awful demeanor. "Yes?"

"I was terminated from my position, but you can certainly speak to my employer and HR about the details. I would like to elaborate on why if you find it necessary."

"Yeah," he scoffs, "please elaborate."

His behavior begins to tick me off because underneath that forced bravado is a squirmy fuckin' nerd who makes a five-figure salary.

"I was promoted before I was fired. When other employees found out about my promotion, there was some tension in the office, which my boss couldn't handle. I suppose my coworkers couldn't fathom that a test-subject alien could do better and get paid more than them," I smirk.

Thomas squints. "Interesting."

"You are welcome to contact my boss. I can provide you information—"

"That won't be necessary. Tell me about yourself. Have you been disciplined by the company or by the agency in the workplace?"

"No, sir. Never." I can't even revisit that one time.

"So, why the chips?"

"I think it's just protocol. They were not implanted after an incident, as I have no history of violence. It's just to give people relief."

"So, you're aware people look at you differently?"

"Inevitably."

"Hm. How do you handle those situations?"

"With grace, I imagine. I try to take pleasure in the endless, inane exclamations like, 'You're Lee!' or, 'Can I get a picture with you?' 'Can you take a picture with my friend?'"

"And you're saying that attention benefited the last company you worked at."

"I believe so, yes." Not sure if that's true.

"Okay. Do you have hobbies?"

"I…" Can't think of anything. Come to think of it, I don't partake in many hobbies. "I like to read. I studied sociology for a brief period, and I recently joined the gym. I also journal," against my will.

"Nice. You seem interestingly well-rounded," he says in a tone that seems halfheartedly sarcastic.

"Thank you."

He clicks away on his computer a few times, and I can tell, based on the light reflecting onto his face, that he's turned it off. "Well. Thank you for your time, Lee." He doesn't get up to shake my hand, and I'm unsure whether the conversation has ended.

"Thank you again for taking the time to meet with me. Do you have any more questions?"

"No. Do you?"

I've read somewhere that it's good to have questions prepared for an interview, but since I have a strong hunch that this was not a successful interview, I decide against following up with any more curiosity. "No, sir."

"Cool. Bye now."

Bye, I guess? "Looking forward to hearing from you, Thomas." I look at him one more time, and he's already occupied with his phone. I purse my lips and see myself out.

With the tip of his finger mischievously in his mouth, Marcel looks at me. His swivel chair is near the end of the desk. It's as though he was eavesdropping. "Thank you, Marcel," I say graciously.

"Have a great rest of your afternoon," he nasally wishes me. I do a double take to see if he's got a bitchy look on his face because I'm fucking confused. Did I interview at a cutthroat fashion magazine company? To avoid somewhat of an awkward exit, I make up a question. "Do you know how long it takes for people to hear back?"

Marcel's mouth is open, but no words come out—just a strange noise. "Ummm, I'm not sure," his tone descending apologetically, implying rejection.

"Okay," I say softly.

"Usually, employees are hired on the spot," he burns me. "Okay," I say again.

"I mean," he pops gum and chews violently, "maybe it'll take a day to consider because your case is a little different. Your experience doesn't really matter because you're interviewing for an internship, right? I mean, like," he rolls his eyes, "I ran an Etsy shop before this."

"Right. So, should I give it a day or two?" I ask, displaying my fragility and desperation. "Correct."

"Thank you, Marcel."

"Hope you get the job," he winks. I think Marcel's not a cunt, he's just cunty. I leave the office and take the stairs instead to get myself out of the building faster. When I push open the heavy door, the reality kicks in: Marcel's not calling the shots. He was nice, and he gave me some momentary hope, but let's face it, Mel 2.0 didn't fancy me all too much.

I don't know what I'm going to say to Dr. Barberry, and I don't know how much longer I can remain homeless. It's really kicking my ass. My skin's begun to peel, and I can't tell if it's from dehydration or excessive sun exposure. To ease myself from the panic in my chest, I decide to eat at the diner with the red awning. Food will comfort me.

I walk briskly, investing the remainder of my hopes into the possibility of finding a hot meal resting at the top of the dumpster. Maybe there's a box of pancakes, strawberry pancakes. Strawberry pancakes with strawberry syrup saturating the pancakes. I have faith that there's space for seasoned potatoes in the box. I can practically taste the salt and feel the heat of black pepper down my throat. I hope there are eggs in there, too.

When I get there, I see half of a smoked cigarette on the ground. I pick it up like a crow with silver and carefully place it in my pocket, ensuring it doesn't spill loose tobacco. I check my surroundings by cartoonishly looking left and right. No one is around to take note of IRAAB's extraterrestrial climbing into a dumpster. I apply the same method. Propping my leg on the outline of the dumpster, letting the bottom of my shoe collect friction. Then, I hoist myself over.

I realize I am jeopardizing the well-being of my suit. What does it matter? I first take inventory of the colors of trash. I look for white, as many takeout and to-go bags are that translucent color. Nothing. I roll up my sleeves and get to unpaid work, sifting through mounds of shit-smelling garbage. I find nothing on the first level. I employ my legs and kick around trash. Nothing again. "Fuck!" I let out and look up. "Why?"

Aggressively, I climb out of the dumpster and fall into a crouched position. I see someone in my peripherals, a red-eyed homeless man. He's baffled and unable to stand still. His eyes are bloodshot, and he looks threatening because I think I look enigmatically threatening to him. I look away to prove submission, and after a minute, I forget he's there.

I wipe my snot and pick out the cigarette. The homeless guy is still watching me, coming closer. "You got a lighter?" I ask, sniffling.

I look away, subservient again. Then, a blaring noise hits me from my left. "Fuck did you say to me?" Instinctively, I cringe at the noise and look at the man barking at me. His spit hangs at the bottom of his cracked lips. He takes a step closer, his eyes adjusting in a way that makes me assume that he's probably on drugs. "Go back!" I shift away from him on command, but he still rocks forward.

The cigarette slips from my trembling hand. "Dude, I think you have me mistaken for someone else." He grabs me by the collar of my suit, forcing me near his face. I smell the alcohol and tooth decay, but it doesn't affect my gag reflex. "I'm sorry," I look away.

"This is where *I* live! This is mine! This is me," his aimless slurring projects through the alley. I hope we're in someone's earshot. "Go back!"

"Let me go first!" I've never been in a fight before. I don't know how to go about one. To not let surveillance be notified, I keep myself calm. I don't want to get my ass beat and then also seize. Temperamentally, he pulls on the skin of my eyelid. God knows I want to push him away, but I defensively close my eyes instead. I think of other things to regulate my heart rate. His finger continues to prod until he takes me by the neck and rams my body against the dumpster. "Please," I beg. How is it Virginia made me seize and not him?

His lips tighten. "Disgusting." He punches me in the gut while his hand is still on my neck. I'm winded, and I can't keep my composure any longer. I wonder if I can push through the seizing to fight him back. He punches me again and then moves back. I fall to the ground in a fetal position, clutching my stomach. The ache of hunger could never compare. The derelict backs away. He watches me for a few minutes but not carefully. He paces up and down to tend to various noises, some potentially in his head, and then circles back. This ritual goes on until official disinterest and my adrenaline subsides—the natural pain blooms. I have no strength to get up, so I lay there with a few involuntary tears. From an unusual angle, I watch the homeless man wander off.

I have made my decision. I need him.

CHAPTER 11

THE SALIVA

I know the surgery is over and done with when I feel my first pain. It is sharp, and it is a jab in my abdomen. At first, I assumed my vital chips had been replaced, but that would mean IRAAB was aware of my legal negligence. To avoid excess worry, I focus on the present. My eyes flutter open, lacking the strength to transition smoothly into functionality. I'm lying on the concrete floor in the robe used for my lengthy operation. I can hear garbage trucks collecting trash from dumpsters. I wince at the awful reminder of dumpsters, but I wince more at the pain.

Everything outside is very loud to my sensitive ears. I move my eyes around to locate any source of light. Every bulb is off, just natural light from the small windows installed above. I use the cast of light to locate Dr. Alec and that other foreign surgeon, but no one is here. "Hello," I barely let out any noise.

At some point, I have to help myself, and while it seems quite cruel to be abandoned in this state, this is a cautionary tale. If Dr. Alec evacuated the scene, it was for good reason. And at the end of the day, you must put your oxygen mask on first, right?

I let myself rest and recall the night that led me here. On the day of the assault, I committed to the surgery. I need Dr. Alec in my life. He's the only one who's ever looked at me right. I don't think I could live without him. Days after the assault, I took a late train to the location Dr. Alec wrote about in his small note. Waited for what seemed to be hours. The street leading to the warehouse had post lamps, but nothing was lit at the location. I could only spot the outline of the large building in the distance, as it was darker than the city sky. The warehouse wasn't in the city, just near it. The area felt rural, a place where you'd expect to witness UFO sightings or some shit. Maybe my advanced cousins will stop by to check on me.

As I neared the warehouse, misery shook my bones because, upon evaluating, my shitty life led me to a point where I needed an illegal operation done to free myself from technicalities and scientific fetters. If I died on the table, I wanted everyone to know that it wasn't Dr. Alec's fault. The ones to blame are the ones who decide my fate. I blamed God, too, but I also looked into the night with prayer. Everything was quiet. I could only hear crickets in the distance.

By two, I saw the lights turn on, but when I knocked on the garage door, no one answered within the first five or so minutes. I tried not to worry because Dr. Alec would never ditch me. By the fifth minute, a door opened at the end of the building. I identified Alec Masklig's tall silhouette. He waved me in, and I rushed to greet him with a hug that was so instant, I didn't even give myself time to premeditate it. As if it were instinctual, I buried my head in his chest. He rested his chin on my crown. "I have no words," he whispered gently.

"Thank you," I squeezed him tighter. My fears dissipated, and for a second, I was transported to a time when I'd be the subject of his routine, and we were wandering the halls of a facility only his presence could paint colorful. He let me go first, and I looked at him. "Will it hurt?"

"I'll be gentle," he joked. He pushed the door open, and the gray light from inside flooded the grass. "Come inside, I'd like you to meet someone."

Dr. Alec held my hand. The capacious concrete warehouse wasn't entirely lit. Just a section of it glowed. Under the light, I saw a surgical table. I saw a reasonably old man with white hair only at the sides of his head. He was setting up the table in surgical apparel. "Doctor," Dr. Alec called out. The older man responded by turning to the sound of Dr. Alec's demanding tone. I saw then that the doctor had a mask on already. "This is Lee."

"Hello," I meekly greeted him.

"Pleasure," he waved and then addressed Dr. Alec, "all is a go."

Dr. Alec used his hand as a partition between himself and the surgeon. "He's a man of few words."

I wanted to ask if the doctor whose hands I was putting my body and fate in was qualified, but Dr. Alec's judgment didn't need to be questioned. Also, I was sure he wouldn't want to be questioned. I pondered more about Dr. Alec's fragility. "I see," I looked up at Dr. Alec wide-eyed.

"It's going to be okay," Dr. Alec said. "I promise."

"Alec, what's going to happen?" The doctor resumed setting up while I waited for Dr. Alec to answer my question.

"We'll put you under, extract your tracking chip, and replace your seizing chips. It's a very one-two-three process; shouldn't be a problem." He pointed to a computer on a small desk in the corner of that area. "I'll log into the security system to override any complication and ensure that tracking is not interrupted."

"What if it is? What if it glitches?"

"I wouldn't take that risk."

"Then why surveil?"

"Just in case."

"But—"

"Would you rather I not?"

"I'd rather know there's no need to."

"There's no pressure. This is your decision." Tocuhè, but I couldn't bring myself to agree entirely with him. Dr. Alec didn't wait for my reply. He retrieved a robe for me to dawn in preparation. I took it from him as an act of acceptance because I had made this decision on my own. When I was looking at his face, I remembered how much I yearned for his existence in my life. Without Dr. Alec, I would fail eventually. This truth brought me solace more than disappointment within myself as I realized, after getting my ass handed to me, that I couldn't venture alone toward freedom within Project O.H.I.

"I'm going to wake up, right?"

"You're insulting me," the doctor intruded. We looked back at him. "Are you ready?" Dr. Alec put his hand on my shoulder. "It'll be okay," he affirmed tenderly.

I put my hand on his hand. "I'm ready."

…Retrieving myself from the memory, I twist my head too fast to look for the microchip, and then my body twists internally with horrible agony. "Fuck," I groan, letting my pain echo through the warehouse. I can feel the sutures—each of them. The pain equates to stabbing, and thank goodness they put me under because IRAAB would have easily assumed the worst had they read my vitals. Instead of moving my head around like a screwball, I employ my wrists and inch my hands around to detect the object. I only come in contact with the cool concrete. My heart rate quickens for a moment. Would Dr. Alec seriously fucking forget to give me the chip? "Help." I let out one more time. "Dr. Alec?"

With my last attempt at seeking aid that I cannot give myself, my incapacitated body becomes one with the hollow building. I wiggle my limbs to ensure I am still functioning. It worries me that the physical cost of the surgery is as expensive as it is, and without warning, I consented. Am I stupid—or worse, naive?

I reflect more throughout the hours I spend in recovery. I think about things that induce epiphanies I can later journal about as long as I place them under a different context. Maybe when I journal, I will describe homelessness to get a rise out of Richard. I deliberate whether I should have mentioned Dr. Alec's former relationship with Richard. It might have been distasteful, but I'd like to know more about the CEO.

More likely than not, Dr. Alec would have given me a halfhearted confirmation that Richard's intentions are purely geared toward scientific discovery. Yet the people seated at the conference tables know his attempts to bridge the gap between terrestrial and beyond is a limited portrayal of projection. I remember his name would be spoken of only in whispers. I think the board refused to mix corporate jargon into Project O.H.I. The legalities of the whole experiment are already draining enough. Discretions and lack of disclosure were oftentimes a piece of cake to detect, like the doctor who operated on me. The fact that I never saw his face or learned his name means his identity was intentionally hidden. This isn't something they kept me from figuring out. I think the doctor wanted me to know that I would never know him. I think his accent might be Russian. I don't want to be ignorant, but I think he's not from around here.

I want so badly to sleep, but knowing it isn't safe to remain here forces me to expedite things. I grit my teeth and lift my head again. My limp weight depends on shoulders that press into the concrete. I push myself higher, letting my muscles get used to the pain. The jabbing sensation hurts more when you forget to expect it, so I let my body adjust. Eventually, I am sitting up, and the blood in me plummets, leaving me in cold sweats. My head especially endures dull but heavy throbbing, and I can feel sweat on my scalp. I feel myself dropping consciousness like a plane unintentionally descending. Everything around me loses color, and I see black spots. My cheeks flush for a second.

I hold myself in this position to stabilize my body, but it takes too long, so I shift around to get myself on my knees. When I do, I hear something small drop. The hopefulness in me assumes it's the chip.

I was right! There it lay, like a gem of mined labor. It's black and silver and has a little blood on it. I shove it in my pocket. I know that I will compulsively check this pocket throughout the day. From sitting on my knees, I get myself to crawl on all fours, moving forward in grunts. I see my jumbled suit, too, and cling to it. It was fair of Dr. Alec to remove the robe as it would serve as unsanitary evidence. But he could have dressed me, at least.

I focus on the natural light ahead as a point of direction, and eventually, I see the door. I swat my hand until it lands on the metal knob and shift my weight so that I can safely use the knob to hoist myself up. My breathing suffers, so I deepen my intake, filling my lungs with air. I figure the more oxygen pumping, the less likely I'll pass out. I don't see black spots anymore, but I can tell my face has lost its adorable pinkish shade. I'm not sure where to go, but I have to get back to the city.

When I leave the warehouse for good, the morning air slaps me with a temperature that gives me no choice but to appreciate what I have inside the building. I crave going back and sleeping the day away. I'm desperate for rest, and I can't fathom the "triathlon" of walking all the way to the train, boarding it, and finding a safe place to sleep in the city. It's too much.

I hear a vehicle come around the back lot and turn to see a rickety old pickup truck kicking up dirt as it flies down the road. I don't consider any threat. I stretch out my arm as high as my sutures allow and wave delicately to get the driver's attention. The driver sees me. I know this because he breaks abruptly.

When the driver pulls up, his window is already down. I can practically smell the coffee nested in his cup holder. The blonde bearded driver wears a neon vest, cheap sunglasses, and a hard hat. He hasn't decided on either speaking or carefully driving away, so I just break the ice before it's too late. "Hi. I'm Lee. I'm a product of the International Research Administration of Animalia Biotechnology. Here is my card if you have any concerns," I pull out the card from my jacket. Now realizing that I am in the nude, I ball up my clothes to cover my privates. While I cannot see his eyes, I can tell his guard is up from the visible tension spreading through his upper body. He grips the steering wheel. "Here," I carefully hand him the card. It's fair of him to be suspicious. As he reads the card, I slip into my long sleeve to hide any surgical scars and jump into my pants without underwear.

"Hm," he skims the card. "Do you need something from me? Cuz I got a job to get to, and I really don't like to participate in anything… political. Don't get me wrong, I believe you're real. No Republican can deny that—well, some do, but I—I just don't want to participate," he stammers. He hands the card back to me apologetically.

I calibrate. "It's not a political gesture at all, sir. No one here but me. I just need a ride. I had a rough night, and I'm homeless…" I need the pity.

The man scratches his beard. He glances at the empty passenger seat and then the rearview mirror. "Guess you can." Before he changes his mind, I hurry to the other side of the pickup, but I don't run. I can't run.

"Thank you," I enjoy the heated air blasting on my face and feet. "Mind the temperature?"

"Not at all."

We drive momentarily in silence, and I respect it. "I can get you midtown. Is that okay?" The driver officially bars me from even considering Dr. Alec's place.

"That's completely fine."

"I've never spoken to your kind before. Took my daughter to the zoo the other day. They got a bunch of you there," he taunts me, but I assume this is unintentional.

"Hm," I carelessly grunt.

The driver increases his speed as we take up the highway. "Sorry, I didn't mean to insult you."

"It's okay."

"You got a family or something?"

"I was raised at the facility," I say, resting my head against the seat. "Is it okay if I close my eyes?"

"Hungover?" He asks in a friendly tone. My eyes pop open. "No. No. Just tired."

"Are you sick or something? Because man, I don't think I should—"

I chuckle at his unintelligent innocence. "No, it's not that. I think I ate something spoiled, and it's just kicking my ass." I hope he doesn't ask me why I was naked.

"Okay," the driver carefully switches to the left lane to hurry, giving me less time to decide where I should lay myself. I weigh my options. It's unsafe in my condition to wander alone.

"Do you think you can drop me somewhere specific? It's on the outskirts of the city, so you won't have to travel inward."

"I guess."

I ask the man to drop me at my gym, and he courteously agrees. I wish I could give him something in return because for him to overlook his beliefs and concerns and help me is more than what most strangers have done.

We get closer to my destination in comfortable silence. The man doesn't ask for a picture, and I don't ask for his name. He just pulls up to the building and waits for me to exit, "Thank you again," I say as I rely on my arms to support my descent from his truck.

"Yep," he musters. He gets one more look at me and nods. I shut his door with as much force as possible and enter the building.

Coming downstairs was the manager of the gym. We lock eyes, and his face lights up for a brief moment. "Lee! You're finally here to work out?" Blake cocks his head to the side as he notices my wrinkled suit.

"Um…"

"How'd the interview go? Felicia told me."

"Oh. It went well," my tone hikes an octave. I feel sudden discomfort between us and wish that it was Felicia that I bumped into rather than him.

"So… do you plan on joining us today or?"

"Actually, I'm not feeling well. I just stopped by to say 'hi' to Felicia if that's okay." I can't think of another excuse fast enough, but I suppose paying her a visit wouldn't be the worst thing.

I step to the side to reluctantly climb the stairs, but he gets in my way. "I'm sorry, Lee. Unless you're here to work out, I cannot allow you to use our facilities or request aid, which is something that we are not required to provide in the first place. We do it out of courtesy."

I'm in no mood to give head, but I can't lose my membership. "I'm so sorry. I was actually here to see if there are any pilates classes available in the mornings or early evenings. I'm trying to plan my schedule. Again, I apologize. I'm very grateful for how generous you both have been and am aware of the terms that I need to fulfill," my spiel seems to butter him up a bit.

"Thank you for that," he straightens. "When do you think you could stop by again?"

Fuuuuuck. How long will it take to recover? "I'm waiting to hear back from my job first to implement a steady routine. Is that okay?"

He frowns but accepts. "Well, we do offer classes in the mornings, but the evening ones fill up fast early in the week. Just shoot me an email beforehand. That way, I can update our site."

"Yeah. For sure," I nod. "Cool."

"Okay, well. I'll see you soon," a sharp pang suddenly shoots through the back of my neck, where one of my tracking chips has been replaced.

He turns around and steps up onto the staircase. "If I don't, I'll have to revoke your membership. Hope you understand," he jogs up and away.

"I understand. Thank you!" I holler, hoping my confirmation reaches him. I bite the skin of my thumb. Where do I go from here?

The one who physically assaulted me is my closest option… I know I'm so screwed. I can't think of any place other than a homeless shelter. But that will strike terrible publicity.

She's a subway ride from here.

My body suffers exertion as I accumulate distance from the gym. At the station, since I no longer have it in me to stand, I prop myself against a pillar. It's hard to ignore the pungent smell of piss. I let the crowds invade first because it is difficult to twist and contort to get through the clusters of people only to find an uncomfortable seat. I rest my head against the closed door and hold on to the pole with an arm that can barely extend. My eyes flutter as they are unable to consume the bright lights above.

I plant my feet and use only the muscles in my hand that grip the pole to stabilize myself when the subway picks up speed. The occasional rattling of the cart causes the operated parts of my body to implode, and I feel like I'm going to throw up. I lose my balance. My feet try to find a stance that can save me from falling, but I continue to stumble in the small corner. I can't figure out where I will land next, so I throw myself onto another pole and hold on tightly.

Of course, passengers observe my drunken behavior but do not vocalize their concerns. I wait until my stop arrives and desperately flee the cart. My prayers trail behind me while I rush up and out of the station to locate Virginia's building. I'm praying for her to take me in. I'm just praying for any kind of mercy.

Virginia's building still has a security guard. She'll have to hear from me first, compromising the element of surprise. I press the pad and request entrance by stating Virginia's full name. When I enter, the dude at reception is shocked to see me. He rubs his eyes like a cartoon would and then blows a gust of air. "No freakin way."

"Hi," I act like I didn't notice his excitement.

"Wow," the young guy shakes his head with continued elation. "No one is going to believe me," he mumbles to himself as he punches a code into the front desk phone. "Hi, Ms. Byrne. A gentleman by the name of Lee," he looks up at me and winks, "is here to see you." He waits for a reply with his mouth open. "Okay, great!" He hangs up the phone and points to the elevators. She *answered*. She *allowed* me.

"Thanks," I spin.

"Oh wait!" He holds up a sign-in clipboard. "Autograph."

I sign the clipboard with limp and careless fingers and leave the pen on the board, which fucking rolls off the thing, and of course, instinctively, I bend to catch it. The stabbing sensation returns. "Shit!" I exclaim. The guy looks at me with terror. Must be weird to see an alien yell profanities out of nowhere. "Sorry," I breathe out, clutching to my abdomen.

It's hard to fix my posture at this point, so I proceed with a hunch. I can basically feel my eyes roll out of my head. My face feels flushed again. I press the button several times like it's an emergency and escape into the elevator to fall on the floor. In a fetal position, I lay, looking up at the camera that's watching me back. I carefully stick out my arm to avoid any stretching and press four. The elevator gives me little time to recuperate. I think I really am going to pass out this time. I can't get myself to get up.

I try to collect my thoughts by retracing my well-being since I've woken up. I thought I was okay. I was fine in the man's car. My pain was present but manageable at the gym. Do sudden movements really compromise my capacity? When the doors open, I can only bring myself to crawl out and rest against the wall of the lengthy hallway. I'm afraid of standing alone.

My breathing deepens again. I shut my eyes tight like a dam to water, holding in tears. I wish to the point of begging to go back to page one of my second journal when I'd just started my job. I try to fabricate the smell of my pod in my head. I can't tell if this is a panic attack, but the nostalgia distracts me from the painful notifications my body keeps delivering. The unreasonable worry washes over me.

I open my eyes to see the directions posted on the wall before me. I pick myself up and move ten doors down. I move through my struggle until my knees can't take it anymore.

The agony picks up again and travels through other parts they've operated on, like my legs. My knees weaken, and I collapse, writhing. The sobs expel with pools of spit, "Virginia," I yell. "Virginia!" I don't look up in search of her. Instead, I watch the stream of saliva wet the fresh carpet. It's *red*. "Virginia!" I hear footsteps.

"Oh my god." It's her. I hear her witnessing my state. I continue to sob in relief. She kneels, gently pressing her hands into my arms to unwrap them. I look at her, ashamed. I feel shame overshadowing my needs. She cups my face. She looks like a miracle with frizzed curls tucked behind her ears. She smells new, like vanilla. But her scent is the same. Virginia hesitantly runs her thumbs over my eye bags, and I sense they're swollen. "What happened?" Do I look that bad?

"Don't call for anyone. Please," I cry again.

She pauses but looks up at the ding from the elevator. "Come on," she whispers. "Let's get you inside." Virginia throws my hand around her shoulder and lifts me with all her fragile might.

She carries me inside, and in a swift motion, she sets me on a couch. "Thank you," I say weakly.

She rushes to her kitchen for a glass of water and frantically brings the whole jug over. She puts the beak of the jug to my lips, and I rapidly inhale water to incite more mercy. It may be manipulative, but I need her for more than a few visitor hours.

But then I look up at her face and see that her expression hasn't shifted from trouble. It makes my heart sink, and suddenly, all exploitative tactics break, so I reach out and wait for her hand to touch mine. She holds it with forgiveness. I hold back tighter this time to tell her that I could never be her monster. I hope she understands this. Tears stream down her face in response. I can sense the guilt, but she doesn't ever need any with me. Virginia closes her eyes and presses her forehead against my head. I don't move; I let her remain as long as she'd like, and when she moves back, we wait for a conversation. "Do you have painkillers?" I ask.

A short laugh bursts through her snot. She wipes her nose quickly and gets up. "Yeah."

She leaves me in full view of her clean, two-bedroom apartment. My head rests on a stack of folded and floral-scented laundry. There's a yoga mat rolled in front of a small plasma. I look to the right and see sliding glass doors and a balcony. She has two flourishing plants, a chair, and a tiny folding table. I can see from the half-cigarette and ashtray that she hasn't quit her habits. She obstructs my sight with a bottle of painkillers that she reads with a thin pair of glasses. "Is it maximum strength?" I ask.

"Mhm," but she still reads. "Is this safe for you to take?"

"I've taken worse things," I joke.

Her brows mash together, "I'm serious."

"Yes," I reassure her calmly. She accepts my truth, pours two into the gracious palm of her hand, and drops them into my mouth. She lifts the jug again, and I swallow my relief with water. "Can you tell me what happened?" She levels with me literally by sitting next to the couch. "…Did someone hurt you?"

"No," I chuckle. "Virginia," she looks up and away from my weakened body. "I need to trust you."

She waits for a moment and shakes her head, "I won't tell anyone."

I look up at the ceiling, like a patient on a shrink's couch, and begin my story from the day we departed each other's lives.

BY ZAINAB F. RAZA

CHAPTER 12

GAMBLING WITHOUT MEANS

I wake up to the noise of the microwave slamming, my ears jerk back, and my eyes tighten shut. It's not a bad noise. In fact, it reminds me that I am no longer alone. I'm not even lonely. "Lee," I hear her voice travel to me to announce breakfast. I can't smell it yet, but I know she's microwaving oatmeal. My eyes accept that it is time to get up, so I open them to find myself in a sprawled-out position in the middle of her half-furnished office. I sleep on a makeshift bed of several comforters and couch pillows.

"I'm coming," I shout back happily. Virginia's been taking care of me. She's kind of pushy. She forces a glass of blended greens daily and takes me out on short walks. It didn't take long for my strength to come back. By the fourth day, I was more able. The first three days were hell. The night I arrived at her place in a completely useless state, I saw my reflection in the bathroom. My face had really lost color, and the whites of my eyes were yellow. I considered flagrantly rushing to the hospital but decided it was better to die this way than by termination. To my luck, I survived the fever-riddled nights. I didn't think my life would get to this point, but I'll never be the one to complain as I am letting my ego shatter defenselessly. She's helped me believe that it is okay to depend on someone and that it does not show signs of weakness.

Before I leave my safe space, I check for any morning wood. That would be seriously awkward. She knocks on the door and I open it with an eye roll. She has her hand on her hip. "Good morning," she says sarcastically.

I rub my eyes, "Don't you have somewhere to be?"

"It's Sunday. Go brush your teeth."

I do as she demands. Her bathroom is littered with various hair oils and products to tame her frizz. I hear her damn herself every morning here. My reflection is healthier as my skin is pinker and even hydrated. I share her skincare routine but she doesn't know this. Quickly, I pee, brush my teeth, wash my face, and strip off my feminine pajama shirt. Apparently, she's switched to softer fabrics that she's finally able to afford due to her promotion. It's relieving knowing I won't be a financial burden.

I walk into her room shirtless and wait for her. "Any bad dreams?" Virginia asks with a bottle of vitamin E oil.

"No," I've been suffering from nightmares ever since I've been able to sleep better. Odd. Maybe I've finally found the comfort to delve into fears that have less to do with my physical safety.

"Good," she sits beside me, and I turn my back to her. "Any good ones?" She pours a dollop of E onto her index finger. Some of it will drip into her nails, which will bother her. It's become routine to apply this stuff to my surgical scars.

"Nope," I shiver as the cold oil meets my regulated temperature. She first begins with the back of my neck, then triceps.

"They're healing so fast," she announces. I turn to face her as she applies a small amount on my abdomen, then quads, and then shins. I look down to note her reference. You can barely see the scars. "Okay," she wipes the excess on her jeans and taps my shoulder, "breakfast is ready."

We get to her kitchen, and she's already pouring some honey into my bowl of milk- soaked oats and topping it with a few blueberries and granola. I move the granola to the side as I like to savor them last. She taps cinnamon into her bowl and crushes dried strawberries. For me, the berries are like supplemental vitamins, except they're not. I walk across her living room to have my food out on the balcony. "Make sure you take ten deep breaths," Virginia orders me with oatmeal in her mouth. Apparently, that helps with anxiety.

I give company to her ashtray. Who is she to tell me to take deep breaths? Girl's gotta quit smoking first. I often badger her about it. She can't leave for a smoke without me buzzing in her ear." I think she likes hearing the list of Surgeon General's warnings as much as she hates it. After a moment, she joins me with a cup of coffee. "Deep breaths, Lee."

"I am," I whine. "Are we going to the park today?"

"Let's do something fun."

I look up at her. "No carnivals, please."

Her face lights up from the comical nostalgia. "What do you want to do?"

"I'll tell you what I don't want to do… I don't want that sick hang-over cure—"

"Non-negotiable, buddy," she pulls a cigarette from a crumpled pack and a pink lighter from her breast pocket.

"You're gonna die before me."

She rolls her eyes. "Let's go shopping. I don't want to share clothes with you anymore," she laughs.

I shrug. "It's not fun, but it's something we should do."

"Cool. Get dressed… in my clothes."

I force-feed myself the oatmeal and chew on the few bites of granola I left for myself before heading to her room. I'm only allowed to borrow her old T-shirts and shorts that she was about to toss ever since she revamped her wardrobe. It's still winter, but the weather here warms up fast.

She comes in, reeking of fresh smoke, to apply tinted lip balm. "Ready?"

I nod. We take the stairs to the garage to avoid attention at the lobby because people will notice my redundant appearance at some point. The garage is typically empty, but if I do see someone from afar, I immediately look at the ground.

Her car is dirty. Without the mix of hibiscus and sea breeze air fresheners clinging to the vents, this car would smell of mildew. Also, there are several coffee cups tossed in the back and protein bar wrappers living in all of the compartments. She doesn't wait for the engine to heat up. We begin our trip to a warehouse of discounted apparel. "You're quiet," she notices.

"I'm just enjoying—" She abruptly turns into a parking garage. I slap my palms onto the dashboard to support myself. "What the hell?" I exclaim. She slows down immediately. "Did you see someone?" I panic.

"No!" She gleams. "I saw a costume shop."

"Virginia," I sigh.

"Sorry," she swerves into a tight spot and unbuckles her seatbelt. "Crawl out from the back," she suggests while carefully slipping out.

She's already walking! "Dude!" I catch up to her, "I'd rather thrift."

She laughs. "No. You wanted to do something fun. I wanted to do something practical. We'll just meet in the middle. Besides, maybe we'll score a novelty disguise. Cover up your face a little."

"It's my nose, isn't it?" I joke.

She scrunches up her face a little, "I didn't wanna be the one to tell you," she grabs my hand and jogs. "Come on."

Virginia's kind of weird. You'd think she still does drugs, but somehow, those drugs wouldn't make her cooler, like they do in music videos. She's just randomly ecstatic, but that's always been her. I think Virginia's the healthiest person I've ever met, and she embraces her faults, unlike the many other people I know.

Speaking of which, Dr. Alec hasn't tried to find me. I sent him a few emails, vaguely divulging my whereabouts and intricately describing any symptoms after the surgery. He hasn't responded, so I've quit on the idea of visiting him for now. I think I need a break because the surgery took quite a toll on me, convincing me to hold a grudge against him despite his better intentions.

Virginia picks up a pair of Groucho glasses. "Well, there's your nose job," she puts the glasses on me. Her head tilts to the side.

"Shut up," I take them off and toss them in a clearance bin. We tour the place, and I have no choice but to consider whether any of these costumes will work as a decent disguise. Maybe a wig? I feel the synthetic strands of a pink bob.

"No, I actually love it," Virginia pulls up behind me, snorting. "Try this," she puts a cowboy hat on me. I don't need to look in a mirror to know that a hat that size would just draw more attention. "Maybe if you pair it with a handkerchief to wrap around your face."

"Really?" I say monotonously. I browse the next aisle with her. "A hat's not a bad idea, but maybe a baseball cap? Or just something much smaller." Virginia doesn't listen to me. She's busy with stupid party favors. I fake a sneeze to get her attention.

"Bless you," she picks up a pack of party blowers. "Hey, you think this would be appropriate to bring to the office? It's someone's birthday."

I shrug. "Seems childish, don't you think?"

Defeated, she tosses the pack on the shelf. "It's why I asked." I leave the aisle uninterested, and she comes along with me. We find more hats in the corner of the store. I put on a dark blue one with red stitching. It's not exceptional, but oddly enough, the cap speaks to me. "Oh, I like this one," she exaggerates.

"Yeah?" I chuckle.

"Oh yeah," she turns around and picks up a pair of rectangle shades. "Try this."

I put them on and glance at myself in the mirror. I almost look *human*, and the corner of my mouth lifts a little. I hand the cap and shades to Virginia. "Thank you," I say with embarrassment. She's been paying for everything, and while she never brings it to my attention, I don't forget her generosity.

"You got it," she smiles. We reach the register, and I prefer to stand behind Virginia so as not to catch anyone's sight. I notice a help-wanted sign propped up on the counter with printed applications stacked next to it. I carefully grab an application while Virginia pays for my stuff. I know her kindness will eventually wear thin, and I better get a headstart by applying to other places. These past few days, I've borrowed Virginia's laptop to send out my resume and other paperwork to jobs nearby.

"Thank you," she waves at the cashier and pulls the hat out of the plastic bag. "Here." I put it on. "Do I need the sunglasses?"

Her face twists as she decides. "Yeah. It wouldn't hurt." She hands them to me. I walk out feeling different, like I am one with the world around me. Most people will only assume I'm just super short and have a skin disease. I won't be subjected to terse introductions and speculation, and I won't have to deal with all of the staring. "How do you feel?" It's like she already knows what I'm thinking about. Ever since I've been shamelessly vulnerable around Virginia, she's understood me more.

"I feel like you," I say, smiling at the world. "Should we go on a walk?"

"Do you want to?"

I purse my lips, "I don't know what I want to do. I'm not used to the whole concept of Sunday leisure."

"Ever heard of a Sunday drive?" We turn back to the parking garage and get in the car, but I don't think she's driving us to the park. "Let's just keep driving until we get hungry." She backs out of her spot. "Are you hungry?" I shake my head. My stomach shrank from the perpetual starvation. "You sure?"

I think twice. "Nah."

"Just letting you know, there's a spot that sells really good bagels. Drive-through."

I shake my head again. I used to think Virginia was taking advantage of me to write her own story, but her story is her own, and her life is near perfect. I did not need to play a role in her life, but it still makes me suspicious. "Can I ask you something?"

"Mhm," she turns out of the lot and onto the road. "Are you hungry?"

"No," she says. "I was just making sure."

"Why?"

"What?"

"You don't have to do all this. You can just give me time," I say without making eye contact. Instead, I look out the window.

"That's so cryptic," she giggles. "What do you mean I can just give you time?"

I want to ask how long I have left with her until I'm considered a burden. "Never mind."

We pass the bagel shop. It must be a nice place. "Are you good to me because you're guilty?"

She bites off the skin on her lip. "Yes… But even when I reach the point where I've done enough and can forgive myself, I won't stop being there for you." She looks ahead while I still look away. "You're not here for my atonement. Not really, at least."

"When will you forgive yourself?"

"I don't know." She turns on the radio for some light country. We encounter the highway toward colorful mountains. "I'm not mad at you for asking these questions." Okay? She lowers the window for a smoke. She takes an exit that leads us down a narrow road.

"Where are we going?"

"Look ahead," she lifts her chin to point. I see a handmade sign tacked into the dirt and a stand next to it. As we quickly get closer, I learn that it's a produce stand. "If you're not hungry now, you'll be real hungry later." She slows down and parks on the worn-out dirt patch where other cars must have parked. Virginia lowers the window. "Hi, Gale," she hollers at a middle-aged, sun-tanned lady.

While Virginia's busy catching up with her friend, I inspect her car more out of boredom and discover something else in the bag from the costume shop. It's the funky pair of glasses with the nose. "Is that a new friend?" Gale peers into the window.

I throw on the goofy pair to change the atmosphere between Virginia and me. When she turns around, she snorts. "I guess so." I avoid panning my face to keep Gale from realizing that the thing sitting next to Virginia is not human. Virginia returns to her order, "I just need a couple of tomatoes and sugar snap peas if you have them. Oh! And vidalia onions." Gale gives her a green thumbs-up and tries to sneak a glance at me.

"I kind of like the get-up," I whisper to her.

"She's suspicious," Virginia smirks as she fishes through her glove compartment for cash. Gale returns with a bag of produce in exchange for a couple of bills. "Thank you, Gale. See you!"

Virginia gets back on the highway. We don't talk for the rest of the drive despite my attempt to break the tension. I'm sure she appreciates my effort, but maybe it's not enough. "Virginia. I'm sorry if I was disrespectful."

She sighs as we turn into the city, "I don't think it was disrespectful. I just wish you'd stop trying to figure me out."

I look down at my twiddling thumbs. "It's a bad habit." I want to justify myself by explaining that the tendency to analyze people's intentions towards me provides guidance on how to approach relational dynamics. It's just another ingenuine survival tactic, but explaining this would be a gamble because it'll either get us closer or help her realize that she is the subject of my advantage.

She barely acknowledges the speed bumps as we enter the garage. Virginia parks out of the lines, but this is not from any urgency. Rather, she just kind of sucks at driving. We leave the car in unison to the stairwell, and I hold the bag of produce as we walk up four flights of stairs. It's humid here, causing her hair to flare into frizz. She picks up her speed until she remembers I can't. My shins produce a stinging sensation by the third flight. "Here," she holds out her hand. "Let me take the bag."

"Aw no," I wave her off breathless.

"Let's not waste more time here. My hair's acting funny," she sweetly places her hand under the bag's handle. I relinquish it, feeling relief in my sore arm.

We walk into a fresh-scented, air-conditioned apartment. I take a gulp of air to cool down and make it to the couch to turn on the TV. "Perhaps I should put on a cooking channel?"

Virginia pours herself a glass of wine. "No. Maybe a movie. I'm bored," she chugs the enticing glass of red and pulls the tomatoes from the bag to wash and slice them.

"What do you want to do?" I put the remote aside and walk to the counter. To be of service, I take out the cutting board. She opens the fridge and searches for ingredients that are about to expire.

"How about a caprese salad with bruschetta?"

"Sure." The wine bottle across the counter tempts me, I fear. I don't look away from the wine when she turns back around. "Hey. Remember when we smoked weed?"

Virginia cringes at the memory. "Mhm."

I snap out of it and resume eye contact. "That was so stupid."

She slowly nods and smiles shamefully. "What made you think of that?" I throw my hand up to admit, "I'm bored too."

Virginia, disappointed, cocks her head to the side. "Dude, no. Also, I don't really do that anymore…" She snips her basil into tiny shreds.

"So you smoke cigarettes?"

"Lee." She sets the knife down carefully.

I back away from her annoying prudence and laugh nervously. "Sorry."

"Yes, I smoke. I've been doing that since I met you, but now that's the only thing I do… and scratch lottery tickets." She mumbles.

I cackle. "What was that?"

"I buy lottery tickets, okay!"

We both laugh. I'm glad I could make her happy, but I need to find a way to make her happier. And sure, alluding to illicit activities as a great pastime gives me the tingles, but I don't mean it. "Let's go buy a ticket then—"

"Let's go to Vegas," her eyes flash with excitement, and suddenly, I am taken by her enthusiasm.

"Seriously?"

"Seriously. It's perfect! You have a disguise. We'll hit a casino. How do you feel, though? Can you handle a road trip?"

I purse my lips. "So long as I can sleep in the car."

Virginia stretches her hand out to shake mine. "Deal. I'm gonna pack this into a few sandwiches."

"What am I gonna wear?"

"Your hat and glasses and your suit," she vigorously chops the tomatoes into slices and throws French bread into the toaster. "Go!"

I hurry like a dog would to her hamper to fish out my suit. It's washed. She just doesn't fold. "Do I iron it?"

"Obviously," she hollers back. Her excitement challenges my anxiety, and I wonder if this is a bad idea. I haven't utilized my chip to visit Dr. Alec, but I'm leaving town to freakin' gamble.

I iron the creases out of my suit while Virginia rushes in to rummage through her drawers. She looks at herself in the mirror, and the fine lines around her mouth loosen. "Hey. Will this get you in trouble?"

I shake my head. "I'll just leave my chip here. Doubt anyone will notice me if I just face the slot machines."

She sits next to me with a jumbled teal dress in her hand, "I don't want to hurt you again." It relieves me to know she takes my safety into account. Virginia's grown past her mistakes. But what consumes her peace? What makes her so bored that she'd want to up and leave on a whim? Am I not enough excitement for her? Should I be glad to know that I blend in with her monotonous life? "I mean, we've taken risks before. They don't end well. Never do," she focuses on the old stains on her carpet. "You know how you were talking about your bad habits?"

"Yes," I say feebly.

"I have mine, too," she looks at me. "I get bored of this life. Fast."

I pull the iron's plug. "It's more fun fucking up. I've been there," I smirk, "but eventually… to not have anything to care about ruins the fun. Your life is my dream." It's true; she's an inspiration to me, and without her, I don't think I would have continued to apply for a job and fixed my health. I wouldn't have cared about taxes.

She holds her dress to her chest. "Thank you."

"We're going. Let's break some rules," I nudge her.

Her mouth is agape, forcing a laugh out. She gets up and leaves for the bathroom while I make sense of her remark. Is she living vicariously through me? I know Virginia advised me not to scrutinize her, but I will do anything to remain in this air-conditioned apartment.

Virginia comes out in her sleeveless dress; it's dull, but it suits her rosacea. "You look great!" I resume with a facade to conceal my true feelings. I'll ruminate in the car until it puts me to sleep.

"Let's go," she leads me through the kitchen to pick up a brown bag of sandwiches. "Oh shit. I forgot your juice," she puts her hand over her mouth.

"Virginia. It's fine," I say as I put my chip in a drawer full of miscellaneous items. She groans. "It's important."

"No," I take her hand and leave the apartment. We race down the stairwell to the car as children do. Virginia adjusts herself, starts the car, carefully backs up, and then *blasts* candy store music as she swerves out of the parking garage. It's hard to keep my eyes closed and thoughts composed as she manically switches lanes to free us from the city. After a short while, Virginia hums her song, and it puts me to rest because I know she'll stop humming when there's difficult traffic. I guess there's nothing to worry about for now.

In and out, I return to my concerns regarding Virginia's intentions with a fresh perspective. It was the way she seemed so perturbed about forgetting my green juice that deepened my trust in her. While it might be true that her kindness stems partly from guilt, and perhaps she lives vicariously through me because the exciting part of her life feels long past, her care is also genuine. It pains me to think that I am forbidden to hang with her. If only Richard knew her the way he knew Dr. Alec. Virginia wakes me with a nudge. "Can you hand me a sandwich?" I peel open a saran-wrapped caprese sandwich for her convenience. She dives into a large bite. "Jesus, I'm so hungry."

I dial back the music. "You know what? Me too." I copy her and find the balsamic- soaked bread to be delightful.

"You know how to play blackjack?"

"Nope," I scarf down the rest of the sandwich in two more bites.

"No worries, I'll teach you." Virginia sighs. "We should get there in a couple of hours. Get some shut-eye," she dials the music down a little more, and I am lulled.

I've fallen into a deep cycle, so Virginia can do nothing to interrupt it. Not even her attempts to avoid potholes could wake me. For hours, I sleep with my head lightly bouncing against the cool window until we arrive at a hotel.

Virginia parks up front and directs the valet with cash in her hand. Has she done this before? Probably. I get out of the car with my sunglasses and hat. She gestures to me to follow her as she saunters into the hotel lobby. "I think I look stupid," I say as I catch a glimpse of myself in the lobby mirror.

Virginia tries her best not to laugh. "You're cool," she forgets my embarrassment upon seeing the casino attached to the hotel. Older couples filter in and out. It's not hoity-toity. Most of the women wear capris. "You have your card?"

"You have your ID?"

She smirks and approaches the bouncer. Alarmed, the brawny guy notices me first.

"Fuck?" he whispers. I hold my card for his swollen fingers to grab. I can tell he can't understand jack. He shoots a look at someone else behind the lobby desk. The other guy scuttles to the bouncer's aid. "I don't understand," the bouncer grumbles.

The lanky employee shoots me a look, and Virginia intervenes. "This is Lee. He is—"

I take it from there, "I am the property of the International Research Administration of Animalia Biotechnology. If you read the card, it will give you legally approved information."

The employee reads the card and hands it back. "How interesting. A pleasure, Lee. If you need anything or have any questions, please let us know. I will inform our staff. Welcome," he steps aside to let us in. I raise my brows as I collect my card from him. The oafish bouncer still doesn't get what's going on.

"Come on," Virginia chirps. "Let's go win some money!" Or lose money. I look back at the bouncer with worry. They know me now. I wonder if the news will ever leak. Virginia taps my shoulder and raises her voice to speak over the ambiance that is composed of chatter, the clinking of coins, and music. "Wait over there," she points at the rows of slot machines. I pass a few old ladies glued to the machines, pulling levers. Virginia scopes the area and waves at me to meet her at a green felted table.

I reach her in the middle of a game. "This is blackjack." She picks up a cocktail from a passing waitress. "The objective is to compete against the dealer to get a higher hand than him." She sips the cocktail. "Oh, you can't go over twenty-one." I watch Virginia play as a few people float to the table to join until she pushes me forward. "Your turn," she pats my back.

My eyes widen. "Be for real."

Virginia finishes her drink and turns her head in search of the young waitress, "I am so for real."

Shaky, I play. Virginia places my bet for me, and I begin with ten of hearts. As the round continues, someone reaches twenty-one. We continue the rest of the round. I have now accumulated a ten of hearts, three of spades, and a two of diamonds. I gesture for another hit and reach a bust. Virginia laughs, but for some reason, I take it more seriously.

She browses other games, picking up martinis like dirty business-men pick up women, and I waste away my allowance. Maybe it's the air or how the moon is phased, but my losses feel karmic. And it keeps fucking pissing me off. I motion to stay since I am collec-tively at twenty. The dealer flips his cards after going around, and it's a motherfucking bust! I gather my chips and rush to miss tipsy. "Virginia! I won!"

Virginia's words slur as she congratulates me. I realize that despite my superficial temptations, leaving her to chase trays is unwise. I take her to the bar to order water, and she hounds the bartender, "I'll have another—"

"I got it," I put my hand on her shoulder and mouth 'water' to the bar-tender while Virginia fidgets in her seat. "You okay?" I speak clearly in her ear, and she jumps at the sound of my voice as if she had forgot-ten I am next to her. I hold in my laughter, waiting for her to answer.

She scratches her head. "Should we go?" Anxiety bubbles in her eyes. I worry she cannot get us home safely. "Can you drive?"

She handed me the valet ticket. "Can you get the car?"

I'm almost positive that Virginia will soon discover that her cocktails and martinis are just water, and I've never seen her as an angry drunk. I don't want to be pegged as the guy that's bothering a single woman. I guess we'll wait in the car for her to sober up.

When the valet arrives, I see Virginia swaying left and right as she makes her way to me. I gently hold her arm, and she tosses the keys to me. "You're driving."

I catch them and look up at her. "You can't be serious."

"I can't do it," she whines.

"Virginia, dude. What the hell?" I enter her personal space to whisper frantically. "You know I can't do that."

"I have work tomorrow!"

"Let's just get in the car and wait until you're sober—"

"Nope," she purses her lips.

I wait for her to explain, but she leaves it as is. "Why can't you do that?"

"I have a job, Lee. You wouldn't know," she smirks through a hiccup. "And I can't call in sick! I have my life in order. You said it yourself." When did I say that? "Don't make that stupid face." She tugs on my arm, "I'm not staying here."

"Let's just play some more." Stubborn, she shakes her head. We return to her waiting sedan, and I take the driver's seat. Luckily, no one notices. "Okay," I say to Virginia as she plops into the passenger side. "Now what?"

Her pointer shakes as she motions towards the gears. "First, foot on the break." I press on the gas and the engine revs. We both scream. "Left—left pedal, Lee." She's still pointing at the gear.

"Okay," I press on the break.

"Okay. Okay. Now," she moves the gear into 'D.' "Slowly take your foot off the break and use the other pedal to move. Slowly!" She giggles. For fuck's sake, I need a booster seat. My heart jumps as we roll forward. I smash on the break, and Virginia flies forward. "Ow!"

"Put on your seatbelt," I command her. I put on mine, too. Slowly, I lap the hotel to get used to the mechanics and then carefully exit the vicinity onto an empty road. It's late.

"Virginia, we should really wait." I reach a green stop light, but I don't know if I should go.

"Go!" I pick up speed, but a pack of cars passes me, shattering my confidence. "Can you at least put in your address?"

She presses a bunch of incorrect buttons until the navigation routes us home. She presses a triangle button. "So people avoid you. And both hands on the wheel. Also, use the indicator to switch lanes." Indicator?

"If you can remember so much, then you drive!"

"I will get us killed!"

"Then let's wait," I beg her. "You can still get to work tomorrow."

She bangs the back of her head against the car seat, "I've been taking care of you for two weeks, Lee! I had work to do over the weekend that I freakin' forgot about because of *you*." She looks out the window. "Take me home."

I tried. I tried to make her happy. "Can you stay up at least?"

"I'm up." She points to the lane next to me. "Go there." Unsure what she means by this, I look at her. "Eyes on the road!"

"Shit!" I hit the break.

"What are you doing?" She looks behind us. "Drive!" I speed up again. "Okay, just stay away from trucks. Avoid the exit lane." She focuses on the road with me.

"Sorry, sorry," I regain control...

After a good hour, I understand that driving isn't all that hard when the roads are clear. To be honest, it's kind of fun. Nerve-wracking but fun. I just wish I was in a better mood. I think today was a rough day altogether, and I could easily write off these two weeks as rough, provided that I haven't heard back from any jobs, but honestly, I believe things are gradually getting better. Being around her palliates the foregoing anxieties. Today was a bump in the road, so to speak. "I was a few months sober," she bites her nail.

"Hm?" I hate to divide my attention right now.

"This evening—well, today was the first time I drank in a long time." I try to understand Virginia's urgency to escape Vegas. It can't just be work, right?

"Why did you do it? Because you're bored?"

"I don't know," she answers in dejection. "I'm sorry if I upset you."

"No. I would've done it without you… at some point, at least. I don't feel good enough, you know?" She touches the cold window, "I have the job, the promotion. But I feel like I don't belong." She puts her heavy hand on my shoulder, "I always get you mixed up in my shit." We don't talk for a long time after her indirect apology.

The navigation directs me to an exit, leading us into the city. "Do you think I should leave?"

"You do what's best for you," her response bothers me. "Virginia. Are you using me?"

"No," she sighs. "You don't change me. You don't change anything. Can you just accept that I'm good to you?"

"Well, I'm not used to it." Sometimes, I wonder if my skill of insight has gone soft or if everyone in my life is deceitful. It could be that people contain their authenticity to avoid unnecessary vulnerability. Maybe it's my fault that I won't accept Virginia's motion to keep me in her life. I'm being unfair to her, as I've always been.

"If you can't trust, you won't ever be human," she scoffs. "Oh, *shut up.*"

"What?" she exclaims.

"Just because I'm hypocritical doesn't mean I don't have a good reason to be—"

"I hope that even if it doesn't guilt you, I hope that you at the very least know this is so wrong of you. You can believe you can be trusted, but you can't… You read others but hate to be read. Jesus, Lee." She slouches in her seat. "So what if I had an ulterior motive? I'm my own person, and yeah, I'm running away from my shit. But you're getting what you need out of this friendship. If you can call it that! What about *your* ulterior motive?"

"What do you mean?" I know I've been caught.

"*Please*. You ask me if you're a burden after I told you I ruined my sobriety." She faces me. "You won't make it out alive."

I bite my lip to conceal the shame that could effortlessly morph into rage. "None of us do," I sass her. I make it a point to abate the severity of her comment by replying with something so stupidly emo.

"Pull over," she snaps her fingers and points to the side of the road. "Now." I doubt her sanity. "No."

"Lee. I've sobered up. You can't drive in the city."

She has a good point, but I know damn well that she hasn't entirely sobered up. "We're almost there." Virginia doesn't argue with me, and we drive through another period of silence. At this time, to take my mind off our minor altercation, I think about the casino. It wasn't a bad time. In fact, the feeling of winning sparks a lust for dominance—a trait I believe resonates primarily with cis-American men, as this form of dominance often manifests through monetary entitlement. I felt like a rich man despite being unable to cash my chips. It's the feeling more than the money.

I've been chasing that feeling. I've been calling it independence.

When I reach the city, I use street lamps to locate the stop signs and pavement markings. A few cars pull around me as I drive slowly with the hazards on. Virginia, petty as she is, doesn't care to help me. After pulling into the garage, I park the car in a very vacated area.

Without her, I climb flights. Is it appropriate to pack my items and travel to Dr. Alec's residence since my time is most likely up? Maybe I should leave before she says anything. When I reach her floor, I find Virginia exiting the elevators. So petty.

She unlocks the door and lets me in first. I feel like she's gonna stab me again. We disperse in different directions. I gather my things and pack the bed in her office. Maybe she'll pity my initiative and allow me to stay even longer. In case, I check the laptop to see if Dr. Alec replied to my email. A different subject line titled, "We are Offering You the Position…" catches my attention. It's a message from Thomas from this past Friday. My heart drops, "Virginia!" I walk away from the laptop.

Her demeanor adopts maternal instinct. "Yes? What?"

My mouth falls open, and air flows through in gusts. "I think… I think I got the job." She puts her hand to her mouth. "Are you serious?"

I return to the email with her and open it to find an offer. We look at each other and scream. She jumps up and down, and I raise my fist triumphantly, like a dork. "I did it! I fucking did it!" I hurry to her. "What should I say?"

She squints. "Don't reply on a Sunday!"

"It's Monday."

She taps her foot and thinks. "Wait three hours. It'll look professional. It's as if you get up early, and you have your shit together."

CHAPTER 13

NEW AND FINALLY

I turn my cheek against the onlookers sitting in front of me, not because I am reluctant to socialize, but because I need to inconspicuously check if I smell like ass. The concoction of cologne, aftershave, and deodorant hasn't worn off yet, but neither has the scent of Virginia's place, I imagine. After a quick whiff, I rest my head against the subway wall and review the list of discoveries I have attained to appeal to Dr. Barberry and maybe Richard. I wouldn't be surprised if he were to attend the routine check-up since my life's trajectory has significantly shifted since our last meeting.

The pages in my journal fill up the details of my daily life. That's promising. Maybe even Dr. Phillips would be impressed with the emotional occurrences I documented. Dr. Alec would tell me that the genius is in the detail, so I've been detailing my entries with interactions at the office, gym, and at home. Of course, in my best interest, I haven't been honest about who's adopted me without rent, but it would be unconvincing to claim homelessness.

My skin's been vibrant lately due to a good diet and, yes, occasional yoga. I only frequent the gym to keep the membership as a backup because, despite the current joy of liberation, I always trace where I stand to know where the edge is. Oftentimes, I'm on it— many times, I've fallen. It's better to know where to turn back. But, I can say with relief that things have been good.

My stop presents itself today as an opportunity because I'm looking forward to tomorrow for the first time in a long time. Tomorrow's only Wednesday, but it's another day to make an allowance. I hope to invest in a place of my own. It has nothing to do with Virginia; she's been massively hospitable, and frankly, it'll be tough to part ways because she has a way with friendship. I won't miss her, though, which sounds shitty, but I swear it's not my fault yet. She's excellent at taking care of me, and thanks to her, even my scars have dissolved without vestige.

On the way to the lab, I count my proposals. I am a working man now. I have goals, I answer to someone, and I find it redeemable to receive praise from my boss. There are just a few things I want to leave out. Such as Virginia, the surgery, and maybe even the last conversation I had with Thomas.

He suggested I take a course in tax preparation to prove that I am a viable employee worth keeping, and if I do well, I can build a career at his firm. Of course, he hired me for the hype and free advertisement, but it's still a risk if I'm incompetent. Fair.

Thomas is a little better than Mel because he cares for his job. So he's a little bit more interactive than that bald, benign lump I worked for. No matter the income, Thomas acts like "the man," and people want to listen to him. Our last chat about me remaining as an employee permanently was sorta exciting, so maybe that's why I have had eyes for him lately. After the check-up, if it goes well, I'll have to head to work with at least an inclination toward a decision.

The facility's doors are cracked open, but I shut them as I enter. Are they testing my manners? There's no one in sight, yet I hear chatter and the echo of loafers down the hall. I walk in that direction, hoping to be met with zeal. It's just an intern. I politely wave this time for a good change. It takes an intern to know an intern, right? I used to never acknowledge them as they were the least of my concerns. I mean, it's not as though their opinions determine me. The intern, surprised, waves back at me. "Do you know where Dr. Barberry is?"

The intern eyes go wide for a second. "I think he's in a meeting. Sorry, I'm sectioned for a different project, but I can escort you to your pod."

"No," I raise my hand to stop him, enjoying the dominance. "I'll find the lab instead.

Would you relay the message?" The intern nods, and I leave him to organize his spinning thoughts.

The lab is empty, so I drop my suitcase on the sanitized counter and wait for Dr. Barberry on the examination table. Dr. Barberry knocks before entering. I don't know why, but I thought it was Dr. Alec. "Hello, Lee," Dr. Barberry greets me as if nothing's happened between us.

The brief illusion of Dr. Alec throws me off, but I respond with a copied demeanor, "How are you, Dr. Barberry?" I hop off the table to shake his hand.

He looks at his clipboard. "You feel good?" He spots my briefcase. "Journal's in there?"

I pull it out for him. "Yeah… for both questions." He skims through my entries for updates. Captivated, he finds a stool to rest on and carefully rereads my pages.

He closes the book with his thumb in it. "You made a new friend? How?"

I want to pick a playful banter with him, but I'm afraid he just might misinterpret it. "Yes, they've been quite hospitable."

"How does the trust factor work between you both then?"

"Just a matter of getting to know each other," technically, I'm not lying.

"And the job? Tell me more about that. What's required of you? What qualifications did you claim?"

"Well, the job is entry-level. So it's really a position to earn qualifications, right? I guess I got lucky. I didn't think they'd hire me. I've been shadowing preparers and learning about income tax returns. I'm learning how to handle client transactions and reconcile bank accounts. It's interesting. The world isn't as simple as I thought it was. Do you know what an equity loan is?"

He smirks. "You learned about equity loans at your job?"

"No, not exactly. I was talking to a coworker, and he was telling me about the home he was about to buy with his girlfriend. It just got me thinking about what I can do with my money. I used to think life was just give and take, buy or sell, win or lose. Like a two- way street. I get that this isn't an emotional discovery per se, but I feel a sense of belonging…" My heart races.

Dr. Barberry lets the confession linger like it's meaningful and then clicks his pen to record evidence. "It's odd that you're working there."

"How so?" I nervously whisper. Have I done something wrong?

"One of the more civilized things we do is pay taxes. You don't see animals doing that, right? Your first job was just a job. If I'm not wrong, I didn't see much correlation between sentience and a company that sells weight loss pills, but this—this is a good choice, Lee. It's disciplined," he shrugs, "I could be wrong."

"My boss is happy with my dedication."

"That's great," he nods.

I lean forward to courageously share the good news. "He said I might find a permanent position there if I continue to work hard."

He sets the clipboard down and opens a drawer that's stuffed with folded hospital gowns. "I'll leave you in peace to change. Meet me at the lab. I'm going to make a copy," he waves the journal.

"Sounds good." As soon as he exits, I strip. Quickly, I take the chip out and hide it in my socks, then hide the socks in my pants pocket. I put on my robe and leave for the neighboring lab. As I face my fate, I don't feel the sting of potential loss because I've been too good to worry as much as I used to.

The lab is dim. Dr. Barberry is in the other room behind the glass. He speaks into the microphone. "Keep your thoughts composed." I nod as I lay at the base of the X-ray machine. The mechanical operation begins with sudden whirs and then takes me in. I scratch away the flaking skin around my thumbs while I wait to be studied. I can hear the machine observe me from a series of different angles. Eventually, the test ends suspiciously quicker than usual, and I am birthed out of the massive cylinder.

Dr. Barberry exits the room with his clipboard, "Lee! I don't think I need to defer your scans to other biologists." He looks like he's going to pop a bottle of champagne.

"Huh?" I sit up.

"I see so much in your limbic system… Do you want to see?" He offers his hand, and I think twice before taking it. Do I care to witness proof of who I'm turning into?

I do. We go to the back room. Dr. Barberry leans over his chair to point to the screen, which displays an image of my brain. "This here suggests growth within the insula region. Insula manages emotions and empathy. Could it be the budding friendship?"

I scoff at the idea, "Dr. Barberry, while it's not in my favor to admit, I must be candid. I don't experience sympathy. I don't think I could ever experience empathy! It scares me."

He sighs. "Well. Your species isn't prone to large communities. It's just the way you evolved."

"Why do agencies experiment on us?" I purse my lips and look down. Dr. Barberry doesn't cast reciprocity. He's unable to.

He refers back to the image, "I also noticed some development in the frontal lobe. It's general, but based on your notes, I assume the change speaks on your emotional control and judgment," he glances back at me. "You've definitely matured."

I smile softly. "Thank you."

Dr. Barberry signs out of the computer. "Okay, Lee. I guess you're good to go. There's no point in waiting for confirmation. It's obvious you've done good work."

While that is great to hear, I can't help but focus more on the fact that it will only get harder to generate development. The last mile is often the hardest. "By the way," I blurt. "What happened to Dr. Phillips?"

Dr. Barberry returns to practicality. "She's around. Just busy." I don't think I have much more to add. She and I never got close. I just wanted to review the members of Project

O.H.I. because I haven't put in a lot of face time with the fallible, weak Gods of my existence. "And Cambry?" I ask with an undetected smirk.

He cocks his head to the side. "You miss them?"

I laugh. "No. I haven't seen them in a while." I take a step towards the door, "I should probably change."

Dr. Barberry acknowledges my distance with one nod. "Take care."

In the other room, I dress for work and leave the facility with a sense of integrity, which is something I rarely achieve.

Instead of taking the usual way home, I look at the woods behind the vast facility. I remember talking about a shortcut with Dr. Alec a while ago and never found the courage to discover whether he's true. There was a time when I was less afraid of taking risks, but the more I become a person, the more afraid I am of loss. I think it's the living I don't want to give up, not being alive. Does that make sense? When I was younger and more animalistic, the urgent priority was to stay alive, which I still maintain, but I think that, as of late, I enjoy knowing there is a tomorrow and there may be a future.

I try the shortcut to find balance, and if I get lost, I have my chip on me. I have a phone too, thanks to my new job. I walk around the fence that perimeters my former home and take my first step into a world untouched. The sun is rising, and few of its rays pass through to reach dirt and bark. It's pretty. I've witnessed this before when I needed to take a quick piss in the woods, but I don't think I allowed myself to enjoy it. Based on my understanding, it should just be a straight shot through the woods, and then I'll just need to bear right towards the station. It's not all that quiet as the birds sing, and an owl vocalizes its call in the distance. I hear the twigs snap beneath my step. It smells like nothing, but the air's scent is still distinct. It smells like outside. I touch the trees to memorize the sensation. I can't remember the last time I've really breathed fresh air. "This is as good as it gets," I mumble.

There isn't any point in acknowledging where I stand between humanity and alien life as I know I stand on the border, on the precipice, facing the direction of whichever whim. Lately, I have been facing the enticement of social construct and maybe even the reward of capitalism. The mood dies when I realize that loitering in the woods does not serve my purpose—in fact, it never did—so I cut through the rows of oak to find the station, wondering about my said purpose. It's already been established, and I know what I live for, but it's not so much the purpose itself that concerns me but the origin.

Since those visits to the library, I've learned many schools of thought and even selected one to live by, or rather, I've identified it. I consider myself an existentialist, you know? The type that leaves it all on the field, never leaving my happiness to chance. I don't believe in theism, but I do believe in God. It's all too miraculous to not believe in a higher being, regardless of whether the jurisprudence of religion applies to me. I live the life of a religious existentialist and didn't even know it until I learned, but that's beside the emphasis because I'm focusing on the origins of the reason I exist. Maybe I was already written about somewhere up there, but all I can perceive as a being, be that an alien or person, is the logical performance of life that leads me to my purpose. I believe I exist as a consequence of discovery or curiosity. I can ask, 'why me?' But I think I was subjectively at the right time and place of capture and could have been arbitrarily replaced by others. It's hard to say that the trees that grow here were from winds that carry dwindling seeds because though the necessity of flora is primary, and that necessity is a science, and that science is a concept—it's still a thought when nothing existed, and someone must have thought of it.

The shapeshifting perspectives on the theory of everything I know keep me company until I arrive on the other side. Dr. Alec was right. The station exists behind the trees. I wait patiently on a bench at the empty station when my phone rings. I jump at the sound of the abrupt tune and answer. "Hello?".

"Hey!" Virginia enthuses. "Are you okay? Are you still there?"

"No, I'm at the station—"

"So it went well!"

"Yes! Yeah," I cough out. "Yeah, turns out I made some major growth, so I'm good to go for the next cycle."

"Oh, that's awesome! We should celebrate."

My train arrives. I board with Virginia on the line. "Oh man, I should have asked for printouts of my CT scan. I think you'd find them super cool."

"Oh yeah?"

"Yeah—"

"You have your chip, right?" I check again. "Yeah."

"Cool. Do you want to go out for dinner or something?"

I rest my head on the seat and sigh. "Honestly, I'm so tired."

"Okay, any requests for dinner?" I think she called dibs on the excitement of successfully passing another check-up. I wanted to share the big news, but I'm content as long as she's happy. Besides, it's not something to celebrate too much—time's already begun to tick. "Lee?"

"Oh. I think… You know? Let's order takeout. On me," I smile, taking pride. I can do this now. I can pay for shit. It goes against my innate frame of vantage as I need to save to afford big-city things, but I consider kindness an investment. "Let's have Thai!"

"Sure. I like Thai."

"Yeah, it's this place I used to go to. I'll text you the number."

"Sounds good… So, watcha doin'?" I think she's bored at work.

"Literally waiting until I reach work. You think I should try for a license?"

"Like, you wanna drive?"

"Yeah," I shrug, "I don't know. I'm getting tired of taking the train. It's boring."

She sighs. "Dude, anywhere you sit for long periods is boring."

"That's not as profound as you think," I scoff as I bite the skin around my nails. "Oh shit. Did I tell you what Thomas said? About the courses?"

"No, I don't think so."

"He said I should take a tax preparation course. That way, I can stay at the company permanently. That's pretty cool, right?"

"Is that something you want to do? I mean, if you have the option to study for something, shouldn't it be a subject that excites you?"

"Dude, even when I had interests, I wasn't allowed to indulge them. Maybe they were time-consuming or expensive. I don't know," I smack my teeth and look out the window as we pass the town at reasonably high speeds.

"Well, if you like the idea, then do it." I think Virginia realizes she's in no position to suggest a career because she likely didn't want to end up in human resources.

"Right?"

"I'm gonna do my work, but I'll keep you on the line."

"Mhm," I busy myself by flipping through my journal.

The train ride passes easily as I become entrenched in the stories I'd tell and how they would make me feel. For a few fleeting moments, I embody the version of myself that was fascinated with the experience of new emotions and considered each phrase of encouragement a Pavlovian treat. This was when the scientists were more involved in my progress.

I hear Virginia stir in her seat and cough a couple of times, and it pulls me back into the world I'm in. She sneezes. "Excuse me."

I bless her the way you'd hold the door for someone who's a foot away from you—not because I want to, but because it feels weird not to. My stop approaches, and I pack my journal away in the briefcase. "Looks like I'm here."

"Nice," I can hear her type something important. "What's a good way to sign off?" I wait by the doors about to slide open. "What do you mean?"

"Like for an email."

The locomotive releases me to my own means of bipedal travel, and I begin my route of a few blocks. "Regards?" I suggest carelessly.

"That sounds rude."

"Okay. Kind regards."

"Whatever, I'll just figure it out myself… Sorry, I'm just kinda hungry. Oh! Did you drink your smoothie? I left it in the fridge."

I sigh, "Virginia—"

"Oh my god, Lee. It loses nutrients if you don't drink it as soon as it's made. I can't stand over your head every time. Speaking of which, did you apply vitamin E?"

"Yup."

"Did they notice any scarring?"

"Nope! They're basically gone."

"Cool," she types again. "I think I'm just going to say 'best'."

I reach the steps of my building. "Okay, well, best, because I'm at my job." My nerves briefly accelerate as I haven't ever been late to work. "Hm," she sounds preoccupied, "best."

I hang up and let myself in. I've become accustomed to taking the stairs, which is what I often do at Virginia's place, so instead of using the elevator, I exercise. I can hear office chatter from a distance and find bagels near reception. "Hey guys," I politely greet my coworkers. A sense of belonging crashes over me.

Marcel waves with a plastic knife, "Thomas wants to see you."

"Save me a bagel," I flash a smile. Thomas's door is wide open, which is a rarity unless his office is vacant.

He doesn't look away from his computer to greet me, nor does he show any relief that I've returned safely. "Alright, Lee. I need an answer, buddy."

"Hey, Thomas," I take a seat. "Can we discuss how this is all gonna go? What would I have to do and—"

Thomas reclines in his swivel chair and looks at me. "It's a course you'll have to take. It ranges from thirty to seventy-two hours. I want you to put in the full seventy-two. I want you to stay after work and study with me until *I* feel you can do it alone. When you take the exam, I will be there to ensure you have not arranged any loopholes, and if you fail the first test, I will not accept a retake. I will have no choice but to terminate you. Keeping an intern who cannot be trusted is senseless. The course costs around eight to nine hundred dollars. Let me know when I can enroll you?"

"I need to go over this with IRAAB before proceeding. Also, I have to see if I can afford the course."

Thomas doesn't like evasion, so he clicks his pen several times. "I have a responsibility to execute." I hate that word, or both of those words, for that matter. "I need an answer promptly. It's a pain waiting when I should be doing—do you understand the risk of hiring you? Sure, you're a spectacle. It's considered politically incorrect to question your belonging in the workplace. You got a bunch of hippies rooting for you on college campuses. But as soon as you mess up, it's on me."

"Okay. I'll do it. I'm sorry for any hesitation. I've never done something like this before, and if you think I'm up for it, then I trust you." I don't.

Thomas runs his fat fingers through his hair and smiles. "Cool. I'll email you more info on the course."

I wait for anything else and then carefully rise from my seat. "Great. Thank you, Thomas."

"Yep. Oh!" He points his pen at me. "When did you get in?"

"Not sure, maybe a few minutes ago."

"Well, you're paid hourly, so email HR about it… Sorry," he purses his lips. I nod and leave his office without haste to avoid any aggressive impressions.

I resume the office culture with a smile and a bagel in my hand. Marcel hangs with a couple of coworkers, and I join them. "What did he have to say now?" Marcel rolls his eyes.

"Aw man, nothing bad," I'm afraid the big guy's listening.

Marcel leans in to whisper. "Don't worry about him. He's always on edge."

I chuckle. "Really? I didn't notice." We both laugh, and I subject myself to the other tax specialists. "Have you guys taken the same tax courses or?"

"No. Most of us took different courses, but it's pretty much the same thing," some blue button-down answers.

"Why?" Marcel asks.

"Thomas suggested that I study and take the exam." Marcel raises his brows. "*Wow*. That's exciting."

I smile humbly, unsure if he means it. "We'll see." I look back up to judge the common expression on most people's faces. They all appear to be encouraging, disarming my anxiety. "Okay, well. I think I'm gonna see what Payton is up to."

"See ya, Lee," Marcel says. We're actually on good terms.

The main floor of the office is designed to be a fucking cubicle maze, and in the beginning, it would take me at least five minutes to find my mentor. I recognize Payton now from his blonde flyaways sticking up. "Hey," I pull up a chair next to him. "How's your morning going?"

"Good," Payton chugs an energy drink followed by a protein shake. "You wanna take over?" Why? So you can swipe on Christian dating apps? He pulls out his phone, and I can tell from the motion of his thumb that he's doing what I suspected. Payton scoots back so I can take over. "Just review the information in the message box and line it up with previous returns."

"Okay," I log into the portal to access mundane information. Thomas didn't set me up for failure. Payton is not always hands-on, but it gives me space to make mistakes, which he comes in to correct before sending out any information. He's taught me well, and I'm able to fly solo for the most part.

"Hey…" Marcel approaches me with a face so apologetic. Jesus, I hope he's not firing me. "Thomas wanted me to let you know that you will have to work through lunch since you came in late. Sorry," he puts his hand on my shoulder.

CHAPTER 14

TO BE LET GO OF IS TO BE LOVED

It's been seventy hours. Seventy hours and three-fourths of it were spent under the supervision of Thomas until he deemed me an independent "pupil." His encouragement motivates me, of course, but I know if I don't perform as expected, I'll end up on the chopping block. The pressure of passing is getting to me despite any approbation from him. He says I've made great progress throughout this time.

Even with the door closed, I can hear Virginia nearly gasping for life as she endures seasonal allergies, or at least she says they're allergies. I think it's a nasty cold, but my opinion matters to neither her nor me. She knocks on the door and opens it slowly. "Hey," she sniffles.

I turn away from the painfully bright computer screen. "How are you feeling?"

"Not great," she wipes her nose with the sleeve of her overwashed robe. The irritation enhances the redness on her nose. "I think you're right," she surrenders, "I'm fucking sick."

"Do you want me to run to the store?" I would hate it if she agreed to interrupt my studying. I feel bad for the girl, but not enough to make room for her on my list. I know it's such an awful thing to say, but I trust that I yearn for the day I feel accountable.

"No, it's fine. I think I need some rest. I was just checking on you."

"Okay, yeah. I'm almost done, and then we can spend some time together," I smile, "does that sound good?"

"No rush," she rubs her temples and leaves me to my privacy. My stomach rumbles, reminding me that I haven't eaten since lunch, which is not good because I spent a substantial amount of the night burning my energy.

My stomach churns again. I guess this is an opportunity to prove to Virginia that I am a worthy member of the household by cooking for both of us. I emerge from the room and see her lying on her belly on the floor. She sees me, "I read somewhere that this position relieves your sinuses."

I remember the times when Virginia took care of me. "Are you hungry? I'm going to make some pasta for us."

She lifts her limp hand to wave away my offer. "You go study. I'll just—"

"Suffer?" I pull a pot from the cupboard, fill it with water, and wait for it to boil on the stove. "You have to have something before going to bed. It'll make you feel better." Instead of standing above the pot of water, I come to Virginia's aid with my hand out for her to grab. "This isn't going to help your sinuses."

Virginia refuses to grab my hand. "I'm fine, Lee." I sit next to her. "Why are you avoiding my help?" Virginia raises her shoulders, "I don't need it."

"I didn't refuse your help when you offered."

"Because you needed it."

I lay down with her. "You're so annoying." No, she's actually so great. Virginia doesn't ask for much in return, and it worries me because I don't know if she's counting her kindness, waiting for me to fuck up.

I've been emailing Dr. Alec more often. At least twice a week, I reach out to him, but I haven't received an answer. I gave him my job address in hopes of gaining even an obscure response from him. I imagine him waiting at the steps of the building with a look of shame and softness. I don't need Dr. Alec in my life anymore, but he was part of my support system, so to accept that loss gives me a troubled sense of instability.

"Come on," I nudge Virginia, "let's get you on the couch. You look stupid." She sends a muffled laugh into the shag rug, which she's dug her face in.

She finally listens, and I drape a fleece throw over her before returning to the boiling pot. I dash salt for taste. Should I blend a juice for her, too? Will she notice the extra mile? While I decipher the code of ethical exchange, I hear a direct ping from the office. Is Thomas tracking my progress? That line sounds too familiar.

I rest a wooden spoon over the pot—something I've learned from cooking articles—and follow the ping. The bright screen informs me that I've received an impersonal email—a notification, rather. It's from Dr. Alec. In a panic, I click "delete" by accident. My heart drops, "Virginia!" I forget everything else. I forget her illness. "Virginia!"

She's kind enough to step around my unmade bed. "What? What?" She asks wheezing. "What happens when you delete an email?"

"It goes in the trash," she coughs and rubs her temples. I pull on my face. "Fuck!"

"What? Do you want it back?"

"Yes! Yes, obviously!" I tug her robe in sick desperation.

She retrieves the email. "Here, jeez." We both look at the email together. I can hear the water in the pot overflowing. I can't read what it says; my adrenaline is spiking. Virginia looks over at me. "I think he deleted his email."

My face grows in horror, and the tears well. "Why?" Virginia wipes the tears that are first in line to shed. There isn't a threshold. "What did I do wrong?"

She leans to reach my height, but I feel like I'm shrinking. "No," she coos in a raspy voice, "it's not about you." I put my head against her shoulder to let the robe soak my cries.

I hear another ping and return to the computer immediately only to learn that I've been approved for an apartment tour the day after tomorrow. This brings me to my senses, and it's as though the universe is telling me to move on. I pull myself together fast. Maybe it's not always about me.

I rush to the stove. Hastily, I switch off the heat and strain the pasta, slather it with butter, and leave a steaming plate for Virginia. She is just a few paces behind me, watching, observing my well-being. "Aren't you gonna eat?" She asks.

I shake my head and wipe my face, "I have a couple of hours to put in. You go ahead. I'll eat later."

The last two hours drag, and I spend nearly the rest of the night reviewing until Virginia is asleep in her room. My brain is numb now. Before retiring, I look back at the bounced email. I grit my teeth and read the context reinforcing Virginia's point—he did delete it.

This time I can hear my blood boil, and I jerk back from the computer in rage, knowing damn well I could trigger surveillance. I leave the room and breathe the anger out. My peripheral vision utilizes the moon's natural light to spot anything I might accidentally knock over, as my gestures are heavy with rage. Virginia's keys catch my eye.

Without another thought, I choose to look for him.

I swipe the keys from the counter, replace them with my chip, stuff my track phone in my pocket, and carefully unlock the door. The freedom feels surreal for a moment, and without a doubt, I venture to the garage from the stairwell.

The garage is eerily silent, dramatizing my situation. I start the car and wait for a minute or two to see if Virginia somehow figured out I left. She hasn't, she's sick. I back out without fluidity, as this is literally my second time driving. I break over and over again to avoid hitting anyone behind me and then straighten myself out. I test the pedal several times, too, to get used to the control of speed and then exit the garage.

After punching in Dr. Alec's address, I turn on the radio to calm my frantic heart. The static-filled music feels distant, like a soundtrack to someone else's life, but it's better than the silence pressing on my chest. I'm glad that each of the times I've chosen to drive illegally, it's when no one is out. The highway roads are empty, and the trees are too tall; I can barely see the moon. The headlights carve tunnels of light through the darkness, illuminating stretches of asphalt and fleeting glimpses of the forest. My grip tightens on the wheel as I rehearse what I'll say, though I know I'll abandon every word the second I see him.

It doesn't take long to reach Dr. Alec's place at this hour. I park on the curb instead of the driveway to avoid reversing. My stomach turns. To alleviate the sudden nausea, I remind myself of who I'm seeing. It's not just anyone. It's not a penalizing authority figure; it's Alec.

I see a light in the house, and the luminescence carries to the front lawn. The weeds have outgrown themselves, and the shrubbery is unkempt. I feel this barrier around me, and like a warning, it keeps me from calling his name as if the silence is intentional. I can only prevail by ringing the doorbell. And when I do, I hear no response. After a minute or two, I repeat this cycle several times until I reach frustration. "Alec," I voice sternly. "Alec, it's me." I knock this time. "Open the door."

I survey the light to see if he communicates in one way. Nothing changes. "Alec, please!" I beg.

Like a literal fucking psycho, I put myself back on my feet and walk around the house. Of course, I'm scared. It's dark out, and I can barely see anything. What if a serial killer is lurking or a fucking fox? What if Dr. Alec's watching me? He knows I fucking need him. He was never offended by my necessities; he understood my emotional range. "Fuck! Dr. Alec!"

I am at the back of the house. I put my face against the sliding door and see my breath fog up the window. I go towards the location of the room in which this fucking light is in. The curtains are closed. Of course. "Alec, if you can hear me… what the fuck, man? I didn't bring my chip!" I wait again, "I still need you."

I lie in the dirt, staring at the night sky, hoping he will come around. But he doesn't, and even in his proximity, I am alone. Relatively speaking, this isn't the worst night of my life, but it cuts deep. I know this is the end of my relationship with him. While my knocks and incessant ringing have been denied before, there used to be a reason. Our relationship was taboo, if not illegal. But I am here with *total* freedom.

The light turns off.

I don't do anything this time; I don't even look in its direction. I just lay beneath the stars until my eyelids grow heavy and my sight turns blurry. It's over.

With this probable assumption, I sleep. I suppose I'll head out in the morning before Virginia realizes I'm not home. It isn't safe to drive anyway. The hours slowly pass as I wake from every snap of a twig and chirp of a cricket. My instincts are heightened, but not in anticipation of him checking on me—he won't. Instead, I stay alert, watching for a natural threat—something mundane, something that wouldn't be deemed an anomaly.

When I wake, the sun is barely rising. It occurs to me that there's going to be traffic. I press my head into the fucking dirt, hoping the earth will consume me from this treacherous ordeal we poetically call life. I wiggle my phone out of my pocket and dial for Virginia. "Hello," she answers in a drowsy, stuffy tone.

"Hey. Please don't be mad."

"Where are you?" She sniffles. "Oh my God. Are you not home?" I hear her get up from her bed and groan when she realizes that I am not, in fact, home. "Lee," she gasps, "did you take the car?" She exclaims wildly. It's pretty impressive she's able to connect the dots so fast. "Are you insane? This can get you in so much trouble. Are you hurt? Did you get into an accident? Answer me!"

"If you'll let me," I retort.

"Oh, this is not the time to give me sass!"

"I'm at Alec's place. I figured I'd visit him since he didn't fucking respond to my emails—"

"So I would have taken you!"

"I was upset, okay!"

"You could have gotten into a lot of trouble. You could have put me in trouble, too. Does that ever occur to you?"

"…I'm sorry."

"You're not," she says. "Where are you? What's the address?"

"I'll text it to you. Can you also bring my suit? I need to go to work. And my toothbrush. And maybe some toothpaste?"

She hangs up. I text her the address and wait in the same spot. I hide from the revealing daylight. I don't want Dr. Alec to see me, and I don't want to see him anymore, either. That part of myself has hardened.

It doesn't take too long for Virginia to arrive. I lift myself from the burial soil and dust myself off. Virginia thanks the cab driver with cash. She leans against her car with equal parts exhaustion, grogginess, and disappointment. Her pensive stare doesn't last as her coughs bubble. She trades my suit for her keys. I look for the toothbrush and toothpaste. "It's in the pocket," she says with a petty eye roll.

I get in the passenger seat and wait for her to break the ice, but she just groans at the sight of the lit dashboard after starting the car. "We need gas."

I twist myself to check what she's looking at. "Can you drop me at work first?" I know my persistent ignorance further adds to her dismay, and quite frankly, I can't even make a case for myself that is worth listening to. "I'm sorry," I wisely put out.

She spins out of the cul-de-sac and accelerates, rushing us out of the neighborhood. "Really? For what? Which part are you sorry for?"

I shrug innocently, though I know I won't get away with everything just by channeling an unassuming demeanor. "For everything, Virginia?"

Virginia pushes the threshold of sarcasm with a wind of laughter. "You're not sorry. You don't even know what it's like to feel sorry. You're just sorry for yourself," her words bite into me.

"I didn't want to inconvenience you, but if I drove back at night, I would have crashed on the wheel—"

"No! You shouldn't have left! What the hell does it matter to defend why you didn't come back when you shouldn't have left in the first fucking place! The threat of being pulled over, an accident, the threat of getting us caught—not just you, but us. That wouldn't occur to you, of course. Not when you have something more important to do." She embarks on the highway, collecting more speed. "Was this even important? What answers are you searching for when he's not even *answering*? Get the fuck over it!"

"I don't think you can speak on my relationship, Virginia," I warn her. "Do not evade the point!"

"Then what should I say?" I yell.

"I don't think you need to say anything more."

My breathing is shallow. "Are you asking me to leave?" My chest trembles with each pull of air.

She doesn't answer. She doesn't answer for a long time. We return to the city, and at a stoplight, she begins to cry small tears, "I don't know why I care for you—to this extent, at least."

She stops at the front of my office, and I change into my suit quickly, shedding the crumbs of dirt onto her seat. She looks at the mess thoughtlessly. I get out of the car but cannot shut the door because I know something needs to be said. I bend to see her. "Do I take the subway home or not?"

She nods. I shut the door, and she drives off. I enter the building with a coworker, but it's hard to pay any mind to him. He rushes to push the elevator button for me as I am busy fixing my tie. The first thing I do before heading to my desk is greet Marcel to alter my frequency. "Good morning," I say with a salesman smile.

"Morning, Lee."

"Is Thomas in?"

"I'll have to see. Would you like me to pass on a message?"

"No, that's alright. I'd like to give him the news myself," I walk to the individual bathroom and immediately lock the door behind me. Instead of occupying myself with the list of typical concerns, I focus on my job. I have a job. That's a beautiful thing.

I pull out the toothpaste and toothbrush to quickly scrub my mouth of all the selfish things I had to say to Virginia to confirm my residence.

I spit the remnants of gingivitis blood and mint foam into the sink and look up at the mirror to inspect my smile. I'll have to give many while at work. A knock interrupts my practice, and I whip open the door to see Payton with a pen in his hand. Is he gonna stab me, too? I kind of chuckle at the sight of it.

"Oh," he hands me the pen, "I didn't realize I had this. Can you take it back to the desk?"

"Yeah," I say as I step out of his way.

He sniffs the air of the single bathroom. I leave him to his sleuthing and reach Marcel again. "Is he free?"

Marcel glides near his office and raises a thumb. "He has a meeting in thirty."

"Shouldn't be long," I mumble in the direction of his office. Before entering, I politely tap on his door. Thomas signals me in. "Good morning, Thomas."

"Morning. What's up?" He sips from his thermos.

"I just wanted to let you know that I finished my course."

"Oh great!" He lights up, but his voice is still heavy. He returns to his screen. "Let's schedule you for an exam. How about two weeks from now?"

"Sounds good," my voice is frail, unsure. I think about failing more than I think about taking the test.

He catches my insecurity and shoots me a look without moving his face away from the screen. "You're booked."

I nod. "Where do I take it?"

"You can take it here… with me. You know we had an intern pass like yesterday. He finished the course faster than you."

My jaw locks. A fucking kid surpassed me at something I care for? Is this fucking envy? "Oh yeah?"

"Oh yes."

I bite my lip and think, "I'm gonna pass better."

He laughs at my rivalry, though I'm grammatically flawed. "I sure hope so."

I exit his office without another comment to signal my commitment because, though this entire process has burnt me rough around the edges, I intend on inhabiting my place in this world. I've seen it in glimpses and as a dream, but so long as I'm willing, it will happen. If some intern who graduated from community college passed, I will, too. And yes, I'll do it better.

I grip Payton's pen. He returns with the scent of cheap soap. "Hey man," he chuckles as he sits next to me. I scoot to give him space. "Did you brush your teeth in there?"

Embarrassed, my mouth opens without an explanation. "Oh—"

"No. It's cool." He opens his lunchbox like a bear and unwraps a protein bar. Is everyone health-conscious here? And how conscious are they if they're investing in gas station protein? He bites into it. "You're a weird little guy."

I purse my lips, "I had a rough morning."

"Took the wrong subway?"

"Not exactly," I click through emails. A personal email for me pops up from another tab, and I rush to it. It's from the gym.

Payton reads the letter of revocation. I'm no longer a member. That's great. There goes my Plan B. "Oh, that sucks," Payton chimes in.

"You talk to the interns here?" I look at Payton, skipping our current topic. "I don't know which gyms they go to, but sure, yeah."

I nod, calibrating the transition into self-fulfilling curiosity. "Are they all trying to work here as an employee?"

Payton shrugs. "Not everyone dreams of working here like us," he pretentiously presses his hand to his chest.

I digest his sarcasm without a laugh and delve deeper. "You know about the guy who passed recently?"

"Braxton?" That's his name?

"Yeah, good kid. I don't know his ethnicity, though…" Payton wonders about tangential things—the wheel is spinning, but the hamster is dead. "Why? You need help studying for the exam—"

"No." My mouth twitches with that envy. Who is this Braxton? And what good is he to me?

"Okay, man," Payton raises his hands and backs away like a douche.

I resume work as usual, uninterested in entertaining the topic of Mr. Braxton. Good to know that he's a good kid and can finish the course faster than the average duration.

The rest of my day is spent independently flipping through paperwork and matching information. Payton's become pretty confident in my ethics. I have my lunch at the desk. Sometimes, I don't even look up at the coworkers around Payton as I've learned that this world is not reliant on kindness. Kindness is, to me, observed as a privilege that people can afford if they can firstly afford their necessities. I fear that kindness is fundamentally another manifestation of the primitive inclination to bargain.

At the end of the day, I leave with nothing more than a goodbye to Payton and Marcel. I get why men marry quiet wives. After a long day of work, the last thing you want is to answer to unnecessary bitching that doesn't even make you any money. And the first thing you look for at that point is scotch—at least, that's what I've seen in most marital sitcoms.

Taking the subway home feels like purgatory. I've officially adopted the habit of picking the skin off my thumbs because it makes me feel like a distressed bird that rips its own color. A signal of distress is something I've become used to parading. I know Virginia is not a bitch, so she's not going to bitch, but neither is she going to be hospitable. Maybe I should pick up dinner. Ah, but what if it further frustrates her that I'm taking too long to get home? I hurry to my stop.

Shit, it frustrates me that anything I do is never enough at the end of whatever segment of my life. I climb the stairwell, skipping steps to get to Virginia's four twenty-one. She's sitting on a barstool by the counter, reviewing documents and bills. I immediately assume the worst and believe she's trying to make the point that I'm a financial burden. Her nose is red from pinching it with cheap, textured tissues. "Hey," I greet her.

She asks me with a line between her brows. "How was your day?"

"It was good," I inch towards her. "I'm sorry about this morning," I hope she doesn't again remind me that I'm not sorry.

"I want to know how you feel about the Alec thing."

"Really?"

"Of course. I misspoke this morning. You are entitled to your feelings."

I open the fridge, drop the notion of anticipated punishment, and pick up a premade juice.

"I don't even know what to say. I didn't spend the day thinking about it," I take a sip of the watery mix. "It's more feeling than logic. It's whatever."

"No, it's not whatever. It bothers you, and well," she looks down at the bills again, "while that is *so* important for you to process, you have to understand that how you act on it will define your future." Virginia chews on the inside of her cheek. "You remember my story?"

"Yeah."

"I had to pay my dues, Lee. Bad choices don't lead to good outcomes, and I know this must be so painful for you to hear because it's redundant, and it makes you feel trapped, but…"

I sigh. She's right. Her enrollment in this topic is anxiety-inducing. I subconsciously shift my weight to lean away from her. "But?" I barely ask.

She builds her case, and the muscles outlining her lips and eyebrows deepen in conflict. "But you have to learn and," she scoffs, "it hurts me to be the one to teach you… It's time to give room for others in your life." She pushes her papers aside and gently curls her hand, gesturing to me to sit.

I want to run away. I want to break out of her organized success by whipping open the front door or even jumping from the balcony. But not to leave, instead to stall the end of our conversation. I need her to chase me through avenues, screaming my name. I want to see how long she'll do it for. But I obediently seat myself next to her, hoping to be healed despite knowing what she's about to do. Her lips curve with sympathy. "Give me your hand."

"Okay," I quietly lay mine in hers, and we both look at the contrast of our skin beneath the Tuscan kitchen light. Her fingers are more prolonged, her palm is more expansive, and she has smaller nail beds. Mine appears ugly next to hers, and suddenly, I feel pitied, and subsequently, I feel vulnerable.

"I can't imagine what it's like to deprioritize yourself to grow when you have to prioritize yourself to live," her thumb grazes my protruding knuckles. "The most painful thing you'll do in your life is care for someone…" I look up into her eyes, "but it won't kill you," she reassures me with her softest tone. "How?"

"It's better this way," she squeezes my hand to ask for my attention.

"Virginia, please," I look with beseech. "I'm sorry for everything. Please don't tell me I'm not. I know I was wrong!"

She shakes her head. "It was never your fault."

The point she's making dissolves into the state of panic that I have been trying to avoid all day. "Where will I go?" How could she send me away?

"You have all the time you need here but not all the time you want. Let's find you a place, okay?" She leans in, waiting for me to make sense of everything. "You can't stay here, Lee. But I won't let you slip."

"Virginia, I can't do it so soon. I haven't saved enough." By 'enough,' I mean for a place that makes me feel like I've actually achieved something.

"Lee, I don't want to make you feel bad, but you have to. You have to. It's good for you—"

"Are you telling me or telling yourself this to avoid the responsibility?" I hate that I have to refer to myself as a responsibility.

Her hand recedes from mine. "You don't have to do this with me, Lee. I know your mechanisms, and I forgive you. There's no need to manipulate me. Firstly, you can't," she says shortly with a chuckle, "and secondly, I won't let you slip. Please trust me."

"So you're manipulating me for a good cause?" I lock in.

She slides the bills and receipts over, "I've been paying nearly double since you've been here. Rent, groceries, utilities, water—you shower a lot. All of this and barely anything from you. Then you say things to me that make me want to invest in a therapist that I can't afford and," she looks away from me as if she's talking to herself, "and I never ask myself why. I never ask why I do it. Especially in a way to imply that I shouldn't." Her pained eyes return to me. "You're using me," her voice breaks. She wipes her nose, "I've known this for some time, but do you?"

"I do," I admit.

"You were right. I don't have much to live for. So I chose you," her words sharpen. "It doesn't take away from keeping you as my good friend. I know a Lee that exists; he just hasn't had the chance to prove it, and I love that Lee. I love you," she pushes the words with duty. "You hurt me."

"Virginia." I try to find a response within the depths of my unresponsive displeasure. She has to know that when I am as human as her, she's the first to be loved. She's my first friend.

"No," she smiles as she blinks away her fresh tears, "you're not ready to tell me." We both know what I'm supposed to say.

I step off the barstool and back away in the direction of a room that soon won't be claimed by me anymore. "Are you hungry?" I timidly ask.

Virginia removes herself soberly from this feeling, "I actually had some soup. What's your plan?" She fairly doesn't offer any charity.

"I think I'll eat in a bit. I actually wanted to journal if that's okay."

She sniffles and nods. "Yeah, of course." Virginia collects the papers and neatly stacks them at the corner of the counter. I don't know what else to look at: the papers, her, or my shoes. Hesitantly, I lower my gaze and return to my room.

Closing the door behind me, I take off my socks and shoes and step into the makeshift bed for comfort. I soak in the cool sheets like it'll be my last time. To enhance this feeling, I shed myself to just an undershirt and boxers, and I close my eyes for a moment before assessing my upcoming priorities, such as journaling, apartment hunting, and dinner. Virginia probably thinks I'll be writing about her, and I truly would if I was allowed, but my mode-of-op is to convince IRAAB that things are getting better on account of the good decisions I'm making, which Virginia clearly disagrees with.

With the pressure of securing my safety, I force my eyes open, though they've already formed a layer of wet crust from exhaustion. I need to shower away the dirt from last night, but would it be inappropriate to use her facilities after our conversation? Anyway, I sit up and pull my journal close to begin writing about the recently encountered feelings that are significantly unfamiliar to me. I start with Braxton and ramble about my misgivings and his fortunes and how they make me feel.

I write about his name, too, because it's unpleasant to say aloud—as if he's raised in the upper tax bracket. Today, I felt heat near my ears and tension in my neck as Thomas pitted us against each other. What made matters worse was that Braxton had never spoken to me.

As I finish my productive rant, Virginia knocks on my door and opens it without peering in. "Can I come in?"

I shut my journal and pull the blanket to cover my legs. "Yeah, sure."

She enters with her laptop resting near her chest. She holds it like you'd hold a child. "I didn't know when would be an appropriate time to mention this, but I've been looking at some apartment listings and even booked a few tours," she purses her lips and looks at me. "We can make this fun, you know?"

"Oh," I press the outer lobe of my ear. This is happening a lot faster than I expected. "When did you have time to do this?"

"When you were at work."

"Okay… okay. Yeah, we can take a look."

"It's within your range. I even looked at a few one-bedroom apartments because you're avoiding studios. Maybe we can wait a while before moving out."

"You think I'll still be able to save enough?"

"Well, yeah. I'm only looking at affordable places." I sigh. "Sounds good, I guess."

CHAPTER 15

PHASE TWO

"It's my last Friday," I express with cheer to a teller as I hand her a check. "I'll have to switch to a closer bank."

The bank teller cashes my check. "We can locate a closer bank for your convenience, sir." I like that she didn't call me by name. I feel important. She checks the computer. "Looks like you're all set here. You can email us the new address, and we'll go from there. Have a wonderful weekend," blasé, she wishes me. To be financially sufficient today brings a sense of finality to things, but in a good way. I trust Virginia, mainly because I have no one else to trust, partly because my intuition rings when I hear her. She's not completely present with me anymore, but her judgment relapses when we share laughter, and I'll sometimes look in her eye to track her hesitations.

The hesitation of being sincere comes and goes, but she finds a way to give a shit about me. I've been trying to find a way, too. As I exit the bank, I call her. She answers differently now. "Hello?"

"I cashed my check!"

"Oh, that's great," Virginia doesn't match my energy. "Where do you want to meet?"

"Well, Linda's gonna drop off the keys at a diner near the place. The one we passed with the funky lights."

Virginia thinks. "This is the apartment close to your job?"

"Mhm."

"Okay, yeah. I know what place you're talking about. Sure. I'll meet you there." She hangs up without a goodbye.

On the way to the diner with the funky lights, I think about ways to rekindle the friendship between Virginia and I. Deep down, I know nothing's changed about me, and I've considered scheduling a check-up with Dr. Barberry, who's recently been awarded the head position of Project O.H.I., to reeducate myself on the anthropological value of things. I'd like to make Virginia smile again because it feels like redemption and safety. She's done more for me than anyone else has, and while it hurts to demote others from my past, she deserves to be acknowledged.

When the diner is within my eyeshot, I text the landlord. Virginia calls as soon as I send the text, "I'm here."

"I'm a minute away."

"Okay, I'll order some coffee. Did you wanna sit outside? It's nice weather." I see Virginia looking for me, "I see you," I hurry to her, laughing.

She turns to locate me and gives a reserved smile. "Congratulations," she says, extending her right arm to hug me from the side. Our friendship has devolved into exchanging formalities, but I don't fight it.

"Thank you," I shift out of the hug and check my phone for any replies. Linda texted me directions to the diner as if I'm half-brained, but instead of following them, I just use my eyes like a normal person would to look for a woman with black hair sitting in a booth near the bathroom. "Guess we're not sitting outside," I mumble to Virginia.

We get to the booth, and there she is, my gatekeeper. The landlord stands to greet me. "Wow! So great to meet you in person. Do you think you can give me your autograph?" She jokes.

"How could I not?" I shake her hand. Seriously, is there a way?

Virginia greets herself with an alias to avoid any violation. "Hi, I'm Candice." Her lack of enthusiasm borders on evident guilt, as if she's giving me away. As much as my demeanor could try to convince her that I am well and good, I know she'll come around accepting things at her own pace.

"Linda," the landlord states. We all take a seat in the booth. "I can't stay, but I've emailed you the building rules and directions to local banks, gyms, grocery stores, and I think a dog park, too," she laughs. She hands the keys. I am officially a tenant. A rent- paying, tax-paying, law-abiding citizen who is employed, no longer a burden to society as many motherfuckers would describe me in the previous phase of my life. I am independent with a one bedroom and one bath. Of course, Richard co-signed, as my credit score is the equivalent of an American teen. "I'd appreciate it if you keep company to a minimum of three. Three's a crowd, right?" She seeks approval from both of us. "We just don't want any noise complaints."

"Oh, of course. And real quick, did you receive the deposit?"

"Yeah! I emailed you a confirmation." She leans against the cushion, preparing to slide out of the booth. "Do you have any questions for me?"

I look at Virginia, expecting her to speak on my behalf, though I no longer need her to. I don't mean that in a cruel way. I just think I'm ready to jump the nest. "No. I think I'm good. Can I move in tomorrow?"

"Technically, you can move in today," she smiles as she scoots out in a hurry. "Also!" Linda lays a napkin and a pen on the table, "I wasn't kidding."

I smirk. *I still got it.* I sign the napkin with a seemingly humble laugh. "Make sure to frame it." Virginia unhappily rolls her eyes.

Linda folds the now valuable napkin and thanks me, leaving us two to sulk. Virginia looks at the menu, which doubles as a placemat. "So, are you excited?"

"Yeah," I'm kind of annoyed at her moodiness. "You shouldn't be upset at yourself," I lean toward her a little to capture her attention from the underwhelming, colorless menu. "I'm happy. Thanks to you!"

She finally looks at me with her eyebrows raised sympathetically. "Yeah?"

"Yes!"

She relaxes, "I just want what's good for you, even if that means—"

"I know," I reassure her.

She smiles and lays her head on my shoulder. "You actually hungry?"

"Eh," I shrug.

"I was thinking we could go furniture shopping. Maybe buy a bed and some kitchenware. Some groceries," she picks her head up. "It'll be a goodbye gift from me." I don't like that she said that, but I comply with her suggestion to ameliorate any guilt she may have built up.

"Okay," I use my chin to point to the exit. I spot her car from the window; she's done a poor job at parallel parking. Virginia shoots me a look before taking the driver's seat.

"What?" I laugh, "I'm not taking it for a spin."

We get in, and Virginia maneuvers through traffic. "When's your exam?"

"Monday."

"Excited?" She accentuates the word.

I sigh and look out the window, "I know I'm ready. That's as close as I'll get to excitement."

"Real," after a few blocks, she turns into the parking garage next to the furniture shop. "Are you preemptively planning to celebrate?" I whine.

"Yes," she declares, hitting the brakes as she fills in a vacant spot. Her confidence prevents her from entertaining my opposing doubts. She rushes to the store, and I follow behind, attempting to change plans.

"Can we pencil it in and see—"

"No."

"Virginia," I nag her. "The results come in immediately. What if I fail?" We enter the furniture store in mild distress over a hill I'd like to die on. Celebrations are for achievements.

She turns around with a lamp, which I did not see her pick up, "I'm sure you'll be hungry then, too." My expression sits between warmth and dismay. How does she persist? "Go get a cart."

Grumbling, I fetch one, and on the way back to Virginia, I see multiples of myself in an aisle of mirrors. The only times I've caught a reflection is either from Virginia's bathroom, my job's bathroom, or from the blackout windows of the buildings I pass on my way to work. I look gray in this light, and my teeth appear opaque. "Gross," I secretly criticize myself. I open my mouth wider to get a better look at the condition of my teeth. IRAAB facilitates most of my check-ups, but I haven't had a dental exam in ages.

"What are you doing?" Virginia interrupts with the *two* lamps in her hand. She sets them carefully in the cart.

"Nothing," I remember that if I get the job as a tax preparer, I'll receive benefits and insurance.

She pushes the cart. "Your bathroom has a mirror, right? Do you need a long one? No, we should get the basics first," Virginia adjourns the debate seemingly with herself and not me, the subject of her charity.

I purse my lips and shrug. "Sure," I've clearly never done this before. The last time I began my life, I just scored a cheap mattress, and that was that. We weave through different "rooms" to make opinions of different palettes, prices, and pieces of furnish. "How about this?" I point at a DIY bed frame folded into a box.

"Hm," Virginia considers the option as she notes the price. "Yeah, put it in the cart."

"I think this should be good, Virginia. You don't have to do more than this," I cock my head to the side, my hand on my hip.

"You sure?" She looks in the cart, "I guess I have some pots and pans I no longer use. We can go grocery shopping when you move in."

"Yeah," I walk towards the cashier. Virginia pays without letting me see the receipt and pushes the cart back to her car. I load up her trunk, and we begin the ride home. I press on the radio and turn the dial until we find a tune because anything is better than static or silence.

"Oh. I like this song." It's some old country tune. "You like this?"

"Mhm," she nods unassumingly.

"Hm," I realize that she is her own person, apart from me. "You like country music."

"Yes," she answers, but it wasn't a question. *She likes country music.* "I think it's comforting."

"What else?" I release my curiosity without reason. "What do you mean?"

"I'm not sure."

Virginia laughs in confusion. "Okay… Anyway, I'm gonna be honest with you, I'm hungry." Our friendship is structured around food, and I can't understand its significance.

"Take out?"

"No. I'll cook," she says with a tinge of embarrassment. I hope she didn't assume that I was expecting her to pay. However, bringing it up would make it worse. We get to her garage. "Let's leave the stuff in the car." Up the stairwell, she remembers more on her to- do list. "Remind me to grab a few lightbulbs for the lamps."

"Okay," my voice echoes as we escape the steep climb. Her apartment is circulating a perfect seventy-two, and I take in the lavender scent. *She likes lavender-scented things.* "What do you want to make?"

"How about that Greek chicken I made a couple of weeks ago?"

It sucked. "Okay," I lie enthusiastically. Virginia quickly puts three frozen chicken breasts in the microwave to thaw and throws water in a pot to boil jasmine rice. I'm not sure if the Greeks use jasmine rice…

Virginia shells out a smaller pot, a pan, a spatula in mint condition, a serrated knife, and utensils. "Lightbulbs," she whispers to herself.

Virginia turns on the TV to fill the room with noise as she begins wrapping up my life. "Lightbulbs, bedsheets," Virginia continues. I go to my room and look at my bed with gratitude. This place was my first home. I think every other place I've occupied was just a place I occupied.

"Alright," I get on my knees and roll up the comforter. Unsure of what to do next, I wait for Virginia to give me instructions, but she's busy single-handedly preparing my future without asking for any assistance. IRAAB could never.

Virginia laughs. "Why did you clean up, dumbass?"

"Was I not supposed to?"

"Are you sleeping on the couch?"

She has all the right to call me a dumbass, and instead of responding, I awkwardly unroll the bed. She buzzes out of my room like a fly, zipping back and forth to collect necessities while I begin stripping to my undergarments. Instead of bunching my suit, I neatly fold it as it is now my responsibility to iron my clothes. I hear Virginia wrapping things together while also stirring the pot, but I need a nap. Sorry.

The comforting ambiance of her activity throughout the apartment puts me away, and the nap turns into a whole night's rest. The first thing that occurs is how Virginia might have felt knowing she went to specific lengths to pack and cook while I carelessly slept in a bed she'd made for me—technically, I unrolled it. My favorite thing about the weekend isn't the absence of work but the chance to remain in bed. And Virginia knows to set the perfect temperature depending on the weather outside. No matter the circumstances, I never wake drenched in sweat or with a sense of impending doom. The air is always fresh and clear, always easier to breathe. My door is closed out of courtesy.

I get up, stretch, check my boxers, and peer out to find Virginia cozied up on the couch with a cup of herbal tea. She's watching a documentary on whales. I walk out and wave at her. Her face lights up as she takes another sip. "Good afternoon," she acknowledges my night of rest with some sass. She points to a large suitcase, "took ages to stuff everything in."

I tilt my head and gasp. "Virginia. Thank you." I really am thankful.

"You've got your sheets, a foam mattress tied to the top of the car, a pillow, pots, pans, and even basic groceries. Oh, I packed your toiletries, clothes, and shoes too." Her lips tighten whimsically at the end of her information, as if we both know that what she said is insane.

I seamlessly patronize her. "You fit everything?"

"Took some rearranging... And. For old-time's sake, I whipped up breakfast for you. It's in the fridge." She waits for me to make something of her insistence. I open the fridge to see a bowl of yogurt topped with oats, honey, and dried fruit. There's a tall glass of green juice, too. "Finish it, get dressed, and let's head to your place." The phrase 'your place' feels so sexy. I have my own place!

I chug the juice and take the bowl to my room. I change into something casual—thrifted jeans and a plain white tee. Before leaving, I fish for my chip from yesterday's pants and stuff it into my right

   BY ZAINAB F. RAZA

pocket. "How do I look?" I step into Virginia's room. She dons a cardigan and wraps her frizz into a bun.

"Presentable," she tells me earnestly. I walk to the living room, pick up the bag, and head to the garage. I don't give the place another look as I know I'll return. But this time on my terms, with dignity, and without helplessness.

Virginia pops the trunk, and I use my strength to gently lay the suitcase in it while she starts the car. Normally, Virginia doesn't like it when people stand behind the exhaust pipe of the car because they might inhale toxins, so for her not to remind me clearly indicates that her mind is preoccupied. I can feel her feelings more than I can feel mine.

When I get in, I try not to notice the melancholy. "I hope the place doesn't have roaches."

"Seems like a clean building."

"It doesn't have a lobby," I make a point.

"We all start somewhere," she drives south without direction. My place is close to my job, and she's quite familiar with that route. "Please never hesitate to call me, okay? Seriously. If you need instructions on how to use a stove," she laughs, "fucking call me."

I laugh with her, "I think I'll just look it up." I want her to know that I won't ever use her, but from the expression on her face, I can see she isn't pleased with my remark. "But I still need help doing laundry," I nudge her.

"Shut up," she chuckles. We are near my job, so I pull up the directions on her phone and navigate her to the front of the building. "Oh, I remember this place!"

"Yeah," I nod. "It's the second one we checked out."

"Yeah," Virginia looks at the place with hope, then at me, "you ready?" I flash a smile in response and hop out of the car. I genuinely am ready. Virginia opens the trunk and I lug the suitcase inside the building. She unties the mattress. There's no elevator in sight, which is ass, but I've gotten used to lengthy flights.

"At least I'll have a good view," I make light of the job as we amount to my floor. I pull the keys from my back pocket and instantly check for the existence of my chip in the side pocket. I glance at Virginia for reassurance before unlocking the door. I jab the key into the lock, relying on the fifty-fifty chance of getting it right. I didn't.

The second time's the charm, and we finally step into my quiet yet cozy, as-advertised, apartment. I breathe in the air to familiarize myself with the new scent. It smells like someone's lived here, but it isn't particularly terrible. Virginia sets the mattress against the wall, "I'll go get the bed frame. You settle yourself in."

"Okay," I mindlessly reply as I take in the moment of ownership. I'm here, beginning my life. A smile breaks. *My place is carpeted.* My place has a kitchen, a separate bedroom, and a bath, as advertised. My place is mine, and though it is tainted with the scent of people and maybe mildew, these first seconds are cathartic. I take off my shoes and feel the carpet beneath me.

Virginia comes back carrying the weight of my new life, which is packed into boxes. She somehow has the ability to grab everything. "I'm not making another trip," she switches on the light, something I hadn't thought of doing. Virginia puts her hand on my shoulder. "How does it feel?"

"Better than I thought," I try to behave like a normal person, hiding the fact that I am taken by my reality. Holy shit, this is my reality! My reality is carpeted! I hesitantly step further inside and look to my right to see a small kitchen. It doesn't have an island like Virginia's; it surely doesn't outdo her floor plan, but the countertops are clean, and the fridge doesn't leak. The floors are bare linoleum.

She and I tour the place, which takes about two minutes. The bedroom is a little smaller than Virginia's office, and the bathroom isn't spacious either, but the shower's remodeled. Virginia lugs the bed frame box into the room, ripping off the tape. "Oh. You don't have to."

"Are you sure?" She takes a step back and with her hands on her hips. She gives the place another look. "Well. No roaches."

"Yeah," I smirk.

She looks at me and goes in for a hug, "I'm proud of you. For everything." I hold on to her a little longer, pressing my eyes closed. "See you Monday, right?"

"Yes," I can't deny her.

"Okay," she pecks my head, "enjoy your first night."

"See you," I push half a smile as she walks out. It isn't worth making a whole thing out of a mere goodbye, but as she twists the knob, I feel a sense of urgency to not let her leave, "Virginia!" A bit surprised, she turns to me. "The day I met you… my life changed for the better," I don't know how else to describe our entire experience, which I'm supposed to call a friendship. "You're everything."

"Lee," she coos.

This is just the start of my drivel, "I'm so happy you applied to Cut Theory, I'm so happy you asked to meet for an early dinner, I'm so lucky you treated me right." I zone away, "I treated you like an advantage." Looking back at her, I admit, "That wasn't fair, and I hope I can redeem myself."

"I hear you," she hears me sincerely.

"Please don't go home with the feeling that this is wrong. I'm happy."

She smiles at my confirmation. "Thank you for letting me into your world," she opens the door. I hold it for her, letting her leave this time. The pressure of ending this period on a melancholic note has lifted, and I can comfortably sit with myself. Instead of unboxing things, I sprawl in the middle of my living room and rub my palms over the carpet leisurely because tomorrow is Sunday, and today is the first day. I lay down and stare at the ceiling, remembering the times I'd wake up and do the same thing but with this relentless weight on my chest.

After basking in the championship of my motives, I get up to do the practical: setting up my bed. I open the windows in my empty room to let in some city noise. Virginia didn't lie; she really fit everything into a suitcase. I let my sheets take in their first breath like I did in this place. Piece by piece, I assemble the frame to create a stable platform for my mattress. It's more of a mattress topper. How stupid. There are *things* for *things*. I'm not against excess. In fact, I haven't enjoyed the excess of anything, so maybe one day I'll purchase a mattress for my mattress topper.

I drag my bed to the bedroom and let it fall on the frame. Turns out, it's hard to fix your sheets around the corners of the mattress by yourself. My sheets have a paisley pattern, and they're green. I remember Dr. Alec said he hates paisley. I pause at the thought of Dr. Alec for a brief moment before resuming.

Finally, I lay in a bed that I made, and taking a nap feels *easy*. I don't have anyone to answer to. My goodness, it's been ages since I've relished a bed. The way my mattress consumes muscles that I forgot were aching. I love being alone. I fucking love being alone. I love my bed. I love napping.

After an hour of not answering to anyone, my phone rings. It's Thomas. He sends alarms down my body. "Hello?" I fight the grogginess.

"Hey, Lee. Just a reminder. You will be taking the test in the morning before work. I sent you an email and haven't received a response," his voice makes me recoil.

"Apologies, Thomas. I moved in yesterday and haven't been able to look at any emails. What time should I come in?"

"Seven is good. Counting on you," he hangs up. The fuck does that mean? What? Is he my dad? I toss my phone to the other, unoccupied side of my bed. I realize that I am truly alone and enclosed within privacy, which means I can do whatever I want, and I can do it naked. For the first time in ages, my dick is hard. Before hopping in the shower, I rub one out to outdated images as I haven't replenished my imagination. So weirdly enough, I think of that old cook from that Thai restaurant. I'm not sure why he gets me going. Maybe it's the sweat. Maybe it's the way he cooks in a hurry.

Anyway. I finish. I finish, and I pull the bag of toiletries out of the suitcase and arrange the soaps on the ledge of the sink. I brush my teeth in the shower and rinse myself with berry-fragrant scrubs Virginia kindly packed for me. When I leave the shower, I let myself air dry as I unpack and stock my apartment.

The pots and pans take shelter in the cupboards. Virginia donated her pasta, rice, and granola. A sweet gesture. I guess it's important that I gather perishable groceries today, so I throw on the same jeans and a state tee from Virginia's closet of unused apparel. Before locking myself out, I swipe my key, laminated card, and tracking chip. Linda said the grocery store is up the block.

The grocery store is just a bodega, and I'm not sure why Linda wasn't honest about it— did she think it would deter me from moving in? Maybe she just wanted to impress the only sentient alien within her vast radius. The guy at the register doesn't look up from his magazine. I find eggs, butter, milk, and bread. Virginia tried hard to get me into various flavors, but her attempts never made a difference. Albeit, there was that one time food tasted good.

The guy at the register looks up, and his eyes take a rounder shape. "Hi?"

"Hi, I'm Lee." I think it's important to introduce myself to communities I'll be frequenting. A rare inclination, but for the sake of practicality, I lay the laminated card for the cashier to pick up and read. "I moved recently and just wanted to come by and say 'hi,' because well, I'll be here a lot, I guess," I chuckle, trying so hard to appear friendly.

The cashier doesn't understand. "So… you're—"

"Yes," I nod.

"Where are you from?"

"It says on the card. International Research Administration of Animalia Biotechnology."

"No, but," he points to the ceiling innocently. "You're from there?"

"No," I shake my head. "I mean, yes. But I was born and raised on Earth."

The cashier is blown away. "Your English is great." That's wild. Nevertheless, I appreciate his compliment. The cashier gives me a discount and hands me my items in a paper bag.

"Thank you."

"Thank you!" He exclaims with a weird tinge of nervousness.

When I get to my apartment, I remember that I have to climb several steps. I guess there's a price you have to pay for the happiness you buy. When I get inside, I lay my groceries out on the counter and assess what I have. I guess I could make myself egg and toast with a glass of milk? I'm a little afraid to use the stove and am tempted to call Virginia, but I kind of just want to succeed in life, you know? I want to know that I can do it *and* wipe my ass all by myself like a good boy. I twist the knob of the closest stove and place the pan on it. I cut a square of butter and let it melt.

After a minute, I crack a couple of eggs and pour them into the hot butter. The eggs crackle, and I dodge the beads of sizzling butter. Some of them land on my skin at a searing temperature. "Fuck!" I let out. Immediately, I call for Virginia. She answers joyously. "Hey! How's it going—"

"Virginia!" I yelp as I back away from my burning eggs. "My eggs are burning, there's butter everywhere, and I'm too scared to turn it off," I rush my troubles out in hopes of her catching all of them.

"Just turn the stove off, man," she responds nonchalantly but follows it with a giggle. "This is not funny! I can't switch it off. It's going everywhere!"

"How is it that you can sneak out, steal my car, and drive on the highway, but you can't fry an egg?"

"Help!"

"Okay, okay. Instead of turning it off, just quickly push the pan off the stove. It'll cool down pretty fast." With baby steps, I only stretch out my hand and nudge the pan onto the other stove. The crackling recedes. "Did it work?"

I sigh. "Yes."

"Good," she laughs. "Did you unpack everything? Are you creeped out?"

"Creeped out?"

"You know? Is it weird being alone? Do you feel scared?"

I check the overcooked contents with a fork. "No, not at all. I've been sleeping a lot, actually, so I haven't really experienced being alone yet."

"Okay. Well, let me know when you need anything. I gotta get going."

"Yeah. I'm gonna try to eat."

"See ya," she chuckles. I hang up, adjusting to the calmness after the storm. With my fork, I lift the egg from the pan and lay it on the toast. There was a time when I used to fish out half-eaten, tainted meals from a dumpster. I take my food and the pint of milk to the living room window, where I can see traffic pass from below.

For the rest of my evening, I repeat information I've learned with no source of confirmation that the information I've learned is correct. Occasionally, while repeating tax preparation content, I'll take laps around the place, pee if needed, or just hang by the window. I consider grabbing a legal vice, maybe cigarettes. Is kombucha allowed? With these thoughts, I witness the sun decline and set. I conclude my practicality and turn the page to whatever else that's expected of me. It's expected of me to be rested, but I have a lot pent up in my chest, congesting my thoughts, and I know I can't fall asleep with a full mind.

So, I do turn the page—of my journal. And while that is a practical task, I feel the need to document myself therapeutically. Rarely have I cared to express my identity for purposes endemic to the ego. However, today might be regarded as a special occasion.

I title this entry, 'Pride.' That is the emotion I'm suspicious of, and while pride is not a commendable feeling, it is real and often experienced and exploited. Pride is catered to, I think.

I've been daydreaming more. Normally, I think about things that make me afraid, but I've been daydreaming about things that excite me. I'm starting to look forward to it, and I think it's coming from a place of proving myself—not to just pass evaluation.

My daydreams consist of my apartment being intricately furnished. If I think more about the life I want, I get excited about the details. Like my clothes being branded, and I never want to stink again. I don't want anyone to look at me with pity ever again. I never deserved to feel disposable.

I deserve to be respected. So I think buying a house will help. I want to be further educated. I want to look healthy, and I want to actually select the people I want to spend my time with. That is what everyone else did around me, and not everyone chose me. I've met a lot of people along the way. Most of them suck, and I wasn't treated kindly enough. Maybe that's because of who I was. I also don't want to be only around people that I need. I can only think of one person so far that I would want to be around and not need.

I also want to have hobbies and donate, and if I ever donate, I don't want it to be anonymous. I feel the phase of my life of existing to mimic human patterns is over, and it feels good to become one of you. I have to be honest. I'm not referring to community and inclusion. To feel like one of you feels mean. I can't think of a better word.

Maybe selfish. I think I can be good and selfish at once.

It could consequentially be that I don't have what it takes to be like one of them, but I have a suspicion I'm almost there.

Upon drifting to bed, I conceive nightmares. Glimpses of the sterile facility make my stomach turn. I dream of the time Virginia stabbed me, the dirt I slept in when Dr. Alec's bedroom light switched off, and the night I used cheap wine to threaten the survival of Project O.H.I. I dream of Richard, too, but his face does not register, so when I wake in a sweaty panic, I assume the face I saw behind closed eyes is blank.

I run to the bathroom to shit eggs, and my head hangs in relief when I realize that Virginia did pack me toilet paper. On account of beginning my new life, I refuse to devolve into animalistic tendencies. I don't want to be nasty anymore. I should get a bidet…

The next time I wake up, it's at six in the beautiful morning. I open my journal to cite my dreams and convey my daily anticipations before brushing my teeth and buttoning my button-down. I walk to the fridge, down some milk with sliced bread, and throw a few granola clusters in my mouth. I put on my pants, belt, and tie. I'm glad Virginia folded my clothes in a way where they barely creased. By half past six, I leave.

It takes me ten minutes to get to the office, but Thomas isn't here yet. Is he intentionally *this* punctual? Within those early ten, he arrives. Yes, he is that intentionally punctual. I wait with my hands clasped together, imitating a submissive body language. His chest is broad, and his posture is pristine. He tips his head as he unlocks the office. "Morning."

"Good morning, Thomas. How was your weekend?"

"Good," he gives a beat, "I went to a concert with my girlfriend. Is it bad that I don't know the band's name?" I've never had a casual conversation with Thomas, so I cannot track the implications.

"Doesn't make you a bad partner," I reassure him meekly.

"Cool." We walk to his office. He sets up the computer for me to occupy. "You know the rules: no cellphones, this is a timed exam. Most of it is multiple choice. You have sixty minutes, and the timer begins as soon as you enter your name. I've logged you in already." He raises his brows without a smile. "Good luck." Thomas sits a few feet away from me. He opens his laptop and busies himself.

He gestures for me to begin, and I follow with a deep breath to shake away the nerves. I type my name, 'Lee.' The first question is about taxable income. "Jury duty pay, wages, unemployment compensation," I whisper to myself as I click the correct option. In case, I review the other choices and confidently move on. The following questions are conveyed through various scenarios that I've studied. Can a spouse file as a dependent? What is adjusted gross income? Are student loans tax deductible? What is 1040 PR? I breeze through most of the questions and refrain from sweating the complex scenarios I didn't learn about in the course because I only need a passing grade, baby. At some point, I return to the questions I skipped to answer to the best of my ability, and a sudden anxiety welcomes itself.

What if I fail? It's not a unique worry, but it is hard to brush off. I spend the remainder of my time wrangling with the information I recently acquired through hours of coursework and reread the question in a hushed tone. "Two taxpayers married on September 11th," were they trying to throw me off with that date? "That same year,

 BY ZAINAB F. RAZA

the husband enrolled in an accredited college and received a Form 1098-T, Tuition Statement. The wife was employed with an income of forty-five thousand dollars and paid for the husband's education expenses. What is the correct method to report the education credit?" I'm dumbfounded. "Taxpayers must file a joint return." Unsure, I read aloud my answer.

Once I submit my final work, I am logged out. I think I finished faster than Braxton.

Carefully, I lift myself from my seat and look up at Thomas, who is scrolling on his laptop. "Done?" He asks without relinquishing any hint that he's impressed with me.

"Yes," I step away from the computer. He takes over and logs in. "Is it okay if I make a quick call?"

"Sure. You know, I was thinking, you worked hard. You can take the day off," he plays radio hits on his computer as if everything's *cool*.

Is this a test? "No, I'm perfectly fine with working today, Thomas. It's not a problem.". "I mean it, you deserve to chill."

"Wow. Thank you, really," I pull my phone out of my pocket.

Thomas doesn't respond; he's too busy looking through my test, which makes my insides twist, but I walk out into the hall. I dial Virginia, and she answers immediately. "Did you pass?"

"I don't know yet. My boss is looking through."

"When will you get your results?"

"I don't know," I stress the phrase. "Dude, I'm scared."

"No matter what, everything's going to be okay."

"Mhm," I don't listen to her. It's not going to be okay. If I fail, I lose my rights. I won't be able to afford my place. I'll be homeless again. IRAAB won't take me in. I can't suffer twice; I just can't. But if I pass. I'm on my way to have everything—in a sense.

I fight the temptation of turning back to see what Thomas's face divulges. He's pretty stoic anyway, so looking doesn't serve a purpose. I literally don't know what else I can do. "By the way, Thomas said I can take the rest of the day off. Did you want to swing by now?"

"I mean, I'm at work, but I guess I can blow it off," Virginia compromises so selflessly.

"Lee," Thomas calls me in.

My heart drops. "Stay with me," I whisper to Virginia as I shove the phone into my breast pocket.

I enter the office. Half of Thomas's ass rests on the edge of the desk. "How many questions do you think you got wrong?"

"Maybe a few. Some of the lengthier questions confused me. Why?"

He rolls his eyes apathetically. "You failed." He crosses his arms. "It's unfortunate—"

I see my consequential future repeating the unbearable past. I don't think I can suffer again. "Can I retake it?" I know this is the end of my employment.

"You know the terms." Thomas steps forward to shake my hand. "It was a pleasure having you. Best of luck on your endeavors," his words insult me. I didn't expect to feel insulted; I expected fear of the future, and while that feeling is amplified, I feel more so *insulted*.

"Thomas," I hold myself from panicking. "Can I stay until my internship ends?"

He purses his lips, "I don't see the point. I don't need you."

I scoff at his dismissal. I've known this interaction in every circumstance. "Fuck you," I force out. My voice fills the room but stabs him directly.

"You need to leave. Now," he grits his teeth.

I push him out of the way, and my heart rate increases to warn me from taking things too far. "Let me see the results." He gets in the way, but I can see that I barely failed. "I was almost there!" I holler to make a case for myself. Thomas pushes me back, and within the second, I feel the first wave of incapacitation burning my nerves. My body collapses. I put my weight on the desk as I fight through the beginning stages of the seizure.

Thomas's brows mash, and disgust permeates through him. "The fuck?" It might be an unholy sight for sure, but it doesn't matter anymore. It's over. Everything's over. I fight to keep my eyes from rolling back and grip his collar. Thomas whips me away, and I land on my back, groaning. *I cough blood.*

"You ruined it!" I rebel against the pain to scold him. I get up one more time and use whatever strength I have left in my calves to pounce on the motherfucker. I see black splotches. Laughing hysterically at how crazy this must look, I change into myself, rip myself from the commodity of being human.

I tear the flesh from his face with my teeth. Like a thread, I keep pulling until a strip of him is tossed. This is the third time I've tasted blood in recent months, but it's the first time tasting someone else's blood. My species doesn't have a penchant for it, but victory has its flavor. I hear his blood burst from wounded skin, and he shrieks for God. That wet noise sounds good. He flagrantly curses me through his loud agony and simultaneously pleads for mercy, but my fingers are twisting into his exposed facial muscles, and the seizing makes it harder to let go. So we flail together around the office, my legs kicking the air, Dua Lipa playing in the background.

If he bleeds out, I'm sure his obituary will inspire more change than mine. A man's death will spark revolutionaries, but we inhabitants are brought up with the threat of extermination. And yes, some bat an eye, but we all know how blind the rest are.

So this is it. This is my forfeit. I can't see anything anymore, but I can locate his jaw from the stubble and find his jugular. I continue to laugh, overpowering his terror and piercing cries. Thomas attempts to pry me off as I scratch into his neck, undoing his shirt into tatters. But the seizing muscles work in my favor as I latch onto him. I use my fingers to grab the back of his gelled hair, keeping his throat vulnerable. I hear people barging in— employees, maybe.

My body gives up, and I fall off. Thomas kicks me several times before charging to safety. I am left cold and panting, and for about thirty minutes, I remain conscious. The seizing stops, but I still feel sharp jabs where my chips are located, as if I just came out of that surgery.

In these long moments, I can only picture Virginia. I hear men shouting at Thomas and Thomas shouting back. I hear them say I am a product of IRAAB and will be tried and terminated appropriately.

Someone checks my vitals and reports potential hemorrhaging. Someone explains that the implanted technology is foreign to the surveillance systems initially established for Project O.H.I. Someone figured it out. And then I hear that these foreign chips severed my organs upon seizing, and then I smile with finality.

I want to say her name in case she's still on the phone. I want to tell her not to come. That she doesn't need to see any of this. I feel ashamed for inconveniencing her, and all I can hear is the rustling of jackets.

I'm sorry.

ABOUT THE AUTHOR

Primarily a screenwriter, Zainab discovered her passion at the age of fourteen. Before bringing her own ideas to life, she gained valuable experience working as a production assistant for several years. Her films went on to compete in both national and international festivals, expanding her professional horizons. Zainab later served as a script judge and reader for the esteemed Austin Film Festival. It was during this time that she conceived the project *Who Is Lee?*, a story she ultimately realized was best suited as a novel before adapting it into other formats.